Praise for
the Psychic Eye Mysteries

"Intuition tells me this book is right on target—I sense a hit!"   —Madelyn Alt, author of *A Charmed Death*

"Victoria Laurie's books are a delight to devour."
                    —Savannah Russe, author of *Beneath the Skin*

"A fresh, exciting addition to the amateur sleuth genre."
                    —J. A. Konrath, author of *Dirty Martini*

"There are plenty of surprises and revelations in the exciting story line; these keep the heroine and readers slightly off balance, especially in anticipating what's next."   —Gumshoe

"An invigorating entry into the cozy mystery realm. . . . I cannot wait for the next book."
                    —Roundtable Reviews

"Victoria Laurie has crafted a fantastic tale in this latest Psychic Eye Mystery. There are few things in life that upset Abby Cooper, but ghosts and her parents feature high on her list . . . giving the reader a few real frights and a lot of laughs."   —Fresh Fiction

continued . . .

The Psychic Eye Mystery Series

Abby Cooper, Psychic Eye
Better Read Than Dead
A Vision of Murder
Killer Insight
Crime Seen
Death Perception

The Ghost Hunter Mystery Series

What's a Ghoul to Do?
Demons Are a Ghoul's Best Friend
Ghouls Just Haunt to Have Fun

DOOM WITH A VIEW

A Psychic Eye Mystery

Victoria Laurie

AN OBSIDIAN MYSTERY

OBSIDIAN
Published by New American Library, a division of
Penguin Group (USA) Inc., 375 Hudson Street,
New York, New York 10014, USA
Penguin Group (Canada), 90 Eglinton Avenue East, Suite 700, Toronto,
Ontario M4P 2Y3, Canada (a division of Pearson Penguin Canada Inc.)
Penguin Books Ltd., 80 Strand, London WC2R 0RL, England
Penguin Ireland, 25 St. Stephen's Green, Dublin 2,
Ireland (a division of Penguin Books Ltd.)
Penguin Group (Australia), 250 Camberwell Road, Camberwell, Victoria 3124,
Australia (a division of Pearson Australia Group Pty. Ltd.)
Penguin Books India Pvt. Ltd., 11 Community Centre, Panchsheel Park,
New Delhi - 110 017, India
Penguin Group (NZ), 67 Apollo Drive, Rosedale, North Shore 0632,
New Zealand (a division of Pearson New Zealand Ltd.)
Penguin Books (South Africa) (Pty.) Ltd., 24 Sturdee Avenue,
Rosebank, Johannesburg 2196, South Africa

Penguin Books Ltd., Registered Offices:
80 Strand, London WC2R 0RL, England

First published by Obsidian, an imprint of New American Library,
a division of Penguin Group (USA) Inc.

First Printing, September 2009
10 9 8 7 6 5 4 3 2 1

Copyright © Victoria Laurie, 2009
All rights reserved

OBSIDIAN and logo are trademarks of Penguin Group (USA) Inc.

Printed in the United States of America

For my fabulous *editor,*
Kristen Weber.
My friend, fan, and partner in prime crime . . . ☺

Acknowledgments

It takes a team of dedicated, hardworking, and brilliantly talented people to bring a book to print, which is why it's a bit unfair to have only one name grace the cover. This is also why it makes me feel so good when fans tell me they've read my acknowledgments, as it's the only way I can publicly express my gratitude to some of the very best people I know, and if it were left up to me, each one of my books would have about a dozen names next to mine.

So if you are reading this, know you have my sincere thanks for taking the time to wait a bit before diving into the story while you pause to read the names of the people without whom this story could not have been told.

First up, the man I thank profusely each and every time I finish a manuscript—my astounding agent, Jim McCarthy. Jim is one of those people you instantly like, want to get to know better, and can't wait to hang out with again. He's also one heck of an agent.

Next, to the person this book is dedicated to, my

amazing editor, Kristen Weber. Kristen, I don't say it often enough, but I am so utterly grateful you're on my team. Above all you are a woman of your word, and the fact that you've somehow done what three other editors couldn't (namely, kept me focused, on track, and on time) is a feat in and of itself! Thank you so much for your positive outlook, your attention to detail, and your brilliant enthusiasm, and, most of all, for loving Abby and M.J. almost as much as I do.

Special mentions also must go to my copy editor, Michele Alpern (thank you, Michele, for your great care and for allowing Abby's voice to shine through!), as well as NAL staff members Rebecca Vinter and Megan Swartz, who help in every way they can, for which I'm extremely grateful.

A personal thanks also goes out to my peeps— those friends who make sure that I come out and enjoy the sunshine every now and again or check in on me to make sure I haven't fallen off the face of the earth since they haven't heard from me in a century. My hood peeps, Jen Casey, Christine Trobenter, Tess Rodriguez, and Shannon Dorn. My out-of-the-hood peeps, Karen Ditmars, Leanne Tierney, Silas Hudson, and Nora Brosseau. And my new peeps—those folks who were fans first but whom I now call friend: Pippa Terry and her mumsy, Betty Stocking; Ellen George; and my new "BFF" Katie Coppedge—who I must mention is also available for crowd control should my book signings attract more than the usual two people. ☺

Next, I would like to thank my family, who mean everything to me, with one special mention here of my fabulous and beautiful cousin Tee-Tee, who is the Candice to my Abby, and who makes me laugh out loud every single day! Hugs and loves, you, *mi carino* . . . here's to plates of delicious paella and much fun in Barcelona!

Finally, I would like to thank my fans, who have stayed with me through each release and have been noticeably spreading the word. I'm beyond grateful to you for your loyalty, dedication, and willingness to see what happens next.

Chapter One

They say that we all face certain tests in life. Some of us are tested by our jobs, others by personal relationships, others by physical or health issues. And I will freely admit that at some point in my life I've been challenged by all those things, but recently my greatest obstacle was a guy who pushed all my buttons. I couldn't stand him, but had to be nice 'cause he's my sweetheart's boss. Otherwise, I'd probably punch his lights out.

Okay, so maybe *I* wouldn't punch his lights out (did I mention he's tall and muscular, and carries a gun?), but I'd sure hire some big goon to do it! Anyway, I'm getting ahead of myself. This encounter with a major pain in my tochus all started about the time I arrived back home from a rather hairy week in Las Vegas. My significant other—FBI agent Dutch Rivers—and I had recently been involved in a case that involved bureau corruption, greed, murder, kidnapping, and his burst appendix, but that's another story. . . .

The important thing was that Dutch, Candice (my

business partner, PI, and dear friend), and I had all arrived back in the quaint little suburban town of Royal Oak, Michigan, very relieved to still be alive and each of us pretty much swearing off Sin City for the foreseeable future.

Once Dutch had recovered from his surgery for the appendicitis, he was promptly informed that he would be on desk duty until he was cleared by Internal Affairs of any involvement with the shady dealings of his former boss, Raymond Robillard. The reason my sweetie was in the hot seat was that Dutch had been secretly investigating his boss, and when Robillard got wind of it while we were in Vegas, he made it look like Dutch was the criminal. Again . . . that's another story.

Now, the guy above Robillard, Special Agent in Charge Bill Gaston, is actually a decent fellow, who's become something of a fan of mine. And as the case in Vegas was wrapping up, Gaston asked whether I might consider assisting his team with an open investigation into the disappearance of three college kids. Being that I'm a professional psychic by trade, my intuitive skills could be useful, so, like an idiot, I'd said yes.

Fast-forward a few weeks to the news that the new guy replacing Dutch's old corrupt boss was this rising star in the FBI—a guy by the name of Brice Harrison.

The downer came when we learned that Harrison was publicly protesting my involvement and he was making no bones about the fact that he found anyone who claimed to be psychic one fry short of a Happy Meal. I discovered all this on the eve of the plane trip that Candice and I were taking out to Washington, D.C., to meet with the assembled task force on the case of the missing teens, and trust me, I wasn't too happy about it.

"Why do we have to meet in D.C. again?" I asked Dutch. I didn't like this idea of being out of my element.

"The missing kids are all from separate states," Dutch explained. "The task force is meeting in D.C. so that each local bureau's lead agent feels comfortable being on neutral territory. Plus, it was probably a power play by Harrison. He's got some connections up the ranks in D.C. and it wouldn't surprise me if he coordinated this meeting there to garner some internal support at the central office."

"Fabulous," I said drolly. "Just the political minefield I can't wait to walk into."

"You can say no," Dutch reminded me. "No one's going to think less of you if you back out."

I scowled at him, still feeling the brunt of the conference call we'd just had with Gaston. "Can you explain to me, now that Gaston isn't on the phone, why he can't simply order this Harrison dude to let us help him on the case?"

The gist we'd gotten from Gaston was that Harrison was so adamant about my not participating that he'd already filed a couple of complaints with various head honchos at the bureau over what he felt was a denigration to the heritage of the FBI and its investigators in the use of ... and I quote ... "palm readers and sideshow fortune-tellers." Gaston had read a few lines from one of the complaints so that I would be fully prepared for the frigid reception he was quite sure I was about to receive in D.C.

"He *could* order him," said Dutch in a way that suggested it wasn't that easy. "But you've got to remember where Harrison is coming from. His grandfather was the former bureau chief and now his father is one level below that. This guy has political clout that Gaston—having come originally from the CIA—doesn't carry. So even though Gaston outranks Harrison, he's still got to tread carefully here, Abby. The only way Gaston can have you participate is if you go to D.C. and win over Harrison. Gaston has gotten the guy to at least agree to meet you, but that's where his advocacy on your behalf is likely to end."

I glanced at Candice, who was sitting in the other chair across from Dutch's desk in his home office. I'd told Gaston at the get-go that the only way I'd agree to join in the investigation was if Candice came along too. "What do you think?" I asked her.

Candice took her time answering, which is one of the reasons I really like having her as my partner—she's cool under pressure. "I think that, ultimately, this isn't about someone else's personal agenda. It's about the missing kids. It's about the frantic parents wanting an answer, and it's about the bastard who will continue to take other parents' kids and possibly hurt them until he's stopped. I also think that you're damn good at what you do, and I'm damn good at what I do, and we have no reason to apologize to anyone for how we make our living. So I think we should head to Washington and show this prick what we're made of."

I smiled as I mentally checked in with my crew—those spirit guides that help keep me on track and assist with my intuition—and they gave me a light airy feeling on the right side of my body. That's a clear sign that they were okay with my getting involved.

With my mind made up, I turned back to Dutch and said firmly, "We're going."

Dutch was grinning too. "That's my girl," he said, then looked at Candice. "Keep her out of trouble this time, okay, Fusco?"

The corner of Candice's mouth lifted. "Sometimes she doesn't make it so easy."

"Tell me about it," he replied.

I rolled my eyes and got up from the chair. "Ha, ha," I scoffed. "*Hilarity* from the peanut gallery. You two have fun with that. I'm off to pack."

A little while later, Candice called to me from the bottom of the stairs that she'd be back at five a.m. sharp to pick me up for our flight; then I heard Dutch's heavy footsteps coming up the stairs.

"Hey, there, sweethot," he purred in his best Humphrey Bogart from the doorway while I folded a pair of jeans.

"Hey, yourself." I smiled. "Are you gonna miss me?"

"Maybe," he said coyly. Then his look got serious. "I meant what I said downstairs, Abs. You can quit anytime and come back on the first flight home. Put it on my credit card if you need to."

I laughed. "I forgot, I'm hanging out with a millionaire these days." I'd only recently learned that Dutch had a butt load of cash from a private security business he'd set up on the side years ago.

Dutch left the doorway and came to lie across the bed. "So you're only into me for the money—is that it?" he said, lifting one of my thongs out of the suitcase and raising an eyebrow as if to suggest my underwear should be made of a little more fabric.

"Well, it's certainly not for your looks," I deadpanned. "I mean, with that chiseled, perfect face, those blue eyes, and all that muscle . . . jeez, are you a pity date or what?"

Dutch lifted his chin and laughed before he dropped the thong and wrapped one of those delightfully muscular arms around my middle, tugging me to the bed.

Nuzzling my neck, he said, "Part of me really doesn't want to let you out of my sight."

I pulled away just a bit and looked him square in the eyes. "I'll be fine," I said, but couldn't help noticing the tiny bit of energy on my left side that indicated I might need to be careful.

"Oh, I know you'll be all right," he said with a smirk. "You'll be surrounded by federal agents—good luck getting into trouble with those guys around."

"So what's all this about not wanting me out of your sight?" I asked, running my fingers through his short blond hair.

"I'll miss you," he said simply.

I clasped both sides of his face and stared into those gorgeous midnight blue eyes. "I'll be home soon," I promised, and was only mildly surprised when the light and airy energy running along my right side said I'd hit that one on the head.

The next morning Candice and I flew out of Detroit Metro Airport on a direct flight to D.C. Candice slept the whole way. I fidgeted, bounced my knee, and basically drove myself crazy from takeoff to landing. She woke up right before the landing gear dropped. Stretching in her seat and sitting up, she took in my rather anxious appearance and said, "Would you relax?"

"What a fabulous suggestion!" I'm not so friendly when I'm uptight.

Candice rubbed her eyes, yawned, then gave me the once-over again. "Can I ask you something?" she said, squinting at the skirt and blazer I was wearing.

I sighed. "If you must."

Candice made a face of distaste and said, "Did you by any chance purchase that outfit during the Reagan administration?"

I rolled my eyes and my knee bounced more vigorously. "You know my entire wardrobe is casual," I snapped. "This was the best I could come up with given the limited choices I had." Self-consciously I tugged on the sides of my blazer, which, for the record, was *not* purchased during the Reagan administration ... but during the Bush years, and so what if by that I mean the first one!

Candice's face softened. "Well," she mused, "I suppose you did the best you could, but what's up with your hair these days, honey?"

"What's wrong with my hair?" I screeched loudly enough for people to turn in their seats and stare at us.

Candice held up a lock of my waist-length hair. "It's lookin' a little ragged, my friend."

My eye darted to the end of the strands in her hand and I had to admit, it did sort of appear that my last haircut had been performed by a machete. "Yeah, well, I haven't had a chance to get my hair done in a while," I growled.

"You're kidding," Candice deadpanned, but she added a smile.

"This conversation is doing *nothing* to make me feel better about meeting Harrison," I grumbled.

Candice's smile widened. "You're right. Sorry," she said. After a prolonged silence where my knee continued to bounce, she added, "This probably isn't going to be as bad as you think."

"Oh, trust me," I said with absolute certainty, "it's going to be far worse."

Candice shrugged her shoulders and moved her seat to its upright position. Glancing at her watch, she noted, "At least our flight's on time."

"Yippee," I said woodenly.

"Are you going to be like this the entire time we're here?"

"Count on it," I said, bouncing my knee again.

Candice and I got our luggage from baggage claim and went in search of a taxi. We'd been informed that Gaston had made arrangements for us to stay at the Sheraton near the bureau, and we decided to check in first, then head over to meet Harrison.

After depositing our luggage in our rooms, we went back out to hail another cab. We told the cabbie that we wanted to go to the FBI D.C. Field Office, and he looked both of us up and down twice before he faced forward and pulled out into traffic.

"What time is it?" I asked Candice.

"Two minutes later than the last time you asked. Seriously, Sundance," she said, using the new nickname she'd come up with after watching a documentary on Butch Cassidy and the Sundance Kid the week before, "you really do need to chill out. These guys are like dogs. They can smell fear, and if you go into this meeting a big blob of nerves, Harrison's going to intimidate the hell out of you and completely dismiss you. He'll be far more impressed if you show up looking cool. He won't be expecting confidence."

"But I'm not confident," I admitted, and I wasn't even talking about my new self-consciousness over my rather dated outfit and frizzy hair.

"Who says you have to be?" she replied with a wink. "Abby, this meeting is about perceptions. If Harrison can't rattle you, then he'll have some respect for you. Right now we know he's not open to hearing much of what you have to tell him. He's beyond skeptical— he's close-minded. But what he doesn't understand is that you really *are* the real deal. He's not prepared for that, and if you can just *appear* to have some confidence and hold up under his scrutiny, I'm positive he'll be surprised."

I sat with that for a bit, letting the words settle into me, and realized she was absolutely right. Who was this asshole to outright dismiss me without even hearing what I had to say or being shown what I could do? The nerve!

So by the time the cabbie pulled up to the impressive marble Washington Field Office on Fourth Street, I had settled down and had a pretty determined mind-set.

It helped a lot to walk in with Candice, who, at five feet nine inches of elegant ash-blond beauty, is the epitome of confidence. She strolled into the building like she owned the place and walked straight to the information desk. We waited in line behind a few other people with appointments before getting our turn.

"Abigail Cooper and Candice Fusco here to see Assistant Special Agent in Charge Brice Harrison," said Candice as she stepped up to one of the big, burly men with a badge behind the desk.

Big and Burly glanced at his computer screen, clicked a few keys, then told us to wait in reception. We moseyed over to two unoccupied seats and sat down. On a nearby credenza was complimentary coffee. "Cup a joe?" Candice asked, getting up from her seat as soon as she spotted the beverage.

"No thanks," I said. I was jittery enough without adding caffeine to the mix.

I glanced at a clock on the wall. It was ten minutes to ten. Our appointment with Harrison was at ten, so I closed my eyes and took some nice deep breaths while focusing on trying to appear confident. I heard Candice come back to her seat and quietly sip her coffee next to me. Surprisingly I really did feel calmer after a few minutes.

At one minute to ten, I opened my eyes and smiled at my partner. "Feeling better?" she asked with a twinkle in her eye.

"Yep," I said. "I'm good."

"Excellent. He should be here any minute, and don't worry, in this light your outfit isn't so bad." I gave her a withering look. And she smiled radiantly back at me. "Just don't let him see you sweat," she advised.

"Roger."

"And if it starts to get confrontational, and you begin to feel pressured, give me a nod and I'll step in."

"Thanks, I appreciate it," I said, really glad that I'd insisted on Candice's coming along to help out.

The big hand settled on the twelve, then moved at a snail's pace past it, then way past; then it settled on the six and it was really hard to continue to appear calm and collected. Finally, I got up and approached the front desk again. Big and Burly gave me a rather dull once-over. "Yes?" he asked.

I forced a friendly smile onto my face and said, "I was just wondering—do you know if Agent Harrison has been informed that we're waiting for him out in reception? Our appointment was at ten, and it's now half past, so I'm worried that he missed being told we were here."

"He's aware," said Burly.

My eyes widened. "Ah," I said at last. "Okay, then."

Burly just stared at me with narrowed eyes. I had a feeling he didn't like me too much.

"I'll wait over there, nice and quiet-like, then," I said, turning to retreat quickly back to my seat next to Candice.

"What's the word?" she asked as I sat down.

"Harrison knows we're here. That's all I got out of the ray of sunshine at the desk."

Candice eyed the clock. "Oldest tactic in the book," she said, setting her empty cup down on the side table next to her. "Keep them waiting, make them impatient, and get them off-balance. Trust me, he's going to hold out until he thinks we're good and angry, and then show up without an apology."

"So he should be showing up any second, then, right?" I groused. I *was* good and angry.

"Oh, I'll bet he makes us wait a tad bit longer," she said with a smirk before stretching her legs, leaning her head back against the wall, and closing her eyes. "Wake me in an hour, would you?"

"You're joking!" I gasped. "You really think he'll be an hour and a half late?"

"Oh, I think he'll be even later," she said. "If I were him, I'd make us sit here until ten minutes to noon. Then I'd show up with an attitude and announce that I had a luncheon appointment and ask if we could make it snappy."

My mouth dropped open. "Please be kidding."

"You wait," she said. "You'll see."

As it turned out, Candice was very good at predicting Harrison's behavior. At eleven forty-five she got up and motioned for me to follow. We headed to reception again and Candice eyed Big and Burly with her own rather dull expression.

"Yes?" he said with just the tiniest bit more enthusiasm than he'd used to address me.

"Please inform Agent Harrison that we waited patiently for him to make an appearance. However, we have other business to attend to. If he would still like to meet with us, he may reach us via this number." She slid her card toward Burly.

He eyed her card and nodded.

"Please further inform Agent Harrison that if we do not hear from him by five p.m., we will make Special Agent in Charge Gaston aware of what transpired here today, and head back to Michigan." And with that, Candice turned and walked away toward the doors.

I was caught a bit off guard by her sudden departure, but quickly recovered myself and hurried after her. Once outside I asked, "Do you think he'll call us?"

Candice smiled as she raised her arm high to hail a cab. "Yes," she said. "But he'll wait until four fifty-five or so."

I chuckled ruefully and shook my head. "So, what do we do in the meantime?"

At that moment a cab pulled up in front of us. Candice reached forward and held open the door. "We shop, of course," she said, making a point to eye my outfit again. "We need to get you into the twenty-first century, toots."

I sighed as I got into the cab. "Okay, but I only brought along a hundred bucks' spending money, so let's make sure to hit the sale rack, okay?"

Candice and I spent the rest of the day arguing over price tags. "Two thousand dollars? Are you *serious*?" I gasped as she held out a pantsuit to me.

Candice looked unfazed. "While you were in the ladies' room after lunch, I called Dutch and explained to him what happened this morning. I also told him I felt you needed to make a powerful first impression, which would require a complete transformation. Face it, honey—you really need a little *pow* to swim with the fish in this pond."

"I never liked swimming in ponds," I grumbled.

"Anyway, Dutch said he was totally behind your makeover, and to put it on his credit card."

I snickered. "Good luck getting ahold of that," I said, patting my purse protectively. I had Dutch's credit card—which he'd insisted on giving me in case of emergencies—safely stashed in my wallet.

"You mean this?" Candice said with a grin as she held up Dutch's AmEx card.

I gasped and tried to grab it from her, but she was way too quick for me. "Candice," I said evenly as I glared at her, "I can't. It would be taking advantage of him!"

"Don't be ridiculous, Abby," she said, completely ignoring the fact that I was unwilling to take the expensive Marc Jacobs garment from her as she sorted through the other suits on the rack. "Harrison is already sizing us up. He's sent us a message that he doesn't consider you worthy of his time. If you show up looking like something right out of *Vogue*, he'll have to reconsider that, and by getting him to reconsider his first impression, we might just be able to open a crack into that brick wall of his mind."

"Can't we look for something on discount at least?" I pleaded, taking the Marc Jacobs and another three suits she handed me, afraid to actually look at the tags.

Candice sighed and turned away from that collection before heading toward another rack labeled ALEXANDER MCQUEEN. "Dutch has given me a budget," she called over her shoulder when I failed to follow her.

"How much?"

"I'm not telling," she said. "But if you don't cooperate, I'll go over that limit by a mile."

I glared at her again. "I hate this whole thing."

Candice stopped draping items over her arm long enough to regard me soberly. "Welcome to Washington, babe. You want to play in this town, you gotta pony up. Dutch gets that, and let's face it, the guy can afford it. Besides, we already know the FBI isn't going to pay you for your services. So let's say that Harrison is won over by you, and you assist with this investigation. Say it takes a few weeks, as we both know it very well could. I know that you get paid a hundred bones an hour from your regular clients, so you're actually forgoing thousands of dollars by taking time off to help these guys out. This is just Dutch's way of paying you back on behalf of the bureau."

"Gee, if I were only naive enough to buy into that," I said woodenly.

Candice smiled and pivoted me around to face the dressing room. "Forward and march, Sundance," she ordered.

By three o'clock I had three suits that cost more than the down payment on my first house. I'd also been accessorized to within an inch of my life. But I will admit—I looked pretty damn good.

"Now what?" I asked as we left the upscale mall Candice had taken me to.

"We're on to hair and makeup," Candice said.

I paused to look at my reflection in one of the mirrors on the way out. "What's wrong with my makeup?"

"It doesn't say *pow!* It says 'hey.'" She said that last bit with a stifled yawn. "Plus, that jungle you have going on has got to go," she added, swirling her finger in a circle at my hair. "I think we should cut off a few feet to really update your look."

I stopped on the sidewalk and stamped my foot.

"Feet?" I screeched. "You want to cut *feet* off my hair?"

Candice ignored my tantrum and raised her arm again to hail a cab. "Trust me," she said. "I'll take good care of you."

An hour later I was really trying not to cry. Long chunks of my waist-length hair lay on the floor of the hair salon and all I could think of was the years it had taken to grow it out that long. Juan—the hairdresser fussing over me with giddy excitement—was undeterred by my pitiful expression reflected back at him in the mirror as my now-shoulder-length hair dangled wetly from my scalp. "On to the tint and highlights!" he sang with a big fat smile before disappearing to mix up some hair dye.

In the mirror I could see Candice approaching my chair, holding on to her ringing cell phone. When she was right behind me, she wiggled it in the mirror but didn't answer it. "Guess who that was?" she said.

"I hate you," I said meanly, ignoring her question.

Her face softened. "Abby, I promise you, Juan is one of the best. You are really going to love this new look. And think about how freeing it will be not to be a slave to your long hair anymore. I mean, the drying time alone must take half an hour."

"I still hate you," I groused, slumping down in the chair.

Candice smoothed a few of the locks away from my face. "You can hate me now," she said, "but just wait to see the end result before you hate me permanently, okay?"

I sighed heavily and stared at my lap. "Was that Harrison?" I asked, wanting to change the subject before I really did start crying.

"It was," she said. "Or at least the caller ID said it was from the FBI." Candice glanced at her watch. "And he was twenty whole minutes earlier than I thought he'd be, the sneaky bastard."

I raised my eyes and cocked my head. "Why is that sneaky?"

"Well," Candice said, leaning an elbow against the next chair, "it means that I gave him until five to contact us. And if he had waited until about quarter to, or even four fifty, and we had just ignored him, then he knew he'd be given the riot act by Gaston. But since he was earlier than expected, well, now he can say that he attempted to call us and we didn't respond, so Gaston can't accuse him of being uncooperative."

"So now what?" I asked, feeling like I was way out of my political league.

"We blow him off for tonight," she said. "And tomorrow we call him early—before he gets into his office, in fact. We'll leave him a message telling him that our plane departs at ten a.m. If he wants to meet with us, he'll have to rearrange his morning schedule, which will no doubt royally tick him off, but he'll do it just to say he did."

At that moment Juan came bouncing back with several containers of brightly colored hair dye. I gulped and gave Candice a pleading look. "Help me," I mouthed.

She smiled broadly and gave my shoulder a gentle pat. "See you in a bit," she sang, then went back to sit in the lobby.

Two hours later Candice and I had made our way back to the hotel. As we stepped out of the cab and approached the door, loaded down with shopping bags, a man walking down the street jumped right in front of us and reached for the lobby door. "Let me get that for you," he said with a *huge* smile and eyes that looked directly into mine.

I blushed and gave a quick "Thank you" as I hurried past him into the lobby.

Behind me I could hear Candice's soft laughter. "That's the third time in twenty minutes!" She giggled.

I could feel my cheeks flush even hotter and saw the evidence as we passed a large mirror on our way to the elevators. My new look was definitely turning heads and as I caught a glimpse of my reflection, I had to admit, even with those bright red embarrassed cheeks, I looked friggin' amazing.

"I barely recognize myself," I said to my partner as we waited by the elevator.

"You look stunning," Candice said. I blushed some more and looked down at the floor. "Really, Abs, I can't believe the transformation."

"I hope Dutch likes it," I said as we got on and turned around to face the doors again. I noticed then that we were surrounded by men all openly ogling.

Candice raised a hand to her lips to stifle a giggle. "Oh, something tells me he'll like it all right."

We left our bags in the room and then headed downstairs to dinner at the elegant Bistro Bis. As we were seated, Candice's cell began to ring.

"Harrison?" I asked as she looked at the caller ID.

"Nope," she said with a smile. "It's your boy." Candice answered the call. "Hi, Dutch," she said. I scrunched my eyebrows, wondering why my boyfriend was calling my partner before calling me. "... Uh-huh," she was saying, "mission accomplished, and I only had to wrestle her to the ground two or three times." Then she laughed and laughed and I snapped open my menu, thoroughly irritated. "Believe me," she continued, "you wouldn't recognize her if she walked right past you on the street. She looks like one of Charlie's Angels."

Behind the menu I rolled my eyes, but deep down I felt the smallest hint of satisfaction. Candice's hand appeared at the top of my menu and pulled it gently down. "Your man would like to whisper sweet nothings to you," she said, handing me the phone.

I took it and gave an unenthused, "Hey."

"I hear you've had a transformation," Dutch said.

"Something like that," I replied, brushing a bang out of my eyes.

"I can't wait to see you," he said.

I sighed, still feeling a bit miffed that he and Candice had gotten together and made me their science project. "Uh-huh," I said.

"What's up?" he asked, sensing my mood.

"Nothing," I said a little too quickly. "I'm just tired."

"Hey," he cooed in that smoky baritone that always sent butterflies into my stomach. "You understand why Candice wanted to give you a makeover, right?"

"Yes," I said, surprised that my eyes were welling with tears and even more so when I realized that I felt a teensy bit hurt and betrayed. "I was looking a bit matronly or something."

"Abs," Dutch said softly, and I could hear the smallest bit of humor in his voice. "You're as far away from matronly as they come, babe. You're a beautiful woman and Candice wasn't out to try to make you look prettier as much as she was out to make you look powerful."

"Uh-huh," I said, still staring at my menu and blinking back the tears. Out of the corner of my eye I could see Candice staring at me with concern.

"She was trying to give you a big dose of confidence, sweetheart; that's all. She knows the best way for you to get through this interview with Harrison is to show up looking like a million bucks and with the attitude that you don't give a rat's ass what this guy thinks of you, because you are a strong, confident, *beautiful* woman, and you know what, doll?"

"What?"

"She's right."

I let that sit with me for a little bit before I said anything. Finally, I whispered, "Okay, I get it."

"Good," he said. "And sweethot?"

"Yeah?"

"No matter what happens tomorrow, I'm in your corner and I believe in you, okay?"

I swallowed hard, suddenly missing him so much. I closed my eyes and just listened to the sound of his breathing in the background and then, like a switch being thrown in my head, my mind's eye filled with images of moving boxes. My eyes snapped back open and I asked, "Dutch?"

"Yeah?"

"Are you thinking of moving?"

There was the slightest pause before he said, "Moving? Why would I move?"

I closed my eyes again and saw that same image of the boxes and then my radar suggested that this move could be major . . . and soon. "Shit!" I swore into the phone.

"What's the matter?"

"You're moving."

Dutch laughed softly. He thought I was joking. "Oh yeah?" he asked. "Where am I moving to?"

My heart sank. "South."

"Like where? Ferndale?" he asked, speaking of a town slightly south of us.

"No," I said, feeling it in my bones. "To the Southwest. Texas. Arizona. New Mexico. Somewhere around there."

Dutch's laughter intensified. "Abs," he said. "I'm not moving. I've got everything I want right here, okay?"

"Yeah, right. Listen, our waiter is here and I haven't even looked at the menu. I'll talk to you later, okay?"

"Hey," he said seriously. I waited without speaking for him to say something and after a moment he did. "Babe, I wouldn't leave you. You have to know that, all right? I'm not moving. You and me, we make a pretty good team, and there's no way I'd break that up."

I wanted to trust him on that one, but my radar never lied and this new insight I was feeling in my bones. Still, I put a little faith into him as I said, "I hear you. Thanks, Dutch. I'll call you tonight before we hit the hay."

"Love you," he said softly.

"Me too."

The next morning I woke up to the sound of Candice leaving a message for Harrison. Her tone was clipped and direct, and groggy as I was, I still appreciated having her along. "... our flight departs at ten hundred hours. If we do not hear back from you by eight a.m., we will assume you cannot accommodate a meeting and head to the airport. You have my number for a callback. Good day, Agent Harrison."

I rubbed my eyes and stifled a yawn. "What time is it?"

Candice slid her phone into her purse. "It's six a.m."

I blinked a few times and noticed that she was already showered, dressed, and looking pretty spiffy. "What time did you get up?"

"Five."

"Good Lord," I moaned, lying back on the bed. "Why so early?"

Candice came over to my bed and hovered over me. "I had to shower first so that I could help you get ready just in case we need to sprint over to the bureau."

"You don't trust me to pull it off on my own?"

"Not for a minute," she said flatly.

I groaned again but sat up and swiveled my legs over the side of the bed. "Don't tell me," I said moodily. "We're going for 'pow!'"

Candice laughed. "No, honey, this morning we're actually going for '*kaboom!*'"

Candice's cell rang at seven, which was a good thing because it distracted her long enough for me to take some deep breaths and force myself to calm down. She'd been downright militant for the past hour, ordering me into the shower and yelling at me to hurry up. Then she practically wrestled me into wearing a bra that I swear came with hydraulics (but at least now I appeared to have some cleavage, which I'll admit was a small miracle in and of itself). Then came the makeup and hair thing. She's a great stylist but can be a little rough with the roller brush, and as I stared at the face in the mirror wearing what I thought might be a little too much makeup, I wondered whether I was ever going to feel like myself again.

"Fine. We'll see you in fifteen minutes, but Agent

Harrison, we will not be kept waiting longer than ten minutes in the bureau lobby."

I smiled. Good old Candice—Harrison had clearly underestimated her, at least. With one more sigh at the face in the mirror, I got up from the side of the tub, where I'd been perched while Candice tortured me, and walked into our room. My partner was hurrying around trying to get our things together as quickly as possible. "We'll take our luggage with us," she said when she saw me.

We exited the hotel fifteen minutes later—which left us about ten minutes to reach the bureau field office, and we made that with one minute to spare. As we hurried up the steps to the front door, Candice leaned in and said, "Remember, you are a strong, confident woman. You look amazing. You *are* amazing. There's no reason in the world why this guy should intimidate you and throw you off your game. Just go in there and do what you do best."

"I can do this," I said, trying to put a little emphasis on that word "can."

"You will."

Candice held open the door and we marched in like we were all that and a bag of chips. And it almost worked. That is, until we got our first look at Assistant Special Agent in Charge Brice Harrison, who was tall, blond, and—dare I say it?—*exquisite*.

Chapter Two

"Aw, crap," I heard Candice mutter as we caught our first sight of him.

I gulped. We were too close now for me to reply without his noticing. He stood like some sort of Michelangelo-inspired statue, leaning with his back against the front desk. There was no mistaking it was Harrison. Candice and I both knew it was him the moment we set eyes on him. He commanded the room, with his arms folded across his chest, his shirt perfectly creased, his tie impeccably straight, and a face that was hard, masculine, and sexy as hell. His nose was straight but slightly hawkish, his forehead high, broad, and unlined, his chin chiseled, and his brown eyes stared straight ahead—focused and intent as they zeroed in on us.

Candice slowed her pace a fraction and I did the same. I knew she was trying not to appear as if she was in a rush, and were I brave enough to sneak a look over at her, I had a feeling her chin would be slightly tilted and her own eyes would be cool and nonchalant. I'd seen that look on her face a hundred times, and worked to mimic it now, even while my stomach bunched.

Candice stopped right in front of him and spoke in a breezy voice as if she didn't have a care in the world. "We're here to see Brice Harrison. Would you please call him and let him know that Candice Fusco and Abigail Cooper are here for our meeting? And please tell him not to be late this time. We're on a schedule."

I resisted the urge to laugh . . . but just barely. Especially when I saw Harrison's cheeks flush and his eyes darken moodily. "I am *Agent* Harrison, Ms. Fusco."

Candice's eyebrows lifted and she made a show of looking him up and down as if she were inspecting livestock. "I see," she said with the smallest hint of disappointment. "Somehow I expected you to be . . ." She paused, as if searching for a word. "Older."

Harrison cocked an eyebrow. "Trust me," he said in a voice not quite as low as my boyfriend's, but still incredibly smooth and masculine. "I'm old enough."

Candice looked at her watch. "Yes, well, as I said, Abigail and I have a plane to catch, so if you will lead the way, Mr. Harrison."

Harrison leaned in toward Candice and looked her dead in the eye. "That's *Agent* Harrison, Ms. Fusco."

The corner of Candice's mouth lifted a fraction, but I could tell the way Harrison was leaning into her threw her off a bit. "As you wish, *Agent* Harrison."

Harrison then swiveled his eyes to me and I gave him a toothy grin—which was my first mistake. He had my number immediately. I could tell it in the way he looked at me—very much like the way a leopard regards the little mongoose before you have to avert your eyes from the TV. "If you two will sign the register, take your visitor badges, and follow me," he instructed.

We did as we were told without comment, then followed him out of the lobby and to a row of elevators. I avoided looking at anything but the floor. Candice stood close to me with her shoulder pressed against mine. I could tell she was doing her best through body language to support me, but my nerves were starting to fray, and as the bell dinged and we loaded onto the car, I had a moment before the doors closed where I seriously thought about sprinting for the exit.

We rode the elevator up in silence and got out on the sixth floor. Candice and I followed dutifully behind Harrison, our heels clicking on the marble floor. I was quickly becoming aware of how uncomfortable I was. The miracle bra was digging into my rib cage. My skirt was too tight for me to take my normal stride. The collar on my blazer scratched against my neck. And I was fairly certain my strong-enough-for-King-Kong-but-made-for-a-woman deodorant had utterly failed.

I was trying to breathe normally, but my mind kept racing ahead to this little "meeting" and the interrogation tactics that I was certain would follow. My radar doesn't usually work well when I'm freaked-out and I knew that it was only going to get worse from here.

Harrison led us into a small conference room and pointed to the leather chairs set around a mahogany table. He sat at the head of the table, and Candice took the one at the opposite end. I sat right next to Candice.

Harrison looked without blinking at Candice, his hard eyes intent and calculating. She folded her hands and rested them on the tabletop, meeting his gaze with her typical cool, composed self.

I, on the other hand, couldn't help myself. I sat back in my chair and tried to make myself as small as possible. That's when Harrison turned his steely gaze to me. "As you know," he began smoothly, "the only reason I agreed to this meeting was out of professional courtesy."

"We're aware," Candice said before I could say anything. "And we agreed to come here out of that same professional courtesy."

Harrison ignored Candice and continued to stare at me. "Let me get straight to the point. I don't believe in psychics or fortune-tellers or mediums or seers or whatever it is you people are calling yourselves these days. I believe in cold hard facts. And of those, I'm convinced you won't be able to offer me any. Still, I agreed to take this meeting, so I'm going to see it to the end. And to prove to my superiors that I gave you a fair shot, I've set up a series of tests."

I looked at Candice in alarm. Her gaze never left Harrison, but she did reach out a hand and squeeze my arm. "It's okay," she whispered. "Just listen."

"If you fail these tests, Ms. Cooper, I will ask you to return home and resist the urge to comment further on any bureau business. You see, it is actually against federal policy to reveal any fact of any case to someone who doesn't have the proper clearance. And if it were suspected that an agent was leaking details about a specific case to his girlfriend, that agent could find himself out of a job very, *very* quickly."

His meaning was clear. Dutch wasn't allowed to ask me for my intuitive input anymore or risk losing his job. And that got my dander up. "And if I pass your tests?" I asked.

Harrison smiled, amused, the way parents do when their child has just said something ridiculous. "Well then," he said, spreading his hands in an "oh well" gesture. "I might ask you to join our investigation."

"Might?" I pressed.

Harrison gave one small, nearly imperceptible nod. I scowled and he remarked, "Of course, if these terms are not acceptable to you, then you and your associate here are free to leave."

I looked at Candice, trying to decide if she thought Harrison's proposal was acceptable. She looked at me with a kind smile and shrugged her shoulders. "Your call, Sundance."

I crossed my arms and checked in with my crew—but their answer wasn't much help. The feeling I had was that they reaffirmed my own sense that these "tests" were bullshit, and if I wanted to stay, they would work with me, but it wasn't going to be easy. If I felt like leaving—they would support that too.

And I was about to say "Thanks but no thanks" and exit stage left when I looked up again and met Harrison's eyes. There was something so smug in the way he was watching me—like he couldn't *wait* to prove me a con artist. In that instant I opened my mouth and accepted his offer. "Very well," I said, staring coolly at him and forcing myself not to blink. "I accept your offer, Agent Harrison."

One of his eyebrows arched and he glanced again at his watch. "Good," he said, "but you'll need to change your flight—the tests that I've arranged may take some time for you to get through."

I scowled at how confident he appeared, but let it go. I had to be at the top of my game here and getting irritated at the way he was treating me wasn't going to help.

Candice already had her iPhone out and as I leaned over to look, I saw that she was on the airline's Web page. "I'll see if I can get us out of here late tonight so you can take your time."

"Thanks," I whispered.

Harrison got up and walked to the door, pausing before he exited to tell us that he would be back in exactly five minutes with the first of the tests. When the door closed, I leaned way back in my chair and said, "He's a charmer."

Candice smirked while she fiddled with her phone. "I think I may have a crush," she said dreamily.

"Oh, me too!" I replied with breathy excitement. "Do you think he might ask one of us to the prom?"

Candice giggled. "I think the only way he'll be able to dance is if the doctors can successfully perform that surgery."

"What surgery?"

"The one to remove that *gigantic* stick up his butt."

That sent us both into gales of laughter and we were still giggling as Harrison came back into the room looking decidedly displeased that we were both having such a good time. "Are you ready?" he asked when we worked to compose ourselves.

"I doubt it," I told him seriously, and Candice turned her head to hide her smile.

Harrison sighed and held open the door. "If you will follow me, please," he said.

We walked out into the hallway and back toward the elevators. Harrison pressed the button and we loaded onto the car and rode it all the way to the basement. When the doors opened, we looked out into a rather dim hallway lined with doors.

Harrison got out and marched midway down the corridor with us in tow, before stopping abruptly. I had already turned up my radar and immediately my intuition wanted to pull me the rest of the way down the hallway, but I didn't know why. I didn't have time to ponder it as Harrison began speaking. "These offices are all empty except for one," Harrison said to me. "To pass this test, you must correctly guess the door that holds an agent—"

Harrison didn't have a chance to finish as I was already bolting down the hallway. Behind me I could hear Candice's heels following closely. I stopped at the second-to-last door and rested my hand on the door handle. "There's a guy in here," I said, feeling out the energy behind the door. I looked up at Harrison, who was eyeing me suspiciously. Pushing the envelope further, I said, "He's white, between five-nine and five-eleven, brown hair, and, I believe, brown eyes. And he's got a lot of blue around him."

Harrison had come down the hallway, his expression unreadable. "You're sure that is the correct door?" was all he said, and the way he said it would make anyone other than me feel like she'd chosen the wrong door.

I narrowed my eyes at him, and without looking at anything but Harrison's face, I turned the handle and opened the door before I stepped back and with a hand flourish said, "Ta-da!"

"Whoa," Candice said, peering over my shoulder. "Abs, that was awesome!"

I allowed myself to look, and there, sitting quietly but rather stunned at a desk in the back of a room painted a vivid blue, was an agent with brown hair and brown eyes.

Harrison, however, appeared completely unimpressed. "If you will follow me to the next test, ladies," he said before turning on his heel and striding back down the corridor toward the elevators.

Candice shook her head ruefully and held her hand up. "High five!" she said.

I slapped her hand and allowed myself a big happy grin, but something in the back of my mind suggested I might not be as lucky next time.

The next "test" wasn't my forte at all. Harrison clearly had no understanding of how intuition worked, as he sat me down in front of another agent and said, "I have instructed this agent to think about certain specific things. A color, a shape, and a location. You are to name what color, shape, and location he is thinking about and you have thirty seconds, starting now."

My mouth dropped. "Are you kidding me?" I asked him.

"You have twenty-eight seconds," he replied.

I looked at the agent across from me, but he wasn't meeting my gaze. He was staring directly at the top of the table.

I looked back up at Harrison, still eyeing his watch. "I'm not a mind reader, Agent Harrison. I'm an intuitive."

"Twenty-one seconds remaining."

I shook my head and felt Candice's hand squeeze my arm. "Try it anyway," she suggested.

"Eighteen seconds," Harrison announced.

I looked again at the agent in front of me, closed my eyes, and called out to my crew for help.

"Ten seconds."

I snapped my eyes open, completely unsure of myself, and said, "A circle, yellow, and an amusement park."

"Incorrect," Harrison said, lowering his watch, but out of the corner of my eye I saw the agent across from me glance up at Harrison.

Candice caught it too because she said to the agent, "Tell us what the answers were."

The agent looked from Candice to Harrison, who scowled but gave a small nod. "A circle is correct," he said, "but the color was orange and the place was Disney World."

"Two out of three, then," Candice said happily.

"One out of three," said Harrison. "I'm not going to count her guessing an amusement park."

"Of course *you* wouldn't," Candice snapped. "And stop saying 'guess.'"

"Let's move on to the next test. Thank you, Agent Millstone. Please send in the other subjects."

A few minutes later two women came in and sat down. Both held carefully blank expressions and worked hard to avoid eye contact with me. "These two women have a unique relationship. Please tell me about how they are connected to each other. You have one minute."

I was taken aback by this one. There was something about the first subject—an older woman with beautiful porcelain skin but marred by dark circles under her eyes—that I kept going back to. I tried to focus on what the relationship between these two was, but the older woman's energy kept tugging at me and I couldn't let it go. I made up my mind right then to allow myself to fail this test and let the chips fall where they would. "I'm so sorry," I began softly, and I reached out to the older lady and touched the top of her hand. "I know you know you don't have much time, but I can tell that you've taken care of everything you've needed to and you may have a month or two longer than you realize. I also want to tell you that it won't be nearly as painful as you think it'll be. And the very end will feel a bit fuzzy, but that will be a good thing, I promise you."

A rather stunned expression appeared on the wom-

an's face even as tears welled in her eyes and began to
roll down her cheeks. I held her hand, and squeezed
it gently. "There's nothing more you need to worry
about," I continued softly. "You can rest assured that
you've taken care of all the small details, and whomever you're leaving behind will be well cared for
and looked after." And in that moment I knew what
the answer was and I swiveled my eyes to the other
woman at the table. "You're taking care of her—"

"Time!" Harrison called out.

"—dog," I finished.

"We've passed the minute mark, Ms. Cooper. And
I'm afraid you did not arrive at the answer in time."

I ignored Harrison and focused on the other
woman. "You'll be a great caretaker," I said to her before turning back to the first woman. "What kind of
cancer is it?"

"Pancreatic," she said, her voice cracking. "I've
asked Joan to take care of my pets when I die. She's
agreed."

"A dog and a cat, right?" I asked.

She nodded.

"It's the right choice," I told her. "They'll be great.
They'll miss you, of course, but I can tell they're going
to a good home."

"Thank you, ladies. You may return to your desks,"
Harrison said to the two women, and the room suddenly got even more uncomfortable.

Candice shook her head and glared at him. I knew
by her posture she was having a hard time keeping her
cool, but by now it was obvious that no matter how
good a performance I put on, Harrison wasn't going
to accept me or my abilities.

Harrison showed the women out and called to
someone else in the hallway. Another male agent en-

tered and took his seat in front of us. He was a beefy-looking man, with a bald head, beady eyes, and a small, nearly lipless mouth.

I definitely wasn't picking up the warm and fuzzy vibe from him. "This is Agent Turrell. You have sixty seconds to list ten facts about him that would be relevant to a profiler, excluding of course the obvious physical description. Your time starts now."

I eyed Agent Turrell, who was eyeing me back, and I swear, his expression said, "I double-dog-dare you to read me."

Gulp.

I closed my eyes and focused, trying to feel out his energy, but immediately I met with what I can describe only as an energetic brick wall. This happens to me sometimes during a session when I get a client who doesn't really want to be read or has completely closed his mind off to me, and it's pretty impossible to get through.

Still, I scrunched my eyes and focused, but after a few more seconds and Harrison announcing, "Forty-five seconds remaining," I knew I wasn't going to be able to pull it off.

I sighed, opened my eyes, and turned to Candice, shrugging my shoulders. "What?" she whispered.

"His mind is closed," I said.

Understanding lit up her face and she turned to Agent Turrell and nodded. But then she did something that surprised me. She squinted at him, then made a face that suggested she was grossed out and reached for her purse. Pulling out a tissue, she handed it to him and whispered, "For your nose."

Turrell looked at the tissue in her hand in surprise and flushed a nice shade of crimson, quickly taking it and swiping at his nose. For the record, there was no evidence of anything snotty—it was just Candice's way of throwing Turrell off-balance to help relax the mental wall.

I immediately focused again on Turrell while he was looking at Candice, who shook her head, made another face, and whispered, "Try again."

Turrell's color turned from crimson to flame red as he then took a moment to blow his nose loudly into the tissue. Meanwhile Harrison called out, "Thirty seconds!" from the side of the table.

And in an instant I had my first threads of information and I began to quickly rattle them off. "I'm sensing a military background—something with boats, so the navy. I'm also sensing something like a special-ops connection, like the SEALs, but there was an injury, I believe to your left knee. I know it was operated on—twice. There's also a connection to California, the southern portion, like L.A., but I don't think you've been there in a long time. However, Colorado is really calling your name—something about a log cabin, I want to place it just outside of Denver, near a lake at the base of a river that I believe flows into that lake. Also, there is some sort of test that you're studying for, but I don't believe you'll pass it this time. But then, you're not supposed to pass it on your first try. It's a hard test, and you need more time under your belt for practice or study or something before you can pass."

"Time!" Harrison yelled out.

I jumped. I'd been so focused and concentrating so hard that I'd nearly forgotten I was being timed. On the opposite side of the table, Turrell just stared at me open-mouthed, holding the wadded-up tissue in his hand. "You got it," Candice said to him, rubbing her nose nonchalantly before turning to smile and wink at me.

"Fail," Harrison said as he nodded to Turrell to go.

"Hold on there," Candice said, reaching across the table to grab Turrell's arm. "What part of that did she get wrong?"

Turrell looked from Harrison to me and back to Candice, uncertainty on his face. "Er," he said, "none of it really."

"Ha!" Candice said, smacking the tabletop. "She passes."

"No," said Harrison, his face hard and determined. "She fails. I asked for ten pieces of information. She only gave me five." And then he listed them, ticking off on his fingers, "Navy SEALs, a knee injury, L.A., Colorado, and a proficiency test."

Now it was Candice's turn to be shocked. "She gave you *way* more than that!"

"She actually gave me nothing useful, Ms. Fusco. The five I'm allowing her are a gift."

Candice opened her mouth and I knew a whole litany of insults was about to pour out of her, so I jumped to my feet and said, "Can we take a break? I have to go to the restroom. Candice, won't you come with me?"

It took a moment or two for my partner to realize I was tugging on her arm and trying to pull her out of the room, especially since Harrison was still eyeing us with that stupid smug look on his face. "The ladies' room is down the hall and to the left," he said.

I got Candice out into the hallway and coaxed her toward the restroom as she listed off ten things that she hated about Harrison. "That arrogant, narrow-minded, pugnacious, tyrannical, misogynistic, sexist, self-centered, smug, sycophantic son of a *bitch*!"

I smiled, impressed that she'd listed off all ten in rapid succession. "So, you're still crushing on him, right?"

As we reached the restroom, Candice was actually speechless. She merely let out a long, "Arrrrgh!" and we went in.

When we were washing our hands, she regarded me in the mirror. "How is it that you're not furious?" she asked.

"There's just no way to win with this guy," I said. "I could lead him to the Holy Grail and he'd still tell me I was full of shit."

"Then what are we still doing here?" she asked, handing me a paper towel.

"Hell if I know," I said. "But I think that there's something I might need to prove to myself. I think that if I can come through this little obstacle course of Harrison's with some amount of success, I might get that bastard to doubt a teeny bit that we're all scam artists."

"It's just so clear to everyone he's put in front of you today that you're the real deal, Abs. It's hard to believe how blind he is."

"They're out there, Candice. The world is full of skeptics with completely closed minds. And there isn't anything I can do to disprove their beliefs because they're so ingrained."

"So what are we still doing here?" she asked again, more gently this time as we made our way back down the hallway.

I sighed heavily. "Let's just do one more test and call it a day, okay?"

"Good," she said. "And afterward I'm taking you out for a fabulous lunch. I'm really proud of you for going through with this and you have flat-out astounded me today, Sundance."

Her boost of confidence did wonders for my ego. "Thanks, gal pal," I said, bumping her with my shoulder.

Outside the room we'd been in, Harrison was waiting for us in the hallway, wearing his usual pose of arms crossed and steely gaze narrowed and focused on us. "What's the verdict?" he asked as we approached. "Are you in for more or out?"

I tried to keep my cool, but it was hard in the face of such arrogance. "We're in," I said lightly. "But as there appears to be such disparity between what you think is pass or fail, we will only participate in one more test. And that outcome will determine whether or not *I* decide to stick around long enough to help *you* with the investigation." *Take that, you bastard*, I thought.

Harrison's eyebrow arched, but no sign of humor cracked his granite features. "Get your coats," he ordered. "We're going off-site for this one."

We drove in a company-issued black sedan through the streets of Washington, making our way slowly out of the Capitol district and into more dicey-looking territory before finally stopping in front of an older home in need of some major attention.

Harrison parked at the curb and pointed to the house. "Inside you will find a crime scene," he said. "To pass this test you'll have five whole minutes to tell me anything you can about the crime." Just then, Harrison's cell phone rang and while he answered it, Candice and I got out of the car and stared at the house. "Wonder when our time starts," I said to her.

Candice glanced at Harrison, still on the phone as he too got out of the car. "It probably already started," she said, and urged me toward the front door.

I entered the grungy-looking house with Candice close on my heels. Our FBI escort came along a few moments later, after he'd wrapped up the phone call out on the porch.

The interior was a surprise given the house's rough exterior. The wallpaper was from an earlier era, but it was a sunny print that still held some glow. The carpets were worn but well cleaned, and pictures and paintings on the walls had been hung with care.

We entered through the breezeway into the living room. The sofa was upholstered with faded roses, and pink throw pillows trimmed in gold were neatly placed at each end. A crucifix hung on the wall above the sofa and a long-outdated copy of *House and Garden* lay on one side table; the other held a cute yellow lamp and a porcelain angel. Near a window was a light green upholstered wing chair, and next to that a small table adorned with knitting needles and yarn.

I moved into the kitchen and surveyed that too. It was small, with outdated appliances, but spotless and clean. "Are you getting anything?" Candice whispered.

The volume on my radar was dialed up to high— but nothing about this space had as yet signaled an alarm, which made me frown in frustration. Surely if something violent had happened here, I'd know it, wouldn't I? "Not yet," I answered, and drifted out into the dining room.

Six chairs sat demurely around an oval dining room table covered in a crisp white tablecloth. I ran my hand over the fabric—it was soft cotton. I glanced at the walls, which were also covered in wallpaper, but this was a more formal print than in the living room. I glanced around some more, not sure what I was really looking for.

"I'm guessing the bedrooms are down that hall-way," Candice said, motioning to a doorway on the opposite side of the dining room that led to the back of the house.

I nodded and noticed that Harrison had come to stand in the kitchen doorway. "Anything to tell me?" he asked.

"Give me a minute," I said evenly, really feeling the pressure. I moved quickly out of Harrison's view down the hall and into the first bedroom on the right. Dim light trickled in through the peacock blue curtains at the window. A full-sized bed with a white handmade quilt checkered with blue squares was the focal point of the room. To the side of the bed was a simple night-stand and on that was a Bible.

I walked into the room and closed my eyes, willing myself to pick up on anything that might give me a clue about what had happened here. Nothing but soft, warm energy enveloped me. "Damn," I swore softly.

"Nothing?" Candice asked—her tone now worried.

"I'm not picking up a thing!" I said. "Maybe I'm so nervous out here that I'm blocked or something, but I keep coming up with zilch."

"Let's try another bedroom," she suggested.

We moved a bit farther down the hall, passing the bathroom on the right into the second bedroom, which was obviously the master. The moment we turned the corner into the room, we both sucked in a breath and Candice reflexively grabbed my arm tightly. *"Holy Mother of God!"* she gasped.

I was so horrified by the scene before us that I couldn't even breathe. The mattress had been fully exposed—no sheets or bedspread remained on it—but on its quilted surface were giant rust-colored stains so dark that they had to go all the way through the mattress. The headboard and wall above the bed were speckled with thousands of red dots and wretched-looking splatters. A broken lamp lay with shards of porcelain all about the nightstand, and more droplets clustered around the beige carpet near the bed.

I glanced toward the ceiling and was repulsed to see that blood had even been spattered up there, freckling the overhead light fixture.

"Jesus!" I finally managed, and stepped back out of the room, taking in big gulps of air.

"Not a pretty scene, is it?" said Harrison, who had joined us in the hallway.

"What the freak *happened* in there?" I exclaimed as I looked at Candice, who was starkly pale and looking as queasy as I felt.

"You're supposed to tell me," said Harrison, reminding me of our deal.

I took a few more deep breaths and eyed Candice for moral support. "It's okay, Abs, you can do it," she encouraged.

I swallowed hard and tried my best to suck it up, but the last thing on earth I wanted to do was tune in on what horrible fate had befallen the person who lived here, and by the surroundings I was guessing it was a sweet old lady who'd done nothing to deserve the violence that had so obviously been unleashed on her.

Finally I pushed away from the wall I was leaning against and moved back toward the doorway of the bedroom. My focus didn't linger on the blood spatter about the room; instead I closed my eyes and inhaled deeply, doing my level best to try to center my energy so that I could utilize my radar. I called out to my crew and asked, *What happened here?*

I then braced myself for the visions I was certain would flood my mind, but instead I was quite surprised when all I saw was a stage with a curtain. *I don't understand,* I said to my crew. *I need to know what happened in this room!* Again, a stage filled the vision of my mind's eye, but off to one side I noticed some stagehands working on scenery, as if they were getting the set ready for a play.

I squeezed my eyes shut further, and concentrated as hard as I could. *I don't understand!* I shouted at my crew. *I don't get what a stage and set decoration has to do with anything! I need to see the murder! Show me the murder that took place here!*

Suddenly, the image in my brain changed, and I had the distinct feeling I needed to go back to the kitchen. I snapped my eyes open and turned around to walk through the hallway, bumping into Harrison in my hurry to get there. "Sorry," I called over my shoulder as I practically ran there.

I could hear Candice's footfalls behind me as I reached the doorway to the kitchen and looked around, waiting for a sign from my crew. I got one when I felt a tug on my energy pulling me over to the sink. I moved there and looked about. Nothing near the sink called my attention, even though my eyes darted back and forth, searching for the thing that my crew wanted me to focus on.

Outside, I heard in my head, and I immediately looked up and out the little window above the sink. The house directly behind us seemed to glow with urgent energy.

My mind's eye filled with the image of a chalk outline, and a gravestone that said *RIP.* "We're in the wrong house," I said breathlessly. "The murder didn't happen here!"

"What?" Candice and Harrison said together.

I whipped around and stared angrily at Harrison and instantly I realized he knew the truth of it. "That's a staged crime scene in there," I said, yanking my head in the direction of the master bedroom. "The woman who lived here died of natural causes. There was no murder."

Harrison's expression immediately turned to one of shock, but was quickly replaced with a cop's poker face. "That's correct," he admitted. "No one was murdered here."

"That is *totally* unfair!" Candice shouted at him, her hands balling into fists.

"The real murder took place over there," I said, pointing to the house behind us.

Harrison's cop face was quickly replaced with one of triumph. "Wrong," he said as a smug smile crept to his lips. "There was no murder. This house belonged to the widow of a former agent. She left this place to the bureau when she passed away quietly in her sleep a few months back, and we've been using it ever since as a staging ground to train new recruits."

Candice's face was full of rage. "You mean you purposely brought us to a fake crime scene just to throw her off?!"

"It beats having her get to a crime scene staged by a murderer out in the real world and pumping us full of false info," Harrison snarled back. The friction between him and Candice was heating up.

"You have *got* to be kidding me," said Candice, her temper flaring again. "That is total bullshit, Agent Harrison, and you know it!"

I was about to add to Candice's comment and tell Harrison where he could stuff it when my radar insisted that I turn around and look at the house behind us again. I did and kept seeing a chalk outline. "Something happened there," I said again. "Something bad went down in that house right behind us. And it happened recently."

"Nothing happened there," Harrison said, glancing with annoyance at the house I was pointing to. "I told you, *this* is the staged crime scene."

I looked at Candice. "Come on," I said to her. "Let's check it out."

Without another word Candice and I walked over to the rear door leading to the backyard. "Hey!" Harrison called. "You can't go trespassing around out there!"

Candice and I ignored him and walked out the door, my partner making sure to slam it in Harrison's face. "You're sure someone was murdered over there?" she asked me as we trudged through the leaves on our way to the other house.

"I'm positive," I said. "I mean, I don't expect to find a dead body, but I want to get close enough to make sure the energy I'm picking up is right."

Behind us we heard Harrison yank open the door and begin to chase after us. "I'm serious!" he said. "That's private property!"

I flipped him the bird and kept walking. I didn't care if he was Dutch's new boss—he'd finally pushed me over the edge. When I got close to the house, I quickly jogged over to the back door and rapped loudly three times.

Candice stood next to me and rubbed her hands in the cold wind blowing around us. Meanwhile Harrison had come up to us and attempted to grab me by the arm. It was the wrong move in Candice's opinion, 'cause the next thing I knew, Harrison was twisted around with his nose wedged against the wall of the house and his right arm pulled up at an odd and painful angle behind him.

"Ach!" he shouted, and tried to twist out of the lock she had him in, but Candice merely pulled up harder on his arm while pushing her body weight into his back.

"Move a muscle and I'll break it," she told him menacingly.

"You're assaulting a federal officer!" he shouted at her. "I can put you away for good on just that!"

My attention had left the door and I was now staring slack-jawed at my partner, who had apparently lost her mind. "Candice," I said in a low, even tone. "Really, honey . . . that's not necessary."

"Knock again, Abby," she said calmly. "And if no one answers, head around the house and look in all the windows. Let's make sure before we get hauled off to jail."

I gave another three raps to the door and called, "Hello?" but no one answered. I then cupped my hands and peered through the window of the door. There was a sheer curtain over it, but I could just make out the shapes inside.

After a moment I stood back and gave Candice a sober look. "Let him go," I said tiredly. Candice hesitated for a few seconds. "I'm serious," I said. "Let him go."

Candice gave one more small yank on Harrison's arm before releasing him, and he wasted no time in whipping around and grabbing Candice roughly by the shoulder and slamming her into the side of the house, where he cuffed her hands behind her back faster than I thought possible. "You are under arrest!" he snapped, then looked at me as if he was weighing whether to call in reinforcements.

"Go ahead," I said, for once giving him a smug smile. "Call in the cavalry. Oh, and while you're at it, you'll need to call the coroner too. There's a dead guy on the floor in there. By the looks of it, he's been like that for a few days."

Harrison stared at me for a full minute, no doubt trying to decide if I was bluffing. Finally, he pulled Candice along the wall toward the door and ordered me to sit down on the ground with my hands on top of my head.

I humored him by sitting down and lacing my fingertips above my head, but I couldn't help smirking up at him for a change.

After I was sitting all nice and quiet-like, Harrison edged over to the window and peered in. I watched with great satisfaction when his head whipped back as if he'd been slapped. "Son of a bitch!" he said, and yanked up the cell phone clipped to his waistband. "Bentsen?" he barked into the phone. "It's Harrison. I need a team of techs, agents, and the coroner to meet me at the house directly behind the staging house, pronto!"

Candice, who was still pressed up against the side of the house, squirmed her head far enough around to give me a big, gorgeous smile. "Way to go, Abs," she said. "Way to go."

Chapter Three

From where we sat in the back of Harrison's car, handcuffed and freezing our butts off, we were able to catch only small snatches of information about what went down in the home behind the staging house.

One of the investigators had collected a statement from a neighbor right in front of the car we were sitting in, and it was pretty obvious what had occurred a few nights earlier.

The neighbor told the investigator that the house belonged to Russ Cadet and his wife, Patrice, who the neighbor suggested had been arguing and fighting loud enough to be overheard ever since Russ had been laid off from his job four months back. The neighbor admitted to hearing a loud argument between the couple around midnight three nights earlier, but ignored it and went back to sleep, although now that he thought about it, he sort of remembered hearing some faint popping sounds in the early-morning hours, but had convinced himself that he must have dreamed it.

We learned a bit more when one of the CSIs showed

his coworker a suicide note written by Russ, which the tech had found on the kitchen counter near the two bodies.

We were saved from the cold, our discomfort, and hearing any more of the tragic details when Agent Gaston arrived on scene. He drove up in a sleek black sedan and approached Harrison, who'd been directing crime-scene techs and local-police traffic all afternoon. Candice and I watched intently as Gaston and Harrison shook hands and began talking. Everything appeared civil until Harrison said something that made Gaston snap his head in our direction. Candice and I both smiled big "Please help us!" smiles and Gaston lost it. There was yelling, finger-pointing, and a march straight over to the car where we were held captive.

"Thank God," Candice said right before the door was yanked open and the full volume of Gaston's voice echoed about the car.

"This is unacceptable, Agent Harrison!" Gaston yelled as he motioned for Candice and me to come out. "I placed these women in your care and you treat them like criminals?"

"Sir," Harrison was saying in a voice that was cool and unapologetic, "these two disobeyed my direct orders, and that one," he continued, pointing to Candice, "assaulted me."

Gaston's face was red with fury, and he held out his hand and growled, "Give me the damn key, Agent Harrison."

Harrison dropped it into his open palm and I quickly turned at the waist to expose my hands to Gaston, as I was so uncomfortable that I couldn't wait for the cuffs to come off. When I was free, I shot out of the car to stretch and rub my wrists while Gaston unlocked Candice's cuffs and helped her out of the car. When he turned back to me, I smiled gratefully at him. "Thank you, sir," I said.

"My sincere apologies, Ms. Cooper," Gaston replied. "I would understand if you wished to be chauffeured back to your hotel and opt out of helping us further."

I looked at Candice, who was glaring at Harrison. "What do you think?" I asked her.

"Oh, I'm *totally* in," she said, still glaring at Harrison. "I say we go for it."

I ducked my chin to hide a smile and waited until I could speak without laughing. It was the perfect revenge for being put through Harrison's tests all day. "Game on, Agent Gaston. We are at your service."

Gaston looked relieved. "Thank you. If I can convince you to stay in D.C. for another day or two to go over the details of the case we're working on, and to get your input, it would be most appreciated," Gaston said.

Candice whipped out her iPhone and began her quick finger poking at the screen. "Absolutely, sir," she said. "How about I schedule us for a flight out of town on Thursday? That should give us plenty of time to assist you."

"Excellent." Gaston beamed before turning to Harrison. "Agent Harrison, please escort our guests back to their hotel and meet me in my office by six. I want to have a word with you."

It was Harrison's turn to smolder. I watched him bunch his jaw as his eyes pivoted between Gaston, the crime scene, and Candice and me. "Sir," he said carefully. "I believe I'm still needed here. I can have another one of the agents take them back."

"Are you disobeying a direct order, Agent Harrison?" Gaston asked quietly, and I could immediately sense the power struggle between these two.

After a notable pause, Harrison said, "Of course not, sir." Turning to us, he said with forced politeness, "Ladies, if you would please get back into the car."

"And, Agent Harrison," Candice said coolly, "if you wouldn't mind stopping at the nearest Starbucks, I could really go for a latte."

Harrison ignored her and walked briskly over to the driver's side. I shot her a sneaky smile and we both got into the back of the sedan without hurry. I even took time to stretch my sore arms and shoulders—for the record it's damn uncomfortable to have your hands cuffed behind your back.

Once we were back in the car, but before we'd even had a chance to buckle up, Harrison pulled away from the curb. Candice sat with a satisfied smirk on her face and purposely positioned herself in the backseat so that if Harrison even glanced in the rearview mirror, he was sure to spot her looking amused.

The entire way back to our hotel, Harrison spoke only once, and that was simply to ask which hotel we were staying in. I noticed too that we passed about four Starbucks along the way and Harrison made sure to accelerate as we passed—but that only sent Candice and me into giggles and a little whispering in the backseat.

We arrived at our hotel and Harrison pulled to a stop without looking at us or saying a word. Instead, he put the car into park and pushed a button for the trunk. Then, he got out, went around to the back, and put our luggage on the curb before hopping back into the car. Candice and I also got out of the car without speaking to him, and as the doorman hurried to help us with our luggage, we heard Harrison's wheels squeal as he sped away.

"If I didn't know better, I'd think he didn't like our

company," I said drolly as we entered the hotel and made our way to the front desk to recheck in.

"Wonder why," Candice mused in the same light tone. "I found him to be perfectly charming."

Just as Candice was finishing up with the registration, I heard my cell go off and I fished around in my purse to retrieve it. "Hi, Dutch," I said as soon as I saw the caller ID.

"Are you all right?" he asked, his voice filled with concern.

"Glorious," I said, and meant it.

"Gaston called me. He filled me in on what Harrison put you guys through. I'm sorry, doll, I had no idea he was going to be such an asshole."

"It's fine, cowboy. I swear. And we're on the case, so it was worth it in the end."

"I heard," he said proudly. "And Gaston tells me you guys even led Harrison straight to a murder/suicide scene near one of the staging houses?"

"We did," I said with a smile and a wink at Candice as she waved our new room key cards and motioned to follow her. "It looks like we'll be here until Thursday, so will you give Eggy and Tuttle a bunch of extra attention while I'm gone?" I was referring to our two adorable dachshunds.

"Like they need any extra of *that*," Dutch teased. "Are you going to be able to rearrange your client schedule while you're down there?"

I smiled. "My appointment book has been a little thin lately. I don't have any readings until Saturday." It was tough being in a service industry at the moment; Michigan's economy was suffering greatly, and my clientele had fallen off sharply in the last few months as the local folks cinched their belts and buckled down on extraneous expenses.

"Okay, well, you be careful, stay safe, and call me if you get any more crap from Harrison."

Candice and I had reached the elevators by now and I let my eyes close as I felt a deep pang of homesickness for my guy and my dogs. "Thanks, Dutch. We're at the elevators and I might lose you, so let me sign off, but I'll call you tonight before we turn in."

A short time later, Candice and I deposited our luggage in our room and promptly went out to eat. By now it was six o'clock and we were both famished, as we'd forgone breakfast and lunch. Candice was in a fabulous mood, so she suggested a wonderful little Italian place in Georgetown called Filomena's she'd read about in the *Washington Post*.

As we dined on some of the best damn pasta I've ever eaten, I grilled Candice about her obvious familiarity with D.C. "I spent some time here a few years ago," she said, focusing on twirling her linguine.

"On a case?" I asked, my radar hinting in that direction.

"Yep."

I smiled. Candice was monosyllabic only when it came to things I probably shouldn't inquire about. "And you can't tell me any of the details," I said.

"I could," she said, taking a sip of wine. "But then I'd have to kill you, and where's the fun in that?"

I laughed. She'd said it so Valley girl and it was such a switch from her usual cool, smart demeanor that I found her hysterical. "I'm not worried," I said easily. "People know I'm with you. Big, strong, manly people with guns."

Candice sat back and wiped her mouth demurely with her napkin. "That's what I need," she said dreamily. "A nice heaping dose of manly." And then she sighed.

I cocked my head. "I thought you were dating what's his name?" Last I heard Candice was doing the hot and heavy with a trainer down at the gym.

But I immediately knew I was out of touch because she rolled her eyes and informed me, "Honey, I dumped him weeks ago."

"Ah," I said. "Yeah, I never could keep up with your social life."

"What's to keep up with?" she asked me. "Lately it's been nothing but crickets."

"You know what I think your problem is?" I said to her, and ignored another eye roll. "I think you get bored too easily."

Candice gave me one of her famous smirks. "Gee, Abby, *you think*?"

I chuckled. "I know, allow me to point out the obvious, but seriously, honey, what you need is a boyfriend, not a fling. You need someone who can put up with your shit and give it to you right back. You also need someone who doesn't look in the mirror at his own reflection every five seconds."

"Wow," she said with a laugh. "Talk about a one-eighty!" I blushed, as I knew exactly where she was going. "Two years ago you were all, 'Guys, who needs 'em? I'm going to be single forever!' and now *you're* lecturing *me* on boyfriend material? Ladies and gentlemen, the world as we know it has officially ended."

It was my turn to roll my eyes. "I'm serious," I insisted. "Candice, ever since I've known you, you've only had one serious boyfriend."

"See?" she said. "That should tell you I'm not hopeless!"

"He was *married*!"

"Ah," she said, fiddling with her napkin. "So he had one tiny, little, insignificant flaw."

"And his wife came after you with a butcher's knife!" I said, recalling her telling me about that particularly ugly scene years ago.

"What?" Candice said innocently. "She missed, didn't she?"

I shook my head ruefully. "Okay, maybe you're right. Maybe *you* shouldn't get tied down. Maybe you should find someone to fool around with one minute and dump the next. Maybe it's just safer for everyone involved if you do."

Candice made her hand into a gun and said, "Pow! Now you're talking."

The waiter came by and removed our plates, asking us if we wanted to see the dessert menu. I could feel the waistline of my new skirt pinching into me, so I declined, and shortly after, we had paid the bill and were ready to leave.

As we stood up, something from the other side of the room caught my attention and I gasped as I realized none other than Brice Harrison had just entered the restaurant. A short man hurried over to him and I could hear him say, "Good evening, Agent Harrison! So good to have you back in town with us again. May I show you to your usual table?"

Harrison hadn't seen us yet and I elbowed Candice and nodded in that direction. "What the hell is *he* doing here?" she snapped.

"Having dinner," I said.

"Do you think he followed us?"

I asked the question in my head and my radar said no. "I don't think so," I told her. "But from what I just overheard the maître d' say, I believe this is a regular haunt for him."

"Well then, let's go," she said. "This place doesn't have as much charm with him here." I led us over to the other side of the restaurant, keeping other dining patrons between us and Harrison on our way to the exit.

As I reached the stairs, I turned to comment on what a great meal that was when I noticed Candice wasn't behind me. With surprise I realized she was over at Harrison's table, talking to him, the waiter, and the maître d'. I didn't know what she said, but it obviously upset Harrison—his eyes smoldered meanly at her while the waiter and the maître d' appeared in complete shock.

With a little wave to them Candice turned and sauntered over to me on the stairs, chuckling like she'd just cooked someone's goose. "What'd you do?" I demanded, climbing the stairs quickly.

Candice's chuckle deepened. "I merely told Harrison—within earshot of the staff of his favorite restaurant, mind you—that I hoped that pesky little business with Internal Affairs over the sexual harassment allegations from one of his fellow agents was ironed out quickly and that he was eventually cleared of any wrongdoing."

I gasped. "You *didn't*!"

Candice's chuckle became a hearty laugh. "Oh, Abby! You should have seen the look on his face!"

"Oh, I saw it," I said. "And may I remind you that we will be spending a lot of time with him over the next couple of days?"

Candice waved her hand dismissively. "Oh, come on," she said. "The guy obviously needs to lighten up, and if he can't take a little joke, who needs him?"

While I agreed with her that Harrison really could use a little levity in his life, I didn't know if he'd appreciate it coming from us, but as Candice was getting such a kick out of it, I decided not to rain on her parade. Still, these little games between Harrison and my partner were quickly reminding me of a kindergarten playground.

The next morning found us back at the field office. Gaston had left us a message requesting that we report in about ten a.m. We were seated in the lobby again at nine forty-five, and at nine fifty a female agent appeared to escort us up to the sixth floor. She led us down a different corridor from our previous visit, through a maze of cubicles into a large conference room, and asked both of us if we would care for any refreshments. Candice and I both took coffee and waited in the empty room for someone to come in.

As we waited, Candice made a comment or two about the weather, but I didn't feel like talking. For some reason I was even more nervous today than yesterday. I didn't have long to dwell on it because at exactly ten o'clock the doors opened and several agents began filing in, each carrying a Styrofoam cup of coffee or a bottle of water. The mood was expectant and serious as they all took their places. Several of the men took notice of me and I could tell they were curious, but other than a "hello" or "good morning," they didn't engage us in conversation.

The last two to arrive were Harrison—who took his seat without making eye contact with us—and Gaston.

Gaston took his place at the head of the table and surveyed the group gathered around the conference table. "Good morning," he said, his voice confident and strong. "Thank you all for attending this meeting. As you know from your SACs, I've asked each of you here to address the investigation of three missing college students from neighboring states, all with a parent in the state legislature. As the circumstances of each individual disappearance are similar, we wanted to put this task force together to investigate what I feel is a strong connection. And as I am the lead on this task force, I thought it appropriate to call in any available resource at our disposal."

Gaston made a point of locking eyes with me, and I had to give the guy credit, because I knew he was putting his butt on the line by including me. "Agents, with us today are Abigail Cooper and Candice Fusco. Ms. Cooper is a very gifted investigative intuitive, and has helped our local Michigan bureau on a number of cases. Her input into those cases undeniably helped the investigation, and in several of them, were it not for her insight, those cases would still be open."

I felt several sets of eyes swivel to me, but most of the expressions around the table were unreadable—except for Harrison's. He barely hid his contempt. I nodded at a few of the men looking at me, and Gaston continued. "Her partner, Candice Fusco, is a licensed PI and an old friend to the FBI. I won't go into the details of our shared history here, gentlemen, but suffice it to say that I consider Ms. Fusco to also be a valuable asset to this investigation. And I want to make it clear that both women will be allowed access to the facts of this case and utilized to the best of their talents and abilities."

"And I would like to state for the record, sir, that I strongly protest their involvement," Harrison said, and I was shocked by his lack of diplomacy.

Gaston merely waved a hand in Harrison's direction and said, "Yes, Agent Harrison, your objection is again noted. Now let's brief our guests on the facts we have at hand. I am anxious to hear Ms. Cooper's impressions on the evidence gathered so far. Agent Albright, if you would be so kind as to detail the facts."

A man I'd put in his late twenties stood up and began to pass out folders. "What we know is contained within these files," he began. "On May eleventh of this year Bianca Lovelace, of Battle Creek, Michigan, left her dorm room at Michigan State University to attend a study group sometime before eight p.m. She never arrived at the study group and no one has seen or heard from her since."

I opened the folder and pulled out an eight-by-ten glossy photo of a beautiful girl with shiny brown hair and a gorgeous smile. My heart immediately sank. Bianca's image appeared flat to my eye—like a deflated balloon—and I knew the poor girl was dead. I swirled my fingers over the photo when I felt a little nudge from Candice. Looking up into her eyes, I knew she was asking me if I thought Bianca was alive. I shook my head and set the picture on the tabletop.

Agent Albright was continuing with the details. He'd already moved on to the second missing student, a young man named Kyle Newhouse, from Ohio, who had vanished exactly one week after Bianca. "This one is a similar scenario; according to his classmates, Newhouse had attended his last class and was heading to the library to study for finals and was never seen again. Security cameras posted at the front entrance of the library do not indicate Kyle ever entered the building. His father is a state senator."

I sifted through my folder until I found Kyle's photo. He was a great-looking kid, robust and muscular, and I couldn't imagine him being overpowered by anyone easily. But his picture told me that Kyle had definitely breathed his last. Again I could feel Candice's eyes on me. I shot her a side glance and gave another small headshake.

"Five days after Newhouse goes missing, our final victim disappeared," Albright continued. "Leslie Coyle, a resident of Madison, Wisconsin, had just finished her freshman year at the University of Wisconsin and was heading home. Her roommate was there as she took the last load down to her car, and they said good-bye. Coyle never reached home and her car has never been found."

Again I flipped through the folder to a blurry photo of Leslie. The picture was of such poor quality that I couldn't really tell if she was dead or alive, but I had a strong sense that she was still with us. I set that photo to the side—separating her from the other two—and looked up again.

I caught Gaston noting that I had set Bianca's and Kyle's photos on my right, and Leslie's photo on my left, but he didn't interrupt Albright, allowing him to finish giving us the facts. "Here's why we think all three disappearances might be linked: They are all of college age and in their freshman year of school. Each student held a two-point-five or better GPA. All three have at least one parent employed within their home state's legislature. All three had close family ties and were on good terms with both their parents and their classmates. None has a history of mental illness. And as far as we know, none of the missing kids knew one another or has ever made contact. We've checked out their blogs and MySpace pages and there's no mention of anything out of the ordinary or of one another. We've done extensive interviews with each kid's family and their friends, roommates, professors, etc., and no one noticed anything unusual in manner or behavior before these kids disappeared."

My radar buzzed while Albright talked, and I made a note on my folder that read, *Kids* did *know one another.*

"We've also checked bank accounts, cell phone and credit card records, and there's been no activity since the date they disappeared."

"How about any surveillance video of campus at the time they went missing?" Harrison asked.

"So far we've logged about a hundred hours of footage, sir, with about five hundred more to go from various cameras posted in the area, but those that we hoped we might get something from, so far, show us no suspicious activity whatsoever. Just the normal college traffic milling around the area. On one particular digital grouping we have terrific footage of Bianca exiting her dorm to the outside, but as she walks out of view, she does not appear to have anyone trailing her."

"And there's been no ransom note or correspondence to the families?" an agent right across from me asked.

"None."

"Have any of their parents in the state legislature been working on any controversial legislation?" Gaston asked.

"Only Senator Newhouse, sir. He's been attempting to allocate funding for a nuclear power plant on the outskirts of a small town in Ohio, and we do know that there's been some major protest over that from some of the residents near where the plant will be located."

"But Kyle was the second victim, not the first, correct?" I clarified.

Albright nodded. "Correct."

"It could be that Newhouse was the target all along, and the other two were abducted as a smoke screen," one of the agents next to Harrison suggested.

I shook my head. My radar said no. Gaston seemed to notice, because he spoke directly to me. "Ms. Cooper, I'd be interested to hear your thoughts on what you've heard so far."

I gave him a weak smile and cleared my throat. "Of course," I began, and couldn't help noticing that Harrison was rolling his eyes. "My first impressions are the following: These two," I said, holding up Kyle's and Bianca's photos, "are no longer alive. I feel *very* strongly that they have been murdered. However," I added, holding up Leslie's photo, "I believe this young lady is still with us. But I couldn't tell you for how much longer and the energy around her feels very unstable. My sense is that if she is still alive, she doesn't have long."

Again I caught Harrison shaking his head slightly and swiveling his chair, almost as if he was trying to distract me. I ignored him completely and focused on Gaston, who was taking notes and nodding. "I also believe there is more than just a circumstantial link between the kids. I believe they knew one another. I don't know if they were friends, but I do believe that they all met at one time."

"Why do you think that?" Albright asked me, and I could tell that he wasn't so much doubtful as he was curious.

"When you suggested that they didn't know one another, my radar insisted that they did. I don't know how old the connection between the three is, but it's there."

Off to the side I heard someone make a derisive sound and I knew Harrison was doing his level best to unsettle me. And by this time I'd had more than enough of his attitude, so I turned to face him and said, "And I know that *some* of you might not feel that's good enough, but I would like to remind you about a certain crime scene that was only discovered after *my radar* pinpointed its location."

Harrison avoided looking at me, but I could see that his eyes narrowed and at least the swiveling of his chair stopped. After a moment of awkwardness Gaston spoke again. "Are there any other impressions you can share with us, Ms. Cooper? Perhaps where the teens might be located or anything about the person responsible?"

I took a deep breath and focused my radar on the photos in front of me. "This girl," I said, pointing to Bianca. "She's somewhere near water. I don't think she's in it, but she's not far away. I'm not sure right now where Kyle is," I admitted, "but I can keep working on it. As far as the person responsible . . ." My voice faded as I tried to focus, and my eyes kept going back to Kyle and how big and athletic he was. It would take a big man to overpower him, but somehow that wasn't exactly my impression of the killer. I suspected he was average in size, and perhaps he'd used some other method to get Kyle away from campus without making a scene—like move in behind him and point a gun into his back or something.

"I believe this is the work of one suspect, a male. I believe he is intelligent, concise, and very deliberate with his movements, actions, and thoughts. I also believe he is comfortable, or would fit in easily, in a collegiate environment. He might even look like a student."

"Any idea as to why he's specifically targeting these kids?" asked another agent who'd been quiet until now.

I paused, considering the motive for a while, and the answer I got was quite puzzling. "It's the weirdest thing," I said, trying to feel out the energy. "It's almost like this is a smoke screen for something else. I can't help thinking there's some sort of bait and switch going on here. As if the killer wants us to think one way, but the truth is very different. There's also something very personal about all this. Like a nerve has been struck and this is the reaction. There's revenge here too, but the real story is much larger than it would appear."

I could tell that my answer both confused and slightly frustrated the group, and for that I felt bad. I didn't know how this jigsaw puzzle fit together either, but I knew I wasn't off when I told them that there was a lot more to it than the facts at first revealed.

"I have a question," Candice said into the silence that followed.

"Of course," Gaston said.

"I'm pretty amazed that the press hasn't gotten hold of this story yet," she said. "I mean, how have you managed to avoid having this story plastered all over every national paper?"

Gaston's eyes flickered to Harrison. "We owe a bit of that to Agent Harrison for bringing this task force to Washington and away from any one local bureau, where the press would be more suspicious of such a meeting, as well as sheer luck. Both the Coyle and Newhouse disappearances were reported in the local news in their towns when the press picked up the stories from local police blotters, but Bianca's father contacted me right away—keeping it out of the press. That's good for us, because the last thing we need right now is to deal with a bunch of reporters before we know exactly who—or what—we're dealing with. So far, none of the AP wires has connected the dots between the three teens, which has worked in our favor."

"How exactly does that work in our favor?" Candice asked.

"Because if we are in fact dealing with an antigovernment serial killer, he'll be looking for attention, and we believe that if he gets it, the abductions may escalate. That's why we're working to keep everyone outside this room in the dark. Even the families have not been told about a possible connection to other missing kids in neighboring states, because the longer we can work this case quietly, the better chance we have to figure out exactly what we're dealing with without risking an escalation from the unsub.

"Still," said Gaston, "we all know it's only a matter of time before word will leak and some ambitious reporter is going to blow this thing wide open, so I want to reiterate the need to keep the details of this case isolated to members of this group and your own individual SACs. Am I understood?"

All heads around the table, including mine and Candice's, nodded.

"Excellent," said Gaston as he got to his feet, and started issuing orders. "Agents Albright and McKenzie, we'll need you to continue to survey the footage at all three campuses with specific focus on the Ohio State campus. I want you to pay close attention to anyone who was perhaps acting suspicious around Kyle Newhouse who might also have been big enough to overpower him. Agents Walters and Stillwell, I'm assigning you the task of going deeper into the three abductees' past. You're looking for any possible connection that might link them. Continue to discreetly ask family and friends until you hit on a likely connection.

"Also, as I understand it, we still need access to two of the kids' laptops. I know you've had remote access to their blogs and MySpace pages, but we need to search through their hard drives and maybe we can locate a specific Web site or online video game they frequented. You'll need to do a thorough profile of each individual, where they shopped, where they ate, if they belonged to a gym, or had any special memberships. I want travel records of each individual in the past year. Let's see if perhaps they all visited a specific location for spring break, and maybe that's our missing link."

My radar buzzed and I made sure to nod my head vigorously. Gaston noticed and asked, "Something about what I just said feel right to you, Ms. Cooper?"

"Yes," I said. "I really like that spring-break idea. You might be on to something there, sir."

Gaston gave me a crooked smile and continued. "Agent Harrison, I am sending you back to Michigan. I want to reinterview Bianca Lovelace's family, as she was our first victim. You will take Ms. Cooper and Ms. Fusco with you, and please allow them to participate."

Out of the corner of my eye I could see Harrison's head snap up and his posture stiffen. Candice seemed to notice too, because she smiled broadly at him. When he glared back at her, I was actually surprised that she resisted the urge to stick out her tongue and say, "Na-ner, na-ner, naaaa-ner!"

Gaston continued, ignoring the unspoken argument traveling back and forth across the table. "Ms. Cooper, I sincerely appreciate your participation in this investigation. I would like you to personally call me after you meet with Bianca's family and inform me of any further impressions you might hit on. However, as you know, this is a particularly delicate situation. I would prefer that you not share your abilities or your impression that Bianca has died with her family. We would like to wait for solid evidence confirming her condition one way or another before we upset her family."

"Of course, sir," I said.

"And I would also like to reemphasize the point not to discuss the other missing teens with the Lovelaces. Again, the longer we can work this case without causing a panic, the better it works in our favor."

"I understand, sir," I said. And then another thought occurred to me and I checked my radar. "But, one more thing I'd like to mention, if I may?"

"Of course," he said.

"There will be one more victim."

The room became very quiet and I could feel all eyes focus on me. "Do you have a sense of when?" Gaston asked.

"Soon, sir," I said quietly. "Very soon. And I also believe that Leslie is almost out of time as well. I'd give her no more than a month—tops."

Gaston sighed heavily and motioned to the group. "You heard her, gentlemen. Let's get to work."

Everyone got up from the table at once and began to file out the door. Harrison was the first to exit, his fury palpable. Gaston motioned to Candice and me to hang back while everyone else left. When we were alone, he closed the door and began to speak in soft tones. "I'm sorry to have to pair you with Agent Harrison," he began. "But my hands are tied here."

I understood that Gaston meant that the internal politics made it very difficult to exclude Harrison from the case. Something that, I suspected, didn't sit well with the SAC. "It's fine, sir, really," Candice said with a smirk. My sense was that she was relishing the opportunity to rub Harrison's nose in it.

"Still," Gaston continued, "I have had a lengthy

discussion with Agent Harrison about your treatment yesterday, and although I would privately like nothing better than to bring him up on charges of insubordination, he did inform me that he was physically restrained by you, Ms. Fusco."

Candice beamed at him proudly. "I'm surprised he admitted that," she said. "I would have thought someone with Harrison's ego wouldn't readily own up to being bested by a woman."

There was the smallest of smiles on Gaston's face as he replied, "Yes, it surprised me too. However, he was well within his right to place you into custody for assaulting a federal officer. I have convinced him to drop all charges, but I would like you to fully understand the precariousness of my situation. I am the only individual of my rank to be open to utilizing Ms. Cooper's talents."

"I get it, sir," I said. "Your butt's on the line."

Gaston's smile widened. "Yes," he said. "But this case has a personal connection for me. Bianca's father has been a close friend of mine since college, and for his sake, I'd very much like to see it resolved, and resolved quickly. To that end I am willing to take a risk and experiment by using you, but I am limited by the tolerance of my own superiors. Another incident like the one yesterday, where one of my agents is physically assaulted and is more than willing to go over my head to report it, would mean the swift end of your participation."

Candice looked chagrined. "My apologies, sir."

"It's all right, Ms. Fusco. Just, please, don't antagonize Agent Harrison if you can avoid it. Be as professional as possible."

"Understood, sir," we both said.

*   *   *

We made it back to our hotel in time for lunch and ate again at Bistro Bis. While we were waiting, a text came in on Candice's phone. She glanced at the screen and said, "Harrison has booked us on a flight out of Dulles tonight at eight."

"I guess that means we should cancel our other flight out for Thursday."

"It does," she murmured as she began to poke at her iPhone.

I ate my chicken salad in silence until she was finished and put her cell back in her purse. "I wonder if he's got us all sitting together," I mused.

"Who?" Candice asked.

"Harrison," I replied. "I wonder if he had the balls to book our seats in one row."

Candice made a derisive sound and jabbed at a sea scallop. "Don't bet on it. I'm thinking he'll be on the opposite side of the plane."

"I just don't get why he's being so close-minded about my involvement," I complained. "I mean, didn't I lead him straight to a crime scene yesterday? How is he able to reason *that* away? Luck?"

Candice chewed a bite of food for a minute before she spoke. "Abs, don't take this so personally," she said. "This really has very little to do with you."

"Come again?" I asked as I rolled up the sleeves on my arms to point to the thin blue bruises where the handcuffs had pressed on my skin for two hours the day before.

Candice smiled. "Okay, so maybe it has a *little* to do with you. The point is that this is really about Gaston and Harrison. You wait, by the end of this investigation they'll be pulling out their willies and getting out the measuring stick."

I made a face. "Ewwww," I said.

"Too graphic over lunch?" she asked.

"A bit."

"Sorry. Anyway, I've seen Harrison's type before. He's used to being the golden boy. I'll bet he's risen through the ranks very fast, and I'll also be willing to bet his family expects nothing less of him. He's been told his whole life that he's special and all he needs to do is follow the rules, play the game, and he'll continue to get those promotions one after another. But then, right in the middle of that fast track, he gets stymied by someone who isn't following the rules, someone unconventional, who thinks outside the box and is willing to try anything to solve a case."

"You mean Gaston," I said.

"Yes," she said. "And it's really rattling Harrison's cage. The fact that he's been assigned to a new position where his boss and one of his direct reports both like to use a psychic to help solve cases . . . it must feel like he's entered the Twilight Zone or something."

I considered that for a while before asking her, "Okay, I see your point, but if you knew all that already, why are you being so tough on him?"

Candice flashed me a toothy grin. "Entertainment," she said easily. "And the fact that I can't stand it when you get bullied."

I laughed. "My own personal bodyguard."

Candice winked. "Anything for you, Sundance."

"So now that Gaston has given us a little warning, are you going to be nicer to Harrison?"

"It depends," she said.

"On?"

"On whether or not he behaves himself."

"Oh, boy," I said.

Chapter Four

At six thirty p.m. we were at the airport and making our way through security. Neither one of us saw any sign of Harrison. And when we eventually boarded the plane, we didn't spot him either.

Once we landed and were able to flip on our cell phones again, Candice showed me another text from Harrison. It read simply: *Troy bureau office tomorrow, eight a.m. sharp.*

We both sighed and waited until it was our turn to deplane, but as I got out to the gate, I remembered that I left my book on the plane. "Want me to hang here while you go back to get it?" Candice asked.

"Naw. You go on to baggage claim. I'll be down in a few."

It took a little longer than I thought it would to wait out the stream of people getting off, and then I was told that I wasn't allowed back onto the plane for security reasons. I then had to wait for a flight attendant to search for my book, but happily she found it and I hurried down to meet up again with Candice.

Once I got there, I spotted her right away and, to my complete surprise, Dutch. I walked toward him with a big grin on my face, ready to jump into his arms, but his eyes glazed over me and continued to survey the crowd behind me. I glanced over my shoulder, wondering whom he could be looking at, and when I didn't see anyone I recognized, I turned back to him.

I noticed that Candice had started giggling, and I wondered what the joke was until I saw Dutch's gaze wash over me a second time as he impatiently surveyed the crowd. I realized suddenly that he didn't recognize me and I smiled hugely and continued to make a beeline for him. His eyes drifted back one last time to me and I winked at him. He quickly looked away, as if my attention was unwanted. I laughed and ran straight at him and his face registered shock at first as a stranger came dashing toward him, but in the last moment before I threw myself into him, he realized it was me and I heard him gasp, "Holy cow!"

"Hi, gorgeous!" I sang as I snuggled into his chest.

"I didn't even recognize you!" he exclaimed.

"I know," I said, backing up so that he could really see me. "I look totally different."

"You look hot," he said, his eyes smoldering.

I could feel the blush hit my cheeks. "Glad you like it."

"Wow," he said, looking intently at me. "Just, wow."

"Shall we head home?" Candice asked politely.

"Sorry!" I apologized as I grabbed Dutch's hand and we made our way out of the crowded airport. Turning to him as we walked, I asked, "How did you know we'd be here?"

"I got a text from Harrison. He said you would be

in around midnight. And I'm glad someone at least let me know."

"Sorry, sweetie," I said, still smiling at the sight of him. "But I knew we'd be in late and I didn't want you to feel like you had to pick us up."

Dutch wrapped his arm around me and pulled me into him for a squeeze. Kissing the top of my head, he said, "Next time let me know, okay?"

"Got it." Something occurred to me then and I said, "Weird that Harrison texted you at all about our arrival."

"Why is that weird?" Dutch asked.

"It seems almost nice," I explained. "I mean, he's been nothing but a jerk to us for three days, and here he goes doing something that's almost thoughtful."

"I wouldn't get used to it," Candice said derisively. "I'll bet he's back to his cold, calculating self by tomorrow morning."

Candice's intuition would prove to be spot-on: The next morning we arrived with Dutch at the Troy FBI office and he left us at reception with a supportive squeeze of my hand before heading to his cubicle.

As usual, I waited impatiently, my knee bouncing, as the clock over on the far wall edged past eight a.m., but around ten minutes past, Harrison appeared and addressed us formally. "Good morning," he said, although there was no warmth in his tone. "If you will follow me, please."

He led us into what appeared to be his office, and I noticed right away that Harrison was as uptight as I'd suspected. There were no personal effects to speak of in the spacious office, no pictures or mementos or decorations that reminded me he was human. All the items on his desk—and by that, I mean an in-box with two folders, an out-box with three folders, a blotter, a notepad, and a pen—were perfectly aligned. I even wondered if he'd used a level.

Harrison took his seat behind the desk and motioned to the two chairs that faced him. Candice and I both sat down and looked at him expectantly. The ASAC regarded us with his cool-eyed stare for a minute before reaching into his in-box and pulling out the first folder. Flipping it open, he seemed to skim the page before saying, "Candice Fusco, current resident of Royal Oak, formerly of Kalamazoo. You've just renewed your PI license, correct?"

Beside me I could feel Candice's energy stiffen a fraction. "If that's what's in your file, Agent Harrison, then it must be true," she said easily.

Harrison looked up at her, much the way a sleepy cobra looks amusingly at a mouse before deciding whether it's hungry enough to exert the energy to strike. "I'm actually surprised the state granted your renewal," he mused.

Candice refused to take the bait; she just sat there waiting for him to get to his point.

"Had a few brushes with the law recently, haven't you?"

"I'm afraid I don't have a clue about what you're referring to, Agent Harrison," she replied smoothly. "I'm a law-abiding citizen through and through."

The corner of Harrison's lip turned up. "Law-abiding . . . ," he repeated. "Did you know that identity theft is a crime, Ms. Fusco?"

"I do indeed," she replied. I couldn't believe she was being so calm under this line of questioning. One of Candice's little secrets was that she often used the alias of her deceased sister.

And as if reading my mind, Harrison said, "Your

sister Samantha DuBois died in nineteen ninety-three, correct?"

Candice nodded, her face perfectly placid.

"Yes," Harrison mused. "You see, I have her death certificate, but apparently she's either faked her own death or she's reaching out beyond the grave to use her credit card at Neiman Marcus and renew her Las Vegas driver's license. Your sister looks amazingly like you, Ms. Fusco. She could be your twin." Harrison then swiveled to me and said, "What do you think, Ms. Cooper? Is Ms. Fusco's sister reaching out from beyond the grave?"

"Maybe," I said as coolly as I could. "I understand that the lines at the Heavenly Gate DMV can really be a bitch."

Candice ducked her chin to hide her smile, but Harrison didn't seem amused. Setting the first folder aside, he reached for the other one in his in-box and opened that up. "And I see you've also had a few brushes with the law recently, Ms. Cooper."

I mimicked Candice and let my eyelids droop like I was bored.

"Did you know it's a federal offense to impersonate an FBI agent?"

"You don't say?" I said, my heart hammering in my chest as he reminded us about a recent stint in Vegas where Candice and I had done just that.

"Yes," Harrison continued, his voice eerily cool. "It carries a pretty stiff penalty, in fact."

"I would imagine it does," I replied.

"Lying to a federal agent is also grounds for perjury," Harrison continued.

"Well, that makes sense," I said. I didn't really know where Harrison was going with all this, and if he meant to unsettle me, he was doing a damn good job.

But he actually surprised me when he closed the folders and placed them both in the out-box. He then folded his hands and regarded us like a principal about to discipline two malcontent fifth graders. "As you're well aware," he said, his voice low and serious, "I object to your participation in this investigation, but *for the moment*, I have no choice but to bring you along. After I'm through laying the ground rules, we're going to drive to Battle Creek and meet with the Lovelaces. You will not reveal how you are connected with the bureau or to this case. I will not introduce you as federal agents, and we'll just allow the Lovelaces to draw their own conclusions. During the course of my interview with them, do not speak. Just sit there and observe. Do we have an understanding?"

Candice said nothing and she gave no indication that she had even listened to a thing Harrison said. I filled the awkward silence by saying, "We understand, Agent Harrison."

Harrison then rose and grabbed his suit coat off a nearby chair. "This way, please," he said.

When we got to the garage, Candice and I had an awkward moment deciding who would ride shotgun. Neither one of us wanted to sit up front with Harrison. He glared at us and I finally relented, getting into the front seat and quickly buckling in.

Candice sat right behind me and the message to Harrison seemed clear: She was watching my back.

The drive to Battle Creek was long and silent. Harrison didn't speak to us and we didn't speak to him. He didn't even play the radio, so I occupied myself by looking out the window at the drizzly fall morning and wishing I were home, curled up on my couch with a good book and a dog on each side to cuddle with.

It took us a smidgen under two hours to make our way to the Lovelaces'. Their house was perched demurely on top of a hill with a fantastic view of the Battle Creek River. We parked and approached the front door, and Candice sidled up next to me and elbowed me gently. When I turned to look at her, she was smiling so huge, it was obvious she had some kind of inside joke she wanted to share, but I couldn't imagine what it was.

Harrison made sure to give us a warning glare—reminding us of the talk we'd had in his office—and he reached forward and pressed the bell.

From inside we could hear the lovely chimes announcing our arrival, and in swift order the door opened and a tall, leggy redhead with fabulously green eyes greeted us. "Good morning, Agent Harrison," she said softly, her face serious but pleasant. As I took in the first impressions of her, I could swear she looked really familiar, but I couldn't quite place her.

Her green eyes swiveled to Candice and me and her expression suddenly lit up in surprise. "Oh, my God! Candice Fusco? Is that really you?"

Candice chuckled. "Hi, Jessica. It's great to see you. And look who I brought along," she added, turning to me.

And then it hit me: I'd read for this woman. Not recently, but somewhere in the past, I knew, I'd had a session with her. "Abby Cooper?" Jessica squealed. "I can't believe you're here! I've been dying to call you. Do you know that absolutely *everything* you told me three years ago has come true?"

I didn't remember her session, but I couldn't help smiling at how enthusiastic she seemed. "Hi, Jessica," I said shyly. "It's great to see you again."

Jessica then turned to a completely stunned—and

probably furious—federal agent and asked innocently, "Are they with you, Agent Harrison?"

Harrison was speechless and I wanted to laugh at his obvious discomfort. He simply nodded and Jessica waved all of us inside. Grabbing my hand and becoming serious again, she said, "I've wanted to call you for months, but I didn't know if you got involved in things like this. I should have just listened to my own gut and made the damn call." I was looking at her and scrutinizing her appearance. I remembered her face and her eyes, but something about her was throwing me off. "It's the hair," she said as if reading my mind. "It used to be blond, but Jeremy likes me as a redhead."

I didn't know who Jeremy was, but I assumed it was her husband and my mind whirled as I tried to remember her reading from three years before. I might as well have saved myself the effort. I had trouble remembering readings even an hour after I gave them. "We got married exactly when you said," Jessica was saying. "You told me he was going to propose early in May and that we would get married on the beach. Jeremy surprised me with a trip to Hawaii at the end of April, and on the last day there, which was May second, he got down on bended knee and asked me to marry him. When I said yes, he was so excited that he arranged for us to get married the very next morning!"

As she talked to me, I smiled and nodded, barely resisting the urge to turn around and stick my tongue out at Harrison.

"We're all so worried about Bianca," she added. "I love that girl like she's my own daughter, and poor Jeremy hasn't had a good night's sleep since she disappeared. Bianca's mother has been a wreck too, and she's been making our lives hell. Those two never did get along, and this situation has only made the tension between them even worse."

I immediately lost all sense of humor as she reminded us about our real purpose here. "I'm so sorry," I said carefully. "I can't imagine how difficult it must be for you." And I couldn't imagine how much more difficult it would become once they learned that Bianca was dead.

Jessica led us through a dark hallway to the back of the house, which was large and spacious. The kitchen, breakfast area, and family room all opened up as one large space. Jessica gestured to a grouping of overstuffed chairs and two sofas. "Please make yourselves comfortable. Jeremy should be here any minute. He had to go to his office to put his name on a new bill he's submitting, but he promised he'd be here. And Bianca's mother, Terry, should be along soon as well."

As if on cue the doorbell chimed and Jessica hurried off to answer the door.

Candice sat down with a flourish on one of the sofas, crossing her legs and bobbing one foot amusingly as she shot Harrison a look that clearly said, "Ha!"

Harrison took his seat in one of the overstuffed chairs and glared hard at the two of us, but he did not comment. I sat next to Candice and leaned in to whisper, "Did you know all along?"

"Not until we pulled up here," she said. "I heard through the vine that Jess had married a representative, but I didn't know his last name. This house was originally Jessica's. She won it in the divorce settlement with her ex-husband four years ago, which was the case I worked on for her. Her ex was a cheater and a fairly crooked businessman. I dug up enough dirt so that she pretty much got everything she wanted in the divorce. And after it was official, and she was single again, I pointed her your way for a session. I remember she was pretty convinced she was never going to fall in love again, and you told her to hang in there, she'd be happily married within two years."

"Damn, I'm good," I said with humor, and Candice giggled.

"Not good enough to let her know that her stepdaughter would be abducted," Harrison shot out from across the room.

I had no time for a comeback, because Jessica and another woman entered the room. "Terry," Jessica said, "this is Agent Harrison and his associates Abby Cooper and Candice Fusco. I know both Abby and Candice from way back, and I'm thrilled that the FBI is utilizing them."

When Terry turned to her quizzically, Jessica explained, "Candice is one of the best PIs in the business, and Abby is one of the most talented psychics I've ever been to."

At the mention of this, Terry made a beeline for me and sat close enough to invade my personal space. Taking my hand, she asked desperately, "Can you see my Bianca? Can you tell me if she's all right?"

And then, something really weird happened. I'm not normally a medium—someone able to communicate with the dead—but every once in a while I'll feel the presence of a deceased loved one on the edge of my consciousness, and as Terry took my hand and pleaded for information, I knew immediately that her daughter had boldly entered my energy field. But letting her know that left me with a huge dilemma: How could I possibly tell her anything without letting her know that her daughter was speaking to me from the other side?

As if to remind me of his earlier warning, Harrison

cleared his throat, and Terry looked at him as if catching something in the air. "Oh, God," she whispered as she turned her eyes intensely back to mine, and I knew, even though I tried to hide it, that she saw my own sadness there. "Oh, no!" she moaned, her eyes welling up. "Please! No!"

Jessica gasped and her hand flew to her mouth as everyone came to a silent understanding. "I'm so sorry," I whispered to Terry, but all color had drained from her face and huge tears began to slide down her cheeks.

"I knew it," she choked. "I knew it the moment it happened. A mother can tell."

For long seconds no one spoke while Terry began to sob. Finally I couldn't take it anymore and I said gently, "Terry, your daughter is here with me right now."

Terry gulped and her eyes pleaded with mine. She took a small moment to try to collect herself, then asked, "Is she all right?"

"She's fine," I reassured her. "In fact, she's just sad that you're going through all of this."

"Tell me what happened to her," Terry insisted.

I looked to Candice, who nodded, and then, reflexively, to Harrison. His expression was unreadable and I knew that Candice and I were likely going to pay for this later, although I could hardly see how any of this was my fault. I decided then and there to ignore him and focus on Terry and Bianca. "First let me make sure that I have your daughter, Terry. Mediumship isn't my forte, so I want to make sure I'm correct when I tell you I can sense her."

Terry nodded, her eyes wide and unblinking even as the tears continued to fall.

I closed my own eyes in concentration and asked for Bianca to prove to me that it was really her. "She's showing me a book," I began as slowly an image appeared in my mind. "The book is blue," I added. "And it has pictures inside.... Hold on, let me take that back. I think what she's showing me is a photo album and she keeps pointing to you and something about a birthday."

Terry gasped, and I opened my eyes. "Does that make sense to you?" I asked her.

"She took up scrapbooking at college," Terry choked. "For my last birthday she gave me a blue photo album filled with just photos of her and me, from when she was a little girl, all the way up to the week before she disappeared. It was the loveliest thing she could have given me."

I swallowed hard. Facing this grieving mother, I was finding it incredibly difficult to keep my own emotions in check. After I felt I could continue without losing it, I closed my eyes again and asked Bianca if she could tell me anything about her abduction or murder. "I'm asking her to show me what happened to her," I said aloud, so that everyone would know what I was digging for. "She's showing me a notebook. No. Wait. It's not a notebook—it's a journal. Do you know if Bianca kept a journal?" I asked, opening my eyes again.

Terry was trembling next to me and I could tell it was a struggle for her to speak. Jessica came over to sit by her and picked up her hand. "She did," Jessica said. "Bianca was always writing in her journals. There are stacks of them upstairs even."

I looked meaningfully at Candice, who said, "Is it all right if we look through them? There might be a clue in there that we can use."

Terry hesitated briefly, and I knew she was concerned about her daughter's privacy, even as she realized she no longer needed to worry about it. "Yes," she whispered. "Of course."

I focused back on Bianca. "Writing was her gig," I said, feeling my way along the impressions Bianca was giving me. "Did you know that she wanted to be a journalist?"

Terry choked as she made a sound that was half sob, half laugh. "Her idol was Anderson Cooper," she said. "She imagined herself working at CNN someday."

I nodded. "Do you know if she was planning on doing an internship at a newspaper or magazine before she disappeared?" I asked.

Both women shook their heads. "She was only a freshman," Jessica said. "She would have needed another two years under her belt to do that."

Terry agreed. "Her plans for the summer were to come home and go back to the morning shift at Denny's. She earned good tips and had her afternoons and evenings free."

I furrowed my brow. Something Bianca was telling me was counter to what I was hearing from her mom and stepmom, but I let it go and asked her for more. I wanted specific details about her killer or the manner in which she died, but all I could sense from her about that topic was a slight choking sensation around my neck. I decided not to share that with her family. I felt it would be too upsetting. "She doesn't really remember what happened to her," I told them all instead.

"Do you know where she is?" Terry asked, her voice tiny and sad.

The image of a postcard flashed in my mind and I almost smiled, in spite of the somber mood. I opened my eyes while my mind whirred, rejecting the image that I was seeing. "What is it?" Jessica asked, looking at me intently.

"This may sound *really* weird," I said honestly, "but

have either of you ever been to this place way up north called Sea Shell City?"

Terry's eyes became huge. "Yes!" she gasped, her hand flying to her heart. "Bianca loved that tourist trap! When she was little, and Jeremy and I were still together, we had a cabin up at Burt Lake, which isn't far from there. Every summer we'd spend two weeks in August at the cabin and Bianca would cry and complain and whine until we agreed to take her to Sea Shell City. I think in her room at my house she still has a few of the conch shells she forced me to buy her over the years. That is so amazing that you got that detail!"

I smiled, surprised by the hit myself. "I know Sea Shell City well," I said to her. "I spent two summers during college working in Traverse City, and a group of us went there just to check out how awful it really was."

"So what's the connection?" Candice asked, getting us back on track.

"Right," I said, realizing I hadn't gotten the answer to the specific question I'd asked Bianca. In my head I questioned her again about where to look for her remains, and again I was shown the postcard from Sea Shell City, but then I was given another image of a dock. I glanced at Terry and asked, "Do either you or Jeremy still own the cabin?"

"It's my family's cabin," Terry said. "My brother, sister, and I each own a third of a share in it, so yes, I still own it."

"Has anyone been there lately?"

Terry looked surprised by the question. "No," she said after thinking about it. "My brother and his wife spent their vacation this year in Europe, and my sister has moved to Florida and hasn't been there in two years. I was going to take Bianca this past August, but with her missing, I couldn't even imagine going there without her."

I looked at her and felt a wave of sadness for what I now knew I had to tell her. "Terry," I said gently, "I believe that your daughter is somewhere close by that cabin," and I remembered what I'd told Gaston, about Bianca's body being near water.

Terry began to cry again and this time her sobs were all-consuming. Jessica wrapped her arms around Terry and tried to comfort her, even as her own tears fell. The awful atmosphere of the room was broken when a male voice demanded, "What's going on here?"

Jessica glanced up at a man standing in the doorway looking around at all of us in alarm. "Oh, Jeremy!" she said desperately, and the rest of her sentence was caught in her throat.

Mr. Lovelace crossed the room quickly, his face stark and pale. Addressing Harrison, he said, "You've found my daughter?"

Harrison's face held that same stony look. "Not yet," he said before shooting daggers with his eyes at me and Candice.

Candice stood quickly and took control of the situation. "Mr. Lovelace," she said calmly as she extended her hand. "My name is Candice Fusco. I'm a licensed private investigator and this is my associate, Abigail Cooper. I know Jessica from a few years back, and when I heard that her stepdaughter had gone missing, I knew I had to try and assist in any way I could. Abby and I believe strongly that your daughter may be somewhere in the vicinity of your ex-wife's cabin, at Burt Lake."

"Alive?" he asked, his voice filled with tension.

Candice's lips thinned as she shrugged her shoulders

once. "I don't know, Mr. Lovelace, but until we search the property, we won't be sure of our hunches."

Jeremy looked again at the keening form of his ex-wife. "Why is she so upset?" he asked a little more gently, and I noticed that the question was largely directed at Jessica.

"Do you remember that psychic I told you about years ago, honey? The one that predicted all those things that came true for me?"

Jeremy looked at her in confusion. "Yes," he said, again looking down at Terry.

Jessica pointed to me. "Abby is that psychic. And she's just made contact with Bianca."

Jeremy shook his head, and I knew he wasn't grasping what that meant. "Mr. Lovelace," I said to him, still feeling Bianca on the edge of my energy. When he looked at me, I said, "Bianca's spirit contacted me."

I didn't know how Mr. Lovelace was going to react, but I certainly didn't expect him to start laughing. Color flooded his face and he looked at his new wife in relief. "Oh, my God, Jessica! You had me scared to death! I thought you'd heard about some hard evidence or something."

I would have let it go, I swear I would have, but Bianca began shouting in my mind and what I thought I heard was, *Say "chuckles"!* Without thinking, I repeated what was booming around inside my head, "Say 'chuckles' . . . chuckles, chuckles, chuckles."

Jeremy immediately became serious. With large round eyes he looked at me and gasped, "*What* did you just say?"

I backed up a little on the couch, uncomfortable with his intense stare and Bianca still repeating over and over the word "chuckles." "It's not me," I said weakly. "It's your daughter. She's yelling at me to say the word 'chuckles,' and I don't know why, but she keeps pointing to you, then to herself, and I can't figure out whether she's talking about how you just started laughing or something else." When Jeremy continued to stare at me in disbelief, I added, "I don't think she's talking about you, though. I think she's talking about Chuckles as a *name*. Like maybe someone's favorite pet was named Chuckles or something."

Jeremy staggered to a chair and sat down heavily. Looking at Terry, who had regained a tiny bit of her composure, he whispered, "Did *you* tell her to say that to me?"

Terry shook her head and I could tell she didn't know what he was talking about. "Don't you remember, Terry? The nickname I gave her when she was ten and we took her to Sea World. She was laughing the whole time we were there, having a blast, and I started calling her Chuckles. Every e-mail, letter, or card I ever got from her after that, she'd sign it, 'Love, your devoted daughter, Chuckles.'"

The room was silent for several long moments save for the occasional sniff from Terry. Her ex-husband sat dumbfounded in his chair, and my heart went out to him, but I wanted to wait and let him absorb the truth about what I was telling him. Finally, with moist eyes he glanced at me and asked, "What else does she say?"

The answer came immediately. "She says she's happy you've quit smoking and that you've taken up jogging again."

Jeremy blinked and he looked to Jessica, who gave him a small, sad smile. "It really is her," she said to him. "You even told me last week when we were talking about how much we missed her that you just wished you could see her to tell her that you'd finally kept your promise and that you'd quit the cigarettes."

"She knows," I said to them. "And she's relieved."

"Can you tell her I love her?" Jeremy said, his voice ragged and pained.

I swallowed hard again even as my own eyes misted. "She knows that too," I assured him gently. And then I felt Bianca fade away from me, like a tide from the beach. "She's gone," I announced.

The room fell silent and somber again. Jeremy finally got to his feet and walked over to his ex-wife. Lifting her up off the couch, he gave her a tremendous hug and she wept into his shoulder. Then, he backed away from her and held his hand out to his new wife, and she got up to stand next to him. Turning to Harrison, he said, "How soon can you get a team up to the lake to search the cabin?"

Harrison appeared taken aback, but as he looked around the room, I knew he wasn't going to protest the request in the face of so much support for our side. "Give me the address and I'll make a call," he said, getting up. Terry gave it to him and he jotted it into a small notebook before excusing himself and stepping outside.

Candice and I also got to our feet and expressed our condolences to the family. "I'm so sorry," I said to first Jessica, then Terry, and finally Jeremy.

He surprised me again by reaching out to shake my hand at first, and then he pulled me into a tight hug. Whispering into my ear, he begged, "If she comes back to you again, please tell her that I will never stop until I've found the person responsible."

I nodded against his shoulder and he let me go. Overcome now by his emotions, he excused himself and left the room. Candice said to Jessica, "I think we should give you all some privacy."

"You don't have to leave," Jessica protested, but I

could tell she desperately wanted to go comfort her husband.

"Thank you, Jessica," Candice said, grabbing her purse off the sofa. "But we really should be off. I'll call you as soon as I know something, okay?"

We found Harrison on the phone, pacing next to his car. He didn't look happy, but then he never looked happy, just occasionally smug. As we came abreast of him, he clicked off his phone and motioned to the car. "Get in," he ordered.

We loaded up and he started the car again without waiting for either of us to finish buckling up. "Are we headed back home?" I asked into the tense silence.

"No."

"Gee, Agent Harrison," I said moodily, finally irritated enough to be brash, "you're so forthcoming with details. I can hardly keep them all straight."

Harrison's jaw clenched and he shot me a smoldering look. "You say there's a body at the lake? Fine, we're going up there to find it."

My mouth dropped. "That's got to be a five-hour drive!"

"Four," Harrison said, his mouth turning up at the corner.

I looked at the digital clock on the dashboard. It was noon. "Can we at least get something to eat?"

Harrison eyed me skeptically. "All that hocus-pocus whip up an appetite?"

"I could go for a burger," Candice called from the backseat. "But I'd understand if you wanted to steer more toward something with a few less calories. You probably need to start watching the carbs, right? Especially after eating that heavy Italian meal the other night."

I turned my head to hide a smile and the car fell silent again.

Harrison drove with his typical stoic glare, and I almost thought he was going to ignore the grumbling sounds coming from my stomach when he pulled into a lovely little restaurant called Clara's on the River.

Candice and I both ordered burgers, fries, and Cokes, while Harrison got the Cobb salad. Candice made sure to smirk at him when our food arrived. He made sure to ignore her.

We were back on the road by twelve forty-five, and now that my tummy was full and I'd expended an awful lot of energy back at the Lovelaces', I talked Candice into taking the front seat with Mr. Charming so that I could take a catnap in the back.

It seemed like I'd only let my head rest against the backseat for a few minutes when I was being gently shaken awake. "Are we there?" I asked groggily.

"No," Candice said from her twisted position in the front seat. "We're still about twenty minutes out. Harrison just got the call from the local PD in Cheboygan. They've discovered a body and they think it might be Bianca's."

"In the cabin?" I asked.

Candice shook her head. "In the boathouse."

Chapter Five

Candice and I sat in the car for much of the time that we were at Terry's cabin. Harrison was handling most of the dirty work and he didn't seem very open to the idea of my partner and I getting in the way and making a nuisance of ourselves.

Soon after we arrived, one lone news reporter turned up and Harrison immediately cornered the poor woman and her cameraman. I had little doubt he told her nothing of substance and convinced her to leave the scene after her camera guy had taken a few clips of the coroner's van.

After the reporter had gone and Harrison continued to direct the scene, time seemed to drag. With a yawn I wondered out loud to Candice why he'd insisted on taking us here in the first place and Candice said, "He never thought Bianca would actually be here."

My brow furrowed. "Then why make the drive at all?"

Candice's sly smile appeared again. "Because he

thought that he could embarrass you by having the police comb the place over and find nothing, then arrive with you a few hours later and have you fall flat on your face when you couldn't locate her body either."

I sighed tiredly. It had been a long day. "You'd think he'd know better by now."

Candice replied, "Maybe you don't need a lot of common sense these days to join the FBI."

Just then the whirring sound of a helicopter coming in low and fast reverberated across the metal of the car. Reflexively, Candice and I both peered up out the back window as the blinking lights of a chopper came into view. "Someone's come to join the party," she said over the noise.

Sure enough, in the field across from the cabin the chopper set down. When the blades had slowed, out hopped Bill Gaston, Jeremy Lovelace, and my boyfriend. "Dutch!" I exclaimed as I threw open the car door and rushed out to greet him.

Candice was right behind me and we met the men on the road next to the driveway. "Is it true?" Lovelace asked me at once. "Have they really found my daughter?" I noticed that he looked pale and shaken. Even though I'd prepared him earlier, this had to be unbelievably difficult for him.

I shook my head as I answered, "I don't know, Mr. Lovelace. Candice and I only heard that they've discovered some human remains. I'm sure Agent Harrison will be able to fill you in on more of the details."

Gaston, Lovelace, and Dutch all looked up over my shoulder. I turned to see Harrison waving them over. Lovelace quickly hurried toward him, but Gaston hesitated and squeezed my shoulder. "Jeremy told me what happened at the house."

"I'm sorry I didn't follow orders, sir."

"You did great, Ms. Cooper. My friendship with Jeremy goes way back, and I know you brought him some measure of comfort this afternoon. I would like to thank you for what you said to him. I know that sometime later, after the shock of losing his daughter ebbs a bit, he'll bear the loss a little less painfully because you convinced him she's still nearby, in spirit."

I nodded and ducked my chin, a little embarrassed. When Gaston left me for Harrison, I felt a strong arm snake around my middle. "Good work, Edgar," Dutch whispered into my ear, using his favorite nickname for me (after Edgar Cayce), while he pulled me close.

"I wish it could have had a happier ending." I sighed.

"It is what it is, Abs."

I squeezed him tightly for a few seconds before realizing that his being here probably meant good news. "Have you been cleared by IA?" I asked, glancing up into his face.

"Not yet," he groaned. "Hopefully another few days and this mess will be behind me and I can get back to my job."

"How were you allowed to come along, then?" I asked, pointing to the helicopter.

"The same way you were," he said with a grin. "We didn't tell anyone important about it."

"So what now?" I asked, turning to watch Harrison talk to Gaston and Lovelace.

Dutch motioned with his head in their direction. "We wait for my new boss to get finished briefing those two. Then we take you and Candice back home."

"Thank God," I said. "I'm beat."

"Does that also mean we're done with the case?"

Candice asked, and I could tell she'd been reading Harrison's body language as his eyes kept roving over to us.

Dutch sighed. "It might," he admitted. "Gaston told me on the way over here that Harrison called on some big guns last night. People he knows personally in high places. The word on your involvement is starting to leak, and by continuing to have you two around, it could look really bad for the bureau if this thing goes south."

"What does that mean exactly?" I asked. "How could it go south?"

"It means that if any other VIP's kid is abducted and/or murdered, you two could be blamed for sending the FBI on a wild-goose chase and diverting the agents from the real clues."

"That's ridiculous," I snapped. "*I* was the one who told Harrison where to look for Bianca in the first place!"

"Hey, don't yell at me," Dutch said, putting his hands up in mock surrender. "I'm just telling you how it will likely go down if we get one more mysterious disappearance."

I scowled, remembering what I'd told the task force the day before, that there would be another abduction soon. "You know what?" I said, still irritated. "They don't want our help? They don't have to have it."

"Abs," Dutch said with a sigh of his own. "Don't be like that."

I knew I was being childish, but it irked me that all my efforts weren't being appreciated. I didn't really have long to dwell on it because Gaston was soon back with us. "Agent Harrison is going to stay here and work with the CSIs to make sure this is done right. Jeremy is also staying, and he'll catch a ride back to Battle Creek with Agent Harrison. In the meantime, I think we should get these two home," he said, indicating me and Candice. "You both look very tired, and I know we've put you through a difficult few days."

"Thank you, sir," I said gratefully.

"We know you're busy and again, we very much appreciate all your assistance in helping us get this far." He said that last bit like he was confirming what Dutch had hinted at—that Candice and I were officially off the case.

I should have been relieved, but the connection I'd made earlier in the day with Bianca left me feeling bummed about not being allowed to help anymore. I simply nodded when Gaston had finished speaking, and we all walked quietly to the helicopter.

The ride home was thrilling, even though it was dark now and I couldn't see much. Still, I'd never ridden in a helicopter before. . . . Er . . . scratch that. I'd actually been medevaced out of a wooded area once, but that's another story. This ride I could actually remember and I wasn't in and out of consciousness—so it was easier to focus.

We were home around nine and I was asleep by ten.

The next few days were very routine; I got back to my regular schedule, beginning each day with Candice at the gym, and we worked diligently on one of the only cases she had lately. "If this doesn't pick up soon," I heard her grouse as she closed the file with a sigh, "I might have to look for a corporate job."

I could sympathize. My own calendar was woefully thin. I remembered fondly when around this time last year there had been a two-month waiting list to get in to see me. Nowadays you could get in for a session right away.

Still, I wouldn't be a good friend if I didn't at least put out my feelers for Candice's business, and when I did, I came up with something interesting. "You know what, girl?" I said casually as I stared at the far wall and concentrated on the images swirling around in my head. "I think you're going to be okay."

"Really?"

I nodded. "I'm getting that this month there might not be a lot of business, but there's something of a windfall coming your way."

"Ooooo," she said dreamily. "I like the sound of that!"

I smiled. "Yeah, but I want to prepare you: The windfall might come with strings." And then something unsettling poked at me from the ether and I couldn't help but pause to reflect on it.

Candice must have noticed the pause because she asked, "What is it?"

I looked at her curiously, considering what I had to ask her and how crazy it was going to sound. "Have you been crying or depressed lately?"

Candice tilted her head back and laughed. And if you knew her like I did, you'd get why that was funny. Candice defined cool, calm, and collected. I'd never seen her cry, or get overly emotional. "No," she said, cocking her head. "Why? Am I about to dissolve into a puddle of tears?"

I shook my head ruefully. "I know, it's absurd, right? I must be having an off day."

"You're due," she said with a kind smile. "Maybe you should take off and go do something nice for yourself, like get a massage or something?"

"I've got a client in twenty minutes," I said. "Otherwise, I'd be all over that."

"Okay," she said. "I've got some paperwork I could catch up on, but I think I'll take off a little early today and go see my grandma."

"How is Madame DuBois?" I asked.

"Crazy as ever. She wants me to help her paint a new chest of drawers for her bedroom."

"Don't tell me," I said, covering my eyes in mock concentration. "Is the color of choice . . . pink?"

Candice giggled. "Wow, you must be psychic!"

Candice's grandmother was ridiculously fond of pink. Dutch and I had once visited with her, and we'd both felt like we'd fallen into a vat of cotton candy. "Well, have fun with that," I told her as I got up to move into my office and get ready for my client's arrival.

"Thanks, hon. If I don't catch you before I leave, I'll see you on Monday in the gym."

My client arrived right on time and I ushered her into my reading room, which is located just off the lobby that both Candice and I share in a lovely little building in downtown Royal Oak.

I was excited to see that I didn't recognize the woman who booked the session with me—it's always good to be challenged by reading for a total stranger. She introduced herself as Jennifer Callahan and we sat down for our session.

"The first thing that I'm picking up for you, Jennifer, is a man to your side. I feel like he's just a little bit older than you, but it's weird—there's no romance here, but I know you two share the same space. It feels like this relationship has fallen into the roommate rut."

Jennifer smiled. "My brother lives with me," she said.

"Ah!" I said. "Well, that explains it. Okay, so with regard to your brother, does he work in law enforcement? Or is he an attorney or does he do anything with the law?"

"No," she said slowly.

"Weird," I said as the image of a badge kept reappearing in my mind's eye. I told her what I saw and she admitted that her brother had been thinking about applying to the police academy. "He should totally do it," I said with emphasis. "He'd make a great cop."

She looked unconvinced. "Do you think he'd be safe?"

"Abso-tootly!" I said, feeling my right side lighten. Then I focused on another series of images. "Holy cow," I said when I'd gotten a sense of the energy. "Do you work with some sort of hateful woman or something?"

Again Jennifer's eyebrows lowered in confusion. "No," she said. "I love my boss."

I frowned. Swirling around my client was the energy of an awful beast of a woman, clearly unstable, who was causing her a *lot* of havoc. "Then I don't get what this is all about," I admitted, "because there is this woman who is right out of a nightmare and has no control over her emotions. I keep feeling like she's painted you as a target. There is a man in this picture too, however, and I feel like these two used to be a team, but now he's on your side and she's not having it."

Jennifer's eyes lit up with understanding. "I think you're talking about my boyfriend's soon-to-be ex-wife."

And like the missing piece in a puzzle, it clicked

into place. "Oh, yeah!" I said. "That's got to be it! Wow, she really has it in for you. Did you know she spies on you?"

Jennifer sighed heavily. "My boyfriend, Paul, and I thought we heard someone in the bushes outside my house two nights ago, but when we went to investigate, no one was there."

"It was her," I said with conviction. "She's really unstable, you know."

"Oh," Jennifer said with a laugh, "you don't have to tell me twice!"

Just then I heard the phone ringing in my office and something about that buzzed my radar, but I set it aside because I needed to focus on my client. "She's also doing something funky with your boyfriend's accounts or with his money," I added. "Again, I want you to realize this woman is not thinking rationally, and she'll pretty much do anything she can get away with to try and hurt both of you."

"Do you think I'm in physical danger?" Jennifer asked.

I worked that question in my mind for a minute and relaxed when I felt the answer. "No," I told her. "I think she would stop just short of that. Still, you and your boyfriend need to tread carefully here, especially with regard to his finances."

"How can we find out what she's up to?"

As if in answer, I heard the phone in Candice's office start to ring and my radar gave another little ping. "My office mate is actually a private investigator, and she's one of the best in the business. I think she could definitely help you out with a little digging."

Jennifer and I continued with the session for about another twenty minutes before we ran out of time. It was a good session, with some great hits, and she looked a bit dazed at the end. "It's a lot to take in, isn't it?" I asked as she paid me.

"It is!" she said with a laugh. "I've never done this before, so I didn't know what to expect, and I certainly didn't think you'd be so detailed and so accurate."

I resisted the urge to blow on my knuckles ... but just barely. After she left, I remembered the little ping my radar had sounded when my phone rang, and as I moved toward my office, I noticed the light was still on in Candice's suite. Curious, I headed there first and was surprised to find her still at her computer. "I thought you were leaving," I said.

She'd been so focused on her computer screen that she obviously hadn't heard me come into the doorway, and she jumped in her seat when I spoke. "Just the girl I need to talk to," she said, recovering quickly, as she indicated the chair in front of her desk. "Take a seat, Abs. We need to talk."

I frowned. "Uh-oh," I said as I sat down. "That doesn't sound good."

Candice closed the lid to her laptop and regarded me thoughtfully. "I got a call while you were in with your client," she began.

"I heard the phone ringing," I said.

Candice nodded and again hesitated before speaking. "It was Jeremy and Jessica Lovelace. They want to hire us."

My eyebrows shot up in surprise. "They do?"

Candice folded her fingers into a steeple, resting her chin on her hands. "Harrison filled them in on how we wouldn't be asked back on the case. He tried to assure them that he could handle things from here on out."

I smiled. "Don't tell me; let me guess. Jeremy and Jessica didn't exactly find his reassurances reassuring."

"Bingo," Candice said with a wink. "Anyway, they want to hire us as a team to work the investigation."

"What about Bianca's mother, Terry?" I asked.

"She's on board too. She's been making copies of Bianca's journals before she hands them over to Harrison. She wants to ensure we have access to as much information as possible."

My brow furrowed. "Her journals?"

"Don't you remember?" Candice asked, and when I shook my head, she reminded me that I'd mentioned to Terry that there was a clue in Bianca's journal about what might have happened to her.

"Oh, yeah," I said as that came back to me.

"There is a catch to all this, however," Candice said, and I noticed that her eyes dropped to the desktop.

"And that is?"

"We cannot in any way interfere with the FBI's investigation. In fact, when Jeremy Lovelace called in a few favors of his own and attempted to get us back on the bureau's team, he was told by Gaston's superiors to butt the hell out."

"Harrison went above Gaston's head again, didn't he?"

Candice sighed. "It appears so. I think that asshole knows some other assholes in some pretty high places, which means this might get sticky for Dutch if the FBI becomes aware that we're nosing around."

"Great," I said. "Just what he needs. More trouble."

"Still, you and I could really use the cash. And Lovelace was willing to agree to our price—which, trust me, I didn't skimp on when I quoted him an hourly rate."

"Lord knows we could use the revenue," I agreed.

"So what do you want to do?"

I thought it over for a little bit and checked in with

my crew. My right side began to feel light and there was a sense of peace that settled into my abdomen. "My crew thinks we should go for it," I told her. "So I'm in."

"Awesome," she said happily. "I'll call the Lovelaces and tell them we're on. You go home and get some rest. We'll start this thing early Monday morning."

"Great, thanks, Cassidy," I said, getting up.

"Hey, Sundance," she called to me as I moved through her doorway. When I turned back, she said, "Remember, we need to keep Dutch out of it for now."

"In other words, you don't think I should tell him."

"I don't," she said.

I agreed, but my radar let me know that I'd certainly hear about it later.

Monday morning after the gym, Candice and I drove up to Battle Creek again, following the directions we'd been given by Terry Lovelace. We arrived at her beautiful home a few miles east of Jeremy and Jessica's, and as we trailed up the winding driveway, I noticed how sparkling clean and well tended everything seemed. The gardens and lawn were perfectly maintained. The house looked freshly painted, the white so brilliant it made me squint, and the shutters also appeared to have received a fresh coat of deep green. Mentally, I wondered whether this was how Terry had been dealing with the worry and anxiety over Bianca's disappearance. It appeared that maybe she'd kept busy on the house to avoid having too much time to think, and I had to give her credit for not crumbling into an unmoving mess, as I might have done in her situation.

We parked next to a silver Mercedes and headed

to the door. It opened even before we had a chance to ring the bell. Terry stood there looking pale and frail, and I wondered whether now that she knew Bianca was really gone, the crumbling would begin. "Hello, ladies," she said with a forced smile. "Please come in."

We entered the house and were immediately warmed by the heat of a fire in the front room. My first observations were that the inside of the house was even more perfect than the exterior. The carpet had been meticulously vacuumed, each line a symmetrical parallel to the next. No clutter dotted the espresso-stained side tables. Just a bowl of potpourri and a side lamp.

The furniture was simple but tasteful; two olive wing chairs faced a chocolate brown leather couch, and olive throw pillows were placed just so.

"Please have a seat," she offered, taking our coats to the front closet.

Candice and I both perched carefully on the edge of the couch. Neither one of us wanted to disturb the tidiness of the room. "Would you care for some coffee or tea?"

"Coffee would be lovely, Mrs. Lovelace," said Candice.

"Make that two," I added.

I noticed that Terry seemed relieved to have something to do with her hands before getting down to business. I imagined that she must be trying very hard to hold herself together.

She returned after a bit with three cups of steaming-hot coffee on a tray and set that down on the coffee table. After offering us cream and sugar, she picked up her own cup and seemed to stare blankly into it, lost in thought. "I've made copies of all Bianca's journals," she said at last. "I gave the originals to the FBI."

"Thank you for taking the extra step," Candice told her. "Hopefully there will be something useful in them."

Terry nodded, but her face didn't look convinced. "I've been all through them," she said. "Last night I combed through all seven of her journals. Even those going back to high school. I couldn't find anything in there that stood out. Nothing she wrote triggered any alarm."

"What do you know about Bianca's friends or the people she hung out with?" Candice asked, and I noticed that she'd discreetly placed a pocket-sized tape recorder on the coffee table.

Terry eyed the device but didn't object to its use as she answered. "Bianca had tons of friends. She was such a warm and outgoing person, she made friends easily. There were three girls up at school that she hung around with the most. I can give you their names and e-mail addresses if you think that will help."

"It would," said Candice. "And what about boyfriends? Did Bianca date?"

Terry inhaled deeply, appearing to struggle to hold herself together. "No," she whispered. "There was a boy that she was crazy about named Craig Stevenson. Those two were great friends all through high school, but he was captain of the football team and always had a new cheerleader on his arm. Bianca had the world's biggest crush on him and I knew that she was privately waiting for him to notice her as something more than just a buddy."

"Do you think he ever did?" Candice asked.

Terry seemed to catch the implied meaning in Candice's question, which was, did Terry think that maybe Craig finally noticed Bianca and things got out of hand and one thing led to another and Bianca ended up dead? "No," Terry said. "The last time I heard Bianca refer to Craig, which was about two weeks before she disappeared, he was overseas in Spain doing four semesters as an exchange student. To my knowledge, he's been out of the country this whole time."

"What about acquaintances? Did Bianca ever mention anyone hassling her or giving her a hard time over something? Even a misunderstanding?"

Terry shook her head and took a tiny sip of her coffee. "No," she said. "Never."

Candice looked down at a small notebook she'd taken from her purse and asked, "Can you forward me all the e-mails you might have received from Bianca while she was at school?"

"I can."

"Also, is it possible for you to get me a copy of her last school schedule?"

"Why would you need that?" Terry wondered.

"I'd like to retrace her steps," Candice explained. "I'd like to know the places she walked on a daily basis. For her to have disappeared so quickly, and with no one noticing, tells me that someone might have known her routine. They were familiar with her schedule, where she went on a regular basis and when she might be vulnerable."

Terry audibly gulped and her complexion grew paler still. She nodded her head numbly and my heart went out to her. Instinctively, I searched the ether for her daughter, wanting to give her even the smallest bit of comfort, but Bianca's energy was absent from my sixth sense today.

Candice too seemed to pick up that Terry was close to losing it. Setting her coffee down, she stood up and said, "I believe that's enough for us to get started on, Mrs. Lovelace. Thank you so much for meeting with us. I know last week had to have been especially difficult for you and you have our sincerest condolences."

Terry and I stood up as well and our hostess said, "I appreciate all your efforts, Candice. I just want them to release my daughter so that we can hold her funeral."

"The coroner still has her?" Candice asked.

Terry inhaled deeply, even as tears welled in her eyes. "They do," she whispered. "We hope it will only be another day or two. They don't want to miss documenting any evidence."

An awkward kind of silence followed and neither Candice nor I seemed to know what to say to offer any comfort to Terry. She was the first to break the silence, though, when she said, "Jeremy has been handling the press, thank God."

"Press?" Candice asked curiously.

"Yes," Terry said. "I believe one newspaper reporter and someone from channel seven contacted him. His friend Bill Gaston told Jeremy to tell them as little as possible. They've all but concluded that Bianca's death was either an accident or a suicide, which bothers me a lot." Suddenly Terry's eyes focused hard on Candice. "I'd like to call them and tell them what the FBI really suspects, Ms. Fusco. I don't want my daughter being thought of as mentally unstable enough to commit suicide. What do you think?"

Candice seemed to shift slightly. "I think that it's better for the time being to follow the FBI's instructions, Mrs. Lovelace. I think that whoever could have done this to Bianca might really hope to get the story in the papers and on TV. You might be feeding right into them by saying anything."

"But what if someone out there can help? What if

someone saw something that can point to the killer and all they need is to hear about it on the news?"

I looked at Candice, knowing she was in a tough spot. She really couldn't explain why the FBI wanted to keep this case on the down-low right now without revealing to Terry that there were two other missing teens—one of whom might still be alive. If Tracy said anything to the press, that could incite the killer to murder Leslie and move on to another victim.

Candice handled the delicate situation very well by saying, "Mrs. Lovelace, I know that more than anything you want the person responsible for your daughter's death to be captured and brought to justice, and if that is truly your goal, I think it's best to listen to the advice of the FBI. They know what they're doing, and all they're asking for is a little time to get to the bottom of this and put some of these clues together without tipping off the killer that they're on to him. It would also help us with our investigation if you said nothing to the press. I mean, the last thing Abby and I need is some reporter sniffing around our investigation."

Terry gave Candice a weak smile. "Well, when you put it like that, Candice, it makes a lot of sense. I just hope whoever did this to my daughter is caught soon."

Candice stuck out her hand. "We'll do our best to make sure that happens, Mrs. Lovelace, and we'll call you the moment we find anything relevant."

After handing us the copies of Bianca's journals and getting our coats out of the closet, Terry looked at me and asked softly, "Did she come to you again?"

"No," I said honestly. "I was open to it, but she's not with us at the moment."

Terry seemed concerned. "Do you think she's all right?"

I squeezed her arm gently. "Of course she is," I reassured her. "What I know about the dead is that it takes a lot of energy for them to come through to someone like me, and once they use up that energy, it can sometimes take them a little while to recuperate. Don't worry, I'm absolutely positive that she's okay and that she hasn't gone far away from you."

Terry swallowed hard. "Thank you," she said.

We left her and began the long trip back to Royal Oak. I'd made sure to wait until after Dutch had gone to work to meet Candice, so I wasn't worried about him wondering where I was or why I was dressed in a suit. And as my phone with the tracking device linked to his phone had been lost in Vegas, I wasn't worried about him checking some GPS system to figure out that I was far outside of town.

About the time we were approaching our exit, Candice said, "Want to grab some lunch?"

My eyes went to the clock on the dash and my stomach answered first with a loud gurgle. "I do."

"What sounds good?"

"Coney Island?" Strange though it may sound, the Detroit metro area offers the best damn hot dog and chili combo *ever*.

Candice smirked. "You and your junk food."

I shot her a look. Candice spent a lot of time trying to convince me to eat right. I spent an equal amount of time trying to get her to cheat a little. "If I offer to get a side salad, can we go to Sparky's on Woodward?"

"They've closed down," Candice told me.

"*What?*" I gasped. "When?"

"Three weeks ago," she said. "A lot of restaurants and small businesses have closed around these parts," she reminded me. "Some of them can't survive."

I scrunched down in my seat and pouted. "Well, that just sucks," I moaned. "I loved Sparky's."

Candice gave me a pat on the head. "Buck up, lil' camper, I know a joint."

About ten minutes later we were on the south side of town and seated in a booth with duct tape on the seats, cracked Formica tabletops, and salt and pepper shakers that had seen better—cleaner—days. "This is great!" I said, looking around in approval.

Candice chuckled. "Remember to order the side salad."

"Yeah, yeah," I said, inhaling deeply as the rich aroma of onions, chili, hot dogs, and mustard filled my nostrils.

We gave our order to the waitress—who, like the salt and pepper shakers, had also seen better days—and began to discuss our game plan for Bianca's case. "Nothing new came to you when we were sitting with Terry?" she asked me.

"Nope," I said, after taking a long pull of my Coke. "The ether was quiet."

"What do you think that means?" she asked.

I thought about that for a minute before answering. "I think it means that we have all the clues we need to get started. And because Bianca specifically mentioned her journals, I think that's where we should start."

Our food arrived and my eyes widened as I surveyed the huge plate of Coney fries set in between Candice and me. "Yum!" I sang happily, diving right in.

Candice gave me a minute to indulge my taste buds before she continued. "I also think I should head up to MSU."

I cocked my head. "You want me to come with you?"

She nodded. "You're better than any bloodhound.

Maybe there's a trace of her up there, some kind of imprint you can pick up on to help us bring out another clue or two."

"You know," I said, pointing a fry at her, "that's a damn good idea. When do you want to head to East Lansing?"

"As soon as her mother sends me the class schedule. If she doesn't e-mail or fax it to me by this afternoon, I'll give her another call and remind her."

"I'm free tomorrow," I said.

"Perfect."

"And give me half of the journal entries today," I added. "I'll take them home and see if my radar hits on anything."

"Done."

"Then what?" I asked after a bit of silence.

"I'll conduct my usual routine and do some digging into Bianca's credit, assuming of course that she had any. I'll contact her friends, teachers, roommates, and acquaintances and see if there're any clues there. I'll look into her bank accounts, e-mails, and any other personal information I can get my hands on and try to find the needle in the haystack."

"Wow," I said. "That's a lot of work. Maybe you'd better give me all the journal entries, then."

Candice laughed. "Done," she said.

We left the restaurant and Candice dropped me at my place with the journal entries. I went inside, changed into sweats, and curled up on the couch with Eggy and Tuttle (our dogs) to begin sifting through Bianca's most private thoughts. I started with the entries just before she disappeared, working my way backward. It bothered me at first to think that I was invading her privacy—it felt so voyeuristic—but I reminded myself that it was Bianca who had suggested I sift through her journals in the first place.

Dutch came home around six, catching me by surprise. I'd been completely absorbed in Bianca's world when I heard his car pull into the driveway. Quick as a flash, I bolted to my home office and stuffed the copies into the bottom drawer of my desk. I then zipped back to the couch and flipped on the TV.

"Hey," he said when he came through the door.

"Hi, sweetheart!" I said happily. "How was your day?"

Dutch eyed me suspiciously. Maybe I was a little *too* happy. "Fine. Yours?"

I shrugged. "Nothing special," I said.

"Why are you panting?" he asked, noting that I was still breathing a little heavy from running back and forth to my office.

I forced a laugh and lowered my lids seductively and purred, "You take my breath away, hot stuff."

"Uh-huh," he said, not buying it. Still, I was grateful when he changed the subject. "You hungry?"

"Aren't I always?"

"I've got some chicken marinating in the fridge that I could grill."

"Sounds perfect. Want some help?" I was a godawful cook, and the kitchen was pretty much off-limits to me these days.

"No," he said a little too quickly before he added, "That's okay. I've got it."

"Suit yourself. Let me know when it's time to set the table and I'll at least do that."

A half hour later Dutch and I were just sitting down to dinner when the doorbell rang. I groaned, knowing full well who it was. "Did you make extra?" I asked, getting up from the table to go answer the door.

"His plate's in the oven," Dutch said with a grin.

I opened the door to a tall, gray-haired hippie. "Dave," I said woodenly. "What a surprise."

"Oh, am I interrupting your dinner?" Dave asked, looking past me hungrily at the table, where the smell of barbecued chicken, baked beans, and mashed potatoes wafted.

"Won't you please join us?" I said in the same flat tone.

"Aww," Dave said, coming through the door and walking purposely toward the table. "I couldn't impose."

I rolled my eyes and headed to the kitchen to retrieve Dave's plate from the oven. Walking back, I set it in front of him and was about to take my seat again when my intuition went *zing!* I looked at Dave in alarm and blurted out, "You're moving!"

Dave had already lifted a forkful of mashed potatoes in the air, but he stopped abruptly when I spoke. Blinking in surprise at me, he said, "I keep forgetting how good that radar of yours is."

"You're moving?" Dutch asked, looking from me to Dave. "When and where?"

"Soon," I answered, sitting down and not feeling very hungry anymore. "And he's moving far away. Down South, right?"

Dave swirled his mashed potatoes, looking guilty. "Business has been really bad lately, guys. I held out here as long as I could, but my old lady is starting to panic about how little we've got in the bank. I can't find much work anywhere these days, and her brother lives in Texas. He owns a construction company and he's offered me a job."

Everyone at the table was silent for a long moment as Dutch and I absorbed that. I might make a stink about Dave's being something of a permanent houseguest—especially at dinnertime—but I'd come to really consider him one of my dearest friends. "Abby thinks I'm moving too," Dutch said, breaking the silence and reminding me of something else I'd predicted.

And my heart was suddenly filled with sadness. Huge changes were happening all around me as my hometown struggled to survive. "When do you leave?" I asked.

"Next week," Dave said. "We're almost done packing up the house and then we're taking off."

I looked at Dutch and his eyes were gentle. "We'll come visit you guys," he suggested.

"We've already found a place in this city called Georgetown—it's just outside Austin. I guess their growth rate is something like forty percent. It's one of the few places in the country doing really well right now, and there are plenty of construction jobs and real estate there is still affordable. We think we can finally afford to buy a place."

"What about your house up here?" I asked. The streets were littered these days with For Sale signs.

"It's a rental," Dave said, color lighting his cheeks.

I was really surprised by that. All this time I'd thought Dave owned his house. "Ah," I said. "That'll make it easier, then."

"If you need any help packing or loading the truck, you can count on us," Dutch offered.

Dave polished off the last of his baked beans. "Thanks, buddy, I appreciate it, but I think we've got it. Anyway, I wanted to come by and tell you the news in person. I'll be back before we leave, though."

I nodded and fought back tears. I didn't want Dave to go. He'd been through so much with me and I was very sad to lose him. So I did the only thing I could think of to give myself a little hope. I checked the ether around him and said, "The move will be a really great thing, Dave. You'll love Texas. I know you'll fit right in. And you're right about the work—there's plenty of it. You'll be busier than you think. I also see you buying your own home in the next year and a half, and it'll be something you'll have a hand in building."

Dave's smile was ear to ear. "Thanks, Abby," he said, and I could see the relief in his eyes.

Dave stuck around to help wash the dishes, which was nice and highly unusual for him. And then he took his leave, suggesting he had more packing to do. When he'd gone, Dutch wrapped strong arms around me and pulled me close. "It'll be all right," he whispered in my ear as I began to cry.

"Everyone's leaving," I said.

"Everyone?"

"Yes," I mumbled, nodding my head into his chest. "Dave, my clients, Sparky's . . . you."

"I'm not going anywhere," Dutch insisted. "It's you and me, right here in this house, for the long haul, Edgar."

But my left side grew heavy and I knew that the winds of change were about to blow my little world apart. I could only hope I was strong enough to weather the storm.

Chapter Six

The next morning, the minute Dutch was out of the house, I tore downstairs to continue reading Bianca's journals. Much of the content was quite ordinary, although I genuinely liked her style and I could definitely see why she wanted to be a journalist. She was very good about detailing the place, time, and date of events, and her entries read more like articles.

By ten thirty a.m. I was at the beginning of Bianca's freshman year when the phone rang. "Hey," said Candice when I picked up the line. "Wanna go for a ride to East Lansing?"

Candice picked me up fifteen minutes later and I brought the journals to read while she drove the hour and fifteen minutes to the Michigan State University campus. En route Candice asked, "How's it coming?"

I sighed and rubbed my eyes. "Nothing looks really interesting to me yet," I said. "Mostly she's documenting her days, her classes, who's going out with whom. Normal teenager stuff."

"Does she mention anyone following her or creeping her out?"

"Nope. She's delightfully sunny about everyone she meets. The girl could find the good in Oscar the Grouch."

"Okay," Candice said. "Keep reading, then. We've still got a half hour to go."

We made it to campus around noon and decided to start with Bianca's dorm. Candice found a place to park in a nearby lot. As we backtracked to the dorm, she took out a copy of Bianca's schedule and a map of the campus. "She lived in Wonders Hall," Candice mused as we walked along. "That must be that big one over there."

"Should we go inside?"

"Can't hurt. Might be a good idea to go up to her dorm room too."

"You want to go into her room?" I asked, feeling a bit nervous about disturbing the students.

"Why not?" Candice asked. When I continued to look at her skeptically, she said, "If someone's there, we don't have to give them any details. We can pretend that we're alumni taking a trip down memory lane and stopped by, hoping to see the old dorm room we shared."

"That is not a bad idea," I said. "Okay, I'm in."

"Turn your radar on," Candice advised as we stepped through the door, held open by an exiting student, and into the large lobby.

We located the elevators and Candice pushed the button for the sixth floor. Once there we went the wrong way out of the little elevator lobby and had to backtrack, but eventually we found Bianca's room. Candice knocked loudly three times. From behind the door we could hear the sound of music playing, and the door was abruptly opened by a young girl with greasy hair and bad skin wearing a skintight running suit that exposed her plump belly. "Hey there," Candice said, flashing her friendliest smile.

"Yeah?" the girl asked, her look guarded.

"So sorry to bother you, but this is my old roommate from the class of 'ninety-five and we were up here on campus taking a trip down memory lane and thought we'd stop by our old dorm room."

"Uh-huh?" the girl said. I could tell she really wasn't picking up what Candice was hinting at.

"We used to live in this dorm, in your room actually," I said, getting to the point. "And we were curious to see how it's changed. Is there any way you could let us take a peek?"

The girl eyed me suspiciously, and then surveyed me up and down, checking out my jeans and thick sweater. Then her eyes roved over Candice and gave her the once-over too.

"We promise, we're harmless," Candice said, holding up her hand like she was willing to swear on it.

The girl finally shrugged and stepped aside, and Candice and I moved into the room—which was a total mess—and took a look around. I had my radar on high, but everything I intuitively sensed came from the girl standing in the doorway, still staring at us suspiciously.

"I love what you've done with the place," Candice gushed, eyeing me to see if I was getting anything. I subtly shook my head and moved toward the bunk beds against the far wall. "Do you remember when we threw that party right around finals?" Candice asked with a laugh.

I knew she was trying to buy me a little time by

making small talk, but the room was so cluttered with energy that it was impossible for me to pick anything out specifically. Whatever had gone on here over the years had included a lot of drama. "I do," I said, and then an awkward silence followed. Turning once more in a circle, I gave up and announced, "Well, we'd better let you get back to your studies. I know I had a hard time with statistics too."

The girl in the doorway nodded; then she seemed to catch what I'd said. "Wait a minute," she said, putting her hand up in a stopping motion. "How did you know I was studying stats?"

I thought quickly and moved across the room to one of the two desks by the window. "Your homework is out on your desk," I said, relieved that it was.

"Oh," she said, still looking oddly at me. I'd been nowhere near her desk, which was partially obscured by the bunk beds, so I knew she was wondering how I could have seen her books.

"Anyway," I said, moving toward the door with a flourish, "let's go, Sharon. We don't want to be late meeting the others for lunch."

"Thanks again," Candice said as we passed the girl and walked back out into the hallway. As we moved down the corridor, Candice said, "Sharon?"

I shrugged. "I didn't want her reporting our real names to the campus police."

Candice eyed me with a smile. "You're a little paranoid, aren't you?"

"Can you blame me after what happened in Vegas?" I asked, referring to a time a few weeks earlier when it had paid to be paranoid.

"Good point. So what did you get from the room?"

I sighed tiredly. "Not a damn thing other than the usual clutter."

Candice arched an eyebrow. "Usual clutter?"

I nodded. "Yep. You find a lot of energetic clutter in places like apartments and dorm rooms. Anywhere there's a constant turnover of people carries energy that feels a lot like static—it's too garbled to pick up anything significant or specific. In other words, I couldn't pick up on Bianca's individual energy—the room was too stacked with the energy of all the other kids who've ever lived there."

"Huh," Candice said thoughtfully. "Good to know."

When we were back downstairs, Candice eyed the schedule again and the map. "Her first class was in the Eppley Center."

I peered over Candice's shoulder. "Holy cow!" I said as I took in the distance on the map between the dorm and Bianca's first class. "That's way across campus!"

"Welcome to MSU," Candice said. "The campus where the smart students travel by pack mule."

We spent the next hour going from one location to the next, walking the long route that Bianca had for her classes. We were halfway through her schedule when we found ourselves close to Grand River Avenue and downtown East Lansing, so we stopped for a bite to eat and to rest our feet.

"I can't believe she walked this route every day," I complained as I took my foot out of my boot and rubbed the sole.

"She only needed to walk it twice a week," Candice said. "She scheduled all her classes for Tuesdays and Thursdays."

"What time did her first class start?"

Candice looked down at the schedule. "Nine a.m."

"What time did they end?"

"Two were in the morning, one was in the late afternoon, and her last class, Intro to Journalism, was an evening class. That started at six and let out at seven thirty."

My radar dinged and my eyes widened. "Bingo," I said.

"What?"

"I'm not sure yet," I admitted. "But we need to go next to the hall where her last class was held."

"You got it," Candice agreed, and I could tell she was relieved that I'd finally hit on *something*.

We finished our lunch and set out at a brisk pace back across Grand River toward campus. Walking southeast, we eventually arrived at a dark brick building labeled North Kedzie. Going inside, we toured the hallways for a bit, finding Bianca's classroom—which was empty— and following my radar, which kept pulling me toward a set of stairs. Instinctively I headed up them. When we arrived on the third floor, I pushed through a set of double doors, with Candice right behind me, and came to a hallway lined with offices of the various professors who taught here. I walked slowly down the corridor, glancing at the nameplates by the doors, and asked Candice, "Who did Bianca have for journalism?"

"Someone named Houghton."

"Professor J. Houghton?" I said, turning around and pointing to the nameplate I'd just stopped in front of.

"Ooh." Candice beamed. "You're good!"

I could see light coming from the crack under the door so I knocked. "Come in," called a voice.

I opened the door wide and stepped into the room. "Good afternoon," I began. "My name is Abigail Cooper, and this is my associate, private investigator Candice Fusco."

Professor Houghton's face registered surprise. "Private investigator?" he asked nervously. "Is this about my ex-wife?"

I bit my lip so as not to laugh and replied, "No, sir. This is about a student who went missing late last spring named Bianca Lovelace. We were wondering if you had a moment to talk to us about her?"

The professor relaxed a little. "I've already spoken extensively to the police and the FBI," Houghton said. "Bianca came to class, took her final, and left."

"How'd she do?" Candice asked.

"She got a four point," the professor said proudly. "She was by far my best student."

I could tell that the professor didn't really want to get involved any deeper, and I couldn't blame him. Being connected to a student who disappeared could cause anyone to get nervous, but my radar didn't want me to let Houghton go. There was something I knew I needed to dig for, but I didn't know what. "Can you tell us anything more about her?" I asked.

Houghton shrugged. "What more *can* I tell you?" he said, turning the question back on me. "Bianca was a great kid. She was enthusiastic, paid attention, never skipped class, studied hard, and got good grades. At least in my class she did. She was eager to get on my good side for obvious reasons, but she never did anything inappropriate or out of line."

I shook my head. That last sentence didn't make any sense to me. "I'm sorry, she was eager to get on your good side? Why exactly?"

Houghton waved his hand at the walls of his office and I suddenly realized they were covered with framed newspaper articles. "I'm the administrative editor of the *State News*," he explained. "I appoint all the student reporters and writers to MSU's paper."

"And Bianca wanted to join the paper," I said as the memory of asking Terry if Bianca was trying to get an internship at a newspaper for the summer rang some bells.

"She did," he said. "But she was only a freshman. Because there's such an interest in the paper, it's more traditional to appoint second-semester juniors or seniors to those positions. I told her to work on a story or two and come back to me in the fall. I might be willing to make an exception if she came back with something really good."

And like that, a few of the puzzle pieces that had been swirling around in my head clicked into place. "She was working on something," I said softly.

"What's that, Abs?" Candice asked.

I shook my head, snapping my eyes back into focus and momentarily ignoring Candice's question. "Professor Houghton," I began urgently, "did Bianca by any chance tell you about a story idea she had, or something she might have been working on?"

Houghton looked slightly chagrined. "Maybe," he said.

I cocked my head. "Maybe?"

Houghton nodded and cleared his throat. "As I said, Bianca was anxious to get onto the school newspaper's staff, and I knew that her father was a state legislator. We haven't really had any interesting political stories lately, so I told her to use her connections and bring me back something working that angle. I also let her know that it would have to be a big enough story to warrant an exception to the rule of assigning someone so young to the staff. I recommended that she nose around her father's office, and see what she could come up with."

I could feel a sense of adrenaline rush through me as my radar dinged big-time. Candice, however, didn't seem at all pleased with the professor's response. "So let me get this straight," she snapped. "You told an eighteen-year-old girl to basically rat on her father or one of his colleagues?"

Houghton's face immediately flushed. "Of course not," he said defensively. "I would never suggest such a thing. But she did have the perfect cover for some undercover reporting, which is done in journalism all the time."

Candice's frown turned into a full glare. "This is why no one trusts the press anymore," she muttered, then looked at me as if to ask if I was ready to go.

But I wasn't quite done with Houghton yet. "Professor," I said, making sure to remove any sense of condemnation from my voice. "Did Bianca suggest to you that she might already have a story idea?"

Again, Houghton looked uncomfortable. "She never told me directly, but yes, I believe she had something in mind."

"How do you know exactly?" I asked.

"When we had this discussion, she asked me if there was perhaps a line that she ethically shouldn't cross, and when I pressed her on that, she said she'd heard rumors regarding a powerful politician that could end a career."

"And what did you tell her?" Candice pressed.

Houghton swallowed. "I told her that the public had the right to know about the ethics and morals of the people they'd elected to government, and if she could uncover anything of substance, then it was her obligation as a journalist to bring it to the public's attention."

I closed my eyes for a moment and tried to collect myself. I really hated this asshole. Finally I looked back at him and said, "You're sure Bianca never let on who she wanted to expose?"

"No," said Houghton, and I could tell he was growing impatient with our line of questioning.

"And you didn't think that her disappearance was in any way connected to the story she was going to work on?"

"No, I didn't," said Houghton. "We had that conversation only a week before her final exam and her disappearance. With all of her other classes and finals, she couldn't have had time to work on the story, so I assumed it was unrelated."

But my radar wanted to suggest otherwise. I knew there was something here, but I also knew it was only a small thread in this bigger puzzle. I turned to Candice and motioned with my head that I was ready to leave.

"Thank you for your time, Professor Houghton," she said. "We'll let you get back to your work."

We left the professor's office and hurried down the hallway, Candice pestering me for details along the way. "What's your radar saying?" she wanted to know.

I waited until we were outside so that I could face her and talk about it without being overheard in the crowded hallways or stairwell. "Bianca was absolutely working on that story," I said.

"And you think that whoever abducted her was the target of the investigation?"

I opened my mouth to say yes, but I felt my left side immediately grow heavy, which totally confused me. "No," I said, and was surprised to hear it come out of my mouth.

"No?" Candice repeated, looking as confused as I felt.

I nodded. "Yeah, my radar says that's off," and as I said that, immediately my right side felt light again and I was even more confused. "Hold on," I said, and closed my eyes to concentrate. There was a mixture of thoughts running through my intuitive filter. I knew that the story Bianca was working on had something to do with her disappearance, but I couldn't figure out how. Finally I shrugged my shoulders and said, "Maybe."

"Maybe what?"

"Maybe her disappearance is connected to the story," I said, and when Candice shot me a rueful look, I added, "Sorry, toots, that's the best I can do."

"How do the others fit into this, then?" she pressed.

That stumped me. "Smoke screen?" I offered, saying it like a question.

Candice seemed to consider that for a minute. "Okay," she conceded. "Or maybe this isn't about Bianca at all. Maybe it's about some grudge the wacko who abducted her has against state political leaders, and killing their children is his way of getting his point across."

I sighed, suddenly very weary. "Yeah, well, it's all I've got."

Candice nodded. "Okay, then, we'll follow your lead and see where it takes us. If you get a chance, go back to her journals and keep digging. Maybe she wrote about her story idea in one of them."

"Will do."

"I'll scour her e-mails for any reference to an article or news story she might have mentioned to her dad. Maybe he even talked to her about it and that's where she came up with the idea in the first place."

"Oh, and make sure you ask her friends if she was working on some juicy story—they might have heard something too."

"I'm on it," Candice promised.

Game plan in hand, we headed home.

That night as I was cozying up next to Dutch and just beginning to drift off to sleep, my radar gave me a really big buzz. I sat up in bed and felt my heart begin to beat faster as my anxiety grew. "Abs?" Dutch asked, setting down the David Morrell novel he'd been reading.

"Something's wrong," I said, working to pull some details out of the ether.

"What exactly?"

I stared at him with wide eyes. "I don't know," I whispered as my sense of dread increased.

"Can you tell me who it might be about?"

I blinked at him and felt out that question. "It's about a female," I said. "No . . . wait," I added. "It's about two women. One older, one younger."

"Is anyone hurt?"

I closed my eyes and my heart sank. "Yes," I whispered. "One of them is close to death, but I can't tell who it is!"

Dutch's hand rubbed my shoulder. "It's okay, honey," he soothed, and I realized I was breathing heavily. "We'll figure it out."

My eyes opened and I stared urgently at him. "It's bad."

Dutch nodded gravely. "Do you think these women were attacked?"

I closed my eyes again, then slowly shook my head. "No . . . there's no attacker."

"Were they in a car accident?"

I frowned. I could feel the fact that one of the women was in grave condition, but how she'd gotten that way I couldn't tell. And the other woman's energy felt so . . . so . . . *familiar* that it was eerie. And then, as if a lightbulb above my head were suddenly turned on, I knew who the second woman was. "Ohmigod, Candice!" I gasped, opening my eyes and reaching over Dutch for the phone on the nightstand.

"She's hurt?" Dutch asked, helping me by handing me the phone.

I didn't answer him because my hands were shaking as I tried to dial her number as fast as I could. I pressed the wrong buttons and hung up, swearing in the process. Just as I was about to click the phone on and try again, it rang in my hands. I jumped, as it was so unexpected, and noticed immediately that the caller ID read *Fusco, Candice.* "What's happened?" I demanded when I answered, knowing she was calling with bad news.

It took a moment for her to answer me. She was crying so hard on the other end of the line that I couldn't make out anything she said. "Where are you?" I pressed. She blubbered something that I couldn't make out, so I tried again, calmer this time. "Honey, I'm on my way, but I can't understand you. Just take a deep breath and tell me where you are and we'll be there in two minutes."

"Hos . . . hos . . . hospital!" she wailed.

"Beaumont?" I asked, hoping it was the local hospital right down the street.

"Yes," she said as her sobs continued.

"We're on our way!" I clicked off the phone before jumping out of bed and grabbing a pair of jeans.

"What's wrong?" Dutch asked me again as he too got out of bed and reached for his pants.

"I don't know," I said, shaking all over. "Candice is at the hospital and I've never heard her so upset."

"Is her grandmother okay?"

I froze and gawked at him. All the clues suddenly clicked into place as the right side of my body confirmed that something was very, very wrong with Madame DuBois. "I don't think so, Dutch," I said. "I think something's happened to her."

"Come on," he said, shoving his bare feet into loafers. "I'll drive."

We arrived at Beaumont Hospital four minutes later. Candice was sitting in the emergency room with her knees drawn into her chest and looking so forlorn that she broke my heart. I rushed to her side and hugged her fiercely. "I'm so sorry," I whispered. "Candice, I'm so, so sorry."

"She had a stroke," she explained, her voice hoarse and nasal. "I tried calling her tonight, and when she didn't answer, I went over to check on her. I found her on the floor in her kitchen."

Dutch sat down on the other side of Candice and rubbed her back. "What can we do for you?" he asked gently.

Tears streamed down Candice's face. Madame Du-Bois was the only family Candice had left. Her parents had both died of different cancers within two years of each other, and her sister had died in a violent car crash when Candice was little. I couldn't imagine what she must be going through right now. "Just stay with me," she begged. "They've got her in ICU, but no one thinks she'll pull out of this."

I hugged her fiercely again and felt my own tears

slide down my cheeks. "As long as you need us, we'll be here, honey."

We waited with Candice until three in the morning. Around one a.m. she was called into her grandmother's room by a kind nurse who suggested that Candice might want to spend some final moments with her grandmother. Dutch and I hovered outside the room, pacing back and forth until we heard the sound of the heart monitor bleep slower and slower; then it finally bleeped its last. Candice's gut-wrenching sobs quickly followed.

As tears poured down my own cheeks, Dutch hugged me tightly and said, "Get in there and be with her. We'll take her home with us tonight. She shouldn't be alone. I'll call off work tomorrow and help her with the arrangements."

I nodded into his chest, unable to speak, then hurried quickly into the room to offer what small comfort I could to my very dear friend.

Chapter Seven

Madame DuBois' funeral was held in the rain. Dutch and I both hovered with umbrellas over Candice, her forlorn figure hunched under the weight of her grief. She looked pale and exhausted as the cemetery employee worked the lift that slowly lowered the frosty pink casket of her beloved grandmother into the grave. I knew that Candice had to be thinking about the funerals of her other family members eased into the earth the same slow, sad way.

I squeezed her hand again and again, trying in vain to let her know that she wasn't alone, that she still had family even if we weren't blood related. As I glanced at the onlookers gathered around the gaping hole in the ground, I felt comforted by the fact that there were so many in attendance. All of Madame DuBois' elderly friends from the senior center had come out. Her neighbors and the woman who did her hair each week were also there.

Many of Candice's clients and friends had also come out, along with Dutch's best friend, Milo. Dave and his "old lady" had come as well, and it touched my heart that they'd even postponed their move a few days so that they could attend the funeral and support a friend. Even my sister, Cat, had flown in for the day, and the area around Madame DuBois' grave was covered with dozens of bouquets of pink roses that my wealthy sister had so generously and thoughtfully purchased. Cat stood on the other side of me and I nudged her with my shoulder.

"How's she doing?" she whispered into my ear.

I whispered back, "I'm worried."

Cat nodded, her own eyes pinched, but she mouthed back, "She'll be okay."

I sighed as I looked absently around again at the flowers and the mourners getting soaked in the rain. I wanted to take Candice away from this somber scene as soon as possible and have her curl up on my couch, where it was warm and dry and I could take care of her, so I didn't notice right away when someone new joined the gathering.

Among the mass of white and blue hair, my gaze belatedly picked out a familiar face and I literally gasped in surprise. Candice's head lifted and her eyes looked at me. "What?" she asked.

I squeezed her hand and nodded to our right. "Harrison is here."

Candice's tired lids blinked in confusion, but she followed my head motion as I indicated him on the other side of the grave. "Huh," she said, her tone flat and lifeless. Gaston had sent flowers and a card to my house, probably hearing from Dutch that Candice was staying with us, and he'd sent his condolences and regrets that he couldn't attend the funeral, as he had business in Washington. I'd been very touched by his thoughtfulness, but for the life of me, I couldn't imagine why Harrison had come.

Candice didn't seem to dwell on it either. Her blank stare returned to her grandmother's casket as it settled into the bottom of its earthen cradle. The priest made the sign of the cross over his chest and concluded the service, thanking everyone for coming and offering his final condolences to Candice.

As the crowd solemnly dispersed, I linked my arm through Candice's and gently pulled her away. "Come on, honey, let's get you home."

Candice stayed with us for the next five days. At first I worried that she wasn't going to pull out of the deep well of sadness that she'd settled herself into. As she sat on our couch, refusing food and my attempts to get her to go outside for a run or at least a brisk walk, I became increasingly concerned that she wasn't going to come back to herself.

But on the evening of the third day I noticed that my friend began to make idle conversation. It started with the weather and moved on to the news and current events. Finally on the morning of the fifth day she found me in my office, poring over Bianca's journals. "Hey," she said meekly.

I'd been so engrossed I hadn't heard her come in and I jumped a little in my chair. "Hi there," I said, smiling a little at my own reaction. "How ya doin'?"

Candice shrugged and came to sit in front of my desk. I tried not to stare at the pronounced collarbone peeking out of her shirt while her clothing hung on her like a sack. I knew she'd barely eaten anything in the last week and the girl had undoubtedly lost more weight than was good for her, but the dark circles under her eyes looked a bit less prominent today and I took that as a good sign at least.

"Have you found anything?" she asked into the silence that followed her sitting down.

I rolled my head from side to side, trying to relieve the stiffness after being hunched over so long. "Not really. I keep looking for clues around her spring-break adventures, but the girl didn't do the usual thing on her vacations."

"The usual thing?"

I nodded. "No beaches, boys, and bedlam for Bianca. Last year she helped build a row of houses for Habitat for Humanity. Her senior year she attended a conference with her dad, then helped organize a cleanup along the Rouge River."

Candice shook her head. "She was a good kid."

"One of the best," I said sadly. "I can't imagine anyone wanting to hurt her."

"Did you go back to her spring breaks from prior years?"

"You mean back through high school?" When Candice nodded, I said, "Nothing that points to anything. She went to London with her mom her junior year, and that's as far as her journals take me."

"I called Jeremy Lovelace after we got back from MSU to ask him about Bianca's big story. He said she never mentioned anything about working on something like that with him, and further, he insisted he never discussed anything that might be inappropriate about his colleagues with Bianca. Also, he was under the distinct impression that she wasn't very interested in local politics in general. She liked bigger stories with broader scope, like foreign wars, global warming, etc., etc."

"It sounds like that's a dead end, then," I said, feeling totally frustrated with this case.

"Yep," Candice agreed. She then ran a hand through her hair and sighed, looking around the room like she needed a distraction before her eyes found mine again. "I think I'm hungry."

I grinned. "Come on," I said, getting up quickly before she had a chance to change her mind. "Let's go find you a good meal."

Twenty minutes later we were seated in my favorite Thai restaurant as two steaming plates of pad Thai were placed in front of us. Candice and I ate in silence for a little while before she worked up the energy for more conversation. "I think we need to change direction."

I swirled my rice noodles thoughtfully with my chopsticks. "Where are we going?"

"It's not so much where as who," she said. When I cocked my head and looked at her quizzically, she explained, "We're not making any headway following Bianca. Maybe it's time we switched our focus."

"To one of the other kids," I guessed.

"Yep."

"Which one?"

"Which one does your radar suggest?" she asked, turning it back on me.

I thought about that for a minute. "The boy," I said, feeling it deep in my gut.

"Kyle Newhouse," Candice said thoughtfully. "Okay, I'll do a little research and maybe we can plan a road trip to Columbus."

"You up for that?" I asked carefully.

"It beats hanging out on your couch and feeling sorry for myself," Candice said with the smallest of grins.

Mentally, I breathed a huge sigh of relief, so glad to see a bit of my friend coming back to life. "I'm game," I said.

Candice and I left for Columbus two days later. Armed with several pages of notes and a map of OSU, we arrived on campus midafternoon. I wasn't sure how Candice had obtained Kyle's school schedule, and thought that the fewer questions I asked about her methods, the less I might have to fess up to if I happened to be asked under oath about it later.

We parked on the street just down from Kyle's old dorm and walked to the front door. Again we'd both dressed very casually. We even came with backpacks to make ourselves blend in. "How did you want to work this?" I asked.

"The same way we tackled Bianca's disappearance," Candice replied. "We'll walk his schedule backward and see if your radar can come up with anything."

We spent much of the next three hours going from hall to hall walking the way we thought Kyle would have gone. On the trip from the last class back to Kyle's dorm, my radar finally dinged. "Hold on," I said, swiveling my head from side to side as I took in my surroundings. We weren't far from the library. In fact we were just on the other side of the parking lot from it.

"What's up?" Candice asked me.

I'd been carrying around Kyle's photo all day, trying to link my energy in with his, and this was the first time I felt a connection. "Over here," I said, hurrying toward the edge of the lot near a few huge buckeye trees.

I could hear Candice following me and I stopped next to the last tree. "What are you getting?" Candice whispered, coming alongside.

I put my hand on the tree and looked down at Kyle's picture. A range of emotions went through me and a connection that I hadn't expected. "Candice?" I said slowly, still feeling out the ether.

"Yeah?"

"Do you remember the name of the third missing girl?"

"You mean Leslie Coyle?"

"Yes."

"What about her?"

"She was here."

Candice didn't speak, so I looked at her and noticed she was squinting at me. "What do you mean, she was *here*?"

"She and Kyle were together right here," I explained, pointing to the ground.

"So you're still convinced they knew each other?"

"Yes," I said. "I'm sure of it."

"And she was the only one out of the three that you think hasn't been murdered?"

"Her picture was too fuzzy to say for certain."

"What do you think now that you're feeling her energy?"

I looked up at her and met her eyes. "I think she's alive."

Candice stared at the tree we were next to. "Do you think they were abducted at the same time?"

"No," I said, remembering the meeting we'd had in D.C. "Remember? Albright said Kyle was the second abduction and Leslie went missing five days later."

"Albright also said Kyle disappeared on his way to the library," Candice mused. "So maybe he got to right here and Leslie showed up."

"What's the connection?" I asked, puzzling over it.

"Maybe she came here to warn him," Candice said.

"Or lure him somewhere," I suggested as a chill went up my spine.

"Does your radar say she was in on his murder?"

I mentally checked that. "I don't think so," I said,

scratching my head. "But there has to be a link between the three of them. Something that ties all this together."

"Well, so far we know that at least two of the kids knew each other," Candice offered. "The missing puzzle piece is how Bianca fits in."

"And that's what I can't let go of," I admitted. "I've been going around and around with all the clues she gave me when we met with her parents, and none of them *go* anywhere. So I have to ask myself why she would tell us to look in places that were all dead ends."

Candice grimaced. "No pun intended, though, right?"

I gasped, realizing what I'd just said. "Oh, God! I didn't mean it that way."

The corners of Candice's mouth lifted. "I know you didn't," she said kindly before she glanced at her watch. "I say we call it a wrap for today. It'll take us a couple of hours to get home and it's already after two."

On the drive back I sifted through Bianca's journals again. There was a clue in there that was staring me in the face, but what it was I couldn't seem to find. My radar kept physically tugging backward, and that, for me, is a symbol to go to the past, so I didn't argue; I dug around in her journals from the beginning of her freshman year and kept feeling that backward pull, so I switched to her senior year of high school, and the tugging stopped, but I couldn't find anything that seemed like it fit.

I picked up the first journal I had from Bianca's senior year of high school and I felt a strong tug forward. "Grrrr," I growled out loud.

"Problem?" Candice asked from the driver's seat.

I rubbed my eyes and laid my head back against the headrest. "I feel like I'm supposed to focus on the latter half of Bianca's senior year of high school, but every time I go through that journal, nothing much pops out at me."

"Is there a specific section that you think you might want to focus on?"

I closed my eyes and concentrated. In my mind's eye I saw an Easter egg. "Easter's usually in April, right?"

"Usually," she agreed. "Right around spring break."

I remembered that strong feeling I'd had at the task force meeting about a spring-break connection, so I flipped back to that section of her journal and began to read aloud the paragraphs that I'd nearly memorized. "'Dad and I are at the MWCFC and this conference is totally cool. There were some interesting presentations and we're meeting all these amazing people and there are tons of kids my age here. I'm hanging out with three kids mostly. They're totally cool.'"

"Things appear to be totally cool," Candice remarked.

I ignored her and kept reading. "'We're going to hang out in L.'s room tonight and watch movies. I think she totally has it bad for N. H., but I don't know whether he likes her back. Anyway, we're going back home the day after tomorrow, which totally sucks, because then I'll have to deal with the twenty questions from Mom about Dad's new girlfriend. . . .'"

"Hold on," Candice said.

"What?"

"Go back up to that part about hanging out in L.'s room."

My eyes scanned the page to that section. "Yeah?"

Candice glanced over at me. "Do you think L. could be Leslie Coyle?"

My brow furrowed. "Maybe," I said. "But who's N. H.?"

"Newhouse," she said simply. "Kyle was a jock, right? He probably went by his last name like most jocks his age."

"Ohmigod!" I yelled as a thousand bells seemed to ding in my head. "*How* did I miss that before?"

Candice smiled. "I think we've hit our first jackpot," she said, reaching for her cell phone and clicking through some screens until she came up with the number she wanted. She had the phone on speaker and we both heard it ring before being answered.

"Representative Lovelace," Jeremy said.

"Hello, sir, it's Candice and Abby."

"Hello, ladies," he replied. "Have you found anything?"

"Maybe," Candice said, then motioned for me to talk.

"Mr. Lovelace, do you remember a conference that you attended with your daughter two years ago during her spring break?"

There was a pause, then, "Sure. She and I went to a caucus for Midwestern politicians. It was held in Chicago, and members of the state legislature were encouraged to bring their families. Bianca had a blast."

I could feel a surge of adrenaline pumping through me. "Sir, do you remember who she hung out with during the caucus?"

There was another pause and then he said, "I don't remember their names, but I do remember one young man was from Ohio. I think his name was Kevin or something. He was a good-looking kid. Then there was a girl. Lisa or something, and another young man that I only shook hands with once. I don't remember his name or where he was from."

Candice and I exchanged a look. "At that caucus did anyone personally threaten you or take a special interest in the group your daughter was hanging out with?"

"No," Lovelace said, his voice suddenly cautious.

"Was there anything that happened at that event that was perhaps controversial?"

"Well, yeah," Lovelace said. "I mean, whenever you get a group of politicians that large in one hotel, there's bound to be some controversy."

"Does anyone at all stand out in your mind that maybe you thought twice about or who seemed off to you?"

The line was silent for so long that I thought we'd dropped the call, but finally Lovelace said softly, "There was one man."

"Who?" Candice and I asked together.

"During a committee meeting that I chaired on the downward spiral of our Midwestern economy, a gentleman who identified himself from my state got up and disrupted the meeting. He claimed to have been a former assembly-line worker and accused us of doing too little, too late to help the auto industry recover from the slide of recent years. He became so disruptive that he was eventually removed by hotel security."

"Did he make any overt threats?"

Again, Lovelace was silent for a few seconds. "He did," he said. "He said we'd all be sorry."

"Who was on that committee?" I asked.

"There were several representatives," Lovelace said. "I can't remember all of them, but I have a copy of the minutes from that meeting somewhere. Can I dig it up and call you back?"

"Absolutely," Candice said. "Please call us back as soon as possible."

"Will do," he said.

Candice and I waited twenty anxious minutes, but finally Lovelace called. "I've got the list," he said.

"Shoot," Candice commanded.

"The attendees were Representative Witlow, from Chicago; Representative Bentley, from Ohio; Senator Newhouse, also from Ohio; Representative Coyle, from Wisconsin—"

"Stop!" I nearly shouted, interrupting the representative, aware that I was bound by Gaston not to reveal any details of the other teens' disappearance. "Mr. Lovelace, we'll have to call you back."

Candice clicked off from what had to be a rather stunned Lovelace and turned to me with a curious look in her eyes. "What're you thinking?" she asked.

"We can't hold on to this by ourselves," I said. "We've got to go to the big guns and tell them about the connection."

"Gaston?" she suggested.

I shook my head. "I think we should go to Dutch first, because if he finds out from Gaston that we've been working the case behind his back, he'll be pissed."

"Good point," she said, handing me the phone.

My hands shook a little as I dialed his number. He hated when I went off on my own without telling him. "Ms. Fusco," Dutch's rich baritone said into my ear. "What's up?"

"It's me," I said.

"Abs?"

"Yeah."

"What sticky situation are you in now?"

I frowned. He knew me too well. "Don't be mad," I began.

Dutch sighed deliberately. "Great," he said. "This is bound to be bad. Okay, out with it, Edgar."

I swallowed, encouraged that he'd used his pet name for me at least, so I got on with it. "You know how Gaston kinda hinted that we needed to butt out of the Lovelace murder?"

Another sigh, then a groan sounded in my ear.

"Well, we didn't *exactly* listen to instructions." There was a long pause, so I said, "Dutch?"

"I'm here," he said. "And I'm not surprised. What did you two come up with?"

"We found the connection between the kids and we think we have a lead on the killer."

There was a low chuckle. "Oh, is that all?" he deadpanned.

The tension left my shoulders. "Pretty much."

"Have you called Gaston yet?"

"We thought we'd start with you."

"Nice of you."

"I *know*, right?"

That got me another chuckle. "Okay, hang on, I just saw Gaston a few minutes ago. Let me go find him and tell him you're on the line."

Dutch put me on hold and I switched to speakerphone. We waited with the hold music filling the car for maybe three minutes before the line was picked up again. "Ms. Cooper?"

"Good afternoon, Agent Gaston," I said. "I'm here with Candice and we're just coming back from a quick visit to OSU."

"Yes, Dutch filled me in on the fact that you've been doing a bit of investigating on your own."

"Sir," said Candice, "we were actually working it legitimately. Representative Lovelace hired us to look into his daughter's death."

"Yes," said Gaston calmly. "He did that on my recommendation."

Candice and I shared an astonished look. "Really?" I asked.

"Really," he confirmed, and in the background I could swear I heard Dutch's soft laughter.

"Er . . . thank you, sir," I said.

"So what do you have for me?"

I filled him in on what I thought I'd picked up at OSU and Candice told him about the phone call to Representative Lovelace. When we finished, there were several seconds of silence, but then Agent Gaston said, "Very good work, ladies, and I mean that. I'm going to contact Representative Lovelace directly and bring the task force up to speed. Can I reach you at this number later?"

"Yes," Candice and I said in unison.

"Excellent. Thank you and we'll be in touch."

Gaston clicked off and Candice and I traded high fives. "We rock," she said smugly.

"Can you imagine what Harrison is going to say when Gaston tells him what we've found?"

Candice's face turned down in a scowl. "Who cares what that asshole thinks?" she said with a wave of her hand.

I nodded, but then thought back to the week before when Harrison had paid his respects at her grandmother's funeral. "Aw, maybe he's not such a bad guy after all?" She looked at me as if I'd just told her that communism was good for the economy. "I'm serious," I insisted. "He came to pay his respects last week at your grandmother's funeral and I think that says more about him than how he reacts to people like me."

Candice rolled her eyes. She wasn't buying it. "Gaston couldn't attend," she pointed out. "So he probably forced Harrison to go in his place."

I sighed. This was an argument I wasn't going to win, so I let it drop.

We drove for the next hour in companionable silence when Candice's phone rang. "Hello, Agent Gaston," Candice said, putting us back on speaker.

"Ms. Fusco," Gaston said warmly. "I'm here with Agent Harrison. Is Ms. Cooper still with you?"

"I'm here," I sang.

"Excellent. We've spoken to Representative Lovelace and we'd like to ask for the two of you to join us tomorrow morning if you're available."

"Works for me," I said, looking expectantly at Candice.

She looked frustrated and I didn't understand why, but she grudgingly said, "We'll be there."

"Shall we say nine a.m. here at the bureau?" asked Gaston.

"That's fine," she said.

"Excellent. Have a good evening and we'll see you in the morning."

When we'd clicked off, I said, "You don't look happy."

Candice squared her shoulders and squinted in the dimming light at the road ahead. "I don't want to work with Harrison again."

"Who said anything about working with him?"

"What do you think they're calling us in for, Abs? A cup of coffee and a chat about the weather?"

"You think they want us officially back on the case?"

"I do."

That stumped me. I had kind of thought they'd bring us back in just to verify the information we'd gathered. I hadn't made the leap that maybe they'd want us back on the case. "But the politics," I said after I'd thought about it. "Wouldn't bringing us back on be a big no-no?"

"Not if we'd made further headway than Harrison had without us," Candice reasoned. "And my gut says we leaped him by a mile."

"So you think he'll be forced to work with us again."

"Yep. And if we blow it or step out of line, he'll blame Gaston and probably Dutch, and trust me on this, heads will roll."

"That hardly seems fair," I said. "I mean, why wouldn't he just blame you and me?"

"Because we don't work for the bureau," she said simply. "We're merely the pawns in this game. An experiment."

I leaned back in my seat feeling tired and irritated with myself for saying yes to their offer before I'd had a chance to talk it over with Candice. "I totally walked into that one, didn't I?"

Candice nudged me with her elbow. "It might not be so bad. Let's just go in there, hear the ground rules, and see if we can play by them. If not, we can always say no to the offer and walk away clean."

"But that might be bad for Leslie," I said with a nagging feeling I couldn't shake that she was running out of time.

"It could be, yes."

"I'm willing to take the political risk, then," I said firmly. "If it might save her life, it's worth it. I'll talk it over with Dutch tonight, though, just to make sure he doesn't mind me playing fast and loose with his career."

"Good plan."

"By the way, are you sure you don't want to stay over one more night?"

Candice's expression became melancholy and she reached over and squeezed my hand. "Thanks, Sundance, but it's time for this cowgirl to get back to her own place and give you and Dutch a little alone time."

I nodded, glad she was feeling strong enough to get on with her life, but worried about her nonetheless.

That night over dinner, Dutch and I discussed the pros and cons of Candice and me getting reinvolved with the missing teens. It aggravated me that there were more cons than pros. For the most part, Dutch completely agreed with Candice. We were damned if we did and damned if we didn't, but at least he was okay with becoming a possible scapegoat if things got bad and the bureau needed someone to blame. "You seem pretty relaxed for someone who could lose his job if this thing goes south," I noted.

Dutch shrugged. "I've still got the security business," he said. "We'll live."

I smirked. Dutch made a whole lot more money managing his side business than he did as an FBI agent. "Still, I'd hate to see Gaston take the hit for this."

"Abs," he said patiently. "Don't you think Gaston is aware of the risks?"

"Why's he pushing so hard on our behalf?" I wondered.

"Because he's an outsider," Dutch explained. "He came into this deal with lots of ideas that were unconventional and ran into a culture that has always rigidly followed the rule book. He's pushing for the bureau as a whole to think differently, to experiment and try out new investigative techniques. It's what his old culture—the CIA—is renowned for."

"They experiment a lot over at the CIA?"

Dutch smiled and nodded. "That they do," he said. "Those guys are famous for pushing the envelope and they'll try *anything*, which is what has made them so successful over the years."

"And so scary," I said.

"That too."

"Okay," I conceded. "We'll give it our best shot and hope we don't screw it up."

Dutch tilted his chin and let out a laugh. When I demanded to know what was so funny, he said, "Oh, you'll screw up all right. The only question is by how much."

I gave him a level look. "You have no faith." But deep down I thought he might be right.

The next morning Candice picked me up at eight and we shared a quick breakfast at the Bagel Factory before heading to the local bureau office. On the way there Candice did her best to pump up my confidence. "Just be yourself," she advised.

"Who else would I be?"

"You know what I mean," she said with an impatient wave of her hand. "Don't let those bastards rattle you. After all, you're the one that came up with the new lead. You're the one that has them finally going in the right direction. You're the one that linked in with Bianca and found her body. You're the one—"

"Candice?" I interrupted.

"Yeah?"

"You're making my stomach hurt."

She eyed me from the driver's seat. "Okay," she said. "No more pep talk."

"Thanks."

We parked the car and headed inside. I noticed that we were five minutes early as we took our seats. I didn't really have a chance to get settled, as, just like in D.C., a female agent came to retrieve us from the lobby and invited us to follow her. We were then escorted to a conference room and told to wait. I fidgeted in my chair, trying not to be nervous as I told myself over and over that I'd been through this before, so how bad could it really get?

The door opened and in walked Agent Gaston, Agent Harrison, and an older gentleman I didn't recognize, but who practically oozed power from every pore. I also noticed immediately the man had a strong resemblance to Agent Harrison. "Ladies," Gaston said pleasantly.

"Good morning, sir," we both mumbled.

"Thank you for joining us. You remember Agent Harrison?"

We both nodded and Harrison nodded back, his stony eyes hard.

"And this is Regional Director of Special Investigations, Agent Harrison Senior, who is also Agent Brice Harrison's uncle."

Candice stood slightly to shake the older man's hand. "Sir," she said.

"Ms. Fusco," he replied before turning to me.

I extended my hand and he shook it once, then sat back in his chair to stare at us bemusedly. "I understand that you two have come across some information that is relevant to this investigation," he began.

Candice and I nodded again.

"And I understand that Ms. Cooper here claims to have some psychic ability?"

I smiled. "Guilty as charged," I said.

He smiled back at me and asked, "Might I see a demonstration?"

I blinked at him in confusion as my heartbeat picked up a notch. "Sir?"

"I would like to see this ability if I may. That is, *if* you don't mind?"

The way he said it left little doubt that he would definitely mind if I turned his request down. But I still wasn't sure what he was asking me. "Who specifically would you like me to demonstrate on, sir?" I asked.

"Why," he said, looking around like it was obvious, "on me, of course."

"Ah," I said. I'd been afraid of that. Like his nephew, Agent Harrison Senior didn't strike me as someone with a very open mind, and I thought he might be hard to read.

Still, at this point I figured I didn't have too much to lose, so I closed my eyes and took a deep breath. "The first thing I'm picking up for you is a connection to the Pacific Northwest. Specifically I'm picking up Seattle, but the connection is slightly off. And what I mean by that is that I believe you might be connected to someone who lives in Seattle, rather than to a specific location within the city. The individual connected to you is a woman, and I believe she has dark brown hair. She's got lovely energy, and she's very soft and kind. I'm seeing Christmas lights around this woman, and if I had to put this information together, I would say that I believe you will receive an invitation to join her for the holidays. You will be tempted to turn it down because you don't think your work schedule will allow you to get away, but I believe you can and that you should in fact accept.

"Also, there is a position opening one level above you. Someone is retiring soon, and you will be one of the candidates up for the position." I opened my eyes at this point and noticed that I definitely had the older man's full attention and keen interest. Looking him straight in the eye, I said, "I don't believe you will be selected for the promotion. I think it's going to another man about ten years your junior and with jet-black hair, but only because he is owed a political favor."

Harrison Senior squinted at me and I wondered whether that narrowed-eyed look was a family trait. "Extraordinary," he said, breaking out into a broad smile.

"I told you she was good," Gaston said proudly, and I took extra pleasure in seeing Harrison Junior fuming in his seat.

"Yes, Bill, you did. And I am very impressed. All right, Ms. Cooper, you've convinced me, even though I'm sure my nephew still remains rather skeptical. I would like to invite you to participate in the rest of this investigation."

Harrison Junior opened his mouth as if to protest, but his uncle lifted his hand slightly in warning and Junior shut his mouth.

"Thank you, sir," I said. "But we have some conditions."

The room went completely silent as all three agents stared at me as if I'd just committed the worst imaginable faux pas. "Conditions?" Harrison Senior finally asked.

"Yes, sir. You see, when we were asked last time to participate, we were told not to ask questions and to only observe the situation, but my intuition is at its optimum potential when I'm engaged with the subject. I will often need to ask some clarifying questions to rule out possible misinterpretations of the images I'm seeing in my head."

Harrison Senior shot a glance at Gaston, who gave him the smallest of shrugs as if he hadn't known I would be capable of such a request.

"The last thing we want to do is to lead you down a false trail," Candice explained, coming to my rescue. "And because Abby's radar works with images and pictures, she will need to rule out certain scenarios before she can commit to recommending a course of action or a specific direction."

Harrison Senior seemed to take that in for a moment. "All right," he said cautiously. "But I shall defer to my nephew to determine whether the line of questioning you're taking is appropriate for the time and place. The last thing we want to do is tip our hand to anyone who might be involved in these abductions, so we will need to proceed with caution."

"Understood," I said. "And that brings me to my next condition."

Harrison Senior appeared to be running out of patience, but I gave him credit for asking, "And that would be?"

I took a deep breath. He wasn't going to like what I had to say. "I understand your nephew's skepticism, sir," I began, looking pointedly at Harrison Junior. "And I am *honestly* not here to try and make him a believer. But I find that working alongside a hostile and negative attitude is detrimental to my ability to focus and concentrate on the things I'm trying to pick up on. My craft is one of subtlety, and I cannot afford to be continually distracted by the attitude of a pessimistic and judgmental person."

Agent Harrison Senior's mouth curled up slightly. "I see," he said. "And what would you like me to do about that?"

"May we work with another agent?" I asked hopefully, even while Harrison Junior seethed at me across the table.

Harrison Senior seemed very amused by my request, but he said, "No, Ms. Cooper. I'm sorry. My nephew is the lead on this investigation and he shall remain so."

Harrison Junior changed the glare into a smug look of satisfaction and he leaned back in his chair like he was all that and a bag of chips. "However," his uncle added, "I do not believe it is outside the realm of protocol to ask Agent Harrison to treat you with the utmost dignity and respect, which I have no doubt he will do now that you've made your concerns known."

It was my turn to look smug and I made sure to rub it in for all it was worth. "Thank you, sir. I *really* appreciate it."

"You are most welcome," he said, still smirking. "Are there any *other* conditions you would like to make me aware of?"

I looked to Candice and she said, "We would respectfully ask that Agent Rivers not be blamed, or used as a scapegoat in any way, should this case not have a satisfactory conclusion. It's very important to Abby and me that his job not come under jeopardy if we are unable to assist you in the solving of this case."

Harrison Senior's face turned a dangerous shade of red, and he gave Candice a look that suggested she'd just insulted him and the bureau. "Of course," he said softly after a long uncomfortable pause. He then effectively ended the discussion by getting up from the table. "Thank you again for coming in and meeting with us. My nephew will bring you up to speed on the latest developments and discuss next steps. Bill, if you would please meet with me privately?"

"Of course, sir," Gaston said, standing up as well.

Before Harrison Senior left, however, he made a point of looking Harrison Junior in the eye and commanding, "Take good care of them, Brice."

"Yes, sir," his nephew replied curtly.

And then we were alone with one surly FBI agent and a hell of a tough case to solve.

Chapter Eight

In the pronounced silence that followed Agent Harrison Senior and Gaston's departure, I tried not to fidget. But it was really, really hard. Especially under the steely glare of Agent Harrison Junior. "Where would you like us to start?" Candice asked pleasantly.

Harrison's eyes swiveled to Candice and she smiled like a cat peering through the goldfish bowl, daring the little fishie to jump out of the water. "Our focus has been on the Newhouse kid," Harrison said after a pause.

"Have you discovered anything relevant?"

"Not really," Harrison said, and I knew he wasn't going to fill us in on the investigation so far, no matter what he'd been ordered.

"I really think he and Leslie Coyle knew each other," I offered, trying to move this along.

Harrison's eyebrows arched in mock surprise, and I could tell he was pretending to be out of the loop, just to be difficult. "And why do you think that?"

I could have called him out on playing dumb, but

decided to be patient and play his game instead. "We found a passage in Bianca's journal that indicated she was hanging out with three other kids at the Midwestern political caucus in Chicago two years ago," I told him.

Candice took over from there, saying, "In the journal entry Bianca indicates two of the kids by the initials *N. H.* and an *L.* We believe the *N. H.* stands for Newhouse, and the *L.* is for Leslie. We know from speaking to Representative Lovelace, who attended the conference with his daughter, that both Senator Newhouse and Representative Coyle were in attendance and we believe that they also brought Kyle and Leslie with them. I'd put money on the kids having hung out together over that weekend." When Candice finished she looked at me expectantly.

"What?" I whispered.

"Tell him what you picked up when we went to OSU."

I could feel my cheeks redden a bit. I hated discussing my intuition with hard-core skeptics. There was always a twinge of fear that I might suddenly be pronounced insane and carted off by men in white coats. Still, I sucked it up and said, "I think that Leslie and Kyle were together the day he disappeared."

Harrison scoffed. "Impossible. Leslie didn't vanish until five days after Kyle."

"That doesn't negate the possibility that she and Kyle met on the day he was abducted," Candice pointed out.

Harrison's jaw clenched and I had a small moment where I almost felt sorry for him. Turning to me, he asked, "Why do you suspect they met the day Kyle went missing?"

My cheeks reddened again. "I felt it in the ether,"

I said meekly. Harrison blinked at me, as if I'd just said something in Martian. "When Candice and I went to OSU, we walked the campus according to Kyle's schedule," I explained.

"Why?"

It was my turn to blink. "Well," I said, searching for a way to describe it to him in terms he'd understand. "Because space is often imprinted with the energy of the person moving through it. Think of it like the residual scent of someone a bloodhound is tracking. If I can connect even remotely to the person I'm trying to track, I can follow their energy path and get a feel for what happened to them at a specific location."

Harrison's expression changed subtly, and for the first time since we'd met him, he had the smallest look of interest. "And what you're telling me is that you got a proverbial whiff of Kyle at OSU and you also got a whiff of Leslie?"

I nodded vigorously. "Exactly."

"So what happened when they met?"

"That, I can't specifically tell you," I said. "And what I mean is that the energy didn't contain any sense of violence."

"What *did* it contain?"

I thought back to what I'd felt under that buckeye tree. "Urgency," I said. "There was a definite sense of urgency."

Harrison sat back in his chair and crossed his arms, regarding me for another one of his famous pauses. "Okay," he said after a minute. "I'll check in with Leslie's roommates and see if she took off around the time of Kyle's disappearance. He went missing on a Thursday evening, so she could feasibly have cut her classes that day and driven to OSU to be back in time for her Monday schedule."

"Have you had a chance to comb through the kids' e-mail accounts for any link to each other?" Candice asked him.

"We have," he said. "We've found none."

"Chat rooms?"

"Yes. No links."

I frowned. "So all we have is this really loose connection to each other in one of Bianca's journals."

"And the fact that we think they may have attended the same conference two years ago."

"I'll contact Kyle's father and Leslie's mother to confirm that they and their children were all at the conference at the same time," Harrison told us as he jotted himself a note.

"I'm also worried about the kids of some of the other members on that committee," I said.

Harrison nodded and made another note about contacting Lovelace to get a description and follow up on the lead.

"So where do we go next?" I asked. I expected him to tell us to go back home and wait for him to need us, which of course he wouldn't.

He surprised me, however, by suggesting that we come along with him to interview Kyle's parents. "Who knows?" he said. "Maybe the kid's ghost will show up and give you a few clues."

I stared at him in surprise, not really believing that he was starting to crack the granitclike resistance he'd put up until now. "Come on," I said good-naturedly. "Even *you* have to admit that Bianca contacting me was a good hit."

But Harrison simply moved his chair back and stood up. "We leave tomorrow morning at seven. Please be downstairs in the parking lot on time."

After he'd gone, I turned to Candice and with

pretend gushiness said, "I bet you he's a *blast* at parties!"

Candice grinned. "Come on, Sundance," she said. "I've got to get going. I have a meeting with my grandmother's estate attorney at noon."

My good humor vanished. "How're you doing?" I asked.

Candice shrugged. "Okay, I guess. I'm not looking forward to the meeting, though. It's just too big of a reminder that she's gone."

"You could postpone it," I suggested as we walked out of the conference room.

Candice sighed heavily. "I'd rather just get it over with. Plus, it's probably a good idea to talk to the attorney about how to deal with any debt she's left behind. I tell you, with business as slow as it is, I don't know how I'm going to manage her mortgage payment and my rent."

"You could forget about renting my place and move into her old house," I suggested. Candice rented the house I'd lived in before I moved in with Dutch, and I didn't want her to think that I wouldn't let her out of her lease immediately in light of the circumstances.

Candice nudged me with her shoulder. "Thanks," she said. "But I'd rather not make such a dramatic move just yet. I think living in that house surrounded by all that pink would make me first very sad, and then very nuts. I'll talk to the attorney and see what he suggests."

On the way out I stopped by Dutch's cubicle, but he wasn't there, so I left him a rather racy Post-it note and we took off.

Candice dropped me at the house I shared with Dutch, and I spent the rest of the afternoon curled up with a good book listening to the gentle rain that was a constant around these parts in the fall.

I was just beginning to consider dinner when the doorbell rang. "Come in," I called.

I was surprised when Candice came through the door. "Hey," she said with a rather odd expression on her face.

"Howdy, Cassidy!" I replied, patting the couch for her to come sit down, thinking maybe she needed a shoulder to cry on now that she'd met with the estate attorney.

Candice came to sit next to me and immediately Eggy, my twelve-pound dachshund, jumped into her lap and began to kiss her with enthusiasm. "He's missed you," I said.

"I can tell," she said with a laugh, giving him a hug and curling him into her lap.

"How'd it go?" I asked gently.

"It went . . . ," she said, and her voice trailed off as she searched for the right words. "Unexpectedly well."

I brightened. "Well, that's good, right?" I couldn't get a feel for what was going on with her. Her slightly red eyes suggested she'd been crying, but there was also this odd peace about her.

"Abs," she said softly, "did you know that my grandmother was a millionaire?"

My eyebrows shot up. "She was?"

Candice nodded. "Multimillionaire," she amended.

"So the house doesn't have a mortgage?"

"No," Candice said. "No mortgage on that one, and none on the condo in Arizona that she never told me about, or on the hundred and fifty acres down in Texas currently being drilled for natural gas."

I did a double take. I'd heard so much about Texas lately that it was freaky. "So what does all that mean?" I asked cautiously as I noticed Candice's eyes begin to water again.

"She left it all to me," she said in a voice so soft I could barely hear her. "Real estate, bonds, stocks, treasury bills . . . Abby, the woman had more assets than Donald Trump!"

I gasped. "Candice!" I said, throwing my arms around her. "Honey! You're rich!"

Candice laughed and sobbed at the same time, no doubt overwhelmed by a mixture of emotions. "I guess I am," she said when she could talk again.

I hugged her even tighter, both elated for her and incredibly sad as well. I'd lost my own beloved grandmother many years before, and I still missed her every single day. "With time it gets a little easier," I said, hearing her sniffle. "I swear it does."

The door opened then and I saw Dutch over Candice's shoulder. "Hey there, ladies," he said.

"Hi, Dutch," I said, still hugging Candice.

"Everything okay?"

"Candice is rich," I told him.

"You don't say?"

"Yep."

"Why is she crying, then?"

"She misses her grandmother."

"I have a good cure for the blues," he offered.

Candice backed away from me and dabbed at her eyes. "Oh, yeah?" she asked. "What's that?"

"Lasagna."

Candice and I laughed. "Bring it on," I told him. "And Candice gets the biggest piece."

Dutch cooked dinner while Candice and I shared a bottle of wine. She told me everything the estate attorney had said. How Madame DuBois had been a savvy speculator and had snatched up acreage down in Texas in the early seventies. Ten years ago her hunch had paid off, and her property now produced a healthy income in natural gas. In addition to her two homes, she had various stocks, bonds, and treasury certificates worth a small fortune and she'd bequeathed it all to her granddaughter with specific instructions that Candice feel free to follow her passions and not be held back by any financial concerns.

"What will you do?" I asked her, thinking that she might take a trip around the world or retire young and pursue a life of leisure.

"Exactly what I'm doing now," she said.

"You mean you're going to keep working?"

"Absolutely," she said without a hint of doubt. "I love what I do, Abs. I can't imagine doing anything else."

I thought back to a time when I'd been faced with a similar circumstance over some lottery winnings I'd donated when I'd made the identical choice to continue my day job. Maybe that was what made Candice and me such a good team. We were both doing what we were meant to do, and despite the ups and down of the industry and the occasional dangers, we loved what we did.

"At least now you'll be able to take the cases that interest you and turn down the ones that don't," I said.

Candice winked at me. "Exactly," she said, then sighed contentedly. "God love my grandmother. That old bird was always rescuing me."

"I think it went both ways," I reminded her.

"Dinner's ready," Dutch called, and we headed to the dinning room for some really divine comfort food.

"How's it going with Internal Affairs?" I asked Dutch as he portioned me out a helping.

He handed me the plate and grinned. "I'm all clear," he said.

"Ohmigod!" I yelled. "That's fantastic! Why didn't you say anything when you came in?"

"You guys were having a moment," he reminded me.

I rolled my eyes. "Okay, so what does this mean? Are you back on street patrol?"

"Yes and no," he said, then eyed me with a curious look.

"What?" I asked.

"Did you happen to say anything to Gaston today about my noninvolvement with the missing-teens case?"

Candice and I exchanged a look. "Er ... not exactly that you shouldn't work the case so much as you shouldn't get blamed if it goes south."

"Well, that explains it, then," Dutch said.

"What?" I asked again.

"Gaston pulled me into his office to congratulate me on clearing Internal Affairs and when I asked him if I could join your group, he turned me down flat and said that he doesn't want me anywhere near the case right now. Then he says it's for my own protection."

"So what will you be working on?"

Dutch winked. "That's classified, babycakes."

"Well, at least you won't have to work with Oscar the Grouch."

Dutch laughed. "Aw, come on, Abs. Harrison can't be that bad."

"No," Candice said evenly. "He's worse."

"Still," Dutch reasoned, "he seems to be warming up to you two."

My mouth fell open. "How do you figure?"

"He didn't threaten to resign over being forced to work with you like he did last time."

My eyes bulged. "No way! He threatened to *resign*?"

Dutch nodded and took a sip of wine. "I thought you knew."

"Uh . . . *no*!"

Dutch shrugged. "I will give you credit, though; Denny Harrison you seriously impressed."

"I know," I said smugly. "I love when that happens."

"Yeah, well, tread carefully, okay? Brice might not be as upset as he was about having you on board, but he's still itching to get rid of you two the first chance he gets. Just don't overstep your bounds, follow his instructions, and it should be fine."

"We're headed south to talk to Kyle's parents tomorrow," I told him.

"That's what I hear," he said. "It's a long car ride to Ohio, as I'm sure you two know all too well. Try to be civil."

"We've *always* been civil," I snapped defensively.

Dutch held up his hands in surrender. "Okay, okay, Edgar. Take it easy. You've always been civil."

"Damn straight," I grumbled, thinking that I wasn't really going to like tomorrow.

The next morning Candice picked me up and we drove over to the bureau office's parking lot. We spotted Harrison right away and got into his car without much more than an exchange of "Good morning."

The trip to Ohio was quicker than expected because we didn't have to drive all the way to Columbus. Kyle's parents actually lived in Toledo, which was just

past the Michigan border. It also helped that I'd called
the backseat before Candice, and upon entering Harrison's car, I'd immediately donned my headphones. I
was halfway through the greatest hits from the seventies when I noticed we pulled off the highway and into
a more residential area.

We drove up to the guardhouse at a gated community and Harrison flashed his badge at the guy working the gate. We were waved through without even a
question and I looked out the window at the fairly af-
fluent surroundings.

From the front seat I heard Harrison turn and
say something to me. I pulled off the headphones.
"Sorry?"

"When we get to the residence, I would appreciate
it if you let me do *all* of the talking. If you get any . . ."
His voice trailed off as he looked for a way to finish
his sentence.

"Hits?" I suggested.

"Yes, that's a good word. If you get any hits, I would
ask that you initially keep them to yourself and we
will discuss them later in private. I would also ask that
you not make the Newhouses aware of your abilities
at this particular meeting, as Mrs. Newhouse has had
a particularly difficult time and we've become aware
that she's been struggling with an old alcoholism issue.
I do not want *anything* to upset her more than it has to
at this stage. Am I clear?"

"Crystal," I said woodenly, feeling a little put off
that I was being effectively muzzled.

"I thought we were going to be allowed to ask questions?" Candice said, and I could hear the flinty edge
to her voice.

"We can always request a second meeting," Harrison said easily as he braked for a stop sign. "I want

you here only as observers. I do not want a repeat of the Lovelace interview."

I saw Candice open her mouth to further argue the point, so I said quickly, "It's cool, Agent Harrison. I'll keep my impressions to myself for now."

I saw Harrison's eyes flicker to me in the rearview mirror. "Thank you," he said, while Candice turned her head pointedly away and glared out the window.

Shortly thereafter we pulled into the circular driveway of a traditional colonial with red brick, black shutters, and limited landscaping. At one end of the driveway was a basketball hoop, and I felt a pang as I thought about Kyle playing a game of pickup there probably not too long ago.

The doorbell was answered by a statuesque brunette with lovely features and kind gray eyes. "Agent Harrison?" she asked as she opened the door.

"Good morning, ma'am," he said formally. "Thank you again for agreeing to meet with us."

"Of course," she said, and ushered us into the entryway. We handed her our coats and were shown back to the kitchen, which was open and lovely. She indicated a breakfast table and said, "We might be more comfortable here than in the dinning room."

We took our seats and she offered us a beverage. Candice and I both took coffee, but Harrison declined. As I was taking a sip from my mug, a very handsome man who looked to be in his mid-fifties entered the kitchen. He wore black slacks and a pale yellow shirt that went well with his skin and was unbuttoned at the neck. In his hand he carried a tie that he offered to his wife as he greeted us. "Good morning," he said with a small nod before pivoting his body so that Mrs. Newhouse could help him with his tie. "She always gets it perfectly straight," he explained as we looked on.

"Thomas never wore a tie before I came along," she chided.

Once Mr. Newhouse's tie had been secured, both he and his wife came to the table and sat down. I had a chance to observe them carefully as they went through their morning rituals, and I could sense that these were people who were going through all the motions while holding themselves very tightly. Mrs. Newhouse in particular looked so fragile I was even more nervous about sitting near her, afraid that she'd read my body language like Terry had and be shattered into a million pieces.

"You said you had some new information for us?" Mr. Newhouse said, taking his wife's hand and directing his question to Harrison.

"Yes, sir," Harrison replied, clearing his throat. "We have been suspicious all along that perhaps there was more to the disappearance of your son than first met our eye. And we believe we have uncovered a possible point of origin, a moment that could have acted as the catalyst for a possible abductor."

Mr. Newhouse leaned forward. "Like what kind of point of origin?"

"First, I must ask you if you remember attending a family caucus for Midwestern political leaders two years ago."

Newhouse's face clouded in confusion for a moment, but he answered, "Yes. I attended. It was in Chicago."

"Did your son go with you to the conference?"

Newhouse's expression turned to surprise. "Yes," he said. "He did go with me."

"And do you remember being on a committee focused on bringing some economic relief to the Midwest?"

Again, Newhouse looked confused, but then his eyes lit with understanding. "Oh, my God," he gasped. "Do you think it was that *nut* in the audience?"

"You remember the man who disrupted your meeting?"

"Of course I remember him!" Newhouse said. "He was a wacko with these crazy eyes! Do you think he took Kyle?"

Mrs. Newhouse had gone deathly pale as her eyes flicked rapidly between her husband and Harrison. "Oh, no," she whispered as tears formed and trickled down her cheeks. "Oh, please tell me he's not with some lunatic!"

Harrison's gaze moved to her. "We don't know anything yet, ma'am," he said calmly. "But I feel compelled to tell you that your son was not the only teen who attended the conference to go missing."

"There was another?" Mr. Newhouse asked as I worked to hide my surprise that Harrison was breaking Gaston's rule about keeping the parents in the dark about the other missing kids.

"Yes," Harrison said, and I could tell he was being careful here.

"Who?" he asked. "What was his name?"

"Her name was Bianca Lovelace," Harrison replied. "Her father is a representative from Michigan."

"Jeremy's daughter?" Newhouse gasped.

"You know the representative?"

"Of course," said Newhouse. "He chaired the committee and we shared a few drinks later that night. Kyle palled around that weekend with Jeremy's daughter and two other teens."

"Do you remember who else besides Bianca your son was with that weekend?"

Newhouse rubbed his temple as he tried to remember. "There was a girl from Wisconsin and I believe her mother was also on the committee, but for the life of me, I can't remember her name. And another boy whose name was Matt or Mike, something with an *M*, I believe, but I don't remember his parents either. He was a quiet kid, kind of shy. Just the type Kyle enjoyed befriending and bringing out of his shell," he added proudly, and my heart gave another pang for the man, who clearly loved his son.

"Kyle sounds like a great kid."

"Yes," said his father. "I don't know what I'd do without him, Agent Harrison. You've got to find my son and bring him home for us."

I had to give Harrison credit, because as Mr. Newhouse looked at him with such an open, imploring expression, Harrison held it together, while I had to avert my eyes and take a breath. "We're doing everything we can, sir," Harrison said. After a bit of a pause, he added, "Can I ask you if the name Leslie Coyle sounds familiar to you?"

The Newhouses looked at each other and frowned. Turning back to Harrison, they both said, "No."

"So Kyle never mentioned a girl named Leslie to you? Maybe as a friend or an acquaintance?"

Both of Kyle's parents shook their heads. "Kyle has a lot of friends," his mother explained, and her eyes became teary. "Not a day goes by without one of them stopping by to see if we've heard anything about Kyle."

Harrison closed his notebook and looked gravely at the worried parents. "We will of course keep you apprised of any new developments in your son's case. Thank you very much for meeting with us and we'll let you get on with your day."

The couple looked surprised. "That's it?" Mr. Newhouse asked.

"For now," Harrison said, and he got up from the table.

Candice rose too and I took the cue and got up. We all shook hands, then left the house and went out to the car. Once we were on our way, Harrison eyed me in the rearview mirror again. "Thank you for cooperating."

I shrugged. To be honest, my radar hadn't gotten much and I wasn't really sure why. "We should try and find a place to eat before we get back on the highway," Candice said, pulling out her iPhone and poking the screen with her finger. "What sounds good, Abby?"

"Anything you guys want," I said noncommittally.

"I know of a nice Italian restaurant not far from here," Harrison said cordially. "Or there's also a great authentic Mexican joint I know."

Candice and I both stared at him slack-jawed. He caught us gawking. "What?"

"That's the first time you've been nice to us," I said.

Harrison rolled his eyes. "I'm not a total asshole, you know," he said gruffly.

"Yeah, but who knew?" Candice said, and I started to laugh and then so did she and soon Harrison even cracked a smile.

We put the choice of restaurant to a vote and I was the tiebreaker. We headed to the Mexican place and were seated right away with chips and salsa, which we ate with relish while we each surveyed the menu. "So," Harrison said, his eyes still focused on the menu, "did you pick up any hits?"

I took a big swig of water and sighed. "Not really," I

said. "I mean, I still think Kyle's dead, but when I ask where his body might be, all I see is dirt."

"He's been buried?" Candice asked.

"Maybe," I said. "But it's weird. . . . I don't know that what I'm seeing is underground."

"What do you mean?" Harrison asked, closing his menu and focusing on me.

"I mean that the dirt I see in my mind's eye looks like it's piled into hills. And if I had to guess, I'd say they looked more like sand dunes than mounds of dirt."

"You think he's near some sand dunes?"

I shrugged. "If I had to guess, I'd say yes. But I don't know that I see water around. I mean, all I keep seeing is something metallic mixed in with the sand. I see the dunes and then, like, thousands of little flecks of sparkling silver. It's weird, huh?" And then something else popped into my mind and I cocked my head.

"What are you getting?" Candice asked, reading my body language.

"Agent Harrison?" I said slowly.

"Yes?"

"Can you just confirm one thing for me?"

"That depends on what you want me to confirm," he said in all seriousness.

I smiled patiently and held in a sigh. He sure was a difficult SOB. "I would *appreciate* it if you would call the Newhouses and ask them if Kyle ever spent time racing around in a dune buggy."

Harrison stared blankly at me. "Why exactly?"

I lost patience and growled, "Oh, for cripe's sake! Can't you please just this once lend me this one *tiny* bit of credit and make the call?"

Harrison visibly stiffened and his eyes narrowed slightly, but I was relieved when he pulled out his notebook and his cell phone and punched in some numbers he read off the page. Candice and I waited expectantly and then we heard him apologize for calling the senator back so soon before he asked him my question. "He did?" Harrison said with obvious surprise. "Where exactly did he like to go?" There was a pause; then Harrison's eyes bulged and he shot an alarmed glance at me. "Which side of the state is that?" There was yet another pause and Harrison scribbled furiously in his notebook. "Thank you, Senator. I appreciate the added information. I'll let you know if it's relevant to this investigation shortly." He then clicked off his phone and sat back in his seat, staring at me curiously. "Okay," he finally said. "I'm starting to believe you may *actually* be psychic."

"Gee, thanks for the vote of confidence," I said woodenly. "So what did Newhouse say?"

"He said that Kyle used to go dune buggying each summer with a couple of friends up near Silver Lake. They'd camp and ride dune buggies all day."

Candice beamed at me. "Silver Lake," she said. "No wonder you were seeing flecks of that in your vision!"

"Yeah, but you know what that means, don't you?" When no one answered, I stated the obvious. "Kyle's body is buried somewhere in those dunes."

Harrison picked up his cell again and began to dial and he remained on the phone talking to various police and FBI agents throughout the rest of lunch. As Candice and I were setting our plates aside, Harrison said, "Thanks, Ben, and keep me posted on what you guys find." And then he clicked off.

"They're going to do a search?" Candice asked.

"They are."

"Are you going to drag us up there this time?" I

really wasn't in the mood for another long ride that would end only with me sitting in a car for three hours.

"If I did, would you be able to locate the body?" he asked.

"Maybe," I admitted because I thought I could. But then something else filled my mind and I thought, rather than head up there and sniff around, I might be able to just point the search party in the right direction. "Have your team look near some sort of shack," I said. "I believe one side of the shack is painted aqua. There's also the color red mixed in too."

"His body is in the shack?"

I considered that, then said, "No. It feels like it's buried. But it's near the shack, not in it."

Harrison jumped back on his phone and called that in.

After getting off the phone, he laid some money down for the bill and motioned for us to go. We headed out to his car and were soon under way again. It was quiet in the car, everyone alone with their thoughts, and I could feel my eyelids growing droopy. I really wanted a power nap and was considering taking one when Harrison said, "So tell me how this works, exactly."

I started at the sudden noise in the quiet car. I looked at Candice's face in the passenger-side mirror and saw a small smirk on her face. "Were you talking to me, Agent Harrison?" I asked when she said nothing.

"Yes," he said, eyeing me in the rearview mirror.

"You want to know how my intuition works?"

He nodded.

I sat up straighter in the seat and tried to stifle a yawn. "Well," I began, "it's not that complicated. I focus on something and then certain images fill my mind's eye. The pictures I see are usually metaphoric and the sequence I see them in usually links them together, so as they appear to me, I try and piece together the story they tell me."

Harrison remained quiet for a little bit, and then he asked, "Yes, but *how* does it work? How can you pick up on things that you have no knowledge about?"

I shrugged. "I think you want me to give you the science and I'm afraid I can't do that. It's kind of like asking a caveman how his eyes work. He just looks at something and describes what he's seeing. The actual physiological stuff that is going on with my body and my brain that allows me to get this information is something that I don't have a clue about. I can only tell you that it happens and what it looks like. I can't tell you why or how."

"So why can you do it and other people can't?" he said curiously.

"Why do some people have better vision or hearing than others?" I asked him in return. "Again, you want me to give you the science, and I don't have that. I'm the subject, not the researcher."

"So you do believe that there is something scientifically going on with you. That there are measurable changes happening."

"Absolutely. The question still open is what to measure and how to detect those changes. I don't know that we've developed the right tools yet to be able to measure or identify what exactly is going on with me physically when I'm using my radar, and that's why there are so many skeptics. Everyone wants to be shown the 'proof,' and going after that is all well and good if you've got the right tools to measure and detect the differences between someone using their radar and someone not using it. But if you haven't developed the tools of detection yet—in fact, if you don't even know where to look—then there's no proof to be had. The only thing you can quantify are the results—but that's just not good enough for some people."

"What about all this predicting-the-future stuff, though?" Harrison asked me. "What's your take on how that works?"

"Good question," I said to him. I took it as a positive sign that he was curious. "I think for that we actually can use a bit of science, and I'll point to Mr. Albert Einstein for clarification.

"As you know, Einstein believed that time is not a linear line, that it does not begin at one point and continue out to some finite point in the far distant future. No, he believed that time is actually a loop; that it is possible to consider that time could actually curl back on itself. And if you think of the symbol of infinity, you understand his concept even better. Time as a sideways figure eight in constant motion but swirling back to points already traveled. Now, if Einstein is correct, and time is a loop, then I believe that there are certain things within that loop that are set, or determined. Think of it like time as a stream, and within that stream there might be large boulders which represent specific events where the water—time—bumps into them, and ripples in the water get sent forward and backward.

"What I believe people like me do is look for those boulders, and the reason we can see them is because of the ripples flowing back from them, like an echo effect. Very much like how a bat or a dolphin uses their sonar. They can see in the dark because they're sending out sound waves to find the big objects in their path. I'm using thought waves to find the boulders and the ripples. Now, I can't see everything, of course, but those ripples stand out, and the closer I get to the boulder, the more pronounced the ripple and the clearer the imagery."

Harrison was silent for a while. "So you believe that we have no choice. That our futures are completely predetermined?"

"No, not at all," I said, and I could see the surprise in his eyes as he glanced back at me. "I think the boulders—these specific events—might be set, like they are in a stream, but we're floating along in the water and we're free to choose the course that best suits us.

"So, to give you an example, let's say a certain type of cancer runs in your family. And let's say that one of the boulders in your stream is this cancer. Now, if you don't go in for screening, you might hit that boulder head-on and maybe, because you chose not to get prescreened and it was too late when you found out, maybe you died from the impact. But say you *did* go in for regular screening, and say, because of that screening, your life was saved and you were able to carry on farther down the stream. We can choose which way we'll go when we come to those boulders. We can smack into them, or curl to the right or left and move along down the river to the next set of boulders. It's our choice."

"Huh," said Harrison. And that was the last he said for a long while.

Chapter Nine

As the sun started to set on the horizon and we entered the peak of rush hour traffic, Harrison's phone rang. He answered it in his usual clipped tone and when I heard, "Good work, Ben. I'll alert the family," I knew they had found Kyle. "See what you can do about getting a DNA sample. We might want to consider dental records, though, to get a positive ID. It might be quicker," Harrison added.

After he'd hung up, Candice said, "They found the boy."

Harrison sighed. "They found a body. It was pretty much where Ms. Cooper said it'd be. Near a light blue outhouse at the edge of the camping grounds. The cadaver dogs found him without a lot of trouble."

"Those poor parents," Candice said, and I knew that her own grief over the loss of her grandmother was still close to the surface.

"Yeah," Harrison agreed as he turned off the highway onto the main road leading to the FBI offices. "Informing the parents is the part of the job I could do without."

I stared out the window keeping my thoughts to myself. I felt very sad for Kyle's parents and what they were about to learn. I couldn't imagine having that last vestige of hope taken away from me if my child went missing. Still, at least they would finally know. It had to be better than imagining all the possible tortures that could be happening to someone they loved.

Harrison dropped us at Candice's car. "Thanks," he said gruffly.

"You're welcome," I replied.

"I'll call you when we decide on the next course of action."

"Okay. Good night."

Candice didn't say anything. I figured she was still a little put off by Harrison's stiff attitude. When we got into her car, she said, "And, by the way, Abby, *great* job!"

I smiled. "Thanks. I'm glad *someone* noticed."

"He's not getting my vote for Mr. Congeniality, that's for sure."

"Me neither."

We drove home and I invited her in for dinner. She begged off, saying she wanted to go work the kinks out after the long day in the car by going for a run.

I hurried through the rain to the front door and walked straight into the smell of something delicious. "Hey, doll," Dutch said from the dining room table. "I didn't hear from you, so I started without you."

My eyes roved to the clock on the far wall. It was after seven. "That's cool," I reassured him. "Is there enough left over for me?"

"Always," he said, getting up to retrieve my plate from the kitchen.

"You know," I said, sitting down wearily, "you're pretty much the best boyfriend ever."

"Pretty much?" he said, returning with my plate of roasted chicken with red potatoes and yellow squash.

"Yep. If you picked your socks up off the floor, though, I'd be willing to toss that out and just go with best."

Dutch laughed. "Thanks for the heads-up," he said. The phone rang and Dutch went to answer it. I dug into the chicken and closed my eyes dreamily as I chewed.

In the background I heard Dutch say, "Yes, sir, she's right here." I opened my eyes to see Dutch handing me the phone. "Harrison," he mouthed.

I took the phone. "Hello?"

"Sorry to disturb you so soon after dropping you off, but I was hoping that you and your associate would be able to come with me to interview Leslie's parents tomorrow?"

"Er . . . ," I said, thinking I needed to check with Candice first. "I guess. Can I call Candice and get back to you?"

"Yes."

I waited for him to say something more, but he didn't, so I ended by promising to call him back shortly. I then ate two more forkfuls of chicken (hey, I was hungry!) and pressed the speed dial to Candice's cell. I got her voice mail and knew she'd already left for her run.

I took the time waiting for her to call back to finish my dinner and help Dutch with the dishes; then we sat back at the table and had some coffee.

Candice called back then, and when I answered, she said, "What's up?"

"Harrison wants us to go with him to interview Leslie's parents tomorrow."

"Works for me," she said. "I've got nothing on the books."

"Me either. I'll send you a text with the time."

I hung up with her and dialed Harrison back. "We're in," I said when he answered.

"Seven thirty," he said perfunctorily. "I'll meet you in the parking lot." And then the line went dead.

I sighed and set the phone aside. "Trouble?" Dutch asked, watching me closely.

"I think your boss is an ass," I said earnestly.

Dutch barked out a laugh. "You're just picking that up? Gee, Abby, you're usually quicker on stuff like that."

"No, I mean it, Dutch!" I insisted, all kidding aside. "I think the guy has some sort of social disorder or something."

"Social disorder?"

"Yes. I mean, one minute I think Harrison might be warming up to us and the next he's like . . . a complete jerk!"

"Welcome to the bureau, Abby," Dutch said with a smile. "We're not paid to be nice. We're paid to get results."

"You're not like that," I argued.

Dutch leaned forward and grabbed my arm, pulling me out of my chair to sit me in his lap and kiss me. "When I'm at work, I'm able to conceal my true persona," he said.

"I see," I replied with a giggle. "Your *persona*, is it?"

Dutch nodded earnestly. "Yep. The real charm comes out only when I'm not wearing the badge."

"Ahhhh," I said as he began nuzzling my neck. "It's been a little while since I've seen that . . . er . . . *charm*, you know."

Dutch pulled his face out of my neck and stared at me with bedroom eyes. "Wanna get reacquainted?"

I giggled again. "I'm game," I told him, and he slung me over his shoulder caveman style and carried me upstairs, where we got on with the charm.

The next morning Candice and I got into Harrison's car just as the first rays of the sun were lighting up the east. "Morning!" I said brightly. Candice shot me a quizzical look, but I ignored her. I was going to make Harrison like me if it killed me.

"Ms. Cooper," Harrison said coolly. "Ms. Fusco."

"Agent Harrison," Candice replied tonelessly.

I sighed. This whole getting everyone to be one big happy family was likely to prove tougher than I thought.

I sat up front as we wound our way through traffic. I was surprised when we arrived at a small airport. Harrison pulled into a parking space and cut the engine. "We'll be traveling by charter plane," he said before he got out.

I followed with Candice behind him to a set of three hangars. Harrison led us to the middle one and over to a small white plane with blue piping. "Agent Harrison," a portly man with white hair and an easy smile said warmly.

"Ed," Harrison said. "Are we clear for takeoff?"

"I'm just running through the final checklist," Ed said, running his hand along the underside of the wing. "Why don't you and your guests grab a cup of coffee and I'll come get you after I've gone through the rest of my list?"

Harrison nodded and began walking again without commenting to us. Candice and I followed and we made our way into a small, cozy office with several chairs and the smell of fresh-brewed coffee. Candice headed straight for the brew and she poured us both

a cup. As she handed one to me, we both took notice that Harrison seemed to be waiting for a cup as
well, but instead of pouring him one, Candice merely
stepped aside, giving him access to the coffeepot. I
gave her a contemptuous look, as she was doing nothing to help ease the tension in our little group, but she
just gave me a smart smile.

No one, it seemed, was up for chitchat, so I made my
way over to the window and watched Ed go through
his checklist. And that's when I began to get a really
uncomfortable feeling.

It started as a little sinking sensation in my lower
gut, but the longer I watched Ed as he moved around
the plane, the more unsettled I became. Something
was wrong, but I couldn't quite put my finger on it.
I turned and looked at Candice, wondering if I was
just uneasy about the thought of going up in such a
small plane. I'm generally claustrophobic, so the idea
of being squished into a tight space with a tiny window while flying the turbulent air over Lake Michigan
wasn't very appealing.

"What's up?" Candice asked, noticing my unease.

"I don't think I want to get on that plane," I
whispered.

Candice's attention moved to the window. "Is
something wrong with the plane?" I had to give her
credit for immediately trusting my radar.

I focused on her question and turned back to the
view of the plane in the hangar. "I don't know," I admitted. "I want to say no, but something's not right."

"What's your intuition saying?" she pressed.

"Nothing specific," I admitted. "I just feel really uneasy about it."

"Uneasy as in you think the plane might crash?"

By now Harrison was listening to us and I caught

the look of alarm register on his face as he glanced in our direction.

I ignored him and focused on Candice. The feeling I had was so fuzzy that I thought if she could only ask the right question, I might find the reason for my distress. "Again, I don't think so," I said, feeling that out. "But something doesn't feel right to me." Turning to Harrison, I asked, "Do you know how long Ed has been flying?"

He seemed surprised by the question. "No," he said. "But I know it's been many years. He's the registered pilot with the FBI for this district and you don't get that accreditation without logging a whole lotta flying time."

I took a deep breath and closed my eyes.

"Want to explain to me what she's freaking out about?" I heard Harrison ask Candice.

My eyes snapped open as my temper flared. "For your information, Agent Harrison, I am *not* freaking out! I just don't have a great feeling about going up in that plane."

"Why not?" he asked, and I noticed that his question was asked without attitude. He was genuinely concerned.

"I don't know," I whispered. "But something's not right about this trip."

Harrison's mood turned to irritation. "I can't cancel the trip based on a feeling, Ms. Cooper. We have an appointment to interview Leslie's parents in three hours. If you don't want to come, you're welcome to stay behind and wait for my return."

I eyed Candice, looking for her reaction. "If you want to stay behind, I'm cool with that, Abs," she said. "And I'd be the last person who'd go up in a plane that your radar said was unsafe."

And as she said that, my gaze switched back to the plane. When I focused my energy at it, I knew the plane was fine. But the reason for the unsettled feeling I had still eluded me. I tried to ask myself the question, if I got on the plane, would we make it to Wisconsin safely? I was relieved to feel a positive answer to that. So I knew it was okay to fly, but why I was apprehensive I still hadn't pinpointed. Finally, I shrugged and gave in. "No, it's fine. I think it's just my own nerves about flying in a small plane."

"You sure?" Candice asked, and I could tell I'd now made *her* nervous too.

I nodded with conviction. "Yes. We're fine."

Just then Ed opened up the office door and beamed at us. "She's all set, and I'm ready when you are, folks."

I set my coffee cup down and said, "Let's go."

An hour later I was white-knuckling it over Lake Michigan. The wind had kicked up and Ed was having a hell of time keeping the small plane level as gusts of wind pushed us high, then suddenly gave out and we dropped back low again. My stomach had lurched so many times I found it a wonder that I'd managed to hold on to the coffee I'd drunk. Beside me Candice also looked nervous, and I could tell she was really regretting following me onto the plane. She and I were squished into the two backseats and the sound of the engines right next to us drowned out all other noise. Even with headgear and microphones no one felt like talking.

I stopped looking out the window, as the dips, dives, and surges of the plane were making me motion sick enough. I didn't actually need to see it to confirm how crazy this roller-coaster ride was. Mostly I just took very deep breaths—interrupted by the occasional gasp—and focused on remaining calm. It was really, really hard. Eventually the wind stopped jerking us around and we began our descent into Milwaukee.

With a heart full of gratitude when the plane finally touched down, I let go of the breath I'd been holding and we taxied to another hangar where Ed parked the plane.

As quickly as I could and with trembling fingers, I unbuckled my seat belt, yanked off my headset, and pretty much dived out of the plane.

I heard Ed laugh behind me as I took a few unsteady steps away. "First time in a small plane?" he asked. I nodded, not trusting my voice. "Your first stretch in a strong turbulence is always the toughest. Going home, the wind'll be behind us and it'll be a lot smoother."

I felt the blood leave my face. "We have to do that *again*?"

Ed laughed some more. He thought my reaction was hilarious. "I promise," he assured me, placing his hand on his chest. "It'll be a piece of cake."

My left side grew heavy and I was about to ask him where the nearest car-rental office was because there was *no way* I wanted to do *that* again, but Harrison spoke before I could. "We've got an agent meeting us to take us to the Coyles'. If you two will follow me, please." And he turned and walked away.

"You okay?" Candice asked, eyeing me with concern. "You look a little pale."

I took a deep breath. "Fine," I managed. "Come on. We don't want to keep Agent Delightful waiting."

I believe Harrison heard that, as I saw that his posture stiffened slightly, but at this point I didn't care. If Dutch had been along for that ride, he definitely would have given me a minute to collect myself before marching off. Harrison's lack of decorum was seriously wearing on my nerves.

The corner of Candice's mouth lifted and she took my arm and pulled me along. "Come on, Abs. Let's get you into something with four wheels and no wings, shall we?"

About forty-five minutes later we arrived at the home of Erica and Jim Coyle. I'd learned in the car from the agent who'd been assigned to drive us to their residence, and who'd also initially been assigned to interview them, that Erica was a member of the Wisconsin state legislature and her husband was a district court judge.

Their home was surprising. It was sleek and ultra-modern, architecturally rendered to make it look a bit futuristic. There were three levels to the brilliant white exterior and lots of chrome trim. A circular staircase linked the stories from the outside, and Agent Blass—the agent who'd picked us up from the airport—led the way up the stairs to the second level, where he rang the bell and we waited.

The door was opened by a woman in a brilliant orange pantsuit with matching jewelry, nails, and lipstick. The color did nothing to enhance her looks, which were decidedly plain and forgettable. "Agent Blass," she greeted our chauffeur. "It's good to see you again."

"Representative Coyle," Blass said with a stiff smile before turning to introduce the rest of us. "This is Assistant Special Agent in Charge Brice Harrison, and these are his two FBI associates, Abigail Cooper and Candice Frisco."

"*Fusco,*" Candice corrected as she reached forward and shook Representative Coyle's hand.

We entered the home and I was not surprised by the interior, which was uninspired and plain. The couple seemed to be going for a minimalist look, but they took it to an extreme that removed any sense of cool sophistication. The walls were bare and painted as brilliant a shade of white as the outside. The floors were stained concrete, the color a yucky dung brown, and the two white couches in the central living area were small and stiff. There was nothing in the environment that suggested this was a home. No knickknacks, decorations, or life was on display. It was beyond utilitarian; it was stark.

"Why don't you all take a seat on the couch and I'll get Jim from upstairs," she said before dashing off to another spiral staircase.

We waited until the clink of her shoes had topped the last step before Candice motioned me over to one of the couches, where the two of us took a seat. "Cozy!" Candice whispered as we sat down on the hard cushion, and I stifled a giggle while Harrison shot us both a warning look.

Harrison and Blass stood as stiff as the furniture, waiting without speaking as the seconds ticked by. After what felt like many minutes, two sets of feet clinked down the spiral staircase. All of us looked in that direction as Mrs. Coyle and her husband circled down to the ground. His Honor the judge was even more of a surprise than his wife. Short and slim with jet-black hair and wire-rimmed glasses, he looked far younger than the age I suspected he'd be. When he stood next to his wife, it was almost comical—like the clown car at the circus had just opened its doors and these were the first two occupants to come out.

His Honor nodded to us and remained standing, while his wife moved to the second couch and sat down. Introductions were made again and Harrison took charge. He conducted the interview asking all the questions I assumed the couple had already answered countless times from various law-enforcement officials, and they seemed weary of the repetition but gave their answers without protest or impatience. Throughout it all I waited for some signal from my radar, but try as I might to tune in on her energy, I couldn't really get a bead on Representative Coyle, and her husband was even worse.

Internally I grew frustrated as I realized I'd likely hit on two people whose energy just didn't emit a strong enough vibe for me to pick up on. This happened very, very rarely in my world, but every once in a great while I'd get a client that I couldn't read. I didn't know why this happened, and it wasn't necessarily a bad thing—just some people have very "quiet" energy that doesn't allow my radar to really perceive anything about them. The fact that there would be two such energies together in one room—and married, no less—was what made it so striking to me. And I had to wonder whether all the mixed messages that I'd picked up on for their daughter might also be because her own energy wasn't very "loud" either.

I shook off the frustration, however, and listened to Harrison's interview, hoping for something, *anything*, to ding my radar. At this point he was asking them about the conference two years previously, and the representative acknowledged that she'd been there. "Did your daughter also attend?" Harrison asked.

"Yes," said Mrs. Coyle. "She was there. But what does this have to do with her disappearance?"

"There are two other students who went missing around the same time as your daughter who also attended that conference, and we believe that during that event some of the kids may have hung out together. We think your daughter, in fact, might have spent some time with at least two of them."

Representative Coyle's eyes held a far-off cast as, I assumed, she thought back to that time. "Are you telling me that either Michael, Kyle, or Bianca are missing?"

My eyebrows shot up. I was surprised at the woman's memory. "Bianca and Kyle went missing just before your daughter," Harrison said. "But we're unfamiliar with Michael. Do you remember his last name?"

The representative turned pale as the impact of what Harrison had said about Bianca and Kyle hit home, but she answered his question by saying, "Michael Derby, from Illinois, the son of U.S. senator Matthew Derby. Leslie hung out with those three during the conference. The kids even stayed in our suite and watched movies until about three a.m. one night. Do you think something has also happened to Michael?"

Harrison scribbled in his notebook before answering, "To our knowledge, ma'am, Michael is fine, but we'll certainly check in with the senator to make sure."

"Maybe Michael knows where they are!" Mrs. Coyle said suddenly.

"We'll certainly ask him," said Harrison in his usual calm voice. I knew he didn't want her jumping to conclusions before he talked to Michael and his father first.

"I'll bet they're all together," Coyle continued, looking at her husband pointedly. "I'll bet they're off somewhere laughing it up and making us all sweat. It would be just like Leslie to go off and play that kind of prank on us."

Harrison seemed to shift his position slightly. "Prank?" he asked. "Leslie was given to playing pranks?"

The question seemed to catch Representative Coyle off guard. "Well . . . I mean . . . ," she blustered. "Not really. Not to this extent, of course, but during her senior year of high school, she went through a slightly rebellious stage."

"What did she do?" Harrison pressed.

"Nothing overly dramatic. She ran away from home for a week when we took away her car privileges. But she only went to a friend's house and she came home when she felt she'd made her point."

"Do you think your daughter could somehow be attempting to make a point by disappearing last May?"

Mrs. Coyle's eyes flashed again to her husband, and I had the sense that he wasn't pleased with this line of questioning. He answered for his wife by saying, "No. Leslie isn't pulling a prank. She would have contacted us. She would have let us know she's all right. This is completely out of character for my daughter, who has grown up a lot since high school."

Harrison nodded and moved away from the touchy subject. I had a feeling he'd be doing a lot more digging into Leslie's behavior at school up to her disappearance, but for now he was going to let it drop.

"One last question," he said, and I noticed that his eyes flashed briefly to me. "Did Leslie go somewhere the weekend before she disappeared? Maybe take a road trip or something?"

Representative Coyle nodded. "Yes," she said. "She called to tell me that she and a group of friends were taking a road trip to Ohio State University to visit a friend. I had some concerns about her leaving campus so close to finals, but she assured me that she was well up on her studies, and given her last report card, I had no reason to doubt her."

When Harrison's eyes flashed again to me, I allowed

the tiniest of smiles. "I'd like to hear more about her trip to Ohio," Harrison said. "Can you give me the name of one of the friends she went with?"

Representative Coyle's brow furrowed. "Actually," she said, "Leslie didn't mention anyone by name. I knew she was driving, and she said it was with a bunch of friends, so I didn't think to ask her who specifically she was going with."

"Do you know the name of the friend she was going to visit?" Harrison asked.

The representative blanched again, her fingers finding the orange pearl necklace at her neck. "No," she admitted. "Leslie said it was a friend of a friend."

And I suddenly knew why Leslie hadn't mentioned anyone in particular. She'd gone alone—of that I was certain—and she didn't want her mother to know she was off to see Kyle, but why she didn't want anyone to know wasn't clear. "Do you think her roommate might have gone or might know one of the other kids who did?" Harrison pressed.

"Maybe," Mrs. Coyle said. "You can ask Trish if you like. Do you need her number?"

Harrison glanced at Blass, who said, "We have her contact information on file, Representative Coyle. We'll call her."

After that, Harrison wrapped it up, thanking the Coyles for their time and asking them to keep the specifics of this case out of the press for now.

I thought that his attempts to keep a lid on this case for much longer were going to prove futile, because two dead children of political leaders and one more missing were bound to turn up as more than coincidental really soon. I also noted that Harrison had been careful not to disclose to the Coyles that both

Bianca and Kyle were dead. I figured that was done purposely to keep them cooperative for now.

Harrison was soon folding his notebook closed and looked like he was about to announce his good-byes when Candice asked, "Do you know if Leslie kept in touch with Kyle and Bianca after the conference?"

Again, Representative Coyle looked surprised. "Not that she ever mentioned to me," she said. "But I suppose she could have."

Harrison was clearly giving Candice a warning look, but she ignored him by asking, "And do you by any chance have a better photo of Leslie than the one that was supplied to us? The photo we have on file is a bit too grainy for us to work with."

Mrs. Coyle rose to her feet. "Yes, of course," she said. "I remember that fuzzy photo I gave you, Agent Blass. I wasn't thinking about the picture's quality at the time. When your child goes missing, you lose any ability to think straight." And with that, she left us to hurry out of the room toward the kitchen. I could see her down the hallway and she was back in only a moment pulling apart a small frame. "Here," she said, handing the photo to Candice. "That was taken last year at Castle Rock Lake."

Eagerly I peered over Candice's shoulder and was again a little surprised to see Leslie still looking very much alive. Candice eyed me cautiously and I gave a small nod to indicate that I believed the girl was still with us. "Thank you for the photo, ma'am," said Candice. "We'll make a copy as soon as possible and return the original."

"Thank you," said Mrs. Coyle. "And you'll also let me know as soon as you find out anything about my daughter?"

Candice deferred to Harrison to answer that question and he cleared his throat and said, "We'll keep you advised of any new developments," which wasn't exactly what the Coyles were looking for in the way of reassurances, but it was probably beyond Harrison to consider their feelings.

Soon after this exchange our good-byes were given and we left the couple, heading back to the airport. Harrison and Blass talked in the front seat, mostly about sports, and Candice and I kept quiet. As we unloaded from the car, I had another acute sense of dread when we walked toward the small plane. This time, I knew it was more than just my nerves. Something was telling me that I might want to rethink going up, up, and away.

I stopped on the tarmac just in front of the hangar. Candice eyed me over her shoulder. "You coming?"

"I don't think so," I said.

Candice came back to stand next to me. A cold wind had stirred up and sent leaves swirling in little clusters all around the pavement. "What's up?" she asked softly when she reached my side.

"I can't get on that plane," I whispered as my gut clenched at the thought of flying in it.

Candice eyed the plane and its pilot, who was busy going through his preflight checklist again. "Harrison!" she called out, and he looked back at us in surprise.

"What?"

"We're not getting on that plane," she said, and immediately I was flooded with relief.

Harrison's eyes opened wide. "What do you mean, you're not getting on the plane?"

"Abby's got a bad feeling."

Harrison's brows pulled together and I could tell he really thought we were being ridiculous. "This again?"

he asked, his tone impatient, as he walked back to us. "Listen, we made it here okay, didn't we? Remember how you had a bad feeling before we came, and other than a little turbulence, we made it just fine?"

I nodded reluctantly but held firm. "I'm not flying back in that," I said, pointing to the plane.

Harrison sighed and I knew he was frustrated. "I'm not authorizing a comp on a regular airline," he said stonily. "Either you two fly with me or you pay your own way back."

Candice turned back to me and said, "Are you against planes in general or just that one?"

"Just that one."

Looking to Harrison, she said, "See ya," and pivoted with me to walk back to Blass's car, where luckily he was still parked. Opening the front passenger door, Candice asked, "Can we trouble you for a ride to the airport?"

"We're at the airport," Blass said, and I could see his head pivoting back and forth from Candice to Harrison, who stood angrily with his hands on his hips in the same spot we'd left him.

"I know," Candice said patiently. "But we're looking for the one with bigger planes."

At this point Harrison shook his head and turned away from us. We were on our own. "Sure," Blass finally said. "Hop in."

I called Dutch the moment our nice, big commercial jet came to a stop on the tarmac at Detroit Metro. "We just landed," I said wearily. I'd explained to him as we waited to see if we could get on a flight out of Milwaukee that I'd had a really bad feeling about flying in the charter plane, and Candice and I had decided to fly commercial instead. "Can you come give us a lift?"

"Uh . . . no," he said, and I could hear the tension in his voice and lots of commotion in the background.

"Why? What's up?" I said.

"I don't know how to tell you this," Dutch said, "but Harrison's plane went off the grid somewhere over Lake Michigan."

"What do you mean, 'went off the grid'?" I asked in alarm.

"It went off the radar, babe. We think the plane crashed."

Chapter Ten

Candice and I arrived by taxi at the FBI offices as soon as we could, and by the time we got there, we'd learned that the plane Harrison and Ed were in had been spotted near an old airstrip just off the Michigan coastline, and rescue teams had already been dispatched.

I'd told Candice in the cab that I felt that Harrison was still alive, but Ed's energy felt very grave. I reiterated this to Dutch when I saw him, and I barely got the words out before he yanked me into his chest and hugged me fiercely. "Thank God you didn't get on that plane," he whispered.

Candice too looked a little rattled, and I had the sense that the close call was affecting everyone else a lot more than it was me. Even Gaston seemed anxious. "Why didn't that idiot listen to you?" he asked me when word came that EMTs were on the scene and Harrison was alive but unconscious.

"He's not such a big fan of mine," I replied. "Plus, I didn't know the plane was going to crash. I just knew it gave me the willies to think about getting on it again."

Gaston sighed and I thought he was going to say something else, but at that moment there was more information coming in about the crash. Ed had coded at the scene and paramedics were trying to revive him. My heart thumped hard in my chest as I willed him to pull through. Minutes ticked by as Dutch paced back and forth with his cell phone stuck to his ear while he waited for more word to come in.

Finally after ten long, agonizing minutes he reported that they had a weak pulse on Ed and were en route to the hospital in Pentwater, twenty-five miles away from the crash site.

Much of the rest of the evening was spent waiting for updates, which were slow to come in. But we did hear enough to be able to piece a few things together. Just as they had the Michigan coastline in sight, Ed told Harrison that he was feeling very dizzy and nauseated, and was unable to focus. Feeling like something of a medical emergency might be unfolding, he'd given a very quick lesson to Harrison about handling the plane and what to do in case he became incapacitated, and then he'd suddenly blacked out. Harrison had somehow managed to keep the nose of the plane level, but he'd been too focused on aiming for an old abandoned airstrip that Ed had pointed out to try to radio for help. He'd attempted a landing, hoping that he could help Ed when he got the plane down, but it had been more difficult than he'd imagined and the plane's wing had clipped a tree, sending it tumbling after touchdown.

It was a miracle they'd both managed to survive, as we also received a picture of the crash site. I'd taken a look at Dutch's face as the image flashed across the computer screen. He'd turned ashen and reached for my hand. "I'm okay," I told him. "Really."

But poor Ed wasn't so lucky. The doctors determined that he'd suffered a major heart attack, and he was scheduled for surgery as soon as they could stabilize him enough to take a chance with the operation. Sadly, I didn't have a great feeling about his chances and the next morning we woke up to learn that he'd gone into cardiac arrest on the table and hadn't survived.

On three hours' sleep Dutch was determined to head to the west side of the state and visit his boss in the hospital. I went with him as much for moral support as to make sure he stayed awake during the trip.

We found Harrison grumbling at a nurse on the second floor of the Memorial Medical Center. As the nurse came out of the room, she looked like she liked him about as much as the rest of us. I gave her a sympathetic smile and Dutch and I knocked at the door. "Good morning, sir," Dutch said cordially.

"Agent Rivers!" Harrison said in surprise.

I followed after Dutch into the room and nearly came up short. The right side of Harrison's face was scratched and puffy and his right eye was nearly swollen shut. His right arm was in a sling and a cast had been secured around his hand and lower arm. His breathing seemed a little labored and I could tell he was in no small amount of discomfort, but as his good eye swiveled over to me, I could see he was even more surprised that I'd come too. "Ms. Cooper," he said. "What brings you here?"

It was my turn to be surprised. "Dutch and I wanted to come and see how you were doing, sir."

Harrison's expression was unreadable—but that might have been due to the swelling of his face. His sentiment became clear, however, when he said, "I thought you were here to predict another disaster."

Dutch visibly stiffened, but I'd been hanging out with Harrison long enough to know he was capable of being an ass, so his comment didn't rattle me any more than usual. I forced myself to laugh and turn it into a joke instead. "How about if I just predict your speedy recovery?"

The corner of Harrison's mouth lifted, but it looked more like a grimace and his attention swiveled back to Dutch. "I suppose Gaston's going to make you the lead now that I'm out of commission for a few days?"

Dutch kept his cool and didn't take the bait. "There's been no discussion on that front, sir."

Harrison didn't look like he believed him, but he didn't say anything more on the topic. "I heard about Ed," he said after an uncomfortable pause.

"We're very sorry, sir," I said, and I meant it.

Harrison's eye focused on his bedsheet. The uncomfortable silence returned, but then Harrison said, "Will you stick with the case, Ms. Cooper?"

Again I was surprised, but I answered him immediately. "As long as the FBI finds value in my participation, I'll contribute where I can."

"Good," he whispered so softly that I barely caught the word. Dutch's cell phone rang and he turned to the corner of the room to answer it. I moved closer to Harrison's bedside and asked, "Can I get you anything?"

"I'm fine," he assured me. "Thank you." Then he seemed to notice that Candice wasn't with me. "Where's your partner?"

"She had some details to work out with her grandmother's estate attorney. She told me to tell you to get well soon, though."

This made Harrison chuckle and I couldn't understand what he found so funny. "I'll bet she did," he said with chagrin. "And I'll bet she can't wait to rub my nose in it the next time she sees me."

"Rub your nose in what, exactly, sir?"

"That I got on the plane," he said simply.

My jaw dropped. "Agent Harrison," I said deliberately, "if you *hadn't* gotten on that plane, Ed would most definitely have died. The fact that he was given a chance at all was because you stuck by him and managed without any sort of training and barely any instruction to *land the plane*! As I understand it, before he went into surgery, he was conscious and his whole family was with him. You gave them their one and only chance to say good-bye to him. They would have missed that opportunity entirely if you hadn't gotten on the plane, sir."

Harrison regarded me for a long minute before Dutch came to stand next to me and offered him the phone. "It's the SAC, sir. He would like to speak with you."

Harrison took the phone, and Dutch and I moved out into the hallway to give him some privacy. He called us back a few minutes later. "I was right. Gaston has assigned temporary charge of the case over to you, Agent Rivers. I have been told by the doctors here that I can be discharged as soon as tomorrow and with a day or two of rest I can be back on the assignment by Monday."

"Yes, sir," said Dutch. "I'd be happy to step in until you're well enough to come back on full-time."

"You will of course keep me up-to-date at all times?" Harrison asked, but there was something about his look that suggested he was having a really hard time letting go of the case, even temporarily.

"Of course, sir."

"I would also appreciate it if Ms. Cooper and Ms. Fusco took a step back at this point, Agent Rivers."

Again my jaw dropped. That was out of left field. "But I thought you wanted us to remain on the case?" I said.

"I do," Agent Harrison replied. "But my concern is that the lines between you and Agent Rivers will be too blurred for him to work within protocol. I would appreciate it if you waited until I was back in charge before you joined us again, so that I can maintain a proper atmosphere."

I opened my mouth to protest, but Dutch squeezed my hand and said quickly, "Of course, sir."

We then said our good-byes and left Harrison to battle another nurse who passed us on our way out. When we got into the car again, I turned to Dutch and demanded, "Why'd you cave?"

"Because he's right, Edgar."

"What do you mean, he's right?" I shot back. "He's not right! He's *never* right!"

Dutch grinned as he turned the car out of the parking lot. "Maybe he's not always right," he conceded, "but this time I have to agree with him."

"Why exactly?"

"Because politically it wouldn't look good for me to have my girlfriend too deep into a case that I was in charge of," he said. When I furrowed my brow at him, he explained, "By putting me in charge of this case, Gaston has stepped on all the toes of the other members of the task force. I haven't been in on it from the beginning, and there are definitely other more-seasoned veterans that clearly should have been in line ahead of me, like Blass, or Albright. They're going to be pissed off when they find out they not only have to bring me up to speed but report to me for the next seventy-two hours."

"Yeah, but what does that have to do with *me*?" I asked.

"Everyone knows we're a couple," Dutch said. "Which is why Gaston was careful to keep me out of it in the beginning. He didn't want there to be any appearance of impropriety, and honestly, he probably also thought about protecting me politically should this thing go south—just like you and Candice told him when you guys last met. If things go bad and you and Candice are still on board, I'd definitely be the first person thrown under the bus."

"Do you think he advised Harrison to tell me to step away for a little while?"

"He could have," Dutch conceded. "In fact, he probably did."

"So if everyone is going to be pissed that you're the temporary head of the investigation, and if it's politically risky to you, why move you into that spot at all?"

"Because Gaston needs someone he can trust to head the investigation. This case is personal to him. He and Representative Lovelace go way back. He knows I'll keep him in the loop and keep the level of intensity up on the case." Dutch was silent for a minute before he added, "And it's a short window anyway. He knows Harrison is going to push himself to recover as fast as possible, so I won't be needed longer than a few days, and then he can bring you and Candice officially back on board."

"So what are we supposed to do in the meantime?" I asked.

"What did you two do when you were taken off the case before?"

"We went behind Harrison's back and worked the case on our own," I admitted.

"Well," Dutch said with another smile, "I of course *have* to tell you that the bureau would frown on that, but as long as it didn't directly interfere with our investigation, we certainly couldn't *prevent* you from doing what you wanted."

I shot him a satisfied smile as I sat back in my seat, understanding that the entire course of all this maneuvering had likely been engineered by Gaston, who was quickly becoming a genius in my eyes. The man knew that if he put anyone other than Dutch in charge, I'd probably be underutilized until Harrison came back on the case, and I had no doubt I would have been. None of the other agents besides Dutch would likely be willing to trust my instincts. So he'd set me free until Harrison came back, and by putting Dutch in charge, he had an agent he could count on to let him know what was going on at every turn; plus he could count on Candice and I to continue to work the case and leak our findings to Dutch. He also likely knew that Harrison would want to come back quickly rather than have a green agent unfamiliar with the case in charge. And now, after the plane crash that I'd all but predicted, Harrison might never doubt my instincts again.

In the meantime, I reasoned, Candice and I needed to work this case, and work it hard. I looked at the clock on the dash. We'd be home in a little more than three hours, which still gave us time for a really good powwow.

Later that night my partner and I were munching on pizza and drawing on a large whiteboard in her office. We had a good little flowchart going as we talked through the case and decided on our next move. "As I see it," Candice said, eyeing two boxes at the far right of the whiteboard, "we can either continue to follow Leslie's trail or we can take a chance and follow up with Michael Derby."

"It's a tough call," I said, glancing at the picture on the table in front of me of Leslie Coyle. "I know she's still alive, but there's this awful energy surrounding her. It feels completely unstable and I don't think she can take her surroundings much longer." I gave an involuntary shiver as I felt out her energy, and I knew that wherever she was, it wasn't a place I ever wanted to go.

"What I don't understand," Candice mused, "is why she's been treated so differently from Bianca and Kyle."

"You mean why she's been kept alive and the other two were murdered fairly quickly?"

"Yes," said Candice.

I shrugged. I had no idea. "Maybe the killer likes her," I said. "Maybe he's toying with her or torturing her. Maybe he's just a sick son of a bitch who's not ready to get rid of her yet."

Candice's eye moved to the photo on the table too and then she lit up. "Abs!" she said. "Do you think Leslie is at her old vacation spot, like Kyle and Bianca?"

I looked at the picture again, this time with intensity as I focused my radar on it. The response surprised me. "No," I said after a minute. "She's somewhere with a lot of concrete. It's not the wilderness, and it feels belowground."

"Belowground?"

I nodded. "Like the basement level of a large building."

Candice considered me for a long minute. "It's your

call, Abs," she said, pointing to the two boxes labeled MICHAEL DERBY and LESLIE COYLE.

It was a really hard decision. I knew Leslie was in more immediate danger, but there was something urgent around Michael Derby too. We needed to talk to him, and we needed to talk to him soon. With a growl of frustration I reached for Candice's desk phone, punching in a number as fast as my finger could move. "Hey," I said when Dutch answered the line. "I know I've been asked to stay out of this, but there's a small lead I want you to consider looking into."

"I'm listening," he said.

"I think that Leslie Coyle is being held in the basement of a building. There's a ton of concrete around her, and I don't know how large that would make the building, but it seems big and open on the inside. Also, there's a lot of clutter nearby."

"What do you mean, clutter?"

My eyes were closed as I focused hard on trying to describe what was in my head. "It's weird," I said. "It's not really like there's junk or anything other than chairs. There's just a lot of chairs. . . ." My voice trailed off as I followed that thread.

Dutch arrived at it one nanosecond before I did. "Like a stadium?" he asked. "There's a lot of concrete in a stadium and it's large and open with a whole lot of chairs."

"You know," I said, "that really might be it, Dutch!"

"And you're certain she's still alive?" he asked me.

I opened my eyes and glanced at Leslie's picture again. "Yes. But I could also tell you that I don't know that she has a lot of time. I'd give her a week to ten days. And there's something awful surrounding her too. I wouldn't be surprised if he's slowly torturing her," I whispered. "You guys need to hurry."

"I'm on it," he said. "Thanks, doll."

After hanging up with Dutch, I turned back to Candice. "That's settled," I said.

Candice drew a big circle around Michael Derby's name. "Road trip, to Illinois, tomorrow at six a.m. sharp."

Candice arrived at my house at one minute to six a.m. looking very tired. "Want me to drive?" I asked when I took in the pinched corners of her eyes.

"That'd be good," she said, moving out of the driver's seat. "I want to do a little more research on Derby anyway."

I slid into the driver's side and after Candice had settled herself into the passenger seat, we were off. "What part of Illinois are we aiming for?" I asked.

Candice motioned to the dashboard navigation system. "Just outside Chicago," she said as she pulled out her iPhone and began dabbing at the screen. "I've already plugged in the coordinates. All you have to do is follow the path it lays out for you."

"Where does Michael attend college?"

"Chicago State University," Candice replied, her eyes intent on the screen of her iPhone. "I was up half the night getting as much as I could on him."

"Anything juicy?"

"Nada," she said with a sigh. "The kid's a brainiac. Going for dual degrees in biology and chemical engineering. He's a straight A student, tutors on the side, and at the tender age of eighteen is already two grades ahead of most of his classmates."

"Wow," I said, impressed.

"He's also a member of Mensa."

"So he's stupid," I deadpanned.

Candice laughed. "A real dumb ass," she agreed

with a chuckle. "I used to hate kids like Derby when I was in school. They always ruined the curve for the rest of us."

"What about the father?" I asked. "Did you get anything on him?"

To this question Candice's eyes lit up. "Matthew Derby is one of those oily politicians we all love to hate. He's had a variety of scandals hit his time in office, and the guy has managed to dodge most of them."

"Like what?"

"Well," Candice said, putting down her iPhone to fill me in, "the first scandal was back when Michael was just six years old and the senator was in his second term in the Illinois state legislature. It seems that his wife of ten years was a little fragile—mentally speaking—and there were rumors of her popping pills and having a nervous breakdown, when the *Chicago Sun-Times* broke the news that one of the secretaries in the senator's office claimed he was having a torrid affair with an intern. Both the senator and the intern publicly denied the affair—"

"Surprise, surprise," I interrupted.

Candice chuckled. "I know, right? Anyway, the press wouldn't let go of it. The intern was a knockout and barely out of high school, and the senator was a good-looking guy who had campaigned hard on family values and appeared to stand stoically by his mentally fragile wife."

"Lemme guess," I said, eyeing her. "The wife filed shortly thereafter."

Candice looked at me in surprise. "No," she said, her eyes big as they regarded me. "And I'm surprised you're so far off the mark. She committed suicide."

My jaw dropped and the car swerved slightly. Candice made a squeaking noise as I barely avoided a guardrail. "Sorry!" I said, focusing my eyes firmly forward again. "And I'm surprised that I missed that too," I said after a small pause. I hate it when I'm wrong.

"Anyway," Candice continued after she'd recovered from the fright I'd given her, "as you can imagine, the press went crazy. Instead of backing off, like they should have, they blamed the senator, alluding that his wife's death was his fault because of the affair. And to make matters worse, one particular reporter was caught at the fence of little Michael's playground asking him if his daddy had ever mentioned having a girlfriend and how he felt about his mommy being so sad that she'd killed herself."

"Are you *kidding* me?!" I gasped.

Candice shook her head ruefully. "Unfortunately, I'm not."

"Whoa," was all I could think to say as my mind drifted back to Professor Houghton and what a scum he was to suggest to future reporters that they go for the jugular.

"I know, it's totally despicable!" Candice lamented. "But it actually worked in Derby's favor in the next election. When the school told not only the competing paper what had happened but a local news station as well, the public outcry of what that reporter did was unbelievable. He was fired from his post and Derby won his reelection by a landslide and has been something of a sympathetic character in the public eye ever since. The guy can do no wrong."

"And I'm assuming he pushes that license to the limit?" I asked, knowing there might be more that Candice had dug up.

She shrugged. "I haven't been able to find anything concrete," she said, "but there are rumors out there that suggest Derby's not the man of the people he claims to be."

"Like what?"

"Well," Candice said, digging through her briefcase to pull out her notebook, "there was a little talk three years ago about a vacation home he bought on Lake Michigan. It only set him back three hundred thousand."

"That's a big chunk of change," I said, not understanding the issue.

"He sold it six months later for over a million," she said.

I whistled. "Nice turnaround."

"Exactly. When questioned about it, Derby said that he'd purchased the home from a contractor friend of his who was having cash flow issues, and his buddy had sold the home to Derby at a significant discount. The senator said that he hadn't really wanted the extra house payment and was, and I quote here, 'delighted and surprised' to sell it later for a significant profit."

"Seven hundred thousand dollars would delight the hell out of me too," I said.

"And then there's the fact that in his run for the U.S. Senate to capture the seat of a retiring senator, Derby handily won the election against the opposing party."

"Why is that so shocking?"

"The candidate from the opposing party was a nobody. He had no social skills whatsoever, did very little campaigning, and basically handed Derby the seat."

"Huh," I said. "How do you think that happened?"

"I don't know, but it's weird, you know? Like in all of Illinois there wasn't a better-qualified candidate to run against Derby? It just sounds like someone fixed the election."

"That is weird," I agreed. "And do you know what else I think is weird?"

"What?"

"That of the four kids that hung out at that conference in Chicago two years ago, Michael is the only one who hasn't gone missing."

Candice thought on that for a minute. "Maybe it has something to do with the fact that Leslie is still alive," she said. "Maybe the killer won't think about going after Michael until something changes with Leslie."

I nodded. "You really could be right," I said, seeing her point.

"It could also be that the killer only had a chance to glimpse the three who were abducted. Maybe when they were being observed, Michael wasn't with them. Maybe he was having dinner with his dad or something."

"Another good point," I conceded with a sigh. "I guess we won't know until we talk to Michael. Which brings me to my next question."

"Yes?"

"What's the game plan?"

Candice smiled. "Sorry, forgot to tell you that part. We're heading to the University of Chicago to find Michael and persuade him to talk to us. We're going to have to be pretty sneaky about it too," she warned.

My brow furrowed. "Why's that?"

"Because the FBI will likely have a security detail assigned to him for his own protection, so the task force may become all too aware of our snooping around if we're not careful."

"And while Dutch may be okay with us interviewing Michael, the other guys on that task force won't be so happy about it, so we'll have to be careful not to rub their noses in it," I said.

Candice pointed a finger at me. "Exactly."

"What are we doing after we talk to Michael?"

"Depending on your mood, I thought we might risk an interview with the senator."

"Why does that depend on my mood?" I asked.

"Because I *know* that will get back to Dutch, and he'd be in the hot seat for it. So if you're feeling like you don't want to risk getting him into trouble, then we'll skip it."

I grimaced. "Maybe we should skip it."

"Let's talk to Michael first and see how you feel, but it'll be your call," Candice assured me.

"Okay," I said, already having a bad feeling about it.

A few hours later we arrived in Chicago and I gritted my teeth against the heavy traffic as we slowly made our way over to Michael's school. Glancing at the clock, I was glad Candice had suggested we bring a few extra pairs of clothes, as she suspected we might be in town longer than just the day.

Once we made it onto the campus, it took a little while to find a parking space, but when I mentally handed our need for a slot over to my crew, we found one within about a minute. "You have good parking juju," said Candice as we slid into the spot right in front of Michael's dorm.

"It's the crew," I said, tapping my temple.

We got out and made our way into Michael's dorm. The door was accessible only with a student ID, but Candice overcame this by waiting nonchalantly for a student to walk up and swipe his card, and once the student had entered, she grabbed the door before it closed.

Once in the lobby, Candice consulted her notes and

informed me Michael was on the first floor. We went
through a double set of doors into a very dark hallway
reverberating with loud music and the stench of stale
beer. My feet made a crunching noise and I looked
down to see the carpet littered with cereal, candy
wrappers, and paper. "They don't seem to think highly
of cleanliness," I muttered.

"Did you when you were in school?" Candice
asked.

I thought back. "Not so much," I conceded. "Still,
I'd like to think I was a little neater than this."

We arrived at Michael's door and Candice knocked
loud enough to be heard over the noise in the hallway.
The door was opened about fifteen seconds later by a
short Asian young man with thick glasses and a pronounced overbite. "Hey there," Candice said, flashing him a brilliant smile. "We're looking for Michael
Derby. Is he around?"

The young man ogled her for a full minute before
answering. "Michael's not here. His dad's out of town
and he always stays at the house when the old man's
gone."

"Ah, I see," Candice said, her voice dripping with
sweetness. "He's at the house on Greenwich, right?"

The young man shrugged. "I guess," he said. "I've
never been there."

"Do you mind if we come in and talk to you for a
little while?" she pressed.

I could tell the young man felt a little uncomfortable. He was swallowing a lot and his eyes were large
and unblinking. "Are you guys from the FBI?" he
asked. From his mentioning it to us, it was obvious
they'd beaten us here.

Candice didn't answer him directly, but hinted that
he'd gotten it right by broadening her smile confi-

dently and saying, "You're very observant. I'll bet not a lot gets by you, right?"

To this the boy lifted the corners of his mouth and stepped aside. We entered the dimly lit dorm room to the smell of musty laundry. Once inside I looked around. It was an odd room even for two college boys. Hanging from the ceiling were several models that looked like the latticework of DNA. Yet more models of amazing complexity all but covered one of the desks.

Dirty laundry nearly obscured one corner of the room, and on both unmade beds the linens weren't tucked in at all, just mashed around to cover parts of the mattress. While taking in the room, I tried to keep my face as neutral as possible, especially since I noticed Michael's roommate monitoring us carefully.

"I'm so sorry," said Candice as we entered, "but I don't think I caught your name."

"Cheng," he said, and I couldn't tell if he meant that as his first or his last name.

"It's nice to meet you, Cheng," Candice said warmly, sticking out her hand. "I'm Candice and this is Abby."

Cheng shook Candice's hand awkwardly, giving it two hard pumps, then dropping it. And then he said, "I haven't seen anyone suspicious."

Candice cocked her head slightly. "My associates asked you to keep your eye out for anyone acting suspiciously?"

Cheng nodded.

"Well, I'll bet you've been quite diligent, Cheng. And how is Michael since they paid him a visit?"

"I don't know," Cheng said. "He's been staying at his house for the last two weeks."

"Does his father often go out of town?"

"He's in Washington a lot."

"And Michael always goes to his dad's home when he's not there?"

Cheng nodded.

"And no stranger has approached you about Michael's whereabouts?"

"Only you guys."

Candice smiled again, then changed subjects. "I hear Michael is very smart," she said.

Cheng shrugged. "I guess. He and I usually get the same grades."

"Well then, you must be very smart too."

Another shrug but this time with a blush.

"Are you two close?"

"Huh?"

"Are you friends?"

Cheng looked at her as if he didn't understand her. "I dunno," he said. "We're roommates, so I guess so. I don't really see him a lot. He's at his house more than he's here."

"Did Michael ever talk to you about friends he has at other schools?"

Again Cheng looked confused. "Like who?"

"Like maybe he talked about three other kids that he'd met at a conference. Kids who lived in different states?"

Cheng clearly had no clue what Candice was talking about. "We don't talk a lot about stuff like that," he said.

"What do you talk about?"

"Chemistry and biology," he said simply. "I mean, after that, what else is there?"

I ducked my chin to hide a smile. In a double-entendre kind of way I completely agreed with Cheng. "These models are really cool," I said to him, indicating the DNA hanging from the ceiling.

"Those are Michael's," he said. "He's really got an eye for viruses."

I gave him a curious look. "Viruses?"

Cheng nodded. "That one you're standing next to is hantavirus. The one over there is Ebola."

"Ah," I said, moving quickly away from the models. "Cool."

Candice took a conspicuous glance at her watch and said, "I think we've taken up enough of your time, Cheng. Thanks so much for talking to us."

"Sure," Cheng said, swallowing nervously again.

I waved as I passed him, but he dropped his eyes to the floor. Once Candice and I were out of hearing range, I said, "Nervous little nerd, wasn't he?"

"A little," she agreed. "Wonder why."

We left campus and I followed the directions on the navigator over to the Derby residence. The house we pulled up to was impressive. It had to be at least six or seven thousand square feet in the colonial style with a light tan brick and a shade darker on the shutters. The landscaping was immaculate: every bush trimmed perfectly, not a leaf on the ground, and not a blade of grass out of place. The effect was slightly off-putting and unnatural, like looking at someone who'd gotten too much plastic surgery.

We parked next to a bright blue Jeep Wrangler in the driveway and made our way to the front entrance. Candice rang the bell and we waited for someone to come to the door, but after about forty-five seconds no one had appeared. "Wonder if he's home," she muttered as she pushed the bell again.

I sent my radar to investigate, and I felt sure some-one wasn't just home but watching us carefully. I stepped up to the door and said, "Michael, I know you're in there. We need to talk with you, please."

Five seconds later the door opened a crack and one gray eye stared out at us. "Yeah?"

Candice flashed both her PI badge and her brilliant smile and took command. "Good afternoon, Michael. I'm Candice Fusco and this is Abigail Cooper. I'm sure you've already received a visit from our associates at the FBI, but we were hoping to have a quick word or two with you."

The eye blinked before it swiveled a few times back and forth between Candice and me. Finally, Michael seemed to think it was okay, because he opened the door and let us inside. "Thank you," Candice said, moving past him into the large entryway, which opened up to a huge staircase.

Michael Derby was about five feet eight with dark blond hair and nice features. He was well groomed and clean shaven and nothing about him indicated that he might like spending time in the slovenly dorm room we'd just come from. "I gotta get to class soon," he told us right before his cell phone went off with the awful sound of a metallic mariachi band.

The poor boy quickly yanked his cell out of his pocket and pushed a button, silencing the phone. "Sorry," he muttered, his cheeks reddening.

"No worries," Candice assured him before she got to the point. "We don't want you to be late for your class, so I'll keep it short. We know you've already talked to some of the agents at the bureau, and we know some of our questions will likely be the same as theirs, so I'll keep it quick and not as redundant, okay?"

Michael dipped his chin slightly and crossed his arms. The poor guy looked really nervous and scared.

Candice began the interview by asking him about Leslie, Kyle, and Bianca. "We know that you four hung out at a conference two years ago."

"Yeah," he said.

"Did any of you keep in touch?"

Michael shrugged. "Occasionally," he said. "I mean, Bianca e-mailed me a couple of times right after the conference, but neither one of us really had time to keep it up."

I checked what Michael said against my radar, and was relieved to find he was telling us the truth.

"Did anyone at the conference strike you as out of place or someone maybe who was a little too interested in the four of you?"

Michael looked uneasy. "I dunno. Maybe." Candice waited for him to elaborate and he added, "There was this creepy dude who sorta followed us around and kept listening in on our conversations."

"What conversations was he listening in on?" Candice asked, and I felt a chill go down my spine.

"Mostly about where we liked to go on vacation," Michael said. "Bianca liked to go to her mom's cabin on some lake, and Kyle liked to go to the sand dunes and Leslie said she was going hiking someplace in Wisconsin soon, and right after she said that, this guy starts trying to tell us where he likes to go on vacation."

"And where was that?" Candice asked him.

"He said he liked to go to this place in the UP—"

"The Upper Peninsula?"

"Yeah," Michael said. "And we were all, 'Okay, dude, whatever, we gotta go,' you know?"

Candice nodded like she knew all too well. "Did you see him again?"

"Well, yeah," said Michael. "He followed us into the main conference room and sat near us during the committee meeting that Bianca's dad was chairing, and then right in the middle of it he jumps up and makes this really big scene and was all pissed off and stuff. I told this all to the FBI last night."

"Could you describe him?"

Michael looked impatient. "I already sat with that FBI sketch artist this morning. Do I really have to go over it again?"

"Please," she said, unwavering.

Michael sighed. "He was tall, like, six-one or six-two. He had weird teeth, like they were all jacked up and stuff. And he had this kinda creepy way of looking at you, like he could see inside your soul or something."

"What color was his hair?"

"I dunno. Maybe gray. He didn't have a lot of it—he was kind of bald."

"Did you see him again after he was escorted out of the building?"

"No."

"And what did the other three think of him?"

"They were sort of freaked-out at first, but then they thought it was funny," Michael said, scratching his cheek, then crossing his arms again. "I was the only one that thought he was totally creepy."

Again I checked all that Michael said against my radar, and nothing he'd said seemed fabricated, but there was something I felt I was missing with him—almost like we were asking him the wrong questions, but at the moment I was concentrating too hard on the interview to consider what other questions to ask him.

"I noticed that there's no security detail nearby," Candice said casually, glancing toward the front entrance.

"Yeah, my dad said I didn't need one. He said he'd

be home in the morning and he'd keep an eye on me."

"Your father is a busy man," Candice reasoned. "Why wouldn't he want to ensure that his son was safe while he was otherwise occupied?"

Michael dug his hands into his pockets and his face reddened again. "He doesn't like strangers in the house," he said softly. "And he thought that having the FBI parked in his driveway might make the press curious. They're not really nice to him, you know. They make up crap about my family all the time."

Candice looked at him with sympathy. "So I've heard," she said. "Still, it concerns me that you're on your own here."

"We have an alarm," Michael said, pointing to the wall where an alarm panel was installed. "And I'm being really careful on my way to and from class."

"Has the FBI told you about what's happened to your three friends?" Candice said carefully.

Michael paled. "No," he said after a moment. "They just said that they wanted to check out all the kids my age who attended the conference. When my dad asked why, they said it was because they believed someone might be thinking of kidnapping someone's kid."

"Ah," Candice said, and I knew immediately why the FBI would say that. It was because they didn't want to start a panic among powerful people before they knew what they were up against.

Michael looked at Candice earnestly. "What's happened to them?" he asked, his voice cracking.

"They've gone missing," she said, and I thought, *So much for protocol.* But just then my radar began to hum and a small chill seemed to travel up my spine.

Michael seemed to be having a similar reaction, because his breathing intensified. "Oh, man," he said, and I knew he was now frightened. His eyes seemed to widen and sweat appeared on his forehead. "That's bad, right?"

"It is," said Candice. "Which is all the more reason why you should talk to your dad about letting the FBI assign you a security detail."

And just as she finished that sentence, the chill up my spine intensified and something hit my intuition like a lightning bolt. In my mind's eye I saw a small poster with Michael's picture and the word MISSING as a caption. The image was so intense that I took a step backward, gasping as my hand flew to my heart.

Candice's head snapped over to me and I stared at her in alarm. Michael too seemed to notice my sudden change in demeanor, because he asked, "What's wrong with her?"

"Nothing," I said in a shaky voice before turning to Michael. "Can I use your restroom?" I asked.

He seemed surprised by my request, but he motioned up the steps. "At the top of the stairs," he said.

"Thank you," I said, and bolted. When I'd crested the landing, I went straight into the bathroom and shut the door and sat on the side of the bathtub for a minute trying to take deep breaths. I was used to seeing things that caused me some alarm, but something about the intensity of the vision I'd had downstairs was throwing me. It wasn't just the imagery; it was the level of panic associated with it. My heart was still beating very rapidly. Quickly I pulled my cell phone out of my purse and called Dutch. I got his voice mail and left him a message to call me immediately, then hung up and went to the sink to run some cool water over a clean washcloth to pat my cheeks with. After a minute I felt better and moved to leave.

When I pulled the door open, I was shocked to see

Candice standing there with her hand raised as if she was about to knock. "You okay?" she asked me.

I looked around for Michael. He wasn't in sight. "I need to talk to Dutch," I whispered.

"What's up?"

"Michael's in serious trouble and I don't care what his father says. He needs a security detail assigned pronto."

"You're sure?"

"Positive," I said, feeling a little shaky again as another wave of emotion hit me. "I think our killer is about to go after him."

"What did you see?" she pressed.

"A poster with his picture on it and the word 'Missing' for a caption."

"Shit!"

"I know. Maybe we should keep an eye on him until I can talk to Dutch and he gets an agent assigned."

Candice grabbed my hand and yanked me toward the stairs. "Come on!" she said.

I stumbled after her. "What's the matter?"

"Michael left a few minutes ago. He said he didn't want to be late for class and he took off."

"He *left*?" I gasped as we dashed down the stairs.

Candice glanced at me. "He even punched in the alarm code right in front of me," she said with a mirthless laugh. "Jesus, the kid's so trusting anyone could nab him!"

"We've got to catch up to him, Candice!"

"I know," she said as we reached the bottom of the steps, and Candice moved to the alarm panel, which had a green flashing button like it was in a standby mode. Candice pushed a button on the panel labeled ARMED before she tugged me down a hallway and through the kitchen. "He told me to hit the Armed button and go out through here," she said, pulling open a side door that opened to the garage. Punching the button to the side of the light switch made the garage door creak slowly up. We hurried toward the opening and ducked under the slow-moving door. Candice then pulled up the lid on a side panel mounted on the wall next to the garage, and hit another button, which made the door pause, then creak its way closed again. "Hurry!" she commanded as we dashed toward her car.

I ran to the passenger side and got into the cab fast. There was no question about who would be behind the wheel; Candice didn't have any qualms about driving like a maniac to make up time.

She started the engine and before I even had a chance to pull the seat belt across me, we were rocketing out of the driveway. Tires squealed as she cut the corner and pushed down hard on the accelerator. We wound our way through side streets and I tried not to watch. I also tried not to get carsick.

As we neared campus, she commanded, "Look out on your side for his Jeep!" I did, but it was nowhere to be seen. I even opened up my radar, hoping it would guide me in his general direction, but no information came.

Arriving at Michael's dorm, Candice parked illegally next to a fire hydrant and reached across me to her bag. "I've got his schedule in there," she said. "We'll go to his class and keep him in sight until you can talk to Dutch and get someone else down here to babysit."

As if on cue, my cell phone rang. Caller ID said it was the FBI. "Dutch!" I gasped in relief.

"No," said a hard voice. "It's Agent Harrison."

That brought me up short. I'd been so intent on hearing from Dutch that for a minute I couldn't make any sense of why Harrison was on my phone.

"Tell him that Derby's next class is at Williams Hall, across from the student union!" Candice shouted as her fingers flew over a map of the campus.

My alarm increased. I knew Harrison had heard her very clearly—especially as the silence on his end continued for a beat or two. "Hold on," he said, his voice like ice. "*Where* are you right now, Ms. Cooper?"

"What's he saying?" Candice asked, but didn't wait for my reply. Instead she grabbed the phone right out of my stunned hand. "Dutch, it's Candice. Listen, we need you to get a security detail on the Derby kid ASAP. Abby's had a vision that he's about to be abducted. We're on his tail until you can get an agent assigned. Just tell him to meet us outside Derby's classroom in Williams Hall on the University of Chicago campus."

I was frozen in my seat as I stared at her in horror. She gave me a quick quizzical look and all of a sudden the phone seemed to erupt with noise. Candice immediately pulled it away from her ear and then her eyes also grew wide. Reflexively she hit the End button and dropped the phone in my lap. "Oh, shit!" she said.

"Yep," I agreed. "It has just hit the fan."

Chapter Eleven

I picked the phone up immediately and hit the speed dial, whispering, "Pick up! Pick up! Come on, Dutch, pick up!"

"Hey, sweethot," he sang on the third ring.

"Ohmigod!" I squealed into his ear. "Dutch, you have to listen to me! It wasn't my fault! Candice thought it was you, but it wasn't, and she just sort of blurted out where we were, but I swear *on my life* she didn't mean to! It's not her fault! You can't blame her! I am sooooo sorry!"

"Abs," Dutch said calmly, but I continued to beg forgiveness. "Abby!" he nearly shouted, and I calmed down. "I can't understand what you're saying. Just take a deep breath and tell me what's wrong."

There was a small click in my ear and I knew that Dutch's call-waiting had just signaled. I gasped and shouted, *"Do not answer that!"*

"It's Harrison," he said, and I could hear the confusion in his voice before I sensed that he suddenly caught up to why I was so panicked. "Oh, shit!" he said, echoing Candice's sentiment.

"Dutch, I *swear* it was a total accident!"

"Does he know where you are?"

"Yes."

"Does he know what you're doing where you are?"

"Yes."

There was a pause, then, "I'll call you back." And with that, he hung up and I leaned forward and banged my head a few times against the dash.

"Abby," Candice said gently, but I kept banging. "Hey," she insisted, grabbing my shoulder to prevent another whack. "We've gotta get to Michael, remember?"

"He's going to get fired," I moaned.

She smiled. "It's not his fault," she reasoned, coaxing me out of the car. "We're mavericks, right? Harrison isn't going to blame him for something he had no knowledge of."

I hurried after Candice, my head aching from the pounding I'd just given it and my stomach clenched when I thought about what Dutch must be going through. I felt so bad! If only I'd said something when I realized it was Harrison, like, "Hey there, Agent Harrison! So good of you to call!" If only I had been able to think!

"Come on, honey," Candice urged, grabbing my arm again as I fell behind. "That's the hall where Derby's class is. Let's just make sure he's there. Then we can call Dutch back and tell him what's what." I moaned again and Candice added, "And I can apologize and offer to call Harrison myself to explain, okay?"

Her suggestion made me feel a little better, so I kept up with her as we jogged the last hundred yards and hurried up the steps. Candice kept an eye on the doors of the classrooms, looking for a particular number. She hurried past room 112 to 114 and announced, "This is the one." Without further delay she knocked on the door and opened it, revealing a class of about twelve students all eyeing us curiously. An old man in a bow tie standing in front of the chalkboard asked, "Yes?"

"I'm looking for Michael Derby," she said, still huffing a little from our run. My eyes scanned the students. With a jolt I realized I didn't see Michael among the faces.

"He is not here," said the professor.

Candice looked taken aback. "Oh," she said, "I'm sorry. I thought this was his classroom."

"It is," said the professor. "But Michael has not made it to class today." Candice looked at her watch. I could see from my view that it was ten minutes after two. "Class starts at two, correct?"

"It does," said the professor impatiently. "And if you will allow me to get back to my lesson, it will now continue."

"Sorry!" Candice said, and she shut the door.

"He might be running late," I offered as I noticed her look at her watch again. "Maybe he stopped to get gas, or something to eat," I added, but I had the most terrible sinking feeling.

Candice nodded and stepped back out to the hallway to eye it up and down. "I should have asked for his cell phone number," she muttered.

"He'll show up," I said anxiously, pacing in front of the classroom as my left side felt thick and heavy.

Candice shook her head ruefully. "Damn it!" she swore. "Come on, Michael, don't do this."

I glanced again at my cell phone and made a decision. I flipped through the most recent call list and hit Send. The line was answered almost immediately. "I ought to throw both you in jail for interfering in a federal investigation against my express order!" Harrison roared.

"Yes, sir," I said as calmly as I could. "And I wouldn't blame you if you did. However, sir, there is an issue that demands your immediate attention. And if after I tell you what that is, you still want to haul us to jail, then we will go quietly and cooperatively."

Harrison appeared surprised by my proposal because it was a moment before he said anything. Finally, though, he barked "What?" so loudly I winced.

"Michael Derby did not show up for class, sir. He is currently MIA."

"Where's his security detail?" Harrison barked again.

"His father refused them, sir. When Candice and I went to talk to Michael, we discovered him alone and heading to class. We attempted to trail him, sir, but we lost him shortly after he left his home. So we came here to campus in search of him, but his class started over fifteen minutes ago and there's been no sign of him."

There was a very long pause and for a minute I thought I'd lost Harrison. But then, just as I was about to call out to him, I heard him say, "Stay put. Do not move. Watch out for Derby, and if he shows up, call me immediately."

"Yes, sir," I said meekly, and the line went dead.

I tucked my cell back into my purse and looked up to meet Candice's eyes. "Are we going to jail, Abs?"

I sighed. "Not sure. Could go either way."

"What'd Harrison say?"

"He said to stay put."

Candice nodded and then took to impatiently pacing the hallway.

Time ticked slowly by, both of us watching for Derby. As Candice and I watched the hallway for any sign of either Michael or the FBI, my radar gave me a hint.

"Hey," I said to my partner to grab her attention away from peering earnestly down the hallway.

"What's up?"

"I'm not sure, but I keep getting a strong hit off of the Derby house."

Candice's brow furrowed. "You think Michael might be there?"

My left side felt heavy. "No," I said, scratching my head. "But for some reason I feel like there's something there. Something we might have overlooked."

Candice considered that for a minute. "The kid was awfully fidgety," she agreed. "And scared."

"Maybe he was just being cautious."

"You think he knew something?"

"Yeah," I said. "I think someone or something had him running scared."

Candice sighed and rubbed her neck. "If someone grabbed him while we weren't looking, I'll never forgive myself."

"We don't know that he's been abducted," I cautioned, but then the poster in my head flashed again and I felt a tremendous sense of dread.

"What?" she asked me, and I knew she'd caught the worried look on my face.

"I don't have a great feeling," I admitted.

Candice frowned. "Damn it!" she swore, and went back to pacing.

Finally, at ten minutes to, and when we began to see students emerging from other classrooms, Candice stepped to the door of Derby's class and opened it. "Sorry to interrupt again," she said to the room. "But does anyone happen to have Michael Derby's cell phone number? It's a matter of extreme urgency."

One student in the back row raised his hand. "I've got it."

The professor glared hard at Candice and threw up his arms. "In light of all these interruptions, I suppose we will end class on that note," he snapped, and he began stuffing his briefcase with his notes. "Mr. Jackson, please give the woman Michael's number so that she will stop interrupting classes!"

Jackson stepped forward sheepishly and scrolled through his cell phone's directory. Pivoting the screen around, he showed it to Candice, who hurriedly punched the numbers into her own phone. "Thanks," she said before putting her cell up to her ear and walking back out into the hallway. After several anxious beats she grimaced and shook her head, then said, "Hi, Michael, it's Candice Fusco. We talked at your home a little while ago, and there was just one more question I needed to ask you. Could you please call me back at this number as soon as possible? It's really important. I absolutely, positively need to hear from you the moment you get this message."

She hung up and motioned me over to the far end of the corridor. "What's your gut say?"

I looked down at the ground. It almost hurt to say it out loud. "It's too late," I whispered. "We're too late. Something really bad just happened, Candice."

She was quiet, and as the students streamed past us, she took my arm and led me out of the hallway and onto the street. "We were supposed to wait for the Feds," I protested.

"Yeah, I know," she replied. "But I hear the food in

jail sucks. How about I treat you to something a little more to your liking? Something spicy and loaded with calories."

"Harrison will be furious," I cautioned.

"When is he not?" she shot back.

"Good point," I said. "Let's go."

Thirty minutes later Candice's car was parked in the back lot of a large mall. She'd made me drive while she fiddled with her phone, and after we parked, she unloaded all her gear and advised me to do the same. "We're taking our stuff into the mall?" I asked, reaching for my duffel bag.

"No," she said. "We're catching that bus." And she motioned across the street to a city bus.

"We are?"

"Yep."

"Why don't we just take the car?"

"Because Harrison will have its description and plate number out on every police blotter in town."

"Please do not tell me we are running from the law *again*!"

"Desperate times call for desperate measures, Sundance," she sang as she ran for the bus. I had no choice but to follow.

I joined her in the back of the crowded bus and we passed up four stops before she motioned us off. I had no idea where we were, but Candice had her trusty iPhone and seemed to be following a map on the screen just fine. After walking two blocks, we came to a quant Mexican cantina and my stomach grumbled in earnest.

As we took our seats, my cell rang. I showed Candice the ID, which read *FBI*, and she said, "Let it go to voice mail."

I waited out the rings and bounced my knee anxiously as I imagined either Dutch or Harrison leaving a message. When I felt it'd been long enough, I dialed into my voice mail and heard Dutch's voice say crisply, "Call me."

I did as ordered and he picked up before the first ring ended. "Where are you?"

"At dinner," I said.

"Abby . . . ," he warned.

"Blame my sidekick," I said coolly. "It's all her fault." Candice stuck her tongue out at me and I held in a laugh.

"You need to come in," Dutch said evenly. "I mean it."

By now Candice was leaning in so that she could hear our conversation. To make it easier on everybody, I hit the speaker function and she said, "We will, Dutch. But not tonight, okay?"

"Candice, this is serious shit," Dutch cautioned. "Harrison isn't kidding around anymore. He's had it with you two, and he's had it with me."

"I get it, buddy," she said agreeably. "And I promise we'll make it right. And we'll be in touch." With that, she clicked the End button before I even had a chance to say good-bye.

"I don't want him to get into any more trouble," I told her.

She looked at me with sympathy. "There's really no avoiding it. But maybe we can help undo a little damage." Candice then punched a few digits into her own phone and waited with a perky little smile. I heard the muffled sound of someone answering and then she said, "Good evening, Agent Harrison. It's Candice Fusco." The muffled buzzing sound coming through the earpiece intensified, like a hornet's nest that'd just been poked. But Candice remained cool and collected. "Yes, sir, I'm aware. But you see, we did wait for your agent and they never arrived. We then decided to go to a more convenient location on campus, but we got hungry, so we thought we'd eat first."

I shook my head in amazement. She was playing a dangerous game here. "What's that?" she asked after a short pause and lots of buzzing. "Yes, I know you're furious, sir, and I understand you're ready to toss our butts in jail. And I truly am sorry. However, we feel that by hampering you right now with a lot of pesky paperwork at our expense it would take your focus off the task at hand, which is to find Michael Derby. I would suggest sending an agent immediately to his home to see if he's there. I would also suggest sending word to his father and encouraging him to try to contact Michael. And, of course, sir, if we have any more information that we feel may be relevant, yours will be the first number we dial."

With that, Candice clicked off and beamed me a snarky smile. "If that man doesn't kill you, I will be truly amazed," I told her.

"Maybe he'll spontaneously combust first," Candice said wistfully.

I laughed and toasted her with the margarita the waitress had just set down in front of us.

After dinner we went shopping. Of course, it wasn't the fun kind of shopping where you look for a cute little dress with some really cool shoes and the perfect accessories; no, our kind of shopping was more like what you'd buy for a B&E. "Here," Candice said, handing me a pair of black leather pants.

"Leather?" I said skeptically. "Really?"

"They're warm and functional and you'll look great

in them," Candice said before handing me a tight black knit shirt from another rack.

"Are we going to the club afterward?" I asked sarcastically.

"We may," she said, motioning me over to hats and gloves. "Here," she said, shoving some black leather gloves and a black scarf at me.

I looked at the entire suspicious ensemble in my hands. "And *no one* will ever suspect what we're up to!"

Candice gave me a weathered look. "Leather coats are over there. Come on, Sundance."

Several hours later Candice and I were hiding in a row of bushes along the side of the house next door to the Derby's. We'd already checked into a low-budget hotel under one of the many fake IDs that Candice had on hand, and then we'd taken a cab to a neighboring subdivision and walked a mile or so over to Derby's.

I sat down on the damp ground and rubbed my aching feet, which I was sure were blistered by the new black leather boots Candice had made me buy. "I think you're a little paranoid," I grouched.

"What do you mean?" she asked absently while she peered out of the bushes at Derby's house.

"I mean that there was no reason why the cabbie couldn't have dropped us a little closer. Did we really have to walk the extra mile?"

Candice swiveled round to give me an encouraging smile. "Better safe than sorry, Abs," she said.

"What I don't understand is how you think we won't get caught breaking into Derby's house. I mean, didn't *you* tell Harrison to send an agent over here?"

Candice's smile widened. "I did. And if I were

him, I would have sent an agent right away, and I would have told him to wait for a few hours, and then I would have assumed the kid wasn't coming back home, and I would have focused my resources on campus and anyplace an eighteen-year-old kid might frequent."

"So you don't think they're watching the house for Michael's possible return?"

"Oh, I didn't say that," Candice said, glancing back at the dark house.

"I'm confused," I whined.

"Harrison would have pulled his agent off the surveillance—he wouldn't want to spare one of his guys for babysitting duty. What I would do in his position would be to call the local PD and have a patrol drive by every so often looking for any signs that Michael might be home, like his Jeep or a light on in the house or something."

At that exact moment headlights flashed out on the road. I held my breath and watched in amazement as a patrol car came into view and parked right in front of the Derbys' house. A spotlight was flashed on and pointed into their yard and I instinctively ducked.

Anxious seconds ticked by and the spotlight was turned off just before the patrol car moved on down the road. Candice squeezed my arm. "Told ya so," she sang softly.

"I'll never doubt you again," I said, letting go of the breath I'd been holding.

"Come on," she urged. "We've probably got about twenty minutes to a half hour before they swing by again."

Candice moved out of the bushes and darted across the front lawn of the Derby residence. I followed her crouched posture as she angled toward the left side of the house, near the garage, before ducking even lower and edging around the corner. Once we were in the shadows of the side of the house, she edged carefully along, heading for the back door, and peering through windows as she went. Once we were by the back door, Candice pulled out her iPhone from her coat pocket and tapped the screen a few times.

"Who are you calling?" I asked, shocked that she would choose now to make a phone call.

"I want to make sure Michael isn't here," she said. "If he is, we might hear his phone ring inside."

My mind flashed back to that awful ringtone that had echoed around the front hallway when Candice and I had talked to him earlier in the day. "What if he turned his phone off?" I asked.

"You ever met an eighteen-year-old who turned his phone off?" she asked me. "Kids don't start powering down their cell phones until they get out of school and join the rat race."

Candice lifted the cell to her ear and faintly I could hear it ringing through the earpiece, but all remained quiet inside the house. When Michael's phone went to voice mail, Candice again left him an urgent message and clicked off. "Time to go in," she said.

"How exactly are you planning on getting inside?" I asked doubtfully.

Candice smiled sweetly. "I *may* have undone the dead bolt on the back door before I came up and got you from the bathroom."

"You left his house *unlocked*?" I gasped.

"No," she said innocently as she moved to the door. "It's locked, see?" and she pulled on the handle to prove to me that it was locked. "It's just not locked as securely as usual." With that she took out a very thin piece of plastic and began to slowly jimmy it in be-

tween the doorjamb and the door. I bit my lower lip as
I watched the process. Finally with one last little push
the catch released and Candice stood up triumphantly
as she pushed open the door. Before she had a chance
to celebrate, however, we both heard the high-pitched
warning of the alarm box sounding. We had thirty seconds to type in a code.

Candice moved quickly into the kitchen and over
to the alarm panel. She punched in a code and the
box squeaked once; then a light on the top went solid
green.

"Man," I said appreciatively, "I am just glad you're
my friend and not my enemy."

Candice's smile broadened. "Come on, Sundance,
let's spread out. You take the first floor, I'll take the
second. If anything looks interesting, text me and I'll
be right down, and remember, we need to be out of
here in fifteen minutes."

I didn't comment how crazy I thought she was to
believe that I'd find anything of value in that short
span of time, deciding to argue later when my stomach
wasn't doing so many flip-flops.

Candice shoved a small flashlight into my hands
and moved quickly toward the stairs. I clicked on the
beam and began opening drawers in the kitchen. Finding only the usual cooking utensils and junk drawer, I
searched the countertops. Nothing there. I glanced at
my watch. I'd wasted three minutes.

Hurrying out of the kitchen and into the main hallway, I thought for a moment about my options. To my
left was the living room and, beyond that, what was
likely a den. To my right was the dining room and beyond that I didn't know. My radar tugged on my right
side, so I didn't think twice—I moved off in that direction, allowing my crew to direct me.

Skipping two closed doors, I came to the end of a long corridor, guessing I was now behind the garage when I got to the last door. My intuition told me this was a room I needed to look into, so I opened the door and shone the beam inside. "Jackpot," I whispered when I realized I'd just found Michael's room.

Stepping inside, I flashed the light all around the room, wondering where I should start. Unlike Michael's dorm room, his bedroom was quite tidy—save for the unmade bed and a few clothes scattered on the floor, it was uncluttered and well kept. Moving to the closet, I opened the door. His wardrobe stared back. My radar continued to buzz, but not with any specifics.

I went next to his desk and opened a drawer. Nothing but pens, pencils, erasers, and other knickknacks in there. I opened another drawer and found a stack of textbooks and old notebooks probably left over from the previous semester. Quizzically I opened a notebook and skimmed the first few pages. Michael had taken meticulous notes, his handwriting neat and orderly, and all the subject matter, I noticed with chagrin, was *way* over my head. While I was glancing at his notes, my radar chimed in my head and I looked up. "What?" I asked out loud.

My attention was pulled toward Michael's bed. I pointed my flashlight at the rumpled bed linen, but I couldn't understand what I was supposed to be seeing.

Again I heard another chime in my head and I knew my crew wanted me to investigate the bed.

Setting the notebook back in the drawer, I edged over to the bed and stared down at it, waiting for whatever I was supposed to see to reveal itself. When my eye didn't spot anything suspicious, I began lifting up the bedspread and the sheets, looking for what I didn't know. After searching every square inch, I stood back and eyed it in frustration. My radar was still pulling me toward it.

I got down on my hands and knees and shone the light under the bed. Lots of dust bunnies and a few odd socks reflected in the beam but certainly nothing of interest. I stood back up and put my hands on my hips. "What?" I said out loud as my frustration mounted.

My attention was drawn back to the bed—specifically to the area near the headboard. With a growl I pulled the bedspread completely off; then I tugged off the top sheet. Nothing. There were a lot of extra pillows at the head. I pulled those off one by one, and as I got the last one off, I noticed in the far corner of the bed, right next to the wall was an odd-looking lump.

I got on the mattress and ran my hands over it, noting that it felt like a flat book. Quickly I pulled off the bottom sheet, revealing the mattress pad. The lump was between it and the mattress, so I lifted the corner of the pad off too and found a lavender notebook.

"Whatcha doing?" Candice said from behind me, and I shrieked and fell off the bed.

"Jesus, Abby!" Candice gasped, coming to help me get up again. "You're a little jumpy."

I placed a hand over my heart, which was thumping wildly in my chest. "Gee, Candice, ya *think*?!"

Candice smiled and motioned to the bed. "Better put that back together," she said. "We gotta split."

I nodded and handed her the notebook as I rushed to put the bed back the way I'd found it. "What's this?" she asked, glancing down at the notebook.

"I don't know," I admitted, tugging sheets and pillows back into place. "But my crew thinks there's something in there that we need to look at, and Michael had it hidden under pillows and sheets."

"Cool, we'll read it when we get back to the hotel."

"Did you find anything interesting?" I said as I went to Michael's desk and closed all the drawers I'd opened, setting it back exactly as I'd found it.

"Nada," she said with a sigh. "The old man doesn't leave much out in the open. And you should see his closet! Oh, hey, did you know he's got some woman living here with him?"

"He does?" I asked, turning to her in surprise.

"Yep. And she likes to dress a little on the slutty side, if you want my opinion."

Closing the drawers and looking around Michael's desk, I gave Candice the thumbs-up. "Okay, everything looks like I found it. Let's get out of here."

We moved soundlessly back through the house again to the kitchen. Candice set the alarm and waved at me to exit. We were just closing the door when we saw a beam of light shine through the house all the way into the kitchen. "Eeek!" I squeaked, and Candice clamped a hand over my mouth.

"Shhhhh!" she hissed. She then pulled me deeper into the backyard and over to the walled fence that enclosed the yard.

"We're trapped!" I whispered as I felt the panic rising and I thought about the patrol car out front.

"Here," Candice said calmly, stooping down and forming a cup with her hands. "Step up and climb over."

I stared at her hands for a long moment, trying to make sense of what she wanted me to do. Candice didn't wait for it to sink in. Instead she lifted my leg off the ground and cupped her hands under the sole of my boot. "Grab on to my shoulder for support," she ordered, and in another moment I was lifted high in the air.

I clutched at the top of the wall and swung my leg up, hugging the rim as I panted for breath. Just to the side of me I heard Candice grunt and smack the top of the wall with both hands. She groaned with the effort to pull herself up, then tugged hard on my arm as she dangled over the other side and dropped to the ground. I let go and followed after her—although a bit less artfully.

She was already brushing off the dirt and grinning at me when we heard something growl on the other side of the yard.

"What was that?" I squeaked as my mouth went dry.

Candice's eyes became huge as she turned slowly to look behind her, just before she had my arm and was yanking me forward. "*Run!*" she shouted in my ear.

I took two leaps forward before I heard that deep growl turn into an angry bark, and then all I heard was the sound of four heavy paws charging across the earth. Reflexively I looked over my shoulder and nearly stumbled as the most massive dog I've ever seen chased us down and threatened to tear our throats out.

Chapter Twelve

Candice and I barely made it out of that yard alive. My new leather coat wasn't so lucky. Cujo got hold of my sleeve and I almost didn't manage to escape with my arm intact. Luckily the mutt liked fine Italian leather almost as much as I did.

"That son of a bitch!" I said, breathing hard as we toppled over yet another wall to the grounds outside.

"You okay?" Candice asked me.

"I'm fine," I grumbled while Cujo continued to growl and bark and eat my coat.

A light went on inside the house; we crouched down and waited a moment before Candice motioned for me to follow her.

We dashed across the street to another row of houses and stuck to the bushes, slowly making our way out of the neighborhood as quickly as we could without being spotted.

The patrol car cruised up and down the street—no doubt having been called by Cujo's owner and having the torn remains of a leather jacket on hand to confirm that someone was prowling around the neighborhood. Eventually we emerged from a small patch of woods on the edge of the subdivision and next to a street where several cars whizzed past us and one or two honked as we made our way toward a corner gas station. I walked as close to the inner edge of the shoulder as I could, so as to give Candice enough room on the shoulder not to get hit. Traffic might have been lighter than usual, but at this time of night there was no telling how sober the people driving were.

As if to prove my point, I heard a car approaching us at a fast speed and I turned my head just in time to grab Candice's arm and yank her hard. She barely missed being hit, and as if that weren't bad enough, the car suddenly skidded to a halt with tires screeching as it kicked up a little smoke in the process.

Candice stepped in front of me and I watched with mounting panic as she took up a defensive posture. "If there's trouble," she said through gritted teeth as the car door opened, "you run for that gas station and don't look back."

Trouble was exactly what stepped out of the car, but there was no way I was going to run for it. Judging by the furious expression on the man facing us, I doubted I'd get ten feet before I was shot. "Get in," he commanded, loud enough to be heard over the traffic, but not quite shouting.

Candice relaxed her defensive position and said, "Evening, Agent Harrison. You're looking better than I would have expected for someone who's just been in a plane crash."

His eyes narrowed and his lips thinned as they pressed firmly together. "Get ... in ... the ... *car!*" he roared.

I dropped my chin and tugged on Candice's coat. "I

think we better do as he says." Then, without waiting for her to answer, I ducked over to the opposite side of his car and hurried into the backseat.

I turned in the seat and watched Candice walk calmly over to the other door and open it, smiling wide at Harrison as she smoothly got in.

Harrison slammed her door and then got back into the front seat, his cast making it obviously difficult to steer the car, and likely why he came so close to hitting us out on the road.

He didn't say a word, but the tension inside the car was thick. Candice, however, looked like she was enjoying a nice drive in the country and that happy grin never left her face the whole time we were moving.

Harrison took us into downtown and then into a parking garage. I got a little nervous at the setting, as there was no one around and he still seemed really mad. I wondered whether he might torture us for a while with a Taser gun or something, but he parked near a door and lifted his eyes to the mirror. "One false move from either of you and I will bring down a world of hurt on you so fast it'll make your heads spin."

Candice rolled her eyes, completely unfazed, and opened the door.

"We'll be good," I promised. I seriously didn't know how she could be so cool. I was scared shitless.

We followed Harrison, who was walking with a bit of a limp, through the door to an elevator and rode up two floors. Exiting the elevator, we followed obediently behind him to a double set of glass doors. He swiped his badge through a slot to the right of the entry, and a green light above the doors flashed. Harrison pushed them open with his good arm and motioned us through.

Inside we again followed him over to another set

of elevators and waited while the boxcar descended from the sixth floor. We loaded onto the car and rode up, then stepped out into a brightly lit space divided by cubicles. "This way," he growled, and he led us straight down the middle of the cubicles to an open space at the far end of the room.

As we got close, I could hear muffled voices, and as we drew still closer, I recognized one of them with a pang of guilt. We finally came to a stop among a group of very surprised but very tired-looking men wearing dress slacks and wrinkled shirts with loose ties. "Abby?" I heard Dutch say from off to my right.

"Hey, cowboy," I replied with a small wave.

"Hiya, Dutch!" Candice added exuberantly.

"Sit!" Harrison ordered, obviously irritated by our reunion. Turning to Dutch, he commanded, "Agent Rivers, come with me into the conference room. Now."

"Yes, sir," Dutch said, and eyed me with irritation.

"Crap," I mumbled as they walked away.

"He'll be okay," Candice assured me. "This is just Harrison's way of keeping you in line from now on. He'll yell at your boyfriend the minute you do something stupid, like run around with me."

"Did you have to antagonize him?" I asked. I was really worried about Dutch, especially as we could clearly hear Harrison begin to yell.

"He doesn't scare me," Candice said, looking casually at her nails. "He's all bark and no bite."

I sighed and glanced up, suddenly conscious that we were being stared at by the other agents in the room. "Hey," I said to them.

They all looked away and began whispering to one another. I pouted in my seat and let my eyes wander. Straight ahead was a whiteboard much like the one

Candice and I had used, but taped to the board were pictures of the four missing kids. I shied away from looking at the crime-scene images around Bianca and Kyle and focused on the other two. And then I noticed something that caused me to inhale sharply and sit bolt upright in my chair.

"What's the matter?" Candice asked. When I didn't respond, she said, "Hey, Sundance. Talk to me."

I ignored her and got up, dashing over to the whiteboard. I traced my fingers over Leslie Coyle's photo, the very image that her mother had handed to me only two days before. "Oh, God!" I said, and I started shaking.

Candice was at my side in an instant. "What's happened?" she whispered.

I ignored her and shouted, "No!" as moisture formed in my eyes. "That son of a bitch!" I slammed my hand on the whiteboard with a loud *thwack*, before dissolving into tears.

Candice reached around to hug me tightly and whispered in my ear, "Hey, now," she said. "Take it easy, honey."

"We're too late!" I sobbed, pulling away from her. I was so angry and upset that we'd utterly failed Leslie that I didn't want to be comforted. "We blew it, Candice! We didn't find her in time."

"What's going on?" I heard Harrison's commanding voice say behind me.

"Leslie Coyle's been murdered," Candice said, turning to him.

He stared in shock at us for a beat or two, before he asked, "How do you know?"

"*I* don't," Candice said.

"But Abby does," Dutch guessed, his eyes looking intently at me. "It's her photo, right?" he asked me.

I nodded. "She was alive only two days ago, Dutch! That bastard's killed her within the last forty-eight hours."

"How can she tell?" Harrison said to Dutch, and I noticed that he asked it curiously, not doubtfully.

"It's the way the image looks to her," Dutch explained. "If she focuses on a picture of a person and the image appears flat, or two-dimensional, then she knows they're deceased."

"How accurate is she?" Harrison asked as he stepped over to the whiteboard to pull down Leslie's photo.

"One hundred percent, sir."

Harrison's face turned grave as he considered Dutch, then me, then Leslie's photo. The other agents in the room looked at one another with a mixture of confusion and concern. Dutch came over to me and wrapped me in his arms, and I knew I was forgiven and accepted comfort now without protest. "That's why Michael was abducted," I said. "The killer took out Leslie and that left him with an opening."

A hush fell on the room as everyone seemed to consider that. "Can you find her?" Harrison said to me, holding out the image of Leslie.

I looked at the flat appearance of the young girl so full of promise and choked back a sob. With some effort I collected myself and said, "I need to calm down. Can you give me a quiet room so that I can focus?"

Harrison pointed with his cast toward the conference room he and Dutch had just exited. "You can have a seat in there," he said. I started to walk toward the room and I heard him add, "Can we get you anything, Ms. Cooper? A glass of water or something to eat?"

"Water, please," I said without looking back, and

hurried toward the conference room before I had another meltdown.

Once behind the closed doors I sat on the floor in the corner and cried. I felt so responsible for not coming up with the answer in time, but I'd thought we'd had a little bit more than two days to find her. Something seemed to have sped up the timeline and I didn't know what. I huddled there with my knees pulled up and my head down and let the tears fall.

This had happened to me once before, when I'd acted too late to save someone in time, and then, as now, I felt the weight of the responsibility firmly on my shoulders and how I'd failed the people who'd counted on me the most. I thought about Leslie's parents and winced as I pictured how they might take the news. This would destroy them—I knew it would. It would shatter their calm bravado and tear out their hearts. I'd let them down. I'd let her down. I'd let everyone down.

I heard the door open and imagined that either Dutch or Candice had come in to check on me. I wiped my eyes and looked up and was shocked to see Agent Harrison step into the room with a bottle of water. He saw me sitting on the floor and considered me for a moment before he shut the door and came over to sit down next to me. For a long time neither one of us spoke, and somehow that made me feel a little better.

Finally, he broke the silence by cracking the seal on the water bottle and handing it to me. "Drink a little," he suggested.

I nodded and took a sip, then wiped my eyes. "You must think I'm pathetic," I said.

"Emotional I'll give you," he said calmly. "Along with hot-tempered, irrational, and maybe even a bit delusional, but pathetic? Not so much."

I was stunned by his assessment, but when I turned to look at him, I saw that he was wearing a slight smirk. And then I started to laugh. In the back of my mind I thought how crazy it was that I could be crying one minute and guffawing the next, and I tried to compose myself, but then I heard Harrison chuckle and that made me laugh even harder.

Finally, though, I managed to get hold of my emotions and I wiped my eyes and took another sip of water. "You okay now?" he asked.

"Yeah."

With a grimace of discomfort Harrison stood. "Good. Now focus on finding Leslie. You give me a description of where her body is and hopefully we can narrow our search. And here," he added, handing me the picture from the whiteboard of Michael. "Try and give me anything you can about where you think he might be while you're at it."

"Yes, sir."

With that, Harrison left the room.

I took a deep breath and got up and moved to the conference table. Sitting down, I pulled close to me a pad of paper and a pen that were lying on the surface, and then focused on Leslie's photo. I closed my eyes and called out to my crew for help. I got much of the same imagery as before when I'd told Dutch where I thought she was being held, but this time I kept smelling something like antiseptic. I opened my eyes and jotted the word down on the paper. I concentrated again and begged for more information, but I kept getting the same clues over and over. A large area that was enclosed by concrete. Lots of chairs and the smell of antiseptic. There was also something else here that I couldn't quite grasp, but the energy of the area really upset me. It felt chaotic and dark and full of despair. I knew intuitively that there were grounded spirits in this place and lots of them. Wherever Leslie was, ghosts were abundant and they felt agitated and malcontented.

I shivered involuntarily. "Jesus, honey," I whispered to her image. "*Where* are you?"

I fought for another ten minutes to come up with more, but it seemed there was nothing new to pull out of the ether other than what I'd already gotten. It all felt disjointed and disconnected, and I was so frustrated because I knew I was so close to pinpointing where she was, but I seemed to be missing the one thing that would tie it all together.

Taking a deep breath, I moved on to Michael. Immediately, I felt the very same images that I'd gotten for Leslie and I felt all the air leave my lungs. The killer had him in the same haunting location. I wondered whether all the ghosts that I felt around their energy were other unknown victims. But the thing that I found most frightening was that the killer had obviously changed his pattern. He wasn't killing his victims shortly after abduction. He was saving them for this concrete dungeon, perhaps to torture them for months before finally doing away with them.

I felt my stomach clench and I thought about what horrors he might expose them to, and it was a long time before I trusted my hands not to shake as I got up and went to the door.

I was surprised to see Candice, pacing back and forth just outside. "Hey!" she said when I opened the door, and then her eyes became pinched as she scrutinized my face. "How're you doing?"

"Not good," I admitted. "Are Dutch and Harrison around?"

"I'll round them up," she said. "You go sit down. You look like you're about to drop."

I did feel a little woozy, so I followed her instruction and sat heavily down in the chair while I waited for the cavalry. Harrison, Dutch, Candice, and all the other agents filed into the conference room, which surprised me because I hadn't thought they would take seriously what I had to offer.

As Dutch sat down, he shoved a bag of cashews at me. "Eat something," he ordered, and he looked as concerned as Candice did over my appearance.

"Thanks," I said, popping a few nuts into my mouth. When everyone was seated, Harrison gave me a nod to begin. I stood up and pulled close the pad of paper I'd written on. "Leslie's body and Michael—who I believe is still alive—are in the same location," I announced, and waited for everyone to take that in. "I know I've given a few of these clues to Agent Rivers, but I think I may have gotten a tiny bit more about the physical description of the place.

"The structure they're hidden in is large, but the specific area of that structure where they are located is at least one level belowground. There are no windows that I can sense and no other persons present, which is unusual for such a large structure, so I would venture to say that this might be some sort of abandoned building. There is also lots of seating in the particular room where Leslie and Michael are. It might be an old theater or small stadium of some kind. But the truly curious thing is that I smell a lot of antiseptic, and the only thing I can equate that to is a hospital."

I paused to look around the room. Every face staring back wore the same confused look. "I know it sounds odd," I said to them. "But these are the physical clues that I'm able to pick up on. They describe a structure's characteristics, not necessarily what that structure is utilized for."

"So, we're looking for a small stadiumlike theater-slash-hospital that's partially underground?" asked one agent.

I gulped. "Something like that," I said.

"Abs," Dutch said. "Could it be that the place used to be a hospital and was converted into a theater?"

I let go a big breath and said, "Yes! It absolutely could be that. Which would explain the ghosts too."

"What ghosts?" Candice asked.

"The place is totally haunted," I said. "Lots of grounded energies who are super agitated. And the general atmosphere there is just god-awful! There's this unsettling quality about it, like lots of terrible things happened there over a long period of time. It's no wonder, then, that it's haunted."

And that's when I knew I'd said a little too much because every face in the room save Dutch's and Candice's turned incredulous, then comical. "*Ghosts?*" said Agent Blass from across the room. "Sir," he added, looking at Harrison as if he had to be kidding, "is this bullshit for *real*?"

Harrison didn't have time to answer because Candice came immediately to my defense. "Instead of questioning whether Abby is for real, Agent Blass, I would suggest that you remember that the information she supplied earlier led you *directly* to Kyle New-house when this task force had no leads and had made no progress in locating him for *months*!"

There was a small eruption of noise as Blass took offense and some of his buddies, including Agent Albright, came to his defense, and both Dutch and Candice spat a few more defensive remarks at them until Harrison stood up abruptly and everything got quiet.

"Thank you, Ms. Cooper," he said quietly. "We will take your information under advisement."

"Sure, you will," muttered Candice, and Harrison's eyes narrowed at her.

"Agent Rivers," Harrison said next. "Please escort these two to the airport. I've booked them on the six a.m. shuttle back to Detroit."

"I've got a car in town," Candice growled. I knew she didn't like it when Harrison played travel agent.

"Agent Rivers can drive it back for you," Harrison said coolly. His look suggested there was no way he was trusting us to drive ourselves home, and I had to give him credit for that, as I knew Candice would have found a way to stick around if given the license.

Dutch looked a little surprised and glanced at his watch. I knew we had about two hours to catch the flight, and given that our luggage was still at our hotel room on the other side of town, we'd be sprinting to make it. "Yes, sir," he said, getting up and motioning me and Candice along.

We followed behind Dutch to the parking garage, and Candice muttered and grumbled the entire way. "Spineless jerk!" she growled. "How the hell am I supposed to get around without a car?"

Dutch reached into his pocket and handed her some keys. "Here," he said. "You guys can catch a cab home from the airport and you can drive my car until I come back to town with yours."

Candice took the keys and grumbled some more, but she eventually handed him her keys and gave him the location of her SUV at the mall. Then she continued to sputter and grumble and grouse under her breath.

"Who exactly are you angry at?" I asked when we got to Dutch's company car.

"Harrison," she spat. "Who else?"

I thought back to how he'd sat with me in the conference room and made me feel better. "He's not so bad, you know," I said.

"Of course he is, Abby!" Candice snapped, jerking the car door open and sitting down in a huff. "Did he defend you even *once*? Has he openly acknowledged even *one* time what an asset you've been to this investigation?"

I opened my mouth to reply, but Candice was already answering her own question. "No! He doesn't defend you. He doesn't take you seriously—he doesn't consider anything you offer him to have any kind of value! He's a pompous, no-good ignoramus who couldn't find his way out of a paper bag with a map, a tour guide, and runway lights!"

I glanced at Dutch in the seat next to me, but he had his head positioned so that Candice couldn't see him, even though I could tell he was quietly laughing. "Candice, I think that maybe he's just trying to keep the peace with all these other branches being involved," I said, trying to give Harrison the benefit of the doubt.

"Bah!" Candice scoffed from the backseat as she crossed her arms. "The man's a world-class idiot, Abby!"

I looked pointedly at Dutch. "What?" he asked.

"Tell her he's not such a bad guy."

"No way," he said, glancing at her furious figure in the backseat. "Too risky."

I sighed heavily and buckled my seat belt. I was exhausted and I still had two hours to go before I could catch a catnap on the shuttle home. Candice continued to grumble all the way to the hotel, then all the way to the airport. She barely stopped long enough to thank Dutch for the ride and wish him luck with the rest of the case. "With that asshole at the helm, you're going to need it," she said, wanting to have the last word.

Once we were in the check-in line for our flight, Candice reached behind and under her shirt as she pulled out the lavender notebook that she'd stuffed into the back of her pants many hours ago. "Holy cow!" I said when she pulled it out. "You've had that thing wedged against your skin this whole time?"

Her expression was sober. "Well, I wasn't very well going to parade the evidence of our B&E out for the FBI, now, was I?"

"I'm surprised that Harrison didn't question us about being caught so close to the Derbys'."

"I'm sure he was about to when you informed him that Leslie had been killed." I blanched and Candice said quickly, "Hey, don't go there, Sundance. You know it's not your fault."

"Maybe not entirely," I said. "But I still can't help feeling responsible."

"How could you feel responsible?" she demanded.

"I knew we were running out of time, but I still thought we had longer than two days to find her."

"How long did you think we had?"

I shrugged. "Maybe a week to ten days."

Candice came to the same conclusion I had. "Something sped up the timetable."

I nodded. "Yes."

Candice pursed her lips and flipped open the lavender notebook, glancing at the contents for the first time. I leaned in to look over her shoulder. The notebook was basically empty of content. There were a lot of empty pages after the first two, but on those first pages something struck me. I recognized the handwriting. "No way!" I said, yanking the notebook out of her hands.

"What?"

"This was Bianca's!" I said. I would recognize her distinctive, overly loopy *b*'s, *p*'s, and *g*'s anywhere.

Candice pulled me out of the check-in line and dragged me over to a group of chairs. After we sat down, she hovered over my shoulder as we began to read the script.

It was clear that there were two sets of handwriting on the pages and the writing was like some kind of note passing back and forth. Much of it confusing, as if Bianca and someone unknown to us were continuing a conversation from the middle.

"'Are you absolutely sure?'" Candice read aloud, before reading Bianca's response of, "'I swear on my life it was him!'"

"'Where were you exactly?' " I continued, reading the unknown scribbler before speaking Bianca's reply, "'Out in front of this dive bar called the Cock Tail. We were looking for a pizza place and we walked by just as he was going in!'"

"'What are you going to do about it?'" Candice read.

"'I don't know.'" I read Bianca's writing. "'But this is HUGE, you know?'"

"'Yeah. I'm glad I'm not you.'"

And then the script ended. I flipped the page over and there was nothing on the back. I then turned each page quickly looking for any hint of more text, but there was nothing there.

Candice and I sat quietly for a few moments after I'd reached the end of the notebook. She fiddled with her phone and after a minute she showed me the screen. It was the Web page for the Cock Tail Lounge here in Chicago on Franklin Street. She then said, "You know, Bianca *was* working a story to submit to her professor at MSU."

I was surprised to hear her bring that up but went with her thought process. "Do you think that whomever she saw at the Cock Tail had anything to do with what's happening now?"

"Maybe," said Candice. "I mean, why else would Michael have hidden this notebook under his sheets?"

"It doesn't look like it's his handwriting," I said, pointing to the other script that was clearly not Bianca's.

"How do you know?" she asked.

"I looked through one of his notebooks from school. His writing is much tighter and neater than this."

"It's rough-looking script, though," Candice observed. "Might be male."

"But it sounds female, doesn't it?"

"You think it might be Leslie's?"

And suddenly, my right side felt so light and airy that I sucked in a breath. "Yes, Candice! That's exactly who I think it is!"

"The question is, how did Michael end up with it and why was it important enough for him to hide? I mean, on its own it's pretty innocuous."

"If we answer that, we might figure out why he looked so scared when we questioned him at his house," I said. This notebook held a major clue that wasn't obvious to us at the moment. "So what do we do?"

Candice looked around the airport at people hurrying to get into this line or that. Her gaze then traveled up to a sign indicating baggage claim and ground transportation were one level down. "We blow this joint and go check out the Cock Tail." With that, she got up and began walking with purpose toward the escalator.

*   *   *

Candice and I decided to lie low for most of the day, as it wasn't likely that a bar would be open at six a.m. We were also both exhausted, so we had our cabdriver take us to the first cheap hotel he could find, and slept for a couple of hours. Before turning in, however, I made sure to text Dutch that we'd made our flight and I'd see him at home in a few days. Candice and I both thought it best if we stayed off the grid for a while and didn't let the boys know what we were up to.

When we woke up, it was around three in the afternoon, and my head felt foggy and out of sorts. It was hard to get my body to believe that it was the middle of the afternoon and that I needed to be awake and alert.

Candice suggested a run and I told her to go for it. There was no way I was jogging around in *this* neighborhood. She, however, wasn't deterred and went off by herself.

When she got back, I had showered and switched to a fresh pair of jeans and one of Dutch's sweatshirts I'd brought along, which still carried the scent of his cologne. Candice also took a quick shower and changed, and when she was ready, we went for something to eat. "I think we should hit the bar around seven," she said over dinner.

"There probably won't be many people there until nine or ten," I advised as I munched on my fries.

"Which will give us the opportunity to talk to the staff without the distraction of a lot of other patrons."

"What's our approach?" I asked. "I mean, we can't just go in there and wave the purple notebook around insisting that something big happened there two years ago."

"No, but we can show pictures of Bianca and the others and see if one or all of them ring a bell."

I frowned as I put more salt on my fries. "It's a long

shot," I said, then looked up to see Candice giving me an odd look. "What?"

"It is a wonder you're alive," she said, pointing to the fries and the saltshaker. "You eat worse than a trucker."

"You eat like a gerbil," I replied, waving my hand at her garden salad with lemon and lime wedges. "I mean, jeez, girl! That isn't food. That's landscape!"

At seven o'clock we arrived at the Cock Tail by taxi. The cabbie glanced at us several times in the rearview mirror and I was getting nervous about how he was looking us over, especially when he asked us three times if we were *sure* we wanted to go *there*. But when we unloaded from the cab, I understood fully. The Cock Tail was obviously a gay bar and burlesque club. Candice tipped the driver huge and said, "If you come back by and pick us up in twenty minutes, I'll double that tip."

He saluted her and drove off. "Are you sure you want to go in?" I whispered to her as two somewhat meaty-looking transvestites came out of the bar and stood on the sidewalk to smoke, giving us the once-over before tossing up their noses at us.

"Definitely," Candice said with a smile. "I love the ladies in drag," she sang, and sauntered into the club. We pushed through the door and I squinted. The lights were dim and the floor was flooded with mist from a dry-ice machine. The music was also so loud it hurt my ears. There were very few patrons about, and several waiters (waitresses? it was hard to tell) were loitering around looking very bored. Candice approached the bar with confidence. I followed her so closely I could have ridden piggyback. "Can you give me a little space, Abs?" she said over her shoulder.

I smiled weakly and backed off two inches and smiled when she sighed. "Sorry!"

Candice turned her attention to the queen behind the bar, a colossal, frightful figure in a leather bustier that pumped up the fake cleavage to an unholy degree. I wondered how she breathed. "You two lost?" she said in a deep voice, obviously taking us for tourists.

"Not really," Candice replied. "Couple of Miller Lites, please?" and she delicately placed a fifty on the bar.

The bartender shrugged and uncapped two bottles, setting them down in front of us. "I can't break a fifty this early in the night. It'll use up all my change," she complained.

Candice smiled sweetly and said, "Then keep the difference."

The bartender looked surprised but didn't argue and shoved the fifty directly into her cleavage. I noticed that she'd also failed to ring up the sale. Before she could turn away, however, Candice added, "I was wondering if you might have seen this girl in here before." And she shoved the picture of Bianca forward.

The bartender regarded it and smiled. "She's a little too young and a little too pretty for these bitches to put up with in here, honey."

"She would have been an unwelcome guest?" Candice probed.

"Yep. Just like the two of you are likely to be. I'd suggest you two ask your questions quick and get out before the rest of the party shows up, if you know what I mean."

Candice nodded but showed the other pictures of the kids to the bartender, who continued to shake her head. "Nope," she said. "Never seen 'em."

Candice thanked her and stepped away from the

bar, leaving her beer untouched. I followed after downing about half of mine. (What? A girl can't have a little something to take the edge off?)

My partner methodically wove her way through the staff, asking all of them if they'd ever seen Bianca or any of the others. Each and every one said he hadn't. We were on our last server when someone tapped me from behind. I turned around and got a whiff of the worst breath I've ever smelled in my life. It was so bad, my eyes watered, and I took an involuntary step back as I eyed the owner of the offensive smell. I stared up at *the* ugliest "woman" I'd ever seen.

A veritable beast stared angrily down at me. Six-five in the stiletto heels she wore with a bright yellow skirt that bulged in very inelegant places and a matching feather halter top that allowed scads of flab and fake boobage to droop and dangle and collect in some rather odd spaces.

Above the neckline things grew worse. The head was like something out of a freak show. A headdress of yellow feathers framed a truly unfortunate face. Small beady eyes fringed with gigantic false lashes gave the appearance of two spiders divided by a bulbous nose and puffy cheeks smeared with rouge. Orange-coated lips hung open, revealing the source of the stench—rotting yellow teeth with inflamed gums and small particles of food stuck in the cracks.

I took another step back, and Big Bird noticed. "You afraid I'm gonna bite?" she asked in a voice so deep it made the outfit even more comical.

"A little," I admitted.

Big Bird seemed to think this was hilarious and she opened her gap wide in a freakish smile before focusing on Candice. "Whatcha got there, girlfriend?"

Candice held her composure a little better than

I did, but I noticed that she was careful to breathe through her mouth. "We're trying to find anyone who may have seen this girl hanging around here," she said, handing over Bianca's picture.

Big Bird looked at it with interest. "Did she go missing?"

Candice nodded but withheld saying anything about her murder.

Big Bird studied the photo a little more earnestly. "I don't recognize her," she said. "And if anyone in here would recognize her, it'd be me. I know everybody that comes and goes through these doors."

My radar dinged at that moment and I urged Candice to show the photos of the other kids, each labeled with their names. "Did you ever catch a glimpse of these other kids in here?" Candice asked.

Big Bird studied each picture carefully, shaking her head at all the pictures save one. When she pointed her finger at Michael Derby's name, Big Bird's eyes lit up. "Derby," she said with a sly, knowing smile. "Is this Matthew Derby's kid?"

My radar pinged. "Yes," I said.

Big Bird's awful smile widened. "He looks like his dad," she said, and I knew there was some sort of inside joke that I wasn't getting. "If you see Matt, sugar, you tell him Reba Bell says hi." And with that, she walked away, still wearing that same satisfied smirk.

"*That* was weird," I said as we watched Reba shimmy and shake her butt better than Marilyn Monroe.

But Candice wasn't listening. Her eyes were unfocused and she seemed deep in thought. "Hello," I said, waving a hand in front of her face. "Earth to Candice."

She blinked and looked at me. "Time to go," she said, grabbing me by the hand.

I didn't argue, as I'd really had enough of the burlesque scene, and we headed out. Our cabbie was waiting for us and I don't think I was ever so glad to see a taxi in my life. "We headed back to the hotel?" I asked.

"No," was all Candice said, and without further explanation she simply told the cabbie to drive around the block while she had time to think.

While Candice was "thinking," my cell phone bleeped. I dug it out and looked at the ID. *FBI* was displayed on the screen. "Crap," I said as the phone rang again.

I showed it to Candice, who shrugged. "You might as well answer it."

"Hello?" I said after allowing for one more ring.

"Hey, hot stuff," came Dutch's silky voice.

I breathed a sigh of relief. "Hi, sweetie," I said pleasantly. "How goes it?"

"It goes," he said without further comment. "Did your flight get in okay?"

"Absolutely," I said. I was quite sure the flight had arrived just fine.

"Milo called me a little while ago," he said. "He heard you were alone at the house and he wants to know if you might like some company for dinner."

I was instantly on edge. "Er . . . ," I said, trying to think fast. "I'm actually thinking of turning in early, honey. And I'm not really hungry."

"Ah," he said. "Okay, no worries. How's Candice?"

"She's fine," I said. "I mean, I dropped her off at her place this morning. I'm assuming she's as exhausted as I am."

"Uh-huh," he said. "I thought you guys might be out sightseeing or something."

My stomach clenched and I thought, *Uh-oh*. "Sightseeing?"

"Yeah, you know, Chicago has so much to offer. Maybe you two could take in a show or something while you're here."

My shoulders slumped. "How long have you known?"

"Milo went over to our place to check on you. He said you weren't there, so I contacted the airlines and they said you two never checked in."

I looked at Candice, who was now paying attention to our conversation. "We're busted," I mouthed.

She motioned for me to give her the phone.

I shook my head.

She glared at me and made an insistent hand motion.

I shook my head more vigorously.

She reached out and yanked the phone out of my hand. "Hey, Dutch, it's Candice," she said casually.

I groaned. She was going to say something to make things worse. He'd break up with me. I'd die a spinster.

"Uh-huh," she was saying. "Uh-huh . . . I see. Okay, so let me ask you something: Have you had a chance to interview Matthew Derby yet?" She paused, listening, and then she asked, "What time does he get in?" Another pause. "Okay. We'll meet you at his house at ten. Abby's been getting tons of hits on her radar and she needs to be in the same room when you guys interview the senator."

My eyebrows shot up. What the heck was she talking about? But Candice seemed to be ignoring me. From the buzzing sound coming from the earpiece it sounded like Dutch wasn't thrilled with the idea of our showing up at the interview either. But Candice was undeterred. "Sorry, I didn't catch that, Dutch. What? Hello? I think I'm losing you. We must be in a bad area. I'll see you at ten!" And she clicked off the line, then switched my phone off completely.

"If he breaks up with me, I'm totally blaming you," I growled.

"Oh please," she said, waving her hand at me. "Like he could ever leave *you*!"

I pouted at her for emphasis but switched topics. "What was all that about my radar getting tons of hits?"

"A smoke screen," she said, then leaned over and said to the cabbie, "Can you take us back to our hotel? Oh, and can you turn up the radio? I love this song."

He nodded and the volume to the music became louder.

When we had sufficient noise to cover our conversation, Candice explained, "We need to get the notebook back into Michael's room," she said. "After we put it back, we can tell Dutch to either get the senator's permission to search Michael's room or get a warrant and obtain it legally."

"But the notebook doesn't make much sense," I said. "I mean, the Cock Tail was a bust. No one remembers seeing Bianca."

"I think there's more to this story than we realize," Candice said. "A lot more. You just go sit with Derby while they interview him and see if your radar picks up anything. We'll put these pieces together soon."

I gave her a doubtful look but didn't object. The cabbie dropped us off and he was told by Candice to pick us up again around nine forty-five. He looked hungrily at the cash that Candice shoved into his hand and nodded vigorously before heading off again.

We had about an hour to kill and in that time I watched TV while Candice jotted every word of the conversation in the lavender notebook down on a separate piece of paper. She kept standing up and pacing with her finger tapping her lip in deep concentration, so I asked her, "Want to tell me what you're thinking?"

She shook her head. "It's a weak theory," she said. "I need more intel before I talk about it."

I probably should have pressed her on it, because my radar is pretty good at indicating whether someone is on the right track or not, but I was really exhausted from all the travel and adrenaline and emotion of the last couple of days, so instead of pressing her to reveal her theory, I let the topic drop and settled myself more comfortably on the bed. Within moments, I was asleep.

Chapter Thirteen

It felt like my eyelids had just closed when Candice tapped me on the shin. "Hey, Sundance," she said.

I jerked awake and sat up. "What?"

"Time to go," she said. "And grab your duffel. We won't be coming back here."

I did as she said without argument and we hurried outside to the waiting cab. Candice gave him Derby's address and we zipped off.

We arrived at the Derbys' about ten minutes after ten—traffic was a little thicker than expected—and walked to the door. Candice rang the bell and swiveled to me. "Let me do all the talking," she whispered.

"Don't I always?"

The door was opened by one of the agents who'd laughed at me back in the conference room. "They're expecting you," he said without preamble. "Everyone's in the senator's study."

We shuffled along behind him and into the home office. Senator Derby was sitting straight and dignified behind his large wooden desk. I noticed the resemblance between him and his son immediately. They both had the same good looks and sand-colored hair, but there was a hard edge to Senator Derby that I thought might have evolved over years in a political arena. Nothing much escaped his notice, his eyes moved about the room with a keen intelligence, and I thought he might be something of an expert in body language, able to read people almost as well as I did.

It unnerved me a little when his eyes settled on me and I knew he summed me up in about three seconds. I also knew he correctly assessed that I was someone to be cautious around.

The other people in the room included Dutch, two of the other agents I'd seen around the conference table at the local bureau, and one exceptionally livid Harrison. His face was nearly purple with anger, and I immediately dropped my eyes to the carpet and tried not to tremble in fear.

Apparently, he'd been aware that we were showing up, which surprised me, given how furious he looked. "Sorry for the interruption," Candice said with a casual command I had to greatly admire. "Please continue with your interview." She then shoved me toward an open chair near the senator's desk and I hurried across the room to take it.

Once seated, I was shocked to see Candice motion to Dutch, and the two promptly left the room. I didn't have a chance to ponder over what they could be up to, because Harrison continued the interview he'd been conducting with Michael's father. "So the last time you heard from Michael was Tuesday morning around seven a.m.?"

"Yes," said the senator.

"And in the course of that conversation, did he appear distressed or concerned?"

"No."

"What did you two talk about?"

The senator eyed Harrison as if he were asking too many personal questions, and it amazed me how, after hearing that his son had gone missing and that three other teens had disappeared as well, he would feel the presence of the FBI as an intrusion. "We discussed the precautions I told you about earlier. How Michael was to come home directly after class and make sure to set the alarm on the house."

"And why did you dismiss the security detail we tried to assign to your son?" Harrison asked bluntly.

The senator attempted a smile that reached nowhere near his eyes. "I had to consider how it might appear to the local press to have the FBI surrounding my home. My family has been subject to such idle cruelty by the media that I felt it important for Michael not to be fodder for public conjecture and speculation. After hearing that the last abduction was several months ago, I assessed the risk and decided there wasn't much of it. Michael has certainly been unaware of any impending threat all these months and nothing has happened to him in that time, so I had reason to believe nothing would."

"But something did happen to him, didn't it, sir?" Harrison said, and for once I saw the cool delivery of his questions crack a bit. He was disgusted with Derby for not allowing his team to protect his son.

"Again, I had to go with the information I had on hand at the time," the senator replied. His lack of concern for his son disgusted me too.

"I would appreciate it if you could give me a list of Michael's friends and acquaintances," Harrison said, changing the topic.

"He didn't have many," the senator told him. "Michael kept to himself most of the time. He preferred being alone in his room and working on his studies than anything else."

"We've already interviewed his roommate," Harrison said. "He pretty much said the same thing." Harrison paused as he looked over his notes, then asked, "Can you think of anything that Michael was recently upset about or a reason why he might choose to disappear on his own?"

"No."

"Were there any favorite vacation spots that the two of you liked to travel to?"

"He went with me to Hawaii once right after his mother died," said the senator. "But I doubt he remembers much of that trip. He was quite traumatized during that time and he spent much of the trip in the hotel room watching TV."

Harrison's brow furrowed. "That's it?" he asked. "That's the only vacation you've taken with your son?"

The senator sighed. He clearly didn't like to have his parenting skills questioned. "Michael doesn't like to travel. As I said, he prefers his solitude."

Just then Dutch and Candice came back into the room, and one look from Candice assured me that the notebook had been placed back in its original location in Michael's room.

Harrison looked up as Dutch and Candice entered. I could tell he was wondering the same thing I was about what they'd been talking about. Dutch held up his hand and said, "Pardon me, Senator, but I would like your permission to search Michael's room."

"Why?" the senator asked, and everyone seemed to notice how the guard he'd had up during the interview seemed to intensify.

Dutch smiled easily as if it were no big deal. "I'm just looking for a clue to his whereabouts, sir. That's all."

The senator considered that for a long minute before he said, "I'll want my attorney present before you look through anything in this house, Agent Rivers."

"Of course," Dutch agreed with another easy smile.

The room was quiet for a moment and Harrison looked like he was just about to ask another question when Candice said, "Senator Derby, I was wondering if there might be someone else whom Michael felt he could trust? Another adult that you were close to whom Michael might have confided in?"

Harrison didn't look happy that Candice had interjected a question, but he let the senator reply. "No," Derby said.

Candice nodded and her look was thoughtful. "So there's no friend of the family or female acquaintance that you can think of that he might consider a mother figure?"

Derby's color flushed ever so slightly. "No."

Again, Candice nodded. "You don't have a girlfriend who stays here on occasion or maybe comes by and watches out for him?"

"I'm far too busy for a personal relationship," Derby snapped, and it was clear that Candice had struck a chord.

"I see," she said. And then she went one step further. "Might I ask what size dress your late wife wore, sir?"

I gasped, Harrison looked astounded, and Derby flushed scarlet. *"Excuse me?"* he snapped.

Candice pretended not to notice the shock reverberating around the room. "Your late wife, sir—was she a petite woman? I noticed from the pictures of her on that side table that she looks to be a slight woman, not much taller than five-one or five-two, I'd guess."

Derby appeared too stunned to speak and Candice took that as another opportunity to ask him something else. "I wonder, Senator, do you ever wear heels?"

Derby's eyes widened and flashed to the doorway and the hallway beyond, where Candice and Dutch had recently been out of view. He then swiveled them back to Candice and it felt like some sort of unspoken understanding seemed to pass between them. When Derby spoke next, his voice was lethal. "I'm done answering questions, Agent Harrison. You and your team will remove yourselves from my house *immediately*."

"Of course, sir," Harrison said, looking nearly as angry as Derby. I rose from my chair and hurried to Candice's side. Dutch's lips were pulled tight and he avoided my eyes as he ushered us quickly out of the room and through the house to the front door. Once we were outside and standing next to one of the two black sedans parked in the driveway, Harrison rounded on Candice. "What the *hell* was *that*, Fusco?"

Candice's eyes narrowed and she coolly replied, "It's called detective work, Agent Harrison. Maybe you should try it sometime."

Harrison's face exploded in color and a vein popped out along his temple. I imagined his blood pressure had just risen to dangerous levels. *"Who the hell do you think you are?"* he roared.

Candice's eyes widened uncharacteristically and the cool exterior she was so famous for began to crack. "*I* am the person who will get us to the bottom of this case much faster than *you*, pal! Do you think for one second that asshole in there even *cares* if we find his son? Do you think he wants to cooperate with us? I mean, come on, Harrison! How benighted are you?! The man asked to have his lawyer present for a simple search of his son's room! He doesn't want us anywhere *near* his house! And do you know why? Huh? Do you?" When Harrison didn't answer, Candice yelled, "Well, I do, you pompous, arrogant ass! I know why and it's a doozy, let me tell you!"

"You're going to jail, Fusco," Harrison said, struggling with his good hand to reach into his back pocket for a pair of handcuffs. "I'm charging you with obstruction and lying to a federal officer, and trust me on this, I'll make it stick!"

"Sir," Dutch said quietly.

But Harrison wasn't listening. Instead, after giving up the struggle to get at his own pair of handcuffs, he pointed at one of the other agents and ordered, "Cuff her!"

Dutch stepped protectively in front of Candice. "Sir, if I could just have a moment to ex—"

"Shut up, Agent Rivers! And if you don't step out of the way, I will throw your ass in jail too!"

And just when I thought Candice had really done it this time, another black sedan pulled up and parked behind the others. To my immense relief Agent Gaston got out and approached us. "Good evening," he said cordially while his eyes took in every bit of the tension swirling around our group. "I trust that the interview with Senator Derby is over?"

Harrison visibly worked to collect himself. "It is, sir," he said in a steely tone.

Gaston eyed the house. I sneaked a look too and could see Derby clearly lit in the window of his study, talking on his phone and watching our every move. Gaston then swiveled his eyes back to the rest of us, noting Harrison's red-hot complexion, the handcuffs in one of the other agents' hands, and Candice's defensive posture.

"Ms. Fusco," Gaston said cordially, and she smiled at him pleasantly. "Would you mind riding in my car?"

"I'd be delighted, sir," she said.

"Can I come?" I squeaked.

"Of course," said Agent Gaston. "And Agent Rivers, please join us too."

I glanced at Harrison and thought he might spontaneously combust on the spot. I edged away from him, then darted to Gaston's big black sedan, where I promptly jumped into the back and squished myself into the far corner, hearing Gaston tell Harrison, "I'll see you back at the bureau offices and you can debrief me there, Agent Harrison. Please also be prepared to explain to me why you've seen fit to ignore your doctor's orders and come back to work so soon after the crash."

Candice got in after me, and Gaston sat next to us in the back. That put Dutch in the front seat and the sedan's driver waited until we were all buckled in before he backed out of the driveway. The interior of the car was silent as we drove; everyone was waiting for Gaston to speak, and for a long time he didn't. Finally he did say something, but it was only about the weather. When Dutch swiveled in his seat and opened his mouth to say something, Gaston held up a finger and spoke first. "I trust, Agent Rivers, that you will also give me a full debriefing once we are back at the bureau?"

Dutch closed his mouth for a moment, choosing his next words carefully. "Of course, sir."

Gaston smiled pleasantly at him, then turned to Candice. "And I'll be interested in anything you have to contribute too, Ms. Fusco."

Candice bowed her head politely. "It would be my pleasure, sir."

When Gaston's eyes fell on me, I said, "Yes, sir. If my radar has anything to offer, I'll definitely chime in."

"Excellent," Gaston said, effectively ending the discussion.

The rest of the ride was spent in silence and I thought that Gaston might be something of a political genius. No doubt, Harrison was seething in the car behind us, and very likely imagining all that Dutch and Candice were telling Gaston. But if called to the carpet on it by one of Harrison's upper connections, Gaston could honestly say that he'd had no such inappropriate discussions and that conversation within our car had been limited to the weather. He could also say that he felt it only appropriate to hear any disputes between his appointed team in an open forum. The end result was likely to make Gaston look like a smart and effective leader, and Harrison look like a discontented boob.

"You seem happy this evening," Gaston remarked, and I realized he'd seen me smirking in the corner.

"Just delighted to see you, sir," I said, beaming him the full grille.

"Likewise, Ms. Cooper," he replied with a wink and a smile.

We arrived at the bureau ahead of the other cars and Gaston hurried us along, as I'm sure he wanted to control the debriefing and didn't want tempers to flare anywhere but in the conference room. A little after arriving, Dutch, Candice, myself, and Gaston were all seated in the conference room when we heard the other agents come in. Gaston called to Harrison and as he entered the doorway full of agitation, Gaston said, "Won't you please come in and join us, Agent Harrison?"

"Sir—," he began.

"And if you wouldn't mind shutting the door as well? I'd like it to be just the five of us for the time being."

Harrison seemed to catch himself and his eyes became wary. I could almost read his thoughts as he stood there hesitating in the doorway. He had no idea what we'd said to Gaston, and he was prepared to offer up quite a defense, but at the moment he couldn't really object to sitting down and talking. So he turned awkwardly and shut the door, then chose the chair farthest away from the rest of us and waited to be addressed.

Gaston smiled and spoke with a soft voice. "Agent Rivers," he began, "I would like to hear from you first. What can you tell me about your progress with finding Leslie Coyle and Michael Derby?"

Dutch cleared his throat before speaking. "There have been relatively few leads coming into our office, sir. We've been combing through the records of that committee meeting in Chicago two years ago when the disgruntled man in the audience disrupted the event. But we have no name to place with the man, and we've got one of the task force members working to locate the hotel security detail that had him removed to perhaps offer up any further information.

"Also, before he disappeared, Michael Derby worked with an FBI sketch artist to give us a pretty good picture, and Agent Meyers has supplied us with a likely profile of the abductor, which was offered prior to our obtaining the sketch, and the drawing clearly matches the profiler's description."

"I'd like to hear Meyers's profile of the unsub," Gaston said.

"Meyers has him pegged as a white male, between

forty-five and sixty. He likely lives alone and has a history of broken relationships—maybe divorced and estranged from his own kids. Meyers believes the unsub has been limited in his education, probably denied a chance to go to college either due to financial constraints or lack of academic accomplishment.

"Meyers also believes the unsub has had menial jobs in either the auto industry or steel manufacturing and that he's most likely currently unemployed and might have fallen victim to the recent economic downturn in manufacturing of the past couple of years. The reason he's targeting students is because they represent everything he was denied: the promise of a better life through education and the youthful energy to accomplish it. Meyers believes the reason he's going after these specific teens is because he attributes his most recent downward spiral to the greed and corruption of government. Meyers notes that because the first victim lived in Michigan, that the unsub also lives there. He believes his home is somewhere in the Detroit metro area, with one exception, and that is that he could just as easily be living in Flint."

Gaston listened with focused attention, but when Dutch was finished speaking, he caught my eye. "Something you want to say, Ms. Cooper?"

I realized that subconsciously I was shaking my head. "I'm sorry, sir," I said, feeling awkward about what my radar was implying. "But my intuition disagrees with that profile."

Gaston's brows rose. "Which part does your radar disagree with?" he asked me.

"All of it, sir."

Gaston was silent for a long moment as he considered me. Finally he said, "Can you offer me an alternate description of the killer, then?"

My eyes flashed automatically to Dutch, who gave me a small encouraging nod. "Go for it," he whispered.

"I think the first thing that's way off is the age," I said. "He got the sex right, but this killer feels much younger. I'd put him no older than thirty. He's also incredibly smart—almost too smart. There's something about how he thinks, like he's playing some kind of a chess game and we're just a bunch of pawns. He knows that we're likely to arrive at a set of conclusions and they are exactly the conclusions he wants us to draw. And the connection to the kids—it's more passionate. This is a vendetta against them personally. It's not random. He chose to target each and every one."

"So you feel he may know them?"

"Yes, sir. I do."

"Anything else you can offer me for a description?"

I closed my eyes and focused as hard as I could. "I feel like he's got one of those faces that blends easily into a crowd. I feel like nobody notices him, and that's the point. He doesn't want to be noticed. It's almost like he wants to disappear."

"Do you think he's going to target anyone else?"

I sighed. "Yes, sir. I believe he will. I believe he'll target one more person before this is through."

"Will he go after a male or a female?"

"Male. He's saved the best for last, actually. His greatest revenge is yet to come."

I heard a derisive snort from across the room and I opened my eyes to see Harrison looking skeptically at me. "Agent Harrison?" Gaston said. "You have some comment to add?"

"Sir," Harrison said, "this is ridiculous! You can't be serious about considering her description over an FBI profiler with thirty years' experience!"

Gaston regarded Harrison coolly. "Meyers has been wrong before," he reminded him. "And Ms. Cooper has shown an amazing talent for pulling the unexpected out of thin air and being right about so much that I don't feel obliged to doubt her now."

"Did she tell you about the haunted house where the kids are being held?" Harrison spat. "Did she tell you about the vampires and werewolves and zombies hiding in the forest too?"

"There's no need to get insulting!" Candice snapped.

"Maybe if you spent a little more time doing as you were told instead of interfering in a federal investigation, you might realize how damaging and time-consuming these ridiculous distractions can be!" Harrison spat back.

"And maybe if *you* spent a little more time with your head out of your ass, *you* might be a better investigator, Agent *Hamperson*! While you were in there farting around with Senator Derby, *I* was cracking this case wide open!"

I bit my lip to keep from laughing. I looked at Dutch to see about his reaction, but he appeared only to be truly shocked at the way his own boss was acting.

Harrison threw up his hands and looked at Gaston as if to say, "See what I have to put up with?"

Gaston, however, remained calm and in control. "Ms. Fusco," he said cordially. "You seem to have information for the rest of us?"

"I do," she said with a pointed look at Harrison that clearly said, "Nah-nah-nah-nah-nah-nah!"

"Please tell us, then," Gaston said, waving at her to continue.

"Well," she began, and I knew she'd insert a few fibs to make her point, "it all started yesterday when Abby and I were interviewing Michael Derby right before he was abducted. I had to excuse myself to the powder room and he told me to use the one upstairs. The only one I could find was the one in the senator's bedroom suite."

Gaston's face suggested that he doubted that was the *only* one she could find, but he said, "I see," and let her continue.

"So, after using the powder room, I came out and noticed a pair of stilettos on the floor next to the senator's closet. They were gorgeous and I couldn't help taking a closer look at them, and what shocked me initially was that they were a ladies' size fourteen."

"Size fourteen, did you say?" Agent Gaston said, mildly surprised.

"Yes, sir. And then after looking at them, I realized the senator's closet was wide open, so I just sort of peeked in there and I noticed that half of his closet was filled with women's clothing. We're talking an entire wardrobe of skirts, blouses, dresses, boots, heels, and accessories."

I remembered what Candice had told me about a girlfriend living with the senator and then also remembered how he had denied it to us during his interview, but I still didn't know where she was going with this. She got to her point after Gaston asked her why this was worth noting. "All of the women's shoes in the closet were size fourteen, sir. All of the men's shoes were a size ten. The sizes convert to the exact same sized foot. And all of the clothing was size sixteen—which would proportionally fit the senator as well."

"Oh, for Christ's sake!" Harrison shouted. "Don't tell me you think that a respected United States senator is a *cross-dresser*!"

Candice's eyes narrowed with deadly intent. "I will and he is!" she shouted back. "He's a regular down at the Cock Tail, in fact, and if you or any member of your original team had done *any* kind of investigating, you would have known that, you jackass!"

"Hack!" he snapped back.

"Sycophant!" she retorted.

"Jeez, you two!" I yelled, standing up to get their attention. "Get a room already!"

To my surprise both Candice and Harrison flushed a blistering shade of crimson and looked anywhere but at each other. The effect was so startling that I almost laughed, but Gaston called our attention back to the subject at hand.

"Agent Rivers," he said. "Has any of your background check into the senator suggested that he has . . . maybe a very tall girlfriend?"

"He's single, sir. Both by his own admission and by everything we can determine."

"That explains why he didn't want a security detail in his house guarding his son," said Gaston. "If I had as big a secret to hide as that, I wouldn't want a stranger in my house either."

"And it also explains why he threw us out after Candice started questioning him about his personal life," Dutch said. "He also wanted an attorney present just to search his son's room."

Gaston laced his fingers together and rested his two index fingers on his lip thoughtfully. "I still don't understand what this might have to do with his son being abducted," he said.

It was my turn to chime in as most of the puzzle pieces came together in my head. "Bianca knew," I said, almost in a whisper.

"Excuse me?" Gaston asked, and I realized I'd spoken too softly.

"Bianca Lovelace, sir," I said. "She knew about the

senator's secret. I came across a notebook that Michael had left out in the open while Candice was upstairs using the restroom. It had Bianca's handwriting in it, which I recognized from all the work I did reading her journals.

"In the notebook she had made a notation alluding to the fact that she had recognized someone she knew going into a drag bar called the Cock Tail. When Candice and I went to the bar to check it out, we came across one of the regulars who seemed to know the senator. We also talked to one of Bianca's professors, who claimed that she was working on a huge story she was considering writing for the school newspaper. It was so secretive that she couldn't say much about it to her professor, and she actually even mentioned to him that she thought it was big enough to end someone's career. We know she must have been torn between her own ambitions and the ethics of exposing something so potentially destructive."

"What we further believe," Candice said, taking over from me, "is that at least one of the other four teens that hung out at the conference knew it too. Abby thinks that the other handwriting she saw in the notebook was Leslie's. In fact, it might be a fair assumption to suggest that perhaps all of the teens knew—including Michael. Which is likely how it must have gotten back to the senator, and we believe *he* might be behind all of this. Maybe he took out Bianca, but he wasn't sure which of the other three teens knew, so he methodically removed them too. But he left his own son out of it until it became apparent that we were putting the clues together and it was leading us to the senator."

Gaston's eyes widened. "You think he would cause harm to his own son?" he said.

"He seemed pretty indifferent to Michael's disappearance," I pointed out. "He didn't offer any information that might help us, and has he done anything on his own to find his son?"

"He was remarkably removed for a father whose son might have been abducted by a serial killer, sir," Dutch said.

At the end of the table Harrison sat and stewed. He appeared to be deep in thought, but if he was even listening to our theories, I wasn't sure.

"And I'm assuming the senator has a good alibi for his whereabouts during each and every one of the abductions."

"I haven't had a chance to check that, sir, but I'm sure he wouldn't personally get his hands dirty. I think, if he is involved, he's probably hired someone to do it."

Gaston looked at me. "But the senator is over thirty, Ms. Cooper."

He had me there. "Maybe the guy he hired isn't, sir," I suggested.

Gaston looked conflicted. I knew how our theory sounded, and there was a part of me that couldn't criticize Harrison for being so skeptical—cross-dressing senators who abducted and murdered teenagers in order to keep their secret life hidden sounded pretty absurd to me too, but there was also that intuitive side of me that sensed we really *were* on to something.

"All right," he said quietly. "Agent Rivers, I would like you to follow this theory, but do it quietly. If we're off, I don't, in any way, want the senator's reputation or good name ruined."

"Sir!" Harrison protested, but Gaston shut him down by holding up his hand.

"I will take over the investigation into the alternative theory that our killer is someone along the lines of Meyers's profile and this man who caused a scene at the conference, to make sure that all bases are covered."

Gaston then eyed Candice and me. "You two have done a great job of helping us," he said, "but I believe it would be wise if you now headed back home to Michigan and got on with your lives. We'll take over the investigation from here." His meaning was clear. Candice and I officially needed to butt out. And this time, he wasn't bluffing.

"What would you like me to do, sir?" Harrison asked, and I could see the small bit of triumph in his eyes that we were being dismissed by Gaston.

"You will accompany Ms. Fusco and Ms. Cooper home," Gaston said.

"Excuse me?" Harrison and Candice both gasped in unison.

Gaston appeared unruffled by their outburst. "Agent Harrison, you have been ordered by your physician to take it easy. I am also aware that the hand specialist you saw in Pentwater has recommended surgery for that wrist fracture, and as I do not want to jeopardize the future of such a good marksman, I am ordering you home for two weeks' paid leave. Please schedule the surgery as soon as possible and let me know if you will require more time than the two weeks to fully recover."

"We brought a car to Chicago," Candice said, as an excuse to get away from Harrison.

"Excellent," Gaston said happily. "And as Agent Harrison should clearly not be driving with an injury like his, you would be doing me the greatest favor by driving him home."

"I can take a commercial flight back, sir," Harrison protested.

Gaston stood up and said, "Don't be ridiculous, Agent Harrison. These two are going in your direction and there's no need to waste the bureau's money on an expensive flight home for you. Besides, this time I would like to ensure that everyone I order home actually makes it there. I have no doubt that, should one in your party decide to take a detour, one of the others will let me know about it." And with that, Gaston smiled like the Cheshire cat and gave us his good-byes.

We sat there awkwardly for a minute or two. Dutch was the first to break the silence. "We had your car brought here, Candice. It's parked downstairs in the garage. Here are the keys," he said, giving them to her before kissing the top of my head and leaving the room in a hurry.

With a sigh both she and Harrison rose, glaring at each other. I glanced at my watch and said, "It's going to be a long night, but I'm pretty keyed up, so I can take the first shift at the wheel."

"Shotgun," Candice said immediately.

Harrison sneered at her. "I'd prefer to sit in the back anyway."

Candice's smile intensified. "Oh, I wasn't talking about where I'd be riding," she said easily, and made her hand into the shape of a gun, pretending to line Harrison up in her sights.

Sick of their bickering, I rolled my eyes and left them to continue insulting each other. Something told me this was going to be one *long* drive home.

Chapter Fourteen

We loaded up on caffeine before we started our drive. Candice swore she wasn't tired and argued with me until I allowed her to take the first turn at the wheel. While she drove, I tried to sleep, but I was pretty keyed up—especially after my double latte—so she and I talked for the first hour, then fell silent for the second.

For his part, Harrison could not have been less noticeable. He sat in the backseat, staring out the window and not uttering a sound. I thought at one point he might have fallen asleep, but when I glanced back, he was awake, alert, and silently smoldering. I turned around again quickly and eased my seat back, telling Candice that I was going to try to get a few winks in, and to wake me if she felt tired.

"Want me to take over?" I asked Candice when I'd woken up from my nap about thirty minutes later.

She looked down at the dashboard. "Might be a good idea," she said with a yawn. "There's a gas station two miles ahead. We can refuel there and get some more coffee."

We pulled into the station and before Candice or I had even unbuckled our seat belts, Harrison was out of the car and already had the gas cap off, fixing to pump the gas. Candice scowled meanly at him behind his back and we went into the station. "Maybe you could cut him a tiny break for the rest of the trip home," I told her as we walked to the door.

"Or maybe not," she snipped.

I laughed. "God, Candice! Seriously, he's really not that mean. Do you remember when he brought me water in the conference room? And for a while there, he really was open-minded about my abilities. I mean, until I mentioned the word 'ghost,' he was sort of coming around."

Candice made a face and moved off toward the chips and snacks. I shook my head and went over to the coffee. I poured both of us a cup, then considered that maybe Harrison might like some too, so in the interest of making peace I poured him a cup as well.

When I had my tray of beverages, creams, and sugars all ready, I turned toward the cash register only to see Harrison paying for our gas and saying, "And put whatever they're having on my tab too."

He wouldn't look at me, so I sidled up next to him, presenting the three coffees to the clerk. "Got you a cup of joe," I said quietly.

Harrison nodded with the smallest hint of a smile, took the coffee and one cream, and waited for the clerk to print him a receipt.

As we were settling into the car again, my phone began ringing. "Hi, sweetheart," I said, knowing it had to be Dutch this time when caller ID flashed *FBI*, because Harrison was in the car with us.

"Abs!" Dutch said with a bit of excitement in his voice even though it was well after midnight. "Let me ask you something."

"Go for it," I said, trying to fumble one-handed with the seat belt while holding the tray of coffee and snacks on my lap. Candice held out her hand for my phone and I hit the speaker button before giving it to her to hold while I got settled.

"Do you remember your description of where you thought Leslie and Michael were located?" Dutch asked, his voice filling the cab of the car.

"Yes," I said, wondering why he was asking me about it.

"Do you think that, given all the clues you were getting, it could be an abandoned mental hospital?"

"A *what*?"

"Hear me out," he said, and the excitement in his voice ratcheted up another notch. "I was doing some research into the senator's background and I discovered something rather strange. There was an article in one of the smaller papers in Joliet that reported that Matthew Derby had influenced the closing of a state asylum near the Indiana border. The paper suggested the state mental institution sat on some valuable property that a lobbyist for a local construction company had talked to Derby about. It appears there's a lot of development in and around that area, and the construction company badly wanted the land the hospital sat on, but the state wouldn't sell it because the institution had been in operation for over seventy years and it was filled to capacity with patients."

My brow furrowed. "I still don't see the connection," I said. "I mean, yeah, I guess some of that fits the physical description, but not the section about the stadium-style seating or the theater atmosphere," I said.

"But it does," Dutch insisted. "The asylum was actually a teaching hospital with a large auditorium in the basement of the facility where psychology students could watch through a window as the hospital experimented with things like shock therapy, lobotomies, and various other treatments."

"Whoa," I said as my radar started to ding a loud *Eureka!* in my head.

"There's more," Dutch said. "For sixty years the state hospital was home to the most difficult cases of mental instability along with some of Illinois' most notorious criminally insane. And, Abs, here's where I think you nailed it: The paper said that the senator had managed to get the place closed by arguing that the facility was a hefty liability because the hospital was so understaffed. No one stayed there long and it was rumored by lots of people who went through those doors to be haunted. The paper found scores of ex-employees who swore the place abounded with poltergeist activity and no one liked working there, especially at night."

Candice, who was still holding the phone, beamed at me. "You rock!" she said.

"Where is this place?" I asked.

"South of Chicago," Dutch said. "Near Joliet."

Candice glanced at me, her eyes lit with excitement, and I knew I didn't like that look. "What're you going to do?" I asked Dutch, and took the phone that Candice seemed to be in a rush to let go of all of a sudden.

He sighed into the phone. "Call Gaston and see if I can get clearance to organize a team to go down there and check it out. As far as I can tell, the hospital has been vacant for the past year while the legal red tape gets hammered out for the sale. I just wanted to call and bounce what I'd found off your radar."

I clicked the phone off speaker and put it to my ear. "It all fits, sweetheart," I said, feeling very proud of him. "Way to work those investigative skills!"

"Thanks. I'll call you later and let you know what we find, okay?"

"Sounds good," I told him as I yawned.

"Who's driving?" he asked me, probably sensing my fatigue.

"Me. But I'm fine," I reassured him.

"You're not too tired?" he asked, and I was touched by his concern.

"No," I said. "It's all good. We're all wide-awake, so no worries. You go back to getting clearance and organizing your team."

We said our good-byes and I clicked off, noticing for the first time that Candice and Harrison were engaged in a very quiet conversation. " . . . it'd take us less than an hour," Candice was saying to him as she pointed to the small screen on her iPhone.

Harrison nodded. "You armed?"

Candice reached under her seat and came up with a massive-looking gun and an even bigger grin. "I never leave home without it. You?"

Harrison whipped out his own gun and I was surprised to see it matched Candice's almost exactly. "Nice choice," she said to him. "Can you shoot with that thing?" she added, pointing to his cast.

"Don't worry about me," he said, flexing his fingers. "I'll manage."

"What's going on?" I interrupted, knowing I wasn't going to like the answer, especially when everyone was flashing a gun.

"We're feeling up for a ghost tour," Candice explained.

"You've *got* to be kidding me!" I gasped, looking at both of them in shock.

"It makes sense," Harrison said reasonably. "We're a lot closer than the task force and it's going to take Agent Rivers at least a couple of hours to get a team together and get down here. If we can save him a couple of hours by getting there first, then it's time well spent."

My mouth fell open. "Are you two *crazy*?" I squealed.

"Abby," Candice said soberly. "If you and Dutch are right and Michael is being held in that place, then we don't have a minute to waste. Imagine if something happened to him during the time Dutch was trying to get a team to the location. Remember how you thought we had more time to find Leslie?"

I winced. "Ouch," I said.

Candice's face softened. "I'm sorry, honey," she said. "I didn't mean to bring that up, but we are a lot closer and we can be in and out of there quick if we need to be. If Michael's in residence and we can get there in time to save him, I say we've got to try."

I sighed heavily. When she put it like that, what choice did we really have? "Fine," I groaned. "But I'm staying in the car."

"Duh," Candice said, and she and Harrison laughed like there'd never been any question about where *I* was going to be while *they* investigated the building.

Forty minutes later we were in the middle of nowhere on an old road that was in bad need of repair. Candice's SUV jostled and bumped and gyrated, but as I sat uncomfortably in the passenger seat, I was the only one who seemed to notice. Both Candice and

Harrison craned their necks forward as they peered through the windshield with focused determination. The SUV's navigation system had lost the satellite signal as soon as we turned onto the road, which I thought was really weird, but no one else seemed to want to comment on it. Candice was too intent on keeping the car on the road, and Harrison was also staring straight ahead through the windshield watching for the first sign of the hospital. They were both doubly challenged because of the darkness of the night and the fact that there were no streetlights for miles around, which made it impossible to see more than about thirty yards ahead.

The road dipped and turned sharply and on either side were thick woods, giving a decidedly creepy air to the quest. Goose bumps lined my arms, and the hair on the back of my neck was standing straight up on end. It no longer gave me any comfort to think about staying in the car. I could sense something dark and awful up ahead, like a giant black hole in the ether that I knew I didn't want to be in close proximity to. But I had no choice. We'd committed to the course we were on and my thoughts kept going back to poor Michael.

Finally the headlights lit on a small building to the side of the road and we realized that it was a guard-house. As we approached, we could see that the gates to the grounds were wide open, giving credence to the thought that maybe it was currently in use. We drove past the guardhouse and through the tall gates, and wound up a long drive to the top of a hill where a three-story building of no architectural interest stood in haunting pose.

"Jesus," Candice whispered as her SUV came to a stop, and she cut the engine but left the lights on. "That is one *creepy* building!"

I was now shaking all over and in a moment of weakness I reached over and grabbed her arm. "Don't go in there!" I gasped.

Candice looked at me in shock. "Honey," she soothed. "It's okay."

"I don't like this, Candice!" I insisted. "Really, I think we should wait for Dutch's team!"

"Okay," she said, calmly. "Why don't you call him, tell him we're on-site, and ask him how far away he is?"

I breathed a sigh of relief and fumbled for my phone. But when I tried to make the call, I had no reception. "Damn it!" I swore.

"I've got no bars," said Harrison, and I looked up to see him eyeing his phone skeptically.

"Me either," said Candice. "We're in a dead zone."

I gulped. My radar said that Candice was right on that count. "I'm serious, you guys," I said shakily. "I don't think you should go in there."

Candice eyed Harrison and I could tell they were both nervous, especially given the eerie image of the hospital in our headlights. And I knew I had almost convinced them to turn back when the night was split by the most bloodcurdling scream I've ever heard. It sounded like some poor soul was being subjected to the worst possible torture, and in an instant Harrison and Candice had their guns out and were reaching for the door handles. "Wait!" I begged them, but it was too late—another horrendous scream urged them out of the car.

Candice turned back to me briefly and yelled, "Stay put. I'll be back in exactly fifteen minutes. If I'm not back by then, turn this car around and get the hell out of here!" With that, she slammed the door and hurried through the dark with Harrison and the two disappeared into the shadows.

*　　*　　*

I sat in the cab of the car shaking for several minutes before I realized that I hadn't looked at the clock on the dash to mark the time when Candice and Harrison had left me. Glancing there now only caused more alarm as I realized that the car was turned off, and when I reached over to turn on the ignition, I was horrified to discover that Candice had inadvertently taken the keys with her. "Oh, sweet Jesus!" I squeaked as my eyes peered into the eerie stillness for any sign of Candice's return.

I pulled up the sleeve of my jacket and squinted in the dim light at my watch. I could just make out that it was ten minutes to two. In my head I estimated that Harrison and Candice had been gone at least five minutes—probably longer—so I would give her until two a.m. before I gave in to a full-blown panic.

Time crept by with a slowness that increased my anxiety while I huddled in my seat and swiveled my head to and fro. "Come on, Candice!" I whispered into the stillness of the interior. "Come back!"

At five past two there was still no sign of her or Agent Harrison, and I'd heard nothing coming from the building to indicate that anything was either resolved or amiss. I decided to give it five more minutes . . .

. . . that turned into ten.

And then fifteen.

"Shit, shit, shit!" I swore, shivering in fear. I knew my partner and how punctual she was, and that when she made a promise, she kept it. Something had happened to prevent her from coming back, and I had a *really* bad feeling about it. My choices looked bleak. I could stay in the cab and hope that Dutch showed up sometime in the next few hours, or I could wait until daylight and run back along the road, hoping to stop someone for help. Or—and least appealing of all three choices—I could go into the building and try to find Candice.

What pushed me toward the third alternative was that I had a strong gut feeling that she was in very serious trouble, and that I didn't have the luxury of waiting around for the cavalry to come or for me to go find help.

My mind made up, I took a few deep breaths and with trembling hands I opened the car door. A cold wind whipped my hair around and made the trembling worse. I shivered and tried to swallow, but my mouth was dry as the desert.

I was just closing the car door when three gunshots cut through the night like cannon fire. I dropped to the ground and covered my head, barely resisting the urge to pee in my pants.

My ears waited to hear something else, but the night returned to its creepy stillness and I began to cry. Staying low to the ground, I huddled next to the SUV and peered in earnest for some sign to indicate that the good guys were okay. But nothing moved and no other sounds were heard. I waited another ten minutes just to be sure, and then when the cold wind made me so uncomfortable that I couldn't stand it anymore, I stood partially up and thought about what to do.

I gazed longingly at the cab of the SUV, but something told me that if I stayed there, I'd be a sitting duck for whoever had either fired those shots or done something terrible to my two companions. "Son of a bitch!" I muttered, feeling out of choices and very much like there was no right move to make.

Forcing myself to breathe evenly, I tried to formulate a plan. "Think, Abby, think!" I told myself. I had no idea who had fired those rounds, but I knew

I couldn't go into that building without some kind of a weapon. Quickly I crawled back into the SUV and rummaged around in the back, pulling out Candice's duffel. "Please have a spare gun!" I whined. But I was out of luck. The only thing I did find was the small flashlight she'd given me to use when we broke into the Derby residence and a can of pepper spray. "Beggars can't be choosers," I mumbled, and pocketed the spray and the light.

Moving out of the car, I crouched low and made it over to the side of the building, where I hugged the cold brick and took a few more deep breaths. Moving slowly around the side of the building while looking for a way in, I was almost relieved when I found a window with the pane partially smashed. As quietly as I could, I knocked out the remaining glass with the flashlight, then pulled the sleeves of my sweatshirt over my hands to protect them from any shards and heaved myself carefully through the window.

Landing with a crunching sound on the parquet floor, I ducked low and held still for a long moment, listening for any type of noise or disturbance. Nothing came to my ears, so I stood up and surveyed the room I was in.

It was too dark to see much, so I risked turning on the flashlight, aiming the beam around to get my bearings. The room was small, probably only ten by twelve, and there was an old desk set up against the right wall. Some boxes cluttered the corner, but other than those items, the room was empty.

I moved toward the door and clicked off the light. Pressing my ear to the wood, I held my breath and listened. Nothing sounded out beyond the door, so I grabbed the handle and began to turn the knob when just outside I heard the clomp, clomp, clomp of footsteps approaching. I gasped and held still again, waiting. The footsteps came closer at an even pace, growing louder until they seemed right outside my door. And then instead of continuing on, they suddenly stopped. I pulled my head away from the wood where I'd been listening intently and stared at the handle as my heart hammered in my chest. I was so scared I don't think I took a single breath for the next thirty seconds as I waited to see if the owner of the footfalls would open the door to discover me. But then, as if that person had made his or her point in scaring me nearly to death, the footsteps began to clomp on down the rest of the hallway until they faded away.

My heart continued to thunder in my chest and I rested my head against the door, taking deep breaths. My hand was now shaking so violently that I had to let go of the door handle and I counted to ten, then to twenty, then to a hundred, hoping that would help calm me down. It did and after gathering my courage, I carefully turned the knob and cracked the door open a tiny bit.

Pressing my ear to the crack in the door, I listened. All was quiet. "Please let there be no one out there!" I whispered in the dark, and shivering in earnest again, I pulled the door open just a bit farther.

The door creaked and I winced, then held perfectly still, listening for a moment before I tried short little tugs on the door to keep the creaking to a minimum. When I finally had a space wide enough to allow me out into the hall, I slid sideways through the opening and pressed myself to the wall in the corridor.

It was pitch-black in here and I blinked several times, hoping my eyes would adjust enough so that I didn't have to switch on the flashlight, but it was no use. I couldn't even see my hand in front of my face.

Gripping the flashlight, I turned it on, but kept my finger on the switch in case I needed to turn it off quickly. The hallway was long and there were many doors with empty nameplates. I realized that I must be in the part of the building assigned to the offices of the various psychiatrists who had once worked here.

Taking slow deliberate steps while I hugged the wall of the corridor, I made my way down the hallway back toward the front of the building. Nearing the corner, I noticed a window and that section of the hallway wasn't as dark as the middle section where I'd entered, so I clicked off the flashlight, gave myself a few seconds for my eyes to adjust, and crept toward the corner.

I had gone maybe five feet closer to the window when a large, dark shadow passed right in front of the pane and moved out of view. I clamped my hand over my mouth, barely holding in a scream.

I started to feel dizzy and realized that my breathing was so intense I was on the verge of hyperventilating. I eased myself down to a crouch position and concentrated on holding on to the little bit of air that I could get into my lungs. After a minute or two the panic lessened and I looked back to the window. No sound came to me and no further movement caught my searching eye.

"You can do this, Abby," I said in a tiny whisper. "Come on, girl. Get it together." Using every ounce of courage I had left, I rose to my feet again and made some progress down the rest of the hallway.

When I got to the window, I paused long enough to take a deep breath before allowing myself a small peek around the corner. There was a short hallway in front of me that opened up to what looked like the lobby. The front doors, with their large panes of glass, were allowing enough light from the headlights still on from Candice's SUV that I could make out the eerie shapes quite well.

And even though I could see, I felt no sense of ease as bitterly cold air seemed to fill the space I was standing in. My radar was doing nothing but warning me to be cautious, and I *really* wanted to run out of this awful place and never, ever look back, but I kept thinking about Candice and how my radar also suggested she was in grave danger.

Feeling that my friend might not make it through the night was the only thing that kept me moving, but I didn't really know where to go. The building was huge and it would take me forever to search it thoroughly. Pressing back against the wall and closing my eyes, I whispered, "Can I get some help here? Come on, guys, help me find Candice!"

Go to the stairs, came the answer.

"Stairs?" I mouthed, and peeked around the corner again. Sure enough, in the faint glow of the headlights I spotted something that looked like a banister on the other side of the lobby.

Digging into my pocket for the can of pepper spray, I crouched low and dashed across the lobby to the stairs, pressing myself up against the wall right next to them. "Upstairs or down?" I whispered.

Down.

"I was afraid you'd say that." I gazed at the blackness of the staircase that descended to the lower level. There was the most awful energy coming up from there and nothing in the world could force me to go down those steps except the thought of what would happen to Candice if I didn't. I closed my eyes again, mustering some courage, and I called out to my crew to watch my back before I took the first hesitant step.

I'd gone no farther than that when the interior

of the hospital was split by another bloodcurdling scream that seemed to go on and on, and *on*. I flattened myself against the wall again and held the pepper spray right out in front of me, shaking so hard I could hear my teeth rattle. "Oh shit, oh shit, oh shit!" I gasped.

The echo from the scream finally died away and I was truly paralyzed in fear. I couldn't move and I could barely breathe and I couldn't even think!

Move! My crew yelled in my head. *Move now!*

Somehow, their insistence caused me to do just that. The scream had come from somewhere on the first floor, and I wanted away from that noise and whatever had caused it as much as I'd ever wanted anything in my life.

I nearly stumbled and fell several times down the staircase, but somehow I made it to the bottom, where I again hugged the wall and tried not to faint. *Keep going!* my crew insisted again.

Tears formed in my eyes and slid down my cheeks. I didn't want to.

Abby! they said. *You have to move!*

I was weeping now and trying desperately not to make any noise as I pushed away from the wall and felt my way down the corridor I was now in. *Where?* I demanded in my head when I seemed to be much deeper into the corridor.

To the end, then turn right.

I wiped my eyes and peered into the darkness. I could see nothing; it was pitch-black. I raised my flashlight, about to turn it on, when my crew yelled, *NO!* in my head.

I jumped and almost dropped the light. "I can't see!" I whispered.

Move forward, then right, they replied, and the urgency of the thought made it clear that I needed to hustle.

Sniffling a bit, I edged down the hallway, jumping when someone upstairs slammed first one door, then two more. *Hurry!* my crew insisted. I quickened my pace and squinted. Ahead, about ten yards down, I swore it wasn't as dark. I knew we were belowground, so I wondered where the light was coming from and very faintly I heard the distant sound of a motor.

As I reached the end of the corridor and turned the corner, I could tell that the hallway was lit by a light coming from that far end. *Careful!* my crew blasted into my head, and I ducked down and pulled myself back around the corner. My ears heard the faint sound of something and I strained to hear. It almost sounded like music, but there were voices talking or arguing too. Another door slammed and then something heavy sounded like it got knocked over.

There was another scream, but it wasn't the same bloodcurdling sound as the one upstairs. This one was desperate and it formed the word "Don't!"

Move now! my crew ordered, and I was back on my feet and rounding the corner. *Run!* they encouraged, and I did, closing the distance to the end of the corridor, where the strange light filtered through a set of double doors.

As I closed the distance, I could hear two distinctive voices. "You'll never get away with it!" said a male.

"He's right! Our backup is right behind us!"

"Candice!" I gasped. I'd recognize her voice anywhere.

And then there came a noise that almost stopped me in my tracks. It was the sound of something electric like a dentist's drill, or a small saw. Above that, I heard someone say loudly, "Years ago they used this little gadget to perform lobotomies. I found it and a bunch of other really cool stuff in one of the lockers. I've read all the textbooks, and I think I know how it's done. Of course, this might hurt a little without the aid of anesthesia, but probably only until the probe reaches the center of your brain."

"Don't hurt him!" Candice cried out desperately. *"Please, God, stop!"*

"Holy shit!" I swore, and ran faster. With my heart pounding in my chest and adrenaline coursing through my veins, I kicked through the double doors as the first pain-filled groan from Harrison filled the large room I crashed into.

The room was well lit and I could see him strapped down to a table while Michael Derby hovered over him with a long probelike drill. *"Abby!"* Candice screamed from another table nearby.

I didn't even pause. Instead I charged directly at Michael, yelling some sort of primal battle cry as I lunged at him. His eyes bulged when he saw me coming straight at him, and he brought the drill up defensively, but I had the pepper spray and it had a longer reach. I squirted the contents right at him, but he ducked low and swiveled around. The forward momentum of my charge carried me straight at him and I aimed the spray again, but saw nearly too late that he was throwing the drill right at me!

I ducked at the last second and tripped over something, sending me sprawling to the floor as the pepper spray flew out of my hand. I could hear Michael scrambling toward me and Candice screamed again in warning. Reflexively I reached for anything close by to defend myself with, and my hand curled around the leg of a small table. Pulling that back with all the strength I could muster, I heard it connect with something and a loud "Ooomph" sounded right behind me.

I rolled onto my back just as Michael recovered, and flung the table aside and brought my legs into my chest, kicking them as hard as I could when he threw himself forward to tackle me.

I felt his weight hit me hard, but the adrenaline coursing through my veins was so intense that I managed to recover and shove him back all the way across the room, where he slammed into a tall cabinet. With a crazed look on his face he pushed off the cabinet and charged at me again. This time, I thought he managed to grab what looked like a surgical hacksaw.

"Look out!" Harrison shouted, and I didn't really think I needed the added encouragement, because I quickly crawled underneath the table he was lying on, searching for anything to defend myself with. I found a metal tray on the floor and pulled it with me to the other side, but Michael was quicker than I'd anticipated and I looked up just as he was about to bring the saw down on me.

Somehow I managed to get the tray up in time, and the blade banged loudly against the metal of the tray but still sent a bolt of pain up my arm and caused me to drop the tray.

Whirling away from Michael as he wound his arm up for another crack at me, I heard something rattle next to me and a quick glance showed me that it was the can of pepper spray. Snatching it off the ground, I dived back under the table and shimmied to the other side, where I then jumped to my feet, whirled around and sprayed the shit out of Michael Derby. He dropped the hacksaw, reeling backward and covering his eyes with his hands while he squealed and screamed and thrashed around.

I ran at him and sprayed him again for good measure, then threw the pepper spray aside and picked up the metal tray from off the floor. I then hit Michael as hard as I could over the head. He sank to his hands and knees, squirming and thrashing around, trying to get away from me. I hit him again and again and again until he slumped over and was still. For good measure I hit him one last time and tossed the tray away, panting and squinting through the fumes of the pepper spray as my own eyes watered and teared.

Still in a bit of a panic, I looked around for something to tie him up with, unconvinced he would be unconscious for long. "My coat pocket," said Harrison. "I've got a set of handcuffs in my right front pocket."

I hurried over to Harrison, wincing a little as I noticed his temple was badly cut and bloody. I couldn't get to the handcuffs because of all the straps tying him down, so I loosened them as quickly as I could and he sat up and fished them out himself before handing them to me.

I hurried back to Michael and pulled his hands behind him, struggling as my own hands shook so violently that I had a hell of a time getting his into the cuffs. Somehow I managed it, though, and stood up, my chest heaving as I fought to catch my breath. After a moment I remembered that I probably needed to help get Candice out of her straps too, but when I turned around I stopped short when I realized that Harrison had already beaten me to it. And what further astonished me was that he and Candice were now kissing each other with such mad passion that I actually had to avert my eyes.

"Jeez, you two!" I said, looking anywhere but at them. "Is this really the time and place?"

Peeking out of the corner of my eye, I saw that they were totally ignoring me, groping and hugging each other with fervor. "Okay," I said awkwardly. "Well then . . . uh . . . I guess I'll wait out in the car."

Chapter Fifteen

I sat in the car for maybe ten minutes, still shaking and trembling from everything that had happened, when headlights appeared in the rearview mirror. Two cars pulled alongside the SUV just as Harrison and Candice emerged from the building hand in hand. The moment they spotted the other vehicles, however, they dropped each other's hands and moved slightly apart.

I smirked and rolled my eyes. "Yeah, like no one could tell you two've been mashing," I said to myself. There was a light tap on my window and I felt a flood of relief when I saw Dutch standing there, looking both worried and angry.

I opened my car door and grabbed him around the chest, hugging him so fiercely that he grunted. "What the hell are you three doing here?" he demanded.

I didn't answer him. Instead I hugged him tighter. "Just hold on to me for a minute, cowboy, okay?"

Dutch's strong arms encircled me and he wrapped his coat around me. "You're trembling," he said. "Abs, what happened to you?"

"The scene is secure," Harrison announced, and I turned my head to see him addressing the agents gathering around me and Dutch. "Michael Derby's inside. He's conscious, but he might need medical attention. He fell while being maced and bumped his head. You'll find him inside on the basement level, handcuffed and strapped to a table. In the cooler you'll find the body of Leslie Coyle. Michael killed her, Bianca Lovelace, and Kyle Newhouse. He admitted everything to Ms. Fusco and me. We expect he'll give a full confession without trouble."

Two agents clicked on flashlights and moved in the direction of the front doors.

"Sir," Dutch said, addressing Harrison.

"Agent Rivers," Harrison said. "Good work. We likely never would have found this place if it hadn't been for your research."

Dutch smiled. Then he said, "And Abby's intuition."

I looked at Harrison, expecting him to scoff. He surprised me by saying, "The bureau owes a lot to Ms. Cooper, and I personally owe her my life."

Candice beamed first at me, then at Harrison, and he smiled back at her all a-smitten. "Oh, boy," I said.

Dutch seemed completely confused by everything that was going on. "Would someone please explain to me what's happened here tonight?"

Harrison opened his mouth to tell him when another one of those bloodcurdling screams echoed from inside the building. Dutch immediately pulled away from me and whipped out his gun, as did all the other agents save Harrison, who shocked them some more by laughing.

"Holster your weapons, gentlemen," he said calmly. "There's no threat and no danger. That happens about every thirty to forty minutes or so."

"Derby screams?" Dutch asked, his gun still at the ready.

Harrison and Candice exchanged an amused look. "No," he said. "Not Derby. The hospital *is* haunted, you know. And one of the ghosts likes to shriek every half hour."

"Don't forget the big shadowy-looking thing that came right for you," said Candice, elbowing Harrison good-naturedly. "I wonder if he even felt the three rounds you pumped into him."

Harrison smiled wide and asked me, "Do ghosts notice when you shoot them?"

"Uh . . . ," I said, feeling put on the spot. "I'm not really sure, sir."

Dutch looked incredulously at his boss. "Agent Harrison, sir, are you feeling all right? I notice your head is bleeding."

Harrison wiped absently at his temple and examined the blood on his hands. "I might need stitches," he said to Candice.

"Come on," she said. "I'll drive you." Then she turned to me and asked, "Did you want to come?"

I studied her face and knew that she would rather have a little alone time with Harrison now that they were all friendly and everything, so as much as I detested being anywhere near the haunted asylum, I willed myself to say, "No, that's okay. You two go ahead and we'll meet up for a debriefing later."

As Candice passed me, she said, "Sorry about the keys, Sundance. I found them in my coat pocket and was on my way back to the car when Michael surprised me from behind and shoved some sort of rag soaked in chloroform in my face. I was out before I knew what was happening."

"Don't feel bad," Harrison said. "That little punk did the same damn thing to me."

"I'm just glad you two are okay," I said.

"Thanks to you," Candice said warmly, and reached out to give me a big hug. She must have noticed that I was still shaking a little, because she asked me again more earnestly to come with her and Harrison.

"Thanks, but I think I want to hang with Dutch for a while." And even as I said it, I moved back into Dutch's arms again.

"Okay," Candice said, smiling at both of us. "Take care of her, Agent Rivers. She's had a rough night."

As Candice and Harrison were pulling away, lights in the hospital began coming on. Dutch looked at them and said, "I had no idea this place still carried electricity."

"I think Derby hooked up the hospital generator," I said. "I heard some kind of a motor around the back of the building."

Dutch parked me in his warm sedan while he managed the crime scene. An agent had to be dispatched two miles down the road to get decent cell phone reception and call in the cavalry. Derby emerged from the building on a stretcher, and an ambulance took him away, but not before he fixed his swollen beady eyes on me and screamed, "You ruined *everything*!" To which I simply smiled and gave him a smarty-pants salute.

Leslie Coyle's body was brought out next. She'd been frozen solid. Derby had put her in the freezer right after he'd killed her. Why he'd done that instead of simply burying her was a mystery, but what was even more surprising was a room next to where I'd found him about to lobotomize Harrison and Candice that was stocked with some women's clothing, a blond wig, and a pair of size 14 pumps. Next to these articles of clothing had been a table with straps and a tray filled with every kind of torturous instrument imaginable. There was a bone saw, two drills, several picks, and a few mallets. And next to *that* was a letter addressed to Matthew Derby titled "Atonement."

The letter went on to document every injury and wrongdoing that Michael felt he had suffered at the hands of his father. The first offense sent a chill down my back. *You killed my mother,* it read.

You may not have held the gun to her head, but you pushed her to do it with all your twisted, sick perversions. I was there the night she died. I saw you parade around in front of her in your tight skirt and your high heels as you told her how you couldn't stand the sight of her. How she didn't even look attractive to you anymore. How you made a better woman than she ever did! You made me want to puke, and you made her feel like she'd failed as a wife and a mother. She took her life that night because of YOU!

It wasn't until I read offense number ten that I understood why Bianca, Kyle, and Leslie had all been killed.

And the final reason I'm doing this to you, Dad, is because you had to go to the Cock Tail that night. You had to risk everything during the conference when you knew important people were in town, and guess what? You got caught. You were spotted by two of the kids I was hanging out with, and one of them was about to write a news story on you and all your twisted, sick addictions. But I

*took care of it before it became a big deal, which
shows you that I was a better son to you than you
ever were a father to me. I can't wait until they
find your body. I can't wait until they put all the
little clues I gave them together. They think I'm
dead too, and they'll never know what really happened. They'll always suspect someone else.*

Dutch read the letter out loud to me and in spite
of how bent I knew Michael's mind to be, I still felt a
pang of sympathy for him. He'd obviously suffered a
great deal in his youth, and I knew that with a different
set of parents the bright, hardworking kid I'd caught a
glimpse of would have turned out completely different.
It felt like such a waste that it left me feeling really sad.

We found out later, during Michael's confession,
that his hadn't been the only malicious mind involved
in the plot that started last spring. The other handwriting in the notebook was in fact Leslie's, and it was
Leslie who first broke it to Michael that Bianca knew
his father's secret. Her phone records confirmed she
and Michael had talked several times right before
Bianca and Kyle went missing. The reason the task
force missed seeing it when they were looking into her
phone records was that they were focused on finding
any communication among her and Bianca and Kyle,
so they didn't even look into the calls to a 312 area
code.

Leslie was first tipped off to Bianca's intention to
write the story on Michael's father when she received
a letter from her—later found at the asylum. And I
had to think how ironic it was that in this age of instant messaging, e-mail, texts, etc., Bianca had decided
to use such an old-fashioned method to reach out to
Leslie.

In the letter, Bianca had clearly been going back and forth with her conscience, and she thought that since Leslie also knew the truth about Michael's father, Leslie might be able to give her some guidance.

But Leslie wasn't the friend Bianca thought she was. It turned out that Leslie had had a major crush on Kyle, who'd actually had a thing for Bianca. It was Kyle who asked Bianca to go get pizza with him when they happened to walk past the Cock Tail. Kyle couldn't stop talking about Bianca to Leslie all weekend long, as he believed their shared secret would always keep them connected.

So it was Leslie who suggested that she and Michael abduct and kill Bianca. Michael said during the interrogation that he had taken care of Bianca first, kidnapping and drugging her on her way back from class before driving her up to her favorite vacation spot, where he killed her and hid her in the boathouse.

When asked why he'd gone to all that effort to take her to her family's cabin, Michael had shrugged and said that he thought the least he could do before killing her was to remind her of a happier place and time. He actually found it poetic.

Once Bianca was out of the way, Leslie had gone to see Kyle at Ohio State, faking her panic over Bianca's disappearance and thinking that she could win Kyle's sympathies and start up a romance.

The fly in the ointment to Leslie's schemes was Michael, who'd grown quite unpredictable. Leslie had let it slip that the other person with Bianca when they'd spotted Matthew Derby at the Cock Tail was Kyle. It was actually Kyle who convinced Bianca and Leslie not to say a word to Michael. He felt sorry for the kid whose mother had committed suicide and had a transvestite for a father. But Michael saw Kyle as a liability.

So once Leslie had lured him off campus to talk about Bianca's sudden disappearance, Michael had drugged and killed him.

Leslie had then freaked out, so he brought her to the abandoned asylum and locked her in one of the old solitary-confinement rooms while he thought about what to do with her. In the five months that he'd had her there, he'd used her for various experiments— testing out homemade pathogens and viruses on her. The coroner revealed that at the time of her death from a blunt-force trauma to the head, the poor girl was quite sick, and probably would have lived only a week or two longer.

And that didn't even cover the fact that, alone, in the dark, and terrified by the constant ghostly activity that surrounded her, Leslie had actually gone quite insane, and as Michael told it, once he knew we were on the trail, he'd felt the need to cut his losses, so he'd killed her too.

He was planning on burying her in the very place where the last photo of her had been taken, like he'd done for the others. He knew about all those places because the story he'd told us about the conversation overheard by the disgruntled man at the conference was all true—which explained why my lie detector hadn't gone off and why I hadn't suspected Michael sooner. The kids had actually had that talk about where their favorite vacation spots were. Leslie, Bianca, and Kyle had said that their favorite vacation spots were where they'd spent time with their families, bonding over games of Scrabble, swimming in the lake, hiking in the hills, or driving a dune buggy over the sand.

But Michael had no such stories, because his father had never been interested in spending time with him on any level, especially on vacation, and the one time they did go away together, he'd been left alone in a hotel room with the number to room service and the remote for the TV. From an early age the poor, demented boy had been left to fend for himself, and the result had cost three other families a loved one and everyone else the promise of their youthful, intelligent, hopeful minds.

Dutch, Gaston, and Harrison wrapped up the case and it wasn't long before I saw a news report that had Senator Derby resigning in shame when all his darkest secrets were finally revealed. I didn't feel one ounce of pity for him. If he'd extended even the slightest bit of fondness for his son, I was pretty convinced, none of this would ever have happened. I didn't care if he liked to dress up in women's clothes, and I didn't care that many of his more-shady political dealings were being exposed; I cared about how he treated his child. I don't cotton to people who are cruel to animals and children. Never did, and I never will.

I saw less of Candice for a while after we got back. She and Harrison spent a LOT of spare time together . . . if you get my drift . . . and she wasn't in the office much.

That wasn't so great for me, because my own business had all but flatlined and I spent a lot of time staring bleakly at my bank balance. The timing couldn't have been worse, actually, because in with my mail one morning I found a new lease agreement from the office building's landlord, and to make matters still worse, I discovered that my rent was actually going up.

When I talked to Dutch about it, he seemed unfazed. "I can spot you whatever you need until your appointment book fills up again," he offered.

"Thanks, cowboy, and I know you can," I said with a sigh. "But they want me to sign another three years, and, Dutch, what if my appointment book doesn't recover quickly? What if these tough times continue for a while?"

Dutch wrapped his arms around me and hugged me close. "Then we get through it together," he said. "You need an office, Abs. It's okay to sign on the dotted line."

But my intuition begged to differ. Every time I took the lease out and uncapped the pen, ready to scribble my John Hancock, my left side grew heavy and I couldn't do it. I couldn't see why I shouldn't sign it, but my radar practically yelled at me not to.

Resolving to talk it over with Candice, I decided to take a drive over to my old house, the one she was renting from me—and see whether she was home. As I drove down the street, I noticed two things: One, Candice's car wasn't in the driveway, and two, the house right next to mine was up for sale. Not unusual in these parts—a lot of homes were for sale these days.

I pulled into the driveway, deciding to leave Candice a note on the door, and as I was rummaging around for a scrap of paper, I saw a couple emerge from the house next door, following a woman in a blue blazer. The couple were shaking their heads and talking in a way that suggested they weren't interested in the property. I got out of my car with the paper and pen I'd managed to find in the glove box, and happened to catch their eye. "Hey there," I said, being neighborly. They waved back and then I saw the woman from the couple point to my house. She then said something to the woman in the blazer, who looked at me curiously. It seemed they wanted to ask me something, maybe about the neighborhood, so I waited for her to come over. "Hello," she said, almost shyly. "I'm Cathy Ridge-wald. I'm a Realtor for Coldwell Banker."

"Nice to meet you," I said, shaking her hand.

"Have you lived here long?"

I smiled. "No," I admitted. "Actually I only lived in this house a few months before I moved in with my boyfriend. I'm renting it out for the time being to a friend of mine, actually."

"Only for the time being?" Cathy asked.

I sighed. "Yeah, I think my friend may want to buy her own place soon. Hey, maybe I should get your card for her."

Cathy's smile broadened and before I knew it, there was a card in my hand. "Please do pass on my card," she said. "And if you're interested in selling this place, my clients over there love the exterior, and would really like to see the inside sometime."

That caught me off guard, and I was about to tell her I'd think about it when my radar dinged and I heard *Now!* in my head. "Is now a good time?" I heard myself asking even before I knew what I was saying.

"Of course!" she said, and waved the couple over.

Three hours later I was holding an offer of purchase in my hot little hand, flapping it in front of Dutch in triumph. "And they love it so much they're paying me exactly what I would have asked for it!"

"That's fantastic, honey," Dutch said, and I noticed that he didn't look as happy for me as I thought he should.

"And I talked to Candice and she's totally cool with me selling it. She says all she needs is thirty days to find a new place!"

Dutch nodded, but he still seemed distracted.

"What?" I demanded. "Why aren't you excited?"

He ran a hand through his hair. Something he always did when he was stressed. "I have something to tell you."

I immediately sat down. "Uh-oh," I said.

"It's not bad news," he said with a slight grin.

"Sure," I said sarcastically. "You always start out with happy news by saying that you have something to tell me."

Dutch came over and sat next to me. "It's good news and bad news, I guess," he conceded.

"I'm sufficiently braced."

"The good news is that you were right."

"Shocking," I deadpanned. That won me a chuckle. "What was I right about this time?"

"Do you remember when you asked me if I was moving?"

My stomach clenched. "Uh-huh," was all I could manage to say.

"I've been offered a job."

"Where?"

"Austin."

"Texas?"

"Yes."

I couldn't speak. I'd known in the back of my mind that a massive change was coming to my little world, but not this big. Not that I might lose Dutch to the Lone Star State. "I see," I said after a long moment. My mouth had gone dry.

"Hey, now," he said calmly. "It's not all bad. I've got some other news that might make you feel better."

"Do tell," I said woodenly.

"Harrison was promoted. He's the new SAC for the Austin bureau and he's requested that I come with him. He wants to promote me too."

I was quiet for nearly a full minute. "I'm really sorry," I admitted. "But that doesn't make me any happier."

Dutch broke out into a wide grin. "I'm not done yet," he said. "There's more."

"Stop toying with me!" I yelled at him. I hated it when he dragged these things out.

"Harrison wants you there too."

I blinked at him. "I don't understand."

"He wants to hire you."

I blinked again.

"Not as an agent," Dutch explained. "He wants to give you a special title: civilian profiler."

I blinked a whole lot more.

"You'd be working with us on cases," Dutch went on, "giving your impressions to a field of hand-selected agents that you'd also help train."

I added shaking my head to the blinking. "What could I *possibly* train an FBI agent to do that they don't already know how to do?" I squeaked.

Dutch picked up my hand and squeezed it. "You'd train them to develop their own intuition," he said. "You'd make them better investigators by helping them to trust their own gut."

I sank back into the couch and stared at him with my mouth open and big wide eyes. Finally I whispered, "For real?"

Dutch laughed. "Yes, Edgar. For real."

"How much does it pay?"

"How much are you making now?"

I frowned. "Bubkes."

"It pays only a *little* more than that."

"But we'd have to move to Austin?"

"It's an awesome place, Abs. Have you ever been there?" I shook my head. "There's a great music scene and the winters are mild. It's a beautiful city with tons to do. Trust me, you'll love it."

"You want to take the job, don't you?"

He looked me square in the eye. "Yes," he said. "But not if it means leaving you behind."

My eyes watered and for a moment I was too choked up to speak. My thoughts were tumbling around inside my head and it was hard to make sense of everything that had recently happened. But when I started to assemble the pieces, I was amazed to discover that the universe had been pointing me in this direction for a while now. Dave had already moved to Texas, and I remembered he'd said he was going to be living right outside Austin. Candice had property and investments in the Lone Star State, and I doubted she'd stay long around here if both Harrison and I were down South. She could go anywhere she wanted to now that she was financially secure, and I had a strong feeling she'd come with us if I asked.

My lease was up at my office. I'd just sold my house. . . . What was really keeping me here anyway? Finally, after giving it some thought and noticing that my right side felt so light and airy that it was hard to deny what my crew thought, I said, "Okay, cowboy. Let's do it. Tell Harrison we accept."

Turn the page for an excerpt from
Victoria Laurie's next Psychic Eye Mystery,

A GLIMPSE OF EVIL

Coming in September 2010 from Obsidian.

Just let me state for the record that being the FBI's "intuitive adviser" (i.e. resident psychic) is not the giant ball of laughs it's cracked up to be. Sometimes, my friends, it's a friggin' train wreck.

But on April 1 of last year, I had no idea that I was about to be strapped to the tracks as one mother of a locomotive came barreling down the rails straight at me. No, on that day I was actually feeling pretty upbeat; as the bureau's newest civilian recruit, I felt great about my prospects in my new role.

I should have known that nothing good ever happens on April Fools' Day. Still, as Dutch and I had cruised through Dallas on the last day of March, and then past Waco on our way to Austin, I will admit that I could have been overly optimistic because of all the distractions of the massive changes in our lives.

Toward the end of the year, Dutch had been promoted and reassigned to the central bureau office in downtown Austin, Texas. His boss, Special Agent in Charge Brice Harrison—a man I could not stand for the first month that I knew him—had specifically recruited Dutch and me for the overhaul the Austin bureau was about to go through.

In the past several months, I'd successfully used my sixth sense to help resolve several of the Detroit bureau's toughest cases, and Harrison and his superiors had been so impressed that they'd offered me a job. I'd gratefully accepted, both because Dutch really wanted the promotion, and because my income as a professional psychic had been significantly dampened by the downturn in the Michigan economy.

So after the holidays we'd packed up the house, scouted out a rental down in Austin, and readied ourselves to move. And that's when my test results came back.

See, for all positions within the bureau—even those regarded as "civilian"—you must pass a lengthy and difficult interview process along with one incredibly taxing psychological profile test. On this test, which I assume is largely devoted to determining whether you're a nutcase, they ask you such fun questions as, "Have you ever entertained thoughts of killing your parents?" Ummmm . . . yes? No? Maybe? Hasn't every teenager at one point fantasized about some giant tornado sweeping their parents off to Oz?

Anyway, the tests came back indicating that I was sane, (phew!) . . . but angry. This of course was followed by a rather comedic display on my part of said anger, (hey, I was born feisty, okay?) and a recommendation that I attend anger management classes. Sheesh, some people have no sense of humor!

But it was the only choice I had; otherwise, bureau policy dictated that I could not be hired. After a lengthy study of my struggling bank balance, dwindling client list, and the sad face Dutch showed me every time I looked as if I would refuse to go to the class, I gave in. Which is why our move was delayed two months, from February 1 to April 1.

"Yo, Abs," Dutch said as I stared with concern out the window of his SUV, which had my MINI Cooper hitched behind it. "Penny for your thoughts?"

"It's so stark," I said, pulling my eyes away from the window. "I mean, I had no idea Texas was so flat."

Dutch smiled wisely. "The topography changes just outside of Austin, doll. Don't you worry; central Texas is almost as gorgeous as you are."

I laughed. Dutch was laying on the charm extra-thick these days, mostly, I assumed, because he was so happy I'd agreed to the move. "Yeah, yeah," I said with a wave of my hand. "I'll believe it when I see it." We rode again in silence for a while and I stroked the top of Eggy's head. Both of our pet dachshunds were in the cab, and I had to admit they had been incredibly well behaved on the long journey from Michigan to Texas.

"How're they doing?" Dutch asked as I moved Eggy over into my lap and Tuttle nudged her way closer to my thigh.

"Really well. But I think we're close to the edge here. At some point they've got to be as sick of riding in this car as we are."

"There'll be plenty of room for them to run around at the house," Dutch assured me.

"You swear you loved it?" I asked. Dutch had flown to Texas in late January to look for a temporary rental for us while we decided what part of town to start looking for our own house to buy.

"It's perfect for the time being," he said. "Plenty of room. I promise."

I sighed heavily and tried to think happy thoughts.

I'd lived in Michigan almost my entire life, and no matter how many times Dutch tried to tell me that Austin was the shizzle, for me, seeing was believing.

"You nervous about tomorrow?" Dutch said into another stretch of silence.

I glanced sideways at him. "That's the seventh time you've asked me that, cowboy. I'm starting to think I should tell you something other than 'no.'"

Dutch laughed. "I'm just trying to let you know that it's okay if you are. I mean, these guys can be rough at first."

Dutch was referring to my new job with the bureau, which began the next morning at eight a.m. I would not only be giving my impressions on various cases, but also teaching a select group of agents how to open up their own intuition. "Harrison has my back, though, right?" I said. "I mean, he keeps telling me that he won't allow anyone to show me any overt disrespect, which is incredibly ironic coming from him of all people." Harrison had been one of the most skeptical nuts my intuition had ever had to crack.

"Oh, he'll have your back, all right. Candice would kill him if he didn't."

"I can't wait to see her," I said wistfully. My partner, Candice Fusco, was a licensed PI and had followed Harrison down to Texas two months before. I knew from the few e-mails I got from her that she was ridiculously head over heels for Harrison, and the two were even talking about moving in with each other.

"They've invited us over for dinner," Dutch said. "Apparently Candice laid down a big chunk of change for some swanky condo in downtown Austin and she closed on it last Saturday."

"How is it you know more about Candice than I do?"

"Harrison keeps me in the loop," Dutch said with a bounce of his eyebrows.

I smiled. "You're pretty proud of yourself, aren't you?"

"Little bit," he said.

I shook my head ruefully and stared out the window again, but Dutch's cautionary words about my first day on the job were settling in and making me nervous. "Do you really think they'll give me a hard time?" I asked him after a time.

"Who?"

"The agents I'm going to be advising."

"Yes."

My mouth fell open. "Gee, cowboy, thanks for cushioning it a little."

Dutch reached out and squeezed my hand. "Sorry, doll, but you're better off knowing what you're going to be walking into."

"Do you think it'll be as bad as the first time I met Harrison?"

Dutch considered that for a minute, which made me even more nervous because the first time Harrison and I had met had been *bad*. "Maybe just a little less awkward than that," Dutch said.

"Shit," I said, and that won me a sideways glance from Dutch. My anger management instructor had forbidden us from swearing. "Zu," I amended quickly. "Shit*zu*!"

Dutch laughed and shook his head. "That's a new one."

Since I'd been conditioned the last two months not to swear—my instructor was convinced it led immediately to an anger impulse—I'd been coming up with some rather colorful alternatives. "I'm never going to be able to stop," I admitted. Of all the alternate behaviors we'd learned in the class, the single greatest challenge for me was not swearing. I'd yet to go a full day without letting at least one expletive fly out of my mouth.

"Anything's an improvement," Dutch muttered. And I knew he was right. My mouth could put most sailors to shame.

"Yeah, yeah," I said, then got back on topic. "So, what's your advice for making my first introduction to these agents less awkward?"

"Don't be yourself," Dutch said, and it took me a minute to realize he was kidding.

"I'm *serious*!"

Dutch laughed heartily, but then sobered a little when he saw the look on my face. "I think that it can't hurt to be as professional and down to earth as possible, Abs. You can't go in there and talk about your crew, you know."

That shocked me. My crew was the term I used for my spirit guides, and they were such a part of my intuitive process that I was aghast at his suggestion. "Why the hello-dolly not?"

That won me another smile. "Because the minute you start talking about the voices in your head is the moment these guys will earmark you for a nut job and discount everything you're telling them. Then they'll discount both me and Harrison because we believe in you, and pretty soon we'll have another political mess on our hands."

Now I understood why Dutch had continued to pester me about whether I was nervous and what I planned to say to the agents when I met with them. "So what should I talk about?"

"Well," Dutch said, scratching his chin thoughtfully, "I guess giving them a demonstration would be good. But don't read them. Read a case."

"Why can't I read them?" I asked. That was my

forte after all, and much less difficult for me than solving a case.

"Because you'll intimidate them."

It was my turn to laugh. "Come on," I said, thinking he was still joking.

But Dutch wasn't smiling. "You don't think that going in there and revealing all their hard-held secrets about their personal lives and relationships to an audience will turn them immediately against you?"

My eyebrows shot up. I hadn't considered that. "Okay," I conceded. "I see your point. So I tune in on a case—then what? Have them go out and solve it?"

Dutch shook his head. "Nope," he said. "What you should do is tune in on a case that has already been solved. Something where we've already nabbed the bad guys, but something that took a while to solve, which will be totally relevant because that's this group's forte, after all."

I shook my head in confusion. "You lost me," I said. "What do you mean, their 'forte'?"

Dutch looked at me in surprise. "You do know that the group Harrison was assigned to is the cold case bureau for the Southwest, right?"

My jaw dropped, and it was a minute before I could speak. "Uh . . . no!"

"Oh," Dutch said, looking chagrined. "Sorry, I thought I told you."

I turned my face away and pouted in my seat. "Nope. You didn't."

"Why does that upset you?" Dutch pressed, reading my body language.

I sighed heavily. "Because cold cases are ridiculously more difficult to tune in on than current cases. The energy is all old, Dutch. It's like coating my radar with dust—it's just harder."

"Think of how difficult they are to investigate," he countered. "Abs, we need every available tool and technique we have to try to solve some of these, and no one thinks you'll be able to go in there and solve every one of them, but maybe there are a few we'll get where the energy won't be so old, and you'll bring us one new clue. Sometimes, Edgar, that's all it takes—one new clue."

I sat with that for a bit and realized he was right. "Okay," I said. "I get it. So I'll go in there tomorrow and do my thing—but not overdo my thing—and impress the heck out of these guys and we'll all be singing "Kumbaya" around the campfire by dinnertime."

Dutch laughed. "That's the spirit," he said, adding, "And up ahead is the city of Round Rock. We'll be in Austin in about fifteen minutes, and to the house in twenty."

I looked ahead, and saw that Dutch was absolutely right as I-35 began to undulate over more hilly terrain. We entered Austin exactly when he said we would, and my head swiveled back and forth as I tried to take in as much of my new home as possible.

Dutch took an exit not long afterward and we got onto one highway, then onto another called Route 360. The moment we crossed onto 360, my breath caught. As far as my eye could see were great sandstone cliffs dotted with lush forest, bluebonnets in full bloom, and various other wildflowers welcoming me to the Lone Star State. Dutch glanced over at me as we cruised closer and closer to our destination and asked, "What do you think?"

"I think I'm home, cowboy," I said, my voice cracking. "I think I'm home."